THE LURE OF DANGER

"If you had managed to keep your eyes open during one of your nocturnal visits to my solar," he said, "you would have realized that I can see into your room simply by looking out the window."

"Did you watch me . . . undress?" The sharp question was out before she could call it back.

Her mortification was increased by his laughter.

"You enjoy tormenting me," she said.

"You are so very easy to torment," he murmured, and she realized he was very close indeed. "If I wished to watch you take off your clothes I would simply arrange to have you brought to my room and make you do so."

He was too close to her. He touched her chin, tilting her face up to his, and smiled down at her, a cool wintry smile that didn't reach his golden eyes. She was afraid of him, but she was also fascinated by him, like a fat, juicy mouse being hunted by a snake.

She laughed at herself, breaking the spell he'd cast over her. She half expected fury on his part, but he simply looked at her with a question in his eyes.

"Something amuses you, my lady?"

"My own over-active imagination," she confessed. "There is no reason on earth that I should be frightened of you. Is there?"

"Is there?" he echoed.

And in the distance, she thought she could hear the faint hissing of a snake.

YOU WON'T WANT TO READ
JUST ONE—KATHERINE STONE

ROOMMATES   (0-8217-5206-5, $6.99/$7.99)
No one could have prepared Carrie for the monumental
changes she would face when she met her new circle of friends
at Stanford University. Once their lives intertwined and became
woven into the tapestry of the times, they would never be the
same.

TWINS   (0-8217-5207-3, $6.99/$7.99)
Brook and Melanie Chandler were so different, it was hard to
believe they were sisters. One was a dark, serious, ambitious
New York attorney; the other, a golden, glamourous, sophisti-
cated supermodel. But they were more than sisters—they were
twins and more alike than even they knew . . .

THE CARLTON CLUB   (0-8217-5204-9, $6.99/$7.99)
It was the place to see and be seen, the only place to be. And
for those who frequented the playground of the very rich, it
was a way of life. Mark, Kathleen, Leslie and Janet—they
worked together, played together, and loved together, all behind
exclusive gates of the *Carlton Club*.

*Available wherever paperbacks are sold, or order direct from the
Publisher. Send cover price plus 50¢ per copy for mailing and
handling to Penguin USA, P.O. Box 999, c/o Dept. 17109,
Bergenfield, NJ 07621. Residents of New York and Tennessee
must include sales tax. DO NOT SEND CASH.*

LORD OF DANGER

Anne Stuart

Zebra Books
Kensington Publishing Corp.

http://www.zebrabooks.com

ZEBRA BOOKS are published by

Kensington Publishing Corp.
850 Third Avenue
New York, NY 10022

First Printing: July, 1997
10 9 8 7 6 5 4 3 2 1

Printed in the United States of America

Chapter One

There were monsters who walked the land. Alys had never seen one in the flesh, but she had no doubt they existed. The nuns who'd raised her and her half-sister Claire were full of warnings, and whether the death-delivering creature was named Beelzebub, Grendel, or Satan, they were all equally terrifying to a young and believing soul like Alys of Summersedge.

Unlike Claire, Alys was obedient. Fierce when it came to protecting those she loved, but a devout coward when it came to her own welfare. She hated ghost stories and nightmares, thunderstorms, and restive horses. She hated birch rods and slaps and angry words, but she would endure them all to protect her sister. She would endure anything.

Even marriage to a bone-cracking, blood-sucking monster.

"Are you certain you're willing to marry this creature?" Claire had asked with her usual ingenuousness. "What do we know of him?"

"Most women don't know much of their husbands before marriage," Alys replied with deceptive calm, folding one of the plain linen shifts in preparation for their journey.

"But at least they're not being wed to a. . . ." Fortunately words failed her.

"A wizard," Alys supplied in a subdued voice. "A demon who works wicked spells." Her strong hands crushed the shift. "Oh, Claire, I don't want to go! I don't want to leave this place, I don't want to live at Summersedge Keep. I don't want to be anywhere near Richard, and most of all, I don't want to be married to anyone, particularly a practitioner of the black arts!"

"Richard's our brother," Claire pointed out with uncharacteristic practicality. "We should welcome the chance to return to the bosom of our family."

"If he had any feeling for us he would have brought us home sooner," Alys said bitterly. "We both know it. I don't trust any plans he might have for us. We'd be far better off here. It means nothing that we share the same father. Our father married Richard's mother. The two of us are bastards."

"Royal bastards," Claire said cheerfully. "Roger de Lancie was cousin to the king."

"I'd rather be an unroyal nun," Alys muttered.

Claire looked around the cold stone walls of the convent and shuddered. "Not me. I want bright clothes and sunlight. I want to run barefoot through a meadow, I want to ride fast horses and deck myself in jewels. I want a thousand men to adore me, and all I shall do is snap my fingers at them."

"Grand notions for one who's not much more than a child," Alys said, knowing her attempt at repression would have no effect on her headstrong younger sister.

"Childhood is the time for grand notions," Claire

shot back. "Maidenhood as well. A few grand notions wouldn't come amiss with you either, dear Alys."

"I am well past the age for notions. It's a wonder the wizard consents to marry a crone such as I."

"Maybe he'll devise a magic potion to turn you young again," Claire said brightly. "Change you from a hag of twenty years to a youthful sprig of nineteen."

"I hope Richard weds you to a man who will beat you severely," Alys said.

"Richard won't wed me to anyone for the time being. I'm too young, and he'll be too busy offering you up as a human sacrifice for his pet demon."

That forced a laugh from Alys. "You're a wretch, Claire. I'll see if my lord husband will make a spell to turn you ugly."

"It would take a prodigious spell," Claire said cheerfully.

"That it would," Alys said, completely without rancor. Claire's beauty was a powerful gift, and yet there was no one characteristic that shone above others. Her hair was a glorious ripple of golden blonde that swung to her waist, her eyes a clear, shimmering green, her skin pale and delicate, her form gently rounded. She was an astonishing beauty, a fact both sisters had accepted and the nuns had deplored.

Claire gave her a critical look. "You could do with some improvement, dearest. You don't have to look quite so pale and mouse-like. We could do something interesting with your hair. The color is unremarkable, but I'm certain the arrangement could be bettered."

"Braids and a wimple suit me very well," Alys said evenly. "I doubt the wizard will be marrying me for my beauty."

"You're far prettier than you realize," Claire said stubbornly.

"Don't you understand, I don't want to be pretty? I wanted to spend my life behind the safe walls of this convent, away from prying eyes and pawing hands."

"I suspect the only hands that will paw you will be your husband's. And that is your wifely duty, you know."

"I know," Alys said bitterly. "Let us merely hope they are hands, and not paws. I do not wish to marry a creature of darkness, Claire."

Claire threw her arms around her, clutching her tightly. "If things become desperate we will run back here and take shelter with the good nuns."

"I doubt the good nuns will accept us, Claire," Alys replied. "Not without a hefty dowry and Richard's approval."

"Then we'll become mummers and travel the roads."

"And we'll end up with our throats cut. Or worse."

"What could be worse than having your throat cut?"

Alys sighed. "Any number of things, my pet. Never mind. I'm certain I'm imagining horrors where none exist. Richard may be a wretched, dangerous human being, but he'd hardly marry his sister off to a witch. Would he?" She couldn't keep the slightly plaintive note out of her voice.

"Never," Claire said stoutly. And Alys only wished she had such blind faith.

The wicked wizard of Summersedge Keep always played best to an audience, and at the moment he had an avid one. Richard de Lancie, better known as Richard the Fair, was seated at the end of a dais, his ruddy complexion flushed from too much wine. Simon of Navarre, mysterious magician and all-powerful advisor to his lordship, preferred him that way. While Richard's intellect was no match for Simon's, he had a certain sly cunning that enabled him to see through ordinary tricks, and Simon of Navarre's skill relied on others' gullibility. He took a pinch of sulphur and tossed it on the fire, and the resulting explosion and stench was gratifying indeed. He could see the various knights cross themselves devoutly, and he intoned a few words in Arabic to add to the effect. No one in the household of Richard the Fair understood Arabic, and they thought it was an unearthly language for communing with devils. If they knew its true origins they'd be convinced they were right.

The magician stepped back from the fire, deliberately pushing his long hair away from his face with his bad hand. The young woman draped against Richard shivered and averted her eyes, which amused Simon. There were any number of missing limbs, hideous scars, and marks of battle on the inhabitants of Summersedge Keep, and most people took them in stride. But the sight of the wizard's twisted, claw-like hand made even the strongest knight shudder. It was a sign of the devil, they said. He'd traded the use of his good right hand for the powers of the night.

"The omens are good," Simon intoned in his deep, golden voice. It was well-trained, and could carry over any number of angry conversations, but he seldom had to bother nowadays. When Simon of Navarre spoke, the world hushed in curiosity and fear. Grendel they called him, after Beowulf's bone-cracking, blood-drinking monster. It amused him.

Richard pushed the clinging young woman away from him and stood up, swaying slightly. "Never thought you'd be married, did you, Grendel? To one as high born as my sister?"

Simon of Navarre turned slowly. "Did I mistake the matter? I thought your sisters were bastards."

The silence in the great hall was deafening. Those watching would be hard-pressed to decide who was the more dangerous: the wizard with his untold powers, or Richard the Fair, with his bloody rages that went unchecked.

Simon of Navarre knew which of them was the more dangerous. Richard knew as well. After a moment he managed a boisterous laugh. "Base born of de Lancie blood is better than properly wedded and bedded blood of any other family in all of England. You're a lucky man, Simon of Navarre. Alys may not be as great a beauty as Claire, but her lineage is better, and she's the elder. She's pretty enough, I hear, and all cats are gray in the dark."

"You don't know?" Simon of Navarre murmured.

"Haven't set eyes on the brat since she was a puling child and I had her taken away from her mother. I keep an eye on 'em, though, and they're both pretty-behaved young ladies. Alys will suit you very well indeed. Much more so than Claire. She'd lead you a merry dance, if what the nuns say is true." Richard chuckled.

"And what if I prefer the pretty one?" Simon of Navarre asked.

Richard frowned. "Already sent word to Alys that she was to be married. She's expecting it."

"And you wouldn't want to face your sister's wrath," he said gently.

Richard was just too damned easy to play, particularly after a night of heavy drinking. "The wench will do as I say or I'll have her beaten. You want the pretty one, take her. One sister's as good as another, to my way of thinking. Take 'em both."

Simon of Navarre bowed low, keeping his expression well-hidden. In truth he didn't care which of Richard's sisters ended up in his bed. The fact that one of them would be there was enough to ensure his position and power in the household of a man who was only a few lives away from the throne of England. Granted, the lives that stood in his way were strong and powerful ones, well supported by the Barons of England, but Richard didn't let that daunt his ambitions. And neither did Simon of Navarre.

The magician's own power was mysterious and enormous. One of his secrets was the use of well-placed spies. The woman who last shared his bed had newly come from a visit to the Convent of Saint Anne the Demure, and her knowledge of Richard the Fair's bastard sisters was gratifyingly complete.

Claire, the younger one, was headstrong, flighty, enormously beautiful and strong-willed. Her elder sister, Alys, was fair, calm, and peaceful, and while not the beauty her sister was, in all she was well-enough.

He was pleased to accept the older, plainer, more peaceful one, until Merren added one more disturbing bit of information.

Alys was clever.

While Claire did everything she could to avoid studying, Alys had excelled in Latin and Greek. While Claire had run wild, Alys had studied medicine and philosophy. Even the nuns were in awe of her excellent understanding, and that was one risk Simon of Navarre couldn't afford to take. A clever wife would be the very devil.

No, he preferred something flighty and beautiful to a creature who might possibly begin to see past the mysterious and frightening surface he presented to the denizens of Summersedge Keep. And the wild young Claire would soon enough find someone young and whole and handsome to distract her, so he could con-

centrate on the work at hand and not be bothered by
an importunate wife.

Richard had barely flinched at the idea of substituting
one sister for another, another sign of how powerful
Simon of Navarre had become. Handled properly, Richard would end up doing anything the wizard wanted
him to do, and never realize it hadn't been his idea in
the first place.

"I rejoice to think of my future happiness," Simon
murmured, keeping the light note of cynicism out of
his voice. "I'll make my decision when I see them."

"Well, as to whether you'll be happy or not, I doubt
any woman has the power to make it so," Richard said
with a smirk. "God knows Hedwiga has been a curse
from hell. But that's neither here nor there. They should
be coming soon enough, and I imagine Alys will count
herself lucky if she manages to escape the marriage
bed."

"Entirely?" Simon of Navarre questioned softly. "Or
just with me?"

Richard the Fair's ruddy skin darkened even further.
"Either of them will do as I say, and be glad of the
chance. Still, when I sent word to Alys of her impending
good fortune, she had the temerity to ask whether she
might remain in the convent and become a nun." He
snorted in disgust. "As if I'd waste a sister of mine in
some bloody convent. She'll marry where I tell her, and
if it's not you, then it'll be someone with the money
and power to back me when I need him."

"Back you in what, my lord?"

Richard de Lancie just blinked. Even in his cups he
was discreet, an annoying strength. "A man must keep
his own counsel," he muttered. "Does your damned
stinking smoke tell you when m'sisters are due to
arrive?"

The damned stinking smoke told Simon of Navarre absolutely nothing, but Merren's information had been impeccable. "Within the next two days, my lord," he said.

"Two days?" Richard lurched forward, catching Simon of Navarre's robe in his meaty hands. "We must prepare. No sister of mine is going to be shabbily wed. Even to a low-born charlatan like you," he added, cuffing Simon of Navarre in the shoulder.

The wizard gave him a narrow smile. "Words cannot express my honor."

"Your words express far too little, damn it," Richard said, pushing away from him. "A wedding! Damned if it don't make me feel sentimental. My little sister wed. You'll have to wait till Lady Hedwiga returns from her latest retreat." He snorted his contempt. "She'll see to the details. A wife should be good for something besides praying and plaguing a man to death." He staggered off, dragging the willing young woman with him, clearly in no hurry for the return of his dragon of a wife.

All too quickly the members of the household followed, scattering in various directions, until Simon of Navarre was alone in the empty hall. Even the dogs had slunk away, terrified of him. The fire in front of him had died out, and the room was cool and dark, echoing with emptiness.

He had attended weddings in his thirty-four years. He had seen peasants wed, and lords. He'd watched Arab rites and gypsy weddings, holy feasts and orgies. Oddly enough, he'd never once considered he would attend his own.

It made sense though. The tie of blood would be strong, ensuring Richard of his loyalty. Richard de Lancie was not a trusting man, but he doubtless thought his brother-in-law would be a more faithful tool than a hired magician.

Richard was not a wise man.

Simon walked from the hall, slowly, comfortably certain the brazier would be removed, his tricks carefully disguised. He had servants he could count on, particularly Godfrey, wise and faithful. Another gift in life that he'd never expected. He had wealth, influence, and the support of one of the most powerful men in the kingdom. He had a high-born bride traveling to mate with him. He had everything a man could possibly want.

Except for his immortal soul.

He'd lost that, in the streets of Constantinople. Shed it, along with his blood, on the doomed Fourth Crusade. And it was only on rare nights like these, when the warm wind stirred, that he ever even missed it.

Grendel, they called him. A monster.

The name fit.

"I'm still not certain you should marry him," Claire announced moments after she bounded up on her huge, high-strung mare. They were a motley group, Alys in her cart, Claire setting the pace, the small group of serving women following behind. After five days of travel they were in sight of Summersedge Keep, and their imminent arrival had already been announced.

Alys pushed aside the curtains of the cart that transported her, trying to avoid the horse's heavy breathing. She hated the tight, airless feeling of the curtained carriage, but she feared horses even more. Still, she would have kissed the horse on the mouth rather than finish this dreaded journey. "I don't think Richard will give me a choice in the matter," she replied. "The wishes of his half-sisters have never been of prime importance to him."

"I intend to change that," Claire announced. "I've spent seventeen years immured in a convent, and the only member of the male sex I've seen was old Brother Emory, and I'm not sure he qualifies. I'm ready to live life to the fullest, and I'm not about to let anyone stand in my way."

"I think you underestimate Richard's power."

"Have faith in me, sister dear," Claire said. "I have no doubt I'll be able to charm him. If you decide you don't want to marry the wicked wizard once you've set eyes on him, then we'll simply tell Richard you refuse. After all, he can't force you."

"Can't he?" Alys murmured, unable to keep the gloom from her voice. "You're about to have a chance to try your wiles. If that isn't Richard approaching us then my memory has failed me."

Claire peered at the small group of men. "Either that, or your eyesight. That couldn't be Richard the Fair! He doesn't look like either of us, and he's a gross, ugly old man."

"It's Richard," Alys said flatly. "Older, fatter, coarser, but Richard all the same. I couldn't forget him. The last time I saw him I was four years old and screaming for my mother. He told me I would never see her again. He was right." There was no bitterness in her voice. She'd learned to hide it well.

"At least you remember your mother," Claire said, controlling her skittish horse with remarkable dexterity.

A soft touch, a sweet voice, and the smell of lavender. It wasn't enough, but Alys didn't say so. "Smile at our brother, dearest," she advised in an undertone as the horses thundered toward them. "He holds our lives in his hands."

It took all her strength of will not to cower into the corner of her carriage as half a dozen huge, sweating horses bounded toward them. Richard wheeled his giant black stallion to a halt, inches from overturning the cart, and the welcoming smile on his reddened face was touched with malice.

"Still afraid of horses, little sister?"

Alys was unable to speak as the panic built inside her chest. She wasn't sure whether it was the horses or her brother that frightened her, and she didn't care. She struggled for calm, not certain if she'd find it, when Claire spoke up.

"I'm not," she said boldly.

Richard turned his piercing gaze away from Alys to take in the golden beauty of his younger half-sister. "I can see you're not afraid of anything," he said with a shout of laughter. "That's no horse for a lady."

Claire's eyes narrowed. "She's mine. I raised her from a weanling, trained her. . . ."

"Everything you have is due to my generosity and good will, and I can withdraw both at any time." He glanced with covetous eyes at the magnificent mare, and Alys knew with a sinking feeling that Claire would lose Arabia. And it would break her heart.

For once Claire summoned tact, wise enough to recognize the danger she was in. "And we're most grateful for your generosity," she murmured between her teeth.

Richard put out a leather gloved hand and tilted Claire's face to the sunlight. "By God, you're a beauty, aren't you? They didn't lie. A much lovelier sight than your plain older sister. We'll make a pretty pair, Richard the Fair and his beautiful sister."

Before Claire could summon a response he turned, back to Alys. "Recovered your wits, sweeting?"

"I never lost them, my lord," Alys replied without complete truthfulness.

"And are you looking forward to meeting your husband? He's a prodigious fellow, dark enough to frighten dairy maids, but you have my blood in your veins. You'll bear up well." There was a crafty look in his red-rimmed eyes, one that didn't bode well for the future.

"I look forward to it," she said.

Richard wheeled his horse around, kicking up a cloud of dust. "You may be spared yet, sister," he said over his shoulder.

"What?"

"He said he might prefer beauty to obedience. He'll take his pick of the two of you, and Simon of Navarre's a clever man. He'll most likely go for the beauty."

"No!" Claire cried, Arabia rearing as she sensed her mistress's dismay.

"You'll do as I say. Simon of Navarre is of value to me—a greater value than two pretty bastards. He'll take whichever sister he desires. You needn't worry, Alys," he added. "I'm certain I can find someone who'll warm your plump bones."

He pounded back toward the entrance to Summersedge Keep. The drawbridge was down, the portcullis raised, but the spikes looked like sharp teeth. It was the mouth of a demon they would be entering, and, once inside, the drawbridge would be drawn up, the portcullis dropped, and they would be devoured.

It made no difference that the monster would choose Claire. Alys would rather die than see her sister sacrificed to a demonic creature.

Claire was weeping. She wept easily, but this time there was little Alys could do, short of clambering out of the traveling carriage and hugging Arabia, and she had no intention of attempting any such thing, not even for Claire.

"Don't worry, love," she said briskly. "It isn't going to happen."

" 'Don't worry!' " Claire echoed with a wail. "It was bad enough to think of you wedded to that monster. I can't bear it!"

"Maybe he'll choose me instead."

"Don't be ridiculous!" Claire scoffed, entirely without malice. "Of course he'll choose me. Men are notoriously shallow."

"Even a demon wizard?"

Claire shuddered in horror. "I'll kill myself before I let him touch me. The servants tell me he's an old man, with gray hair and a twisted hand like a demon bird. I couldn't bear it."

"You won't have to," Alys said, very calm. "Haven't I always taken care of you? I wouldn't let that happen."

"Oh, Alys, how can you stop it?" she cried.

"I don't know," Alys muttered. "But I will. He'll choose me. I'll force him."

And Claire, looking down at her small, fierce sister, managed a watery laugh that was half relief, half derision.

Chapter Two

Simon of Navarre was already seated at Richard's right hand when the sisters entered the Great Hall. He found he felt a surprising amount of anticipation, waiting for a first glimpse of his future bride. Not that he had the slightest intention of staying married to her. Permanence was not a way of life for him, and he doubted Richard's grandiose plans would succeed. When they collapsed, and Richard with them, Simon of Navarre would be off in search of new opportunities, and he had no intention of burdening himself with a wife, no matter how lovely she was.

And she was lovely indeed. The noisy court lapsed into sudden silence as the group of women entered, and all eyes focused on the willowy blonde, with her beautiful face, her rippling hair restrained only by a thin circlet of ribbon, her plain clothes caressing her body as most men's hands were itching to do.

He looked down at his own hand. The scarred, twisted one. He felt no urge to touch such beauty, admire it as he might. He glanced up at her again. She hadn't noticed him yet. None of the women were looking at him; they were far too busy taking in the wonders of the court, which suited him well. Her face was astonishingly beautiful, though, as with most young girls, without strong character. He could see she was willful by the slightly stubborn set to her full mouth. He could see she was uneasy by the faint shadow in her perfect green eyes. He could see she was spoiled by the faint swagger in her graceful stride. She was a peacock, surrounded by gray doves, and she knew it, and she reveled in it, even though it made her nervous.

He realized then that he'd been mistaken. There were six women in the group, and five of them were staring about with wonder and curiosity. The sixth was looking straight at him.

Next to the ravishing Claire she was plain indeed. Her face was pale, composed, her hair pulled back into a thick braid of brownish-blonde and mostly covered with a wimple. Her eyes were large, but of an indeterminate color, halfway between brown and green. She was short, sweetly plump, dressed in a gown of some muddy shade that cast her into obscurity. And he had no doubt whatsoever that she was the beauty's older sister. The one he'd originally been chosen to marry.

There was fear in her eyes as she looked at him. Courage as well. He wondered how she'd react when she saw his twisted hand. Would she flinch? What if he touched her with it? Would she gag? He suspected her younger sister would.

"Welcome!" Richard boomed out, all heartiness now that he was getting his way. "Make my sisters welcome! They've been too long from this household. My lady wife is sadly absent, on pilgrimage to Canterbury, but she should return soon enough, and in the meantime we'll do our best to make you welcome. Come sit by me, sweet Alys, and tell me the wonders you've seen."

"In a convent?" Alys said, a faint trace of humor in her soft voice.

Richard's face darkened. He was not a man to make jest of, as Alys would soon discover, Simon thought. She should curb that tongue of hers. That surprisingly warm voice, that dangerous trace of wit. Richard would likely beat her.

Beautiful Claire had said nothing. She'd finally noticed him, but she kept those lovely green eyes carefully averted. Wary of him. She must have heard she would take her sister's place. For some reason her uneasiness failed to excite him. He was more interested in the plain one.

"Tell us your visions then," Simon said, and there was a sudden hush in the noisy room. "Did you see God?"

It was borderline blasphemy, and only the magician could get away with it. The plain sister turned to face him, her fear carefully kept at bay. "No," she said, her warm voice a dangerous delight. There was faint huskiness in it, making him think of scented secrets and long, languorous nights, and he found himself oddly aroused. "But I've seen demons." She looked directly into his eyes, and he wanted to laugh with pure pleasure.

He didn't. She was a danger, with that clever tongue, those wise eyes, that oddly sensual voice. Claire would be prettier, safer, easier. But he found he'd made his choice. Safe and easy had never appealed to him.

He wasn't about to inform any of them. Life was full of opportunities, and he didn't squander any of them. He raised his twisted hand and pushed his hair away from his face. She didn't even flinch.

He could feel Richard's eyes upon him, curiosity rampant. For once, however, he kept his counsel. "Simon of Navarre," Richard called out. "Make my sisters welcome. One of them will be your bride if you so desire. I make little doubt which one you'd choose. Alys, sit by me, and entertain me with tales of life in a convent. My wizard will see to your comfort, Claire."

There was no way either lady could dispute Richard's high-handed disposition of them. And indeed, Simon of Navarre had no desire to interfere. He rose as the Lady Claire approached him, looming over her, and she flounced into her seat with all the appearance of pleasure. Keeping her eyes averted from his face, from his hand.

He was half-tempted to use his right hand to pour her wine for her, but he resisted. He merely sat again, leaning back against the carved wooden back of the chair, and watched her, his eyes taking pleasure in the undeniably lovely sight of her. His body unmoved.

The meal was endless, and for once Alys's appetite had fled. She was used to plainer food at the abbey, boiled fowl and brown bread. The nuns had been sparing with the wine as well, and the stuff she'd grown used to was strong and vinegary, not at all like the delicate, fruity wine in her jewel-encrusted goblet.

She could no longer see the Demon, which was only a slight comfort, knowing that Claire was caught in his company. Ah, but Claire had always been braver than Alys; she would doubtless survive very well indeed.

He wasn't what she had expected. And yet, he was far worse. Given the name they called him, given the whisperings of the peasants, the rumors that had swept over the convent, she had expected someone old, ugly, evil-looking.

My lord Simon of Navarre was none of those things. Indeed, she wondered that anyone even noticed her crude brother with a creature like that by his side.

He was past his first youth—probably in his thirties, though by no means old, despite the streak of gray that coursed through one side of his thick, dark brown hair. He was clean-shaven, when most men wore beards, his face narrow, distant, lit by curiously golden eyes. His skin was tawny, and his clothes were richly colored, long robes in jewel-like hues that accentuated his height and the leanness of his body.

He was a strong man, she sensed it, though compared to her brother's muscular knights he might seem too slight. He wasn't a fighter—she had seen the twisted, scarred shape of his hand, and she hadn't flinched from that either. All she could think of was the pain he must have felt.

And then his eyes had met hers. Those golden eyes, and she'd had the certain knowledge that this was no mortal man. He would be the death of her, perhaps. He would have power over her that no other man could even come close to. And considering how powerless she truly was in this world run by rampaging, war-like men, that was a monumental realization.

She didn't look away from his glance, and she didn't let her own fear show. Wasn't that what Claire had always tried to tell her? You can't let anyone know you're afraid—not horses, not the nuns, not the demons that haunted the night and sent thunderstorms to plague her.

She wasn't about to let this man know she was afraid. Even though she suspected he was well aware of it. Well aware of everything that surrounded him.

She couldn't let her sister be sacrificed to him. He would choose Claire, any man would, and Alys had no idea how she would stop him. But stop him she would. When it came to her sister, to those she loved, she could be fearless.

And it appeared that time had come.

She wouldn't seem much of an opponent. A small, quiet, plain little woman. But she could be absolutely fierce if need be. And the need had obviously arisen.

It was late when they were finally allowed to leave the table. Richard had decreed an endless feast to welcome his long-lost sisters back to the bosom of their family, blithely ignoring the fact that he was the one who'd decreed they be lost. Course had followed course of rich, savory food that tasted like dust in Alys's mouth. The wine was sweet, and she drank too much of it, and when Richard finally let them escape Claire was almost fainting with panic. By the time they reached the tower room they were to share, she was in tears.

Claire flung herself on the bed and howled. "I can't bear it!" she cried. "If he touches me I know I shall die, I just know it."

"Hush, now, love," Alys murmured, sitting beside her and stroking her tear-streaked face. "You won't have to, I promise."

"I saw the way he looked at me," she continued, unmindful of Alys's attempts at comfort. "He couldn't keep his eyes off me. God curse this beauty of mine, if it brings me the attentions of a monster like him."

Alys bit her lip, unexpectedly amused. They both took Claire's loveliness in stride, but there were times when her sister's matter-of-fact attention to her beauty grew a bit tedious. "Go to sleep, love," she said gently, brushing Claire's golden hair away from her face and removing the ribboned circlet.

Claire must have imbibed more than her share of the sweet wine as well. She was asleep almost immediately, breathing deeply, and it was all Alys could do to pull herself away.

But there were certain things that couldn't wait. It might already be too late; the demon wizard might have already informed Richard of his choice. If he had, Alys would simply have to make certain she changed his mind. She hadn't the faintest idea how she would do such a thing, she only knew she had to try.

The halls of the castle were deserted. She crept down the long flight of stairs leading toward the Great Hall, passing no one as she went, silent as a ghost. She half-expected to see her brother and his sorcerer still carousing at the table, but they were long gone, the scarred wooden surface swept clean.

Bodies lay strewn among the rushes, servants and men-at-arms curled up in drunken sleep amidst the dogs and the fleas. She stepped over them, but no one moved. In the corner she could see two people clamped together, moving back and forth in an agitated manner, emitting low, guttural noises, and she quickly averted her eyes. She wasn't about to ask *them* where she would find Simon of Navarre.

She hadn't been in Summersedge Keep since she was four years old. It was an older castle, built along Norman lines, consisting of a central stone keep with four towers, one on each side, surrounded by a stone curtain of defense. The chapel lay along the inside of one of the stone walls. She wondered if the resident demon also lived outside the main keep.

She leaned against the cold stone wall, suddenly dizzy. It was late, she'd been travelling for days, cooped up in that miserable little carriage, and she'd had far too much wine. But there was no way she could sleep knowing the fate that awaited her sister. She had to find the wizard and make him change his mind.

Failing that, she could, of course, kill him.

She found she could laugh at herself, even through her dizzy, faintly drunken confusion. She couldn't bring herself to kill a spider—she would hardly be a match for a man such as Simon of Navarre. Besides, if he had even half the powers he was vaunted to have, he would already know her plans.

Pushing away from the wall, she wandered farther, ending up at the base of one of the towers. Richard and the absent Lady Hedwiga resided in one of them, but she doubted this was it. Richard insisted on pomp and majesty, on rich tapestries and precious gems. This dark, almost bleak curve of staircase wouldn't lead to his sumptuous quarters.

She knew where these stairs would lead, knew without asking. The pale, nervous-looking serving woman who scuttled down them stopped and stared at her, clutching an armload of linens against her thin chest. "You don't want to go up there, my lady," she said hoarsely.

"Why not?"

"Grendel's up there. Them's his quarters. You don't want to go anywhere near that demon unless you have to. Go back to your room, lady. As fast you can. Before he can smell you coming."

"Smell me. . . ?" Alys began, suitably annoyed. She bathed far more frequently than most people considered necessary.

"He's a monster. Eats people. Can sniff 'em out like a hunting dog."

"Then why hasn't he eaten you?" she responded, somewhat mollified.

The woman looked confused. "Maybe I'm too lean for him."

Alys's temporary goodwill vanished. "Well, I'll provide him a tasty morsel if he's in need of a snack," she snapped. "Away with you, woman. Or I'll tell Simon of Navarre you're spreading foul rumors."

The woman blanched, but stood firm. "They are no rumors," she muttered. "You'll see."

Alys had already turned her back on the foolish creature. She wasn't in the mood to climb the narrow, winding stairs of the north tower, particularly since she was already dizzy, but she didn't see that she had much choice in the matter, particularly since the demon who resided there had probably already sniffed her out. Though considering that she'd just bathed in scented lavender water he'd probably have a hard time identifying her as ripe human flesh.

The torches were placed haphazardly along the walls, as if the inhabitant had little need for outside light. She moved slowly upward, keeping one hand on the inside wall for balance. *There's nothing to be afraid of,* she told herself. *Grendel is a legend, a tale to terrify children.*

But why did she feel like such a child?

She climbed to the third floor, breathless, telling herself that the upward climb was the cause of her constricted heart, her damp palms, the fluttering in her chest. She halted there, beneath the battlements. The heavy wooden door was closed tight, and there was no sign of life in the dimly lit hallway. Yet she knew what lay beyond.

Was he a shapeshifter? A demon who changed bodies when no one was looking? Surely there was a reason they called him Grendel, after the despised monster of ancient myth. Did he turn into the bone-cracking beast and stalk the hallways of Summersedge Keep, looking for sustenance?

Or did he wait in his chamber, for those fool enough to come to him, to offer themselves up as his dinner?

She was being ridiculous! It was her idea to face him.

And she'd taken a long, considering look at him before Richard had commanded her attention. The dread wizard Simon of Navarre was a man, no more, no less, and she was a sister to his lord. He would never dare hurt her.

She lifted her hand to knock loudly on the thick wooden door, certain she would never be heard. The door wasn't latched; it swung open silently at the blow from her hand, and the tower room lay before her.

At first all she could see was the blazing fire. It was a chill autumn night, and the stones of the castle seemed to embrace the cold like a lonely spinster. The tapestries that hung on the walls were dark, the furniture sparse.

"You wished to see me, Lady Alys?"

The voice of Grendel came from nowhere, deep and seductive, and Alys had to force herself to remain still, not to run from this place in complete panic. It was no monster's voice. It had an almost eerie charm, rich and beguiling, inviting her to come closer.

Her eyes had grown accustomed to the shadows. He was sitting in a curved wooden chair by the fire, watching her, and the shifting flames made a curious pattern on his enigmatic face. Like the flames of hell, she thought.

She'd come this far, she had to see it through. "I wished to talk with you, my lord Gren . . . Simon." She cursed her slippery tongue. There was always the chance he hadn't noticed. She wasn't going to count on it.

"I am honored, my lady," he said, still from the darkness. "Are you going to stand in the doorway while we discuss things, or are you going to enter? I promise I won't tear your body apart and drink your blood."

He hadn't missed it. He must know what they called him. He might even have been instrumental in coming up with the notion. Fear was a powerful advantage, and

Simon of Navarre was a powerful man. She sensed he would use any weapon he could devise.

She stepped into the shadowy room, noticing with temporary relief that there was a branch of candles on the plain wooden table. That relief vanished when the door swung shut behind her, apparently unaided by human hands.

She didn't shriek, though she wanted to. She merely stood before him, trying to hold herself very tall and straight, wishing she had Claire's impressive height, wishing she wasn't such a hopeless little creature.

He looked up at her from his chair, and she was just as glad he didn't rise. She was already feeling small and helpless. If he towered over her she might just. . . .

She didn't know what she'd do. But he just sat there, looking at her out of his strange, golden eyes. "Pray be seated, my lady," he said, and she looked nervously behind her, half expecting a seat to walk up and present itself.

She knew she was being silly. There was a padded stool nearby, the only choice of seat other than the floor, and she sat down on it, a bit too abruptly. She was too close to him, but in the darkness she wouldn't have been able to see him if she'd moved away, and his rich, disembodied voice was unnerving enough. She preferred to face her enemy.

And that was what he was, she reminded herself. Her sworn enemy, out to destroy her sister.

Silence fell between them, a strangely peaceful silence, considering the oddness of the night. The room smelled of woodsmoke and spices, of leather and rich herbs. It was intoxicating, dangerously so. More lethal than the wine she had drunk. She sat there, dreamily staring into the fire, temporarily at peace. Until he spoke.

"Is there some boon I can grant you, Lady Alys?" he murmured. "Or are you simply here for the pleasure of my company?" He leaned forward, his useless right hand resting in his lap, and poured two goblets of wine with his left hand. He held one out to her, and she could think of no way to refuse. She took it, allowing herself a tentative sip. This was different from the stuff at her brother's table. This was honey sweet, warming her bones, dancing on her flesh. Danger.

"I want you to choose me," she said abruptly.

The darkness must have been deceiving. That couldn't be amusement in his clear golden eyes. "Choose you for what?" he said, leaning back in his chair, his own goblet held negligently in his one good hand.

Horrific doubt assailed Alys. "Richard said he'd offered either of us as. . . . I mean to say, he wanted you to. . . ." It was the wine, she thought, that was making her stupid. Not those eyes trained so steadily on her. She took a deep drink of the golden wine. "He said you would choose one of us to marry," she said in a rush. "I want you to choose me."

"Why?"

A simple enough question. "Because it would kill Claire."

"You've been listening to too many fairy stories, Lady Alys. I don't eat children or maidens. Your sister would survive marriage with me quite handily."

It shouldn't have come as any surprise that he'd made his choice. She'd known there would be no question of who he'd want. She would simply have to change his mind.

"She's high-strung," Alys said. "Willful."

"And you aren't?"

"No!" she protested. "I'm really very meek and quietly behaved."

"I'm not certain your brother would see it that way."

"I would cause you no trouble," she said rather desperately. "I would keep out of your way, I would ask no questions, I would be the perfect wife."

"Was this your sister's idea?" he said, sounding no more than casually interested.

"Oh, no!" Alys couldn't keep the shock from her voice. "She would never ask me to sacrifice myself in such a way. It was entirely my own idea."

The faint choking sound he made was almost like a laugh. "Your years in the convent have taught you well the joys of martyrdom," he murmured. "You must have grieved leaving."

A sudden, glorious thought came to her. "You could choose neither of us," she said suddenly. "Why should you want to be saddled with a wife? The two of us are fairly useless. Granted, Claire's extremely decorative, but she can be very tiresome and stubborn. And while I would promise to keep out of your way and be very, very quiet, I still might be likely to grate on your nerves."

"You won't escape," he said with curious gentleness. "If your brother doesn't marry you to me, he'll barter the two of you to the highest bidder. You won't be getting back to your convent, little nun."

"I don't like to be called 'little,' " Alys said with some dignity, draining the honey-flavored wine. Which was, in itself, a mistake.

"Shall I call you 'large' instead?"

"I don't like you," she said.

"Really? So mild? I assumed you hated me."

"Hatred is a sin."

"Except when its object is evil. Love the good, hate the wicked, isn't that what they taught you?"

"Are you wicked? Evil?"

"So they say."

"What do you say?" she demanded.

"So many questions," he murmured. "Answer one for me. Will you share my bed and lie beneath me? Will you do as I bid and pleasure me?"

He couldn't see that she turned pale in the darkness. The wine had only increased her dizziness, and his low, insinuating words were stifling her.

"If it has to be one of us," she said. "Yes. Let it be me."

He leaned back, his crippled hand curled in his lap. "You're quite brave, aren't you?"

"No," she said. "I'm scared to death."

"I should tell you," he said, leaning toward her. "You wasted your time in coming here tonight. I'd already made up my mind."

Despair washed over her. "You won't change it?"

"Not for all the gold in the holy land," he said.

"My poor sister," Alys cried.

"A pox on your poor sister," he said mildly. "I'd already chosen you."

It was triumph; it was disaster. It was a surfeit of powerful wine. Alys slid off the padded stool and into a longed-for oblivion, right in front of her future husband.

Simon of Navarre looked down at her, sprawled gracelessly on the floor. Her coif had slipped, her braids were coming loose, with tendrils of soft hair framing her sleeping face. Her heavy brown gown had slid part way up her legs, exposing shapely ankles and strong calves. He wondered what her breasts would be like. He wanted to find out.

Instead he sat back in his chair, lifted his cramped right hand and stretched it from its claw-like position. The pain of the original injury had been enormous, the

pain of healing had been even worse. He reached for
the heavy bottle of wine with his strong, scarred hand
and poured himself another goblet full, his eyes resting
on his sleeping bride. She would know, soon enough,
that he was no more crippled than Richard's strongest
knight. She would know, when she was so enslaved by
him that she would never tell.

He knew how to enslave women. He knew tricks from
the far corners of the world, tricks to make a woman
quiver and scream and faint from pleasure.

He was going to enjoy using them on the little brown
wren who would be his wife.

Chapter Three

It wasn't exactly the life he would have chosen for himself, if he'd been given a choice. Sir Thomas du Rhaymer considered himself a simple man, with simple needs. A plain man, a soldier, who feared God, served his lord, championed the weak, and sought justice for all. Who would have thought his life would end up such a tangled mess?

He'd been born of decent stock in the north, soon sent down to Somerset as squire to Richard the Fair. It was a golden opportunity, his father had told him. Richard the Fair was cousin to the king himself, a glorious young lord who would go far in this world and take those who served him along with him.

And indeed, throughout the rigorous years of training, when Richard was young and seemingly fair in nature as well as form, young Thomas had worshipped him, honored to serve so noble a lord. He was knighted, and he gladly took the bride Richard chose for him. Gwyneth had been beautiful, high-born, and delicate.

She had also been Richard's leman, but Thomas had overlooked that small drawback. What he hadn't counted on was her utter faithlessness, her hunger for any man who came within her sight.

That hunger included her husband, and for a while he'd been blinded, entranced, lost in the thrall of her sweet-scented body and rich laughter, her pouts and her tears and her captivating beauty. Until he'd come home from a grueling two-week hunt to find her rollicking in his bed with two of his best friends.

He hadn't gone near her since. All her tears, her pleading had left him stonily unmoved, and gradually she centered her attentions on other, more fertile ground. She'd been gone more than a year now, living like a queen with one of Richard's wealthy barons, and Thomas lived like a soldier-monk. He had made vows before God, and a faithless wife wasn't going to cause him to break those vows.

He had lost his faith in Richard as well. Richard the unjust, the trickster, the sly, amoral fox who owned his loyalty, owned his good right arm and anything else he happened to need. The years had passed, and the other knights mocked Thomas as a man old before his time, a sour plague of a man, but he ignored them. Sooner or later he'd meet an enemy who was faster, more clever, more desperate, and it would be over. He would welcome the end if that was the way it was to come to him. He would never return north to the estates his father had left him, not without a wife and the future of children. That was no longer a possibility, not with Gwyneth cavorting with her wealthy baron.

There was one more possibility left in a bleak life, one chance that he could take. Richard was not noted for his kindness or decency, but every now and then he behaved with becoming generosity. Thomas could only pray that generosity would extend to him.

It was early, just past the first light, but Richard was awake. He slept little, smart enough not to trust in his men-at-arms to keep him safe. It was in the early morning that he conducted most of his business, and he'd agreed to grant Thomas an audience. He was seated at a table, his crimson robe wrapped loosely around his corpulent body, his thinning hair sticking out like straw. His eyes narrowed as he spied Thomas, but his mouth creased in a deceptively affable grin.

He wasn't alone. The wizard stood in the background, watching. The man was the spawn of the devil, Thomas knew that, and it took all his strength of will not to cross himself superstitiously when the man they called Grendel looked at him. But he'd been trained well. He stood straight and tall, facing his master, ready to ask for one last chance to find peace in this life.

"Thomas!" Richard greeted him. "You look grim this morning. But then, you always look grim, do you not? You should partake of more wine and less prayer. How goes your lady wife?"

"I have no idea, my lord. She lives with Baron Hawkesley."

"Ah, yes, I'd forgotten," said Richard, who forgot nothing. "A merry soul, our Gwyneth. Too much of a trial for you, I gather? Learn to hold your women, Thomas. That's the best advice I can give you. You should have beaten her more often. They learn to like it."

Thomas merely bowed, not about to involve himself in a moral or philosophical discussion with Lord Richard. "I request a boon of you, my lord," he said instead.

"So I gathered. And what is this boon? I'm not the man to grant you an annulment—you'll have to go to the pope for that. There are no new crusades for you to shed your blood over, no holy martyrs to follow.''

It would be useless to hesitate. Instead he said boldly, ''I would be released from my duties to join the brothers of Wildern Abbey.''

Richard's expression didn't change. Thomas allowed himself a brief glance at the magician who served him, but those cat's eyes were guarded. There would be neither help nor hindrance from that quarter.

''Why?'' Richard said finally, toying with the goblet in front of him. ''If you wish to leave my service you have lands and family to see to.''

''I feel called to serve God. This world is too shallow and difficult a place for me. I can best fulfill my duties through prayer and meditation, and serving others. . . .''

''You serve me very well in your present capacity,'' Richard said. He looked over his shoulder at his magician. ''Did I ever tell you, Simon of Navarre, about sober young Sir Thomas? He's quite the most prodigious fighting man I've ever had. He can outfight three men to one, and in a tournament he's unbeaten. I count him as one of my most treasured possessions.''

Thomas didn't allow any expression to cross his face, knowing his cause was lost.

''I believe you mentioned it, my lord,'' the man said in his low voice that echoed of magic and madness.

''You know, it's a shame I wasted a fancy creature like Gwyneth on a sober creature like you, Thomas,'' Richard said idly. ''You're much better suited to one like my sister. She wanted to be a nun, but of course I couldn't waste a valuable treasure like her on a convent. Sisters have some value, you know.''

''Indeed,'' Thomas muttered.

''But then, I wouldn't waste her on a lowly knight of indifferent lineage, no matter how renowned his fighting skills. You'll follow me, you'll do as I order, and I don't need to throw away a sister on you. Isn't that the truth of it?''

"Yes, my lord."

"And I have no intention of wasting you on a monastery, either. They sit around and grow fat on the tithes of their betters. You're a man who needs to earn his keep, Thomas. You're a knight, a soldier. A man who lives by the sword, not prayer."

"Yes, my lord."

"Then you know you'll be staying with me?" Richard was enjoying this, God rot his soul. And there was nothing Thomas could do about it. He'd taken a vow. He'd taken far too many vows in this life, and he couldn't break a single one of them. Only if God chose to release him. And it didn't look as if God in His infinite wisdom was ready to do so.

"Yes, my lord." He lowered his eyes, to keep the frustration and rage from Richard's observant gaze. Richard would know, of course. But he would only feed on the proof of it. He started to back away, accepting his dismissal, when the wizard leaned forward and whispered something in Richard's ear, a circumstance that didn't bode well.

"Stay a moment, Sir Thomas," Richard said, holding up a hand. "My Grendel has a most clever idea."

If Simon of Navarre had any objection to being called by a monster's name he showed none of it. "My lord?" Thomas said.

"Since you are so keen on eschewing the ways of the flesh you would be perfect as bodyguard to my sisters, particularly the younger one. While the elder is plain and far from tempting, the other is a bewitchment to stir most males. I can count on your strong right arm to keep those hungry males at bay, and your ascetic soul to keep your own lust under control.''

He'd heard of the sisters already. The one docile, the other a beauty. A heartless, faithless jade like his wife, no doubt. Proximity would be hell, as both Richard and his wicked advisor knew.

They also knew he would scarce object. He simply bowed low in acceptance. "Your faith in me does me honor," he said.

"If any man touches either of my sisters without my express permission," Richard continued, "then you may hack off whichever body part seems handy. There will be no exceptions. You understand? You're responsible for their chastity and obedience."

It was more than he could bear. "My lord, are you certain that women are capable of understanding the concepts of chastity and obedience?" he said.

"Probably not. But that's not my problem," Richard said sweetly. "That's yours."

And he heard the wizard laugh.

"Where were you?" Claire demanded, sitting up in the big, high bed, her hair atangle from a restless night's sleep.

Alys opened her eyes groggily. It was already past dawn, well into the morning hours, and she, who habitually rose at five, was still so tired she could scarcely move. "What do you mean?" she said with a prodigious yawn.

"I woke at midnight and you weren't here." There was no missing the accusation in her light voice. "And don't tell me you had gone in search of the garderobe, for I won't believe you. I was terrified, alone in this place, with none of the serving women nearby. I lay awake for hours, waiting for you to return."

"It must have only seemed like hours," Alys said, closing her eyes as a fierce pain in her head assailed her. The last day and evening were a blur of too many faces, too many voices, too much food and wine. In truth, at the moment she couldn't precisely remember where she'd gone last night. She knew she'd wanted to find the demon wizard, to force him to leave her sister in peace, but all she could remember was a sleep-drugged haze.

Her eyes shot open in sudden horror, as vague tendrils of memory filtered back. She *had* seen him. She'd drunk his wine. And maybe it wasn't sleep that had drugged her at all.

She scrambled out of bed in sudden panic, only to discover she'd slept in her clothes. Her plain, serviceable gown of muddy brown was wrinkled but still tightly fastened, and she still wore her hose, though her soft leather shoes were at the side of the bed. He hadn't touched her, she knew that with a certainty that she could only call relief.

Claire had risen to her knees, staring at her sister with troubled green eyes. "What happened, Alys? What did you do?"

"I'm . . . I'm not quite certain," she confessed, pulling at her crumpled gown. The rest of her clothing was even less flattering than the plain gown, but she would have little choice in the matter of changing. She couldn't present herself to her brother looking like a slattern.

"I believe I had an audience with Grendel."

Claire shuddered. "Don't call him that!" she cried. "I can't bear the thought of marrying such a monster. I'll throw myself from a window before I let him touch me. . . ."

"Put your soul at rest, dearest," Alys said wearily. "He's going to marry me."

Claire's expression was—insultingly—one of shock. "Don't be ridiculous. That's impossible."

Memory was coming back, clearer than ever. The dark, shadowy room, lit only by flickering firelight, the honeyed sweetness of the wine, the beguiling murmur of his voice. She'd been astonishingly bold, but he'd been even more shocking.

The only thing she couldn't remember was what had happened after he told her he would marry her. And how she'd managed to return along those deserted hallways to find herself in bed with her sister once more.

"Not the slightest bit impossible. I went to beg him to leave you alone. He told me he'd already chosen me. There's the end of it."

Claire's expression was one of disbelief. "It makes no sense," she said after a moment. "Not that any decent, wise man wouldn't prefer you, my love, but I have yet to discover that men are either wise or decent. And certainly our brother's wizard could not be counted on to make the right choice. I would have thought he would have preferred beauty. . . ." Her voice trailed off before Alys's ironic expression. "You know what I mean," she mumbled contritely.

"Perhaps he prefers a wife capable of tact," Alys stated, stripping off the rest of her clothes to bathe using the icy bowl of water left by their bedstead. "Or someone who'll fade into the background and leave him in peace. I have no idea, but I'm not about to quarrel with it. Neither should you. Count your blessings that I'm to be sacrificed to the monster and not you."

Claire immediately burst into noisy tears, but for once, Alys made no move to comfort her. She was cold, she was weary, and her head ached abominably. On top of that, she was the one who would wed the monster, not Claire. If anyone deserved comfort, it was she.

Except that Simon of Navarre hadn't seemed quite so monstrous in the midnight stillness of his tower room. He frightened her, there was no denying that, but he fascinated her as well. And if he'd sold his soul to Beelzebub in return for infernal powers, at least that lord of demons had granted him a surprising measure of physical beauty as well. Except for that poor, twisted hand that lay useless in his lap as he watched her, he was quite . . . bewitching.

She pulled on a fresh shift. There was still no sign of their absent serving women, and Alys had no intention of standing around in the drafty room without clothes. She was lost in thought while Claire, unused to being ignored, gradually stilled her noisy sobs to stare at her sister in growing suspicion. "You don't actually fancy the creature, do you?" she whispered.

Alys started guiltily. "Hardly that, Claire," she said briskly. "But neither do I find him repugnant. I'm sure we'll manage a comfortable life. . . ."

"A comfortable life?" Claire shrieked. "Alys, he's a monster! He's enchanted you, with one of his evil spells. We must get back to the convent, to see Brother Emory at once. He'll know what to do to break the spell. Sister Agnes could prepare you a potion. . . ."

"He hasn't enchanted me," Alys said calmly. Wishing she were absolutely certain of it.

"How else could you view marriage to a monster with such equanimity?"

Alys sighed. There were times when her beloved Claire's flair for the dramatic could be extremely tiresome. "If by any chance he happened to bewitch me, then I suppose it's just as well I've been blinded by magic. One of us has to marry him, and we're fortunate that he's chosen me and not you. If I go to my marriage bed under an enchantment then perhaps it's God's mercy.''

"I wouldn't put God and that demon's name in the same sentence,'' Claire said darkly. "You'll bed the creature?''

Alys had her back to Claire, a fortunate circumstance. There was no way she could pretend calm acceptance to that particular aspect of the marriage bargain. "That's usually part of any marriage,'' she said, keeping her face averted. "Unless my lord Grend . . . Simon of Navarre prefers celibacy.''

"I doubt God would be that merciful,'' Claire said. "Perhaps he prefers those of his own sex. 'Tis often said of wizards.''

Alys struggled for common sense. "Well, I suppose in truth I prefer the company of women, so there's nothing so odd. . . .''

"I'm not talking about preferring the company of one's own sex, Alys. I'm talking about bedding them.''

Alys turned at that, shocked. "Wherever did you hear of such things?''

For the first time in days Claire smiled her bewitchingly naughty smile. "The nuns gossip when they think no one's around.''

"How could men prefer to mate with their own sex? How could they. . . ?''

"Some women do as well. Particularly among the nuns.''

"I don't believe you,'' Alys said flatly.

"For a woman as learned as you are, I'm surprised at how innocent you can be.''

"You've spent too much time around the stables.''

"And you've spent too little,'' Claire shot back. "One

can learn a great deal about human nature by watching the beasts.''

"Are you going to tell me that horses mate with their own sex?''

"No, I gather that's a human trait. And if your future husband shares it we can only be thankful. It would also explain why he preferred you to me.''

Alys could only laugh at her sister's ingenuous statement. "Dearest, you really are captivated with yourself,'' she said.

Claire's smile was endearingly wry. "I know. It was ever one of my failings. But it's not my particular accomplishment, to be so lovely. God simply granted it to me, and I'm not certain it was such a great gift after all. There are times when I wish I were a plain, simple woman with plain, simple wants.''

"Like me,'' Alys said.

"No, not like you. You are far too clever, and a great deal more complicated than I could ever wish to be. No, when I see the peasant women, surrounded by children and a loving husband, all their lives in strict order, I wish I could change places with them.''

"I'm certain they'd gladly change places with you,'' Alys said. The silvered glass that showed her reflection was wavery, which was just as well. She doubted her image would please her, particularly in the ill-fitting gray kirtle.

"And when does Grendel make his announcement?'' Claire demanded, climbing out of bed and yawning extravagantly.

"I have no notion. Perhaps he's already told our brother. . . . Don't call him that!'' she said belatedly.

"You called him that yourself.''

"It was a slip of the tongue. He's no monster, Claire.''

All lightness and humor vanished from Claire's lovely face. "Are you certain, Alys?"

"I don't believe in monsters. They're stories from childhood, told by the nuns to scare us into behaving. They don't really exist."

"That's not what I mean," Claire said. "I mean, are you certain you're willing to marry him? Surely we could do something to stop it? Perhaps Lady Hedwiga would help us when she returns. If you really dreaded it I imagine it wouldn't take much to make him change his mind again. You've always taken such good care of me, I would do anything you wanted. I would be willing to . . . sacrifice myself."

And she meant it. Of that Alys had little doubt. Claire's heart was good and kind and generous, beneath her youthful folly and self-absorption. She would marry the monster for her sister's sake. She would die for her sister's sake.

And in return, it was the least that Alys could do for her. Her future had never appeared to be particularly glorious. She was too plain, too clever, too outspoken. Lord Richard's interference would only make things worse, not better.

In all, marriage to the magician would probably be no great disaster. If, as Claire suggested, he preferred his own sex, then that would be a relief. One that would deny her the joy of children, but Claire would have dozens of them, and Alys was prepared to be a splendid aunt.

In all, things were working out as well as could be expected. She had accomplished what she set out to accomplish, and all would be well.

If only she didn't have this looming presentiment of utter and complete disaster.

"I'm not afraid of Simon of Navarre, or of marriage," she said calmly. Lying.

Claire nodded, satisfied. "Then let's go break the news to our dear brother. And see what alternative he has in store for me."

Chapter Four

The Great Hall of Summersedge Keep was alive with activity that late morning. Richard had already broken his fast earlier that day, but he'd grown increasing fond of food and ale, and he ate heartily of bread and cheese and honey while he surveyed his motley household.

Simon of Navarre barely touched the food in front of him. He had few weaknesses, and food and drink were not numbered among them. He was far more interested in observing the inhabitants of the keep and their relationships with their lord and master.

Richard the Fair wasn't quite a prince, though he doubtless wished he were. Second cousin to Henry the Third, the boy king, he could trace his lineage back to William the Conqueror, but then, so could countless others. He had a household of more than two hundred strong, knights and squires, family members and retainers, soldiers and servants. And of course, the castle magician. The wizard, the monster who haunted the corridors and frightened small children. The Grendel.

Simon of Navarre kept his expression calm and clear, ignoring the wary glances, the furtive crossing motions when his gaze would happen to drift across some hapless soul. Even the knights, stalwart and fearless in battle, would do their best to avoid his path. Men like Sir Thomas du Rhaymer would rather face a dozen battle axes than the spawn of the devil.

It was Sir Thomas who particularly amused Simon of Navarre. Sir Thomas, with the whoring wife and the stern morality. Sir Thomas, who never sinned and yet managed to spend a goodly time confessing to Brother Jerome his slightest transgressions.

Simon of Navarre had observed the look in Thomas's eyes when he first gazed on Richard's sisters. The pain, and the longing, quickly repressed when Claire had moved into view. Followed by disapproval as fierce as Thomas's courage.

Which would prove stronger, Thomas's stern morals or Claire's wild beauty? The conflict would be interesting over the next few weeks, and distracting for a brother intent on evil deeds. If Claire didn't do her part, Simon of Navarre had every intention of replacing Thomas with someone more tempting. Richard might think he had the running of his household, but in that he was deluded. For the past three years his wizard had seen to it that he got everything he wanted, and not a soul had interfered. Lady Hedwiga ignored his very existence, too absorbed in her solitude to bother with her household, and Richard was too intent on the pursuit of pleasure. Leaving Simon in power.

He didn't think he was going to have to change Claire's guardian, though. His instincts about such things were infallible, and the flighty Claire would be illogical enough to fancy a stern moralist such as Sir

Thomas. Particularly a married one, forever out of her reach.

Indeed, as Lady Claire cast a glance over the assembled knights, her eyes lingered momentarily upon Thomas. Perhaps it was simply because he was staring at her with fixed disapproval. Perhaps it was because Thomas was undoubtedly an extremely handsome man.

Or perhaps it was just the beneficent workings of fate.

"Claire!" Richard shouted in greeting, dipping a piece of bread in his goblet of dark ale. "Come sit between me and your future husband and tell us what you wish of us. I've a mind to give you a jeweled collar that belongs to my lady wife. Hedwiga has a thick neck but a very great deal of money, and now she has embraced God and eschewed decoration, including her jewels. It would look far prettier on your slender neck."

The beauty had torn her gaze away from Sir Thomas's, and she now looked at her brother with confused dismay, stealing a glance at his companion as well.

So the elder sister had promised her all would be well, Simon of Navarre surmised, and now she didn't know what to believe. He wondered how much Alys remembered of the previous night. The wine had been drugged, and she was already weary and nervous when she approached the solitude of his tower rooms. He'd been both astonished and enchanted by her temerity. There were few men who would dare seek out his presence, and no women. With the exception of this plain, fierce little wren.

She was there, of course, blending in with the somberly-dressed serving women. Her gown today was even more dreary than the brown thing she had worn yesterday, something he wouldn't have thought possible. It was too long for her small frame, too large to show her plump curves to advantage. Her hair was pulled tightly back from her pale face, and she looked as if she were in pain. He suspected she was. The potion she'd drunk down so heartily the night before exacted its own penance by the following morning, with a pounding head and a roiling stomach, particularly if one was unused to it.

She was looking at him as well, with a combination of hope and confusion. Perhaps she thought she'd dreamed her encounter with him last night. After all, she had slept like the dead when he'd had her borne back to her own rooms.

He hadn't wanted to let anyone else touch her, but he couldn't risk being seen. He'd had Piers, a strong young man with no interest in members of the opposite sex, lift her up in his arms and carry her with a maternal tenderness, and Simon of Navarre had followed, watching, intent, half wishing she'd awaken and he could send Piers away.

But she'd slept soundly, as her sister had when Piers set Alys down on the high bed beside her. Claire's silken hair lay spread around her, and her pale, lovely flesh was exposed above the thin chemise, but neither Piers nor Simon of Navarre noticed, for their own, disparate reasons.

He'd dismissed Piers, giving in to the temptation to stand watching Alys as she slept. Alys, with the pale face and the plump body, all fierceness drained from her soul by the drugged sleep he'd offered her.

Christ, but he wanted her! It was an odd feeling, after having kept his hungers in check for so many years. He was used to controlling his needs, but this small, unspectacular woman was having a strange effect on him. If he didn't know better he'd suspect witchcraft.

Ah, but he was the expert at witchcraft around here. He knew, better than anyone, what was possible and what was not. And there was no possibility on this green earth that he would fall under the spell of a woman, particularly an ordinary little creature like Lady Alys of Summersedge.

She should have been a nun. But then, he'd been a monk for a brief period of time, and he knew far too well that holy orders couldn't quell unholy desires. He had looked down at her as she lay in her bed, and wanted her.

Then her sister had stirred, and silently Simon of Navarre had slipped back into the darkness. Claire had sat up, alert, but in the shifting shadows she could see nothing. She simply sank down on the bed again, falling back into a deep sleep.

And Simon of Navarre had wished her at perdition. He wanted to be the one to lie beside Alys's body, feel her warmth, listen to her breathe. He wanted to strip the ugly clothes from her body and discover just what fascinated him so.

He was still distracted by that curiosity the next day, as he sat in the chair beside Richard, watching her. He hadn't slept, though that was not unusual, and now he accepted the fact that it wasn't time for him to satisfy either his curiosity or his inexplicable lust. He was a man used to waiting, to making sure the opportunity offered the most. He would wait for Alys. For a while.

"My lord," Simon of Navarre said gently, but Richard had had enough ale to ignore him, something he was usually too wise to do.

"You may sit on my left hand, Alys," he brayed magnanimously. "Don't worry, we'll find you a husband. Though it might help if you could find something better to wear. That gown looks like it came from the charity box at the abbey. Your looks are nothing to brag of, but you could improve matters with a bit of color. Don't you think so, Grendel?'' he demanded.

"I would hesitate to contradict you, my lord," he murmured. Claire had stopped, unwilling to move closer, and Alys practically barreled into her.

"Well, they can't all be beauties," Richard said with a wet belch. "What shall we do with Alys, wizard? Shall we send her back to the convent after all and make her a happy woman?"

"No, my lord. You should give her to me in marriage," Simon of Navarre said calmly. He could see a flash of something in Alys's eyes, but whether it was relief or despair, he couldn't tell.

Richard turned to stare at him. "Good God, man, you can't really have 'em both!" he shouted. "The church frowns on bigamy, just ask Brother Jerome."

"I'm certain you have far greater plans for Lady Claire," Simon of Navarre said calmly.

For a moment the hall was silent with shock. And then Richard laughed, a hearty bellow that made Lady Alys flinch and put a hand to her pounding head. "By God, you're right, Simon of Navarre! Take the plain one—she'll do for you, and once you're between her legs I doubt you'll know the difference."

"My lord Richard," Brother Jerome spoke up with stern reproof, but Richard just waved an airy hand at him.

"They've been in a convent too long, Brother Jerome. It's about time they knew what women were made for. That's why God fashioned 'em, isn't it? To procreate? I can't think what other use they could be."

Simon of Navarre watched with amusement as Brother Jerome struggled to control his dismay. As far as clerics went, Brother Jerome was not a bad man. A little too serious, a bit too eager to heap on the penances on his unruly flock, but not devoid of true Christian charity. Something Simon of Navarre wasn't always certain even existed.

"Come here, lass," Richard bellowed at Alys. "You're a sly one, cutting out your sister, but Grendel's got the right of it. She'll do far better, and while any baron of England would be lucky to get a bride of my blood, a pretty one will be that much more welcome."

"How fortuitous," Lady Alys said faintly, mounting the dais and taking a seat beside her brother.

"And no more whining about taking the veil, eh? You'll learn to like Simon of Navarre here well enough. He's got a sharp tongue, but he isn't known to beat his horses or his servants. Behave yourself and you'll do very well."

She didn't dare look at him, Simon of Navarre noticed. She kept her eyes downcast like a docile creature. He suspected that she was, in truth, no more docile than her high-strung younger sister. She was just more adept at hiding it.

A clever woman. A danger. But far less dangerous in his bed, where he could keep an eye on her.

Richard swung away from his sister, his quicksilver attention dismissing her as he focussed on Simon of Navarre. "There's but one thing that occupies my mind. Why, my Grendel?" he demanded. "Why take the lesser when I've offered you the greater prize?"

He could feel Claire's curious eyes on him as well, and he suspected she was just as bewildered. "My lord, I could give you any number of satisfactory answers to your question. Perhaps I wished to please you by accepting what you valued less. Or I cared little which one I took, and Lady Alys seemed less troublesome."

"Both admirable reasons," Richard said sagely. "Neither of which are particularly like you, Grendel. What is your real reason for choosing plain Alys over the lovely Claire?''

"Perhaps because I don't consider Lady Alys to be the slightest bit plain, my lord," he said.

It worked, as well as he could have hoped. Brother Jerome nodded in approval. Lady Claire looked suitably pleased at the praise to her sister, something which raised her a notch in his esteem. Lady Alys managed to lift her gaze from the bread in front of her to cast a curious, hopeful glance in his direction. It was, of course, tinged with doubt, but he was already used to the lady's intelligence. She would take nothing at face value. He would have to work hard to keep her off balance, but he always relished a challenge. It kept him alert.

"Reasonable, I suppose," Richard announced. "I should be used to your odd ways by now. When do you wish to be wed?"

If he answered in three months' time, the wedding would be performed that day. And while he had a great deal of interest in seducing shy Lady Alys, he wasn't particularly eager for the complications of marriage quite yet.

"As soon as it pleases you, my lord."

Richard rose to the bait, as always. "We shall see. Lady Hedwiga will have something to say in the matter, and I expect she'll insist on waiting. My sister needs time to accustom herself to the change in her circumstances. She's not used to men, and she's certainly not used to men like you. You need to woo her, Grendel. Court the girl. Write her love poems. Bring her flowers. You'd like that, wouldn't you, Alys?" he demanded.

Alys looked up, her hazel eyes wide with relief. "Yes, my lord," she said softly. And Simon knew perfectly well it was the delay in their nuptials, not the anticipated courtship, that she found pleasing.

"If he wants you, and for some reason he seems to, then he'll have to earn you," Richard pronounced, draining his ale. "Though I shudder to think of what offspring he'll get on you."

And Simon of Navarre noticed lazily that Lady Alys shuddered as well.

The curving stairwell was shadowed, lit only by the narrow arrow slits, but Claire moved swiftly downward, keeping her full skirts tight to her body. She didn't dare change her clothes—it would cause too much comment, and right now the smartest thing she could do would be to make herself as inconspicuous as possible.

A difficult thing, given the looks God had graced her with. Alys loved to tease her about her vanity, but indeed, it was no such thing. As she had told Alys, the pleasing contours of her face and form were no accomplishment of hers, and therefore nothing to take pride in. She had been fashioned a beauty by a generous God, and while she took pleasure in that fact, she took no responsibility.

Brother Emory had warned her, the holy sisters had warned her, and they'd been right. This was her first trip out into the world, and she had discovered she was, indeed, extraordinary. They stared at her when she moved through the halls, the old women with pleasure, the young ones with jealous anger. And the men.

She shuddered. She disliked the hunger she could see in their moist eyes, their thick-lipped mouths. Even her own brother let his red-rimmed eyes travel over her with a look that felt like a touch, and she hated it.

There were only three men in that castle of men

who seemed impervious to her: the magician, Simon of Navarre, who possessed an entirely illogical desire for her older sister; and Brother Jerome, whose calling and whose goodness precluded lustful thoughts.

And then there was the knight. The handsome one, who stared at her with cool dislike, the only one in a crowd of leering men. It was no wonder he'd caught her eye.

Perhaps he wasn't that handsome. He was tall enough, and his pale hair was cut short in the Norman style, presumably to fit under his helm. He looked very strong, very stern, with flinty blue eyes that never seemed to soften, a hard mouth that never seemed to smile. He looked at her with blatant disapproval, and her mischievous nature had immediately been aroused.

She had more important things to think about this morning than a dour knight, however. She'd managed to escape the tower room Richard had allotted them, but just barely. Alys was ill, with a pounding in her head that she insisted was nothing dangerous; she simply needed peace and quiet. While the serving women sat by her side, Claire had slipped behind the tapestry and out into the empty hallway, intent on finding her way to the stables.

She'd been too long without seeing Arabia. She'd raised the mare from a foal, and there was no greater bond between horse and mistress imaginable. She loved her sleek, beautiful horse with a passionate intensity. The only creature who took precedence was Alys, and while Claire loved her more than Arabia, she would far rather spend time with the horse.

She had no idea whether she'd be able to escape the stifling confines of Summersedge Keep and go for a run through the countryside, the wind slapping her in the face. She needed fresh air, away from the smell of men and dogs and smoke. She needed the sun on her face, or the rain drenching her skin, she didn't care which, as long as she was out in the fresh air.

There was a door into the courtyard at the bottom of the tower, and she stepped out, keeping close to the walls. The kitchen buildings were a hive of activity; Richard the Fair obviously put a great store by his meals. In the far corner men at arms were training, and she stopped for a moment, peering in their direction, looking for the stern and handsome knight. Would he fight well? She suspected he would. A man would have to feel very sure of his abilities to pass judgment on women he'd never even spoken to.

"Silly," she said to herself, the soft sound of her voice barely heard over the noise of the midday courtyard. "Who's to say he disapproves of you? Maybe he just has a gloomy expression. It might be the result of a wound."

The more she thought about it, however, the more unlikely it seemed. While that handsome face was not devoid of battle scars, the old wounds were slight, pale, and well-healed. She wondered how the rest of his tall, strong body had fared.

She giggled at the deliciously naughty thought. Alys wouldn't understand. Alys was never tempted to do something wicked, just for the fun of it. Alys thought fun was working hard, loving others, taking care of her sister. Alys was a bore.

Still, Claire loved her dearly. And if she had any say in the matter, neither of them would be sacrificed to Richard's pet demon.

True, he wasn't monstrous looking, if you avoided gazing into his golden, merciless eyes. But there was something about his tall, ominous presence that made Claire shiver with superstitious horror. The very thought of sweet Alys bedding such a man was enough to make her weep.

Still, there would be time. Richard had decreed that Simon of Navarre must court her elder sister, and if the wedding date were dependent on how successful the courtship was, then Alys might very well die a maiden. There was no way a sensible woman could ever be tempted by one such as the wizard, and Alys was a supremely sensible woman.

Claire could smell the stables, ambrosia under the hot sun. No one seemed to realize she'd slipped out of the castle, and she darted forward, intent on reaching the stables before anyone noticed that Lord Richard's golden-haired sister was about.

The shadow loomed up out of nowhere, huge and threatening, cutting off the light, and Claire uttered a small scream, one that was silenced by the hand that clamped over her mouth; the other hand wrapped around her waist and drew her back into the shadows.

She kicked back, furiously, biting down hard on the hand that silenced her, hard enough to bring blood. She was released, just as suddenly, flung away from her attacker into the shadows. The man who'd captured her didn't curse, which surprised her. She was even more startled by the sight of his stern face glowering down at her. It was the grimly handsome knight who'd been watching her.

"How dare you lay hands on me?" she demanded. "Who do you think you are, to assault Lord Richard's own sister? I'll have you whipped. . . ."

"I doubt it," he said calmly enough, his voice low and clipped. "My orders come from your brother himself."

Claire stared at him in disbelief. "You lie."

"I never lie. It's a sin."

"And I suppose you never sin," she snapped back.

"All too often, my lady. But I make my confession, and Brother Jerome gives me penance and absolution. I would think you could do with both of those gifts."

"What makes you think I'm a sinner?"

"We're all sinners," he said heavily. "Particularly women."

Claire was not one to take such words lightly. She moved closer, observing him in the shadows. He was just as handsome close up, with his darkly bronzed skin, his icy eyes, his pale hair. And he was just as disapproving. "If we're sinners, it's because men lead us astray," she said. "You say you're following my brother's orders? And what are they, pray tell?"

He'd drawn a scrap of cloth from beneath his tunic and was casually wrapping it around his hand. "I've been commissioned to watch over you and your sister. To protect you from insult, and from error."

"I don't need your protection, whoever you are. I can take care of myself. Go watch over my sister if you must."

"Your sister is the least of my worries. And I am Thomas du Rhaymer. Knight to your brother, Lord Richard."

"So you said." He didn't smell of ale, or sweat, like most of the other men in the keep. "I absolve you of your duties, Sir Thomas. Go away and watch over some other hapless female." She started past him, but he reached out and caught her, whirling her around to meet his stern gaze. His grip was not painful, but it was unbreakable.

"I'm afraid that's not your choice, my lady. I take my orders from my liege lord and no one else. He's told me to watch over you and make certain you behave yourself, and I intend to do just that."

He was still holding on to her arm, unwilling to release

her, and she told herself he was infuriating. In truth, he was. But he was also interestingly masterful.

Claire, however, was not interested in being mastered at the moment. She was interested in riding. "I'm on my way to visit my horse," she said grandly. "You may accompany me if you wish, Sir Thomas."

"No, my lady. You'll come back inside the keep."

She glared up at him, no longer appreciating the firm grip on her upper arm. "I'll do no such thing. I'm going riding."

He didn't bother to argue. He simply hauled her with him, back to the thick oak door at the base of the tower. She struggled, but it was useless against a man of his strength, and he simply shoved her through the door, following her and closing them into the darkness.

"My brother will cut off your hands," she hissed at him.

He began dragging her up the circular stairs. "I doubt it. My hands are far too valuable to his lordship, and I'm simply following his orders. He told me to beat you if I'd a mind to. In theory I don't believe in beating women, but you may be an exception."

They'd reached the first landing by that time, illuminated by an arrow slit, and acting purely on instinct, she kicked out at him, her leather-slippered foot connecting with hard, solid shin.

It hurt her far more than it must have hurt him, but he uttered a strangled cry and slammed her hard against the stone wall, practically leaning against her in his fury. "Do that again, mistress, and you won't sit down for a week."

She searched her memory for a suitable curse. The Convent of Saint Anne the Demure hadn't been fertile ground for attaining curses, but one emerged when most needed. "Camel-swiving son of a goatherd," she snarled.

He paused, and she thought he was going to hit her then. Instead he choked back a sound that was infuriatingly close to a laugh. But Sir Thomas du Rhaymer didn't appear to be a man intimately acquainted with laughter.

He released her, suddenly. "Get back upstairs, my lady," he said. "And do not make the mistake of kicking me again."

Her sleeve was wet where he'd held it. She glanced down, and saw the dark red stain of blood on her upper arm. "You've hurt me," she gasped.

He sighed, already weary of her. "Nay, my lady. I was bitten by a she-wolf a while back, and I bled on the sorry bitch."

She was speechless. No one had ever dared to speak to her in such a manner. She wanted to slap his cool, disapproving face, but she didn't dare. She wanted to kick him in the vitals, but she doubted she'd survive such an attempt.

"Pig," she said succinctly, turning her back on him and attempting to climb the stairs. Unfortunately her foot had born the brunt of his shin, and she found herself limping quite badly.

Doubtless he knew what had lamed her, and doubtless he didn't care. "Vixen," he replied evenly.

She found her brother in his solar, stretched out in one of the ornately carved chairs, a leg of fowl in his hand, his lips besmeared with grease. He looked none too pleased to see her, but Claire could not have cared less. At least his pet wizard was nowhere to be seen.

"I've been attacked, brother!" she announced.

Richard appeared unimpressed. He took another bite. "Anyone interesting?"

"That . . . that creature you set to guard me!" she cried. "He's insulted me most grievously."

"Thomas? I doubt it. He's hardly a man at all, he's simply a weapon. I doubt he even realizes what you've got beneath your skirts." He tossed the bone down onto the floor and two huge dogs immediately leapt for it.

Claire flushed at his deliberate crudity. "He put his hands on me. He hurt me."

"Beat you, did he? I told him he had my leave."

She was speechless with shock. "I simply wanted to see my horse. . . ."

"You have no horse."

A chill fear settled over Claire's heart. "I mistook your words, brother. I mean Arabia, the mare I. . . ."

"She's not yours, wench. Everything you own belongs to me, including that huge horse. She's too much for a lady to ride; she's far better suited to one of my weight. We'll find you a lady's mount, something gentle and well-bred. When I've decided you've settled down enough."

She stared at him in disbelief. "She's mine," she said helplessly.

"You grow tiresome, Claire." Richard pushed away from the table. "Listen to your elder sister. She'll explain things to you, since you seem curiously lack-witted this morning. The horse is mine, and you are mine, to do with as I please. Body and soul." He was standing too close to her, this brother of hers, and he no longer looked bored. His eyes were suddenly hot and possessive. "Do you understand me?"

Claire couldn't move. She had to be imagining the threat in her brother's eyes. Sheltered she'd been, but she knew which laws were God's laws, and the abomination he was hinting at was horrifying. She backed away, slowly. "I understand, my lord."

"And you won't give poor Thomas any more trouble, now will you?" he continued in a more jovial voice, as if the sudden, twisted threat had been imaginary. "He has enough to distress him, what with his wanton wife."

"Wife?" There was no reason why those words should sound so deadly. She hated the brute.

"Quite a beauty, our Gwyneth. Almost as pretty as you, I dare say. Thomas considered himself quite lucky when he married her. I doubt he still thinks so." He caught Claire's chin with his rough hand, and his thick fingers stroked her jaw, a slow, lascivious stroke. "He's the perfect watchdog for you, Claire. He hates women, particularly pretty ones. So don't push him too far, eh? Have pity on us poor men."

She looked at her brother with undisguised hatred. Alys had never been able to teach her how to hide her emotions, and they lay in her face for all to see.

"Ah, you hate me, don't you? Don't worry, my pet. If you please me, I may grant you that splendid horse as a wedding gift to your husband. Then you may battle with him over which of you will do the riding." He laughed coarsely, releasing her. He looked behind her. "Take this tiresome wench away, will you, Grendel? I've had enough aggravation for the day. You made a wise choice, you know. This one is pretty enough, but tedious in the extreme."

She hadn't realized that Lord Simon of Navarre had arrived. She wondered how long he'd been watching. "It would be my honor to escort Lady Claire back to her sister," he said in his rich, deep voice.

"I can find my way myself," she said furiously, running from the room in a flurry of skirts before they could stop her.

But as she ran, she thought she heard the devil's laughter following her.

Chapter Five

Alys was not made for idleness. She spent the morning in the room she shared with Claire and their serving women, stitching at a piece of fancy work, worrying about her absent sister. A quiet nap enshrouded in darkness had taken care of her aching head, and apart from a lingering queasiness she felt quite well. Too well, in fact. In her brother's castle she had no duties, no tasks to perform, no patients to see. She had always been fascinated by the study of herbs, and Sister Agnes had passed on her limited knowledge. Half the time Alys was afraid she did more harm than good, but at least she'd managed to bring relief to some sufferers.

One of the serving women at the keep had burned herself quite badly, and Alys had seen that the skin was scorched and reddened. Sister Agnes had always sworn on the efficacy of spiders' webs applied to the wound, and certainly Summersedge Keep was more than adequately supplied with the like. With lady Hedwiga on religious retreat, there was no one to oversee the run-

ning of the place, and only the servants' justified fear
of Lord Richard kept the meals halfway decent.

She suspected Richard had no interest in having her
take over the day-to-day task of running the castle in
the absence of his wife. He would probably just as soon
hand her over to his pet monster and have done with
it.

She sat back in the chair, letting her needlework drop
in her lap. She had a stay of execution—she should be
grateful for that much. The wizard would court her, of
all the absurd ideas, and the wedding would take place
in due time. She couldn't imagine any space of time
that would allay her fears. If anything, time would only
allow her dread to grow.

She also couldn't begin to imagine that tall, intimidating creature approaching her with sonnets and posies,
with declarations and requests for a token of her colors.
She couldn't imagine him with a sword—a wizard's staff
seemed far more likely. She couldn't imagine him in
bed with her. . . .

She rose quickly, shutting off that line of thought
before it could lead to murkier places. She knew what
went on between men and women, and she accepted
the fact that the same thing would happen to her,
whether she wished it or not. She simply hasn't expected
it to happen with a man possessed of supernatural
powers.

She wouldn't think about it, or him. Instead she would
gather her soft leather pouch of healing herbs and go
in search of the serving woman. Or someone who
needed her to do something. Her own company was
not the most cheering in the world—she desperately
needed distraction.

She passed Claire on the broad stone staircase that
led down into the kitchens, and her mood didn't

lighten. Her sister looked as furious as only Claire could get, with bright red flags of anger in her cheeks, her golden hair awry, her green eyes blazing. She looked more beautiful than ever, of course, a fact Alys accepted wryly.

"Where were you, dear one?" she asked.

"Being assaulted!" Claire snapped. "I can't bear it here, Alys! He's taken Arabia away from me, and he's put this hideous brute in charge of me. You too, for that matter. I shall fling myself from the battlements, I swear I shall, and then he'll regret his wickedness."

"Calm, my pet. Be calm," Alys said, catching her sister's arm and forcing her to halt her furious dash. "Take a deep breath and explain yourself. What hideous brute? Who's taken Arabia away? And no, you are not going to throw yourself from the battlements, and you know it. It would damn your soul for eternity, and no day's annoyance would be worth the price."

"It goes beyond annoyance!" Claire cried. "It's Richard! He has taken my horse from me, and says she was never mine to begin with."

"In fact, love, he's right. We own nothing that isn't due to his generosity."

"I can't lose Arabia, Alys." Claire's face crumpled, her furious bravado vanishing. "I wouldn't be able to bear it."

"Be patient. Richard is one of those men who like a fight. The more you argue with him, the more determined he'll be to spite you. Be docile and he'll lose interest."

"I thought you hadn't seen him since you were a child?"

"It didn't take me long to realize the kind of man he is. Besides, we've heard rumors all our lives. Richard the Fair is the lord of the castle and all the surrounding demesnes, not to mention his holdings throughout England, and he makes certain all know his power. To defy his will is to court disaster. Now who is the hideous brute? I trust you aren't referring to my future husband?''

Claire looked momentarily abashed. "Certainly not. I'm certain Lord Simon will be an excellent . . . er. . . .''

"Lying is a sin," said Alys. Claire shut her mouth, unwilling to summon another word, and Alys gave her a brisk hug. "Go upstairs and change your clothes. Your gown is sadly soiled. What did you run into?" She reached up and brushed at the rust-colored stains on Claire's tight sleeve.

"A barbarian," Claire replied. "Someone who makes Grendel appear warm and kindly."

"With our kind of luck, he'll be the one Richard chooses to marry you."

Alys watched with fascination as Claire's face paled. "Not likely," she said briskly. "He's already wed to some poor woman. At least I'm safe from that. He's to guard us, both of us, Alys. And a meaner, more brutish creature I've yet to meet. We'll be lucky if he doesn't murder us in our beds."

"You cannot be serious!"

"Can't I?" Claire said tartly. "Wait till he accosts you with his threats and ugly visage. Sir Thomas du Rhaymer is a nightmare come true."

Alys shook her head. "Go lie down, Claire, and stop babbling. If you want I'll brew you an herb posset to. . . .''

"No!" Claire said with a violent shudder. "I need to be left alone. Just a few minutes' peace, please, love."

Alys nodded. "You'll feel better afterwards. And if I run into your hated Sir Thomas I'll give him a swift kick."

"You can try," Claire said morosely, then turned and continued up the stairs without another word.

Alys watched her go, momentarily distracted. Claire's temper was hot and fierce, but quick to blow over. Whoever the brutish Sir Thomas was, he'd best watch his step around her sister. She could make life hell for any man, even a married one who hated women.

She found the injured woman sitting in a corner of the bake house. The smell of fresh bread and rich yeast filled the warm building, and for the first time Alys began to feel at home. The servants regarded her warily at first, but she'd always had a certain gift with people, and their distrust seemed to drop away quite quickly. Soon Morwenna, the injured woman, was chattering away while her fellow servants looked on.

She'd tried beeswax, she said, and spiders' webs, and neither had worked. Her mother had always insisted horse dung was a cure-all, but she hadn't quite decided whether she should eat it or apply it to the wound. What did Lady Alys think she should do?

Lady Alys did her best not to gag at the very notion. She had no strong belief in the efficacy of horse dung, but she tried to keep an open mind, and none of the traditional remedies had seemed to make any difference in poor Morwenna's arm. She wasn't able to work, and Richard wasn't the sort of master to tolerate a nonproductive servant.

"Who does the healing here?" she inquired. "Is Brother Jerome skilled in the arts? Perhaps he might have a suggestion or two."

Morwenna shook her head. "Brother Jerome is useless when it comes to anything but spiritual matters."

"What of the barber. . . ?"

"Not for a servant, my lady, meaning no disrespect," Morwenna muttered.

"But then who takes care of you all?"

Silence reigned in the warm bakery house. And then one of the men spoke up. " 'Tis Grendel. And most of us would rather die than let him touch us. Better to lose your life than your immortal soul. All that monster has to do is look at you and you're done for. If he put his hands on you your doom is sealed."

"His name is Lord Simon," Alys said calmly enough. Their fears came as no surprise to her. Even at the remote northern convent she had heard rumors of Richard's magician, and none of them had been praiseworthy. He was feared by all who knew of him.

"Grendel's a better name for him, I swear," muttered Morwenna. "I'm not letting him touch me. It'll be horse dung or nothing."

Alys sighed. "Dried or fresh?"

"Fresh, my lady. If you'd be willing?"

"If I'd be willing?" Alys echoed.

"It has to be gathered by the healer or it won't work. That's what my mum told me."

For a moment Alys didn't move. At least horse dung was a great deal more appealing than the horse itself, and the castle yard would be littered with the stuff. As long as she didn't have to go to the stables she'd survive.

"Certainly," she said briskly, hiding her dismay. "Do you have something I could scoop it with?"

And that was how she found herself in the courtyard beyond the stables, a trencher of stale bread in one hand, a kitchen spoon in the other, surveying a fresh, steaming mass of manure with strong misgivings.

Thankfully no one was around to watch her, she'd made very sure of that. She bent low, ready to spoon a hearty portion onto the makeshift carrier, when a low, already familiar voice startled her enough to make her drop the trencher.

"Were you planning on eating that, or feeding it to me?"

In the light of day Simon of Navarre should have appeared less threatening. His deep golden eyes should have been a flat brown, his dark hair with its thick stripe of silver should have seemed lifeless. Instead she could practically feel the power pulsing through him. The energy, crackling between them. No wonder they thought him a bewitched creature. She was staring up at him as if she were under an enchantment.

It took her a second to gather her wits about her and rise to her full, unimpressive height. "Neither, my lord," she said. "It was for a serving woman."

"One of the servants expressed a desire to eat shit?"

She blinked. She'd heard the word before, but it was seldom used in her presence. "No, my lord. Though she did suggest that doing so was a possible cure. I was going to use it as poultice on her burned arm." She bent down to fetch the dung-bedecked trencher, but he moved quickly, knocking it out of her hand.

"You're as simple-minded as the peasants," he said sharply, sounding oddly disappointed. "If you put that on an open wound you'd probably kill her. I'm surprised you didn't try cobwebs and goose urine."

Alys rose. It was an odd tableau, with the steaming mass of dung at their feet, her future husband towering over her. Monster, they called him. Why would a monster care if a serving woman died?

"I believe she tried the cobwebs, my lord. Apparently she hadn't heard of the goose urine cure."

"Idiots. And you're as bad as the rest of them," he added. "Why wouldn't she come to me?"

Alys just looked at him.

"Oh, that's right," Simon said with a cool laugh. "I'd

eat her children if I looked at her. So instead she'd rather bathe in horse dung. What's wrong with her?''

"A bad burn on her arm. The skin is red and raw looking, like an angry tear.''

"Is there blackening around the edges?''

"None that I noticed.''

"A sickly smell?''

"No decaying flesh, my lord,'' she said sharply. "I'm not an idiot. I've done my share of healing.''

"If you used horse dung I'm surprised anyone survived,'' he muttered.

"It was Morwenna's idea.''

"The serving woman? More fool you to listen to her. Come with me.'' He turned abruptly and started across the cobbled walkway.

She didn't move. "Come where?'' she said, when he stopped to look behind him and discovered she wasn't following.

"You're to be my wife, Lady Alys. You should learn obedience,'' he said, but there was more amusement than anger in his deep voice.

"You're to be my husband. You're supposed to woo me,'' she replied. And then wanted to bite her tongue. She wasn't supposed to be pert, or bold, to her husband. Particularly not one such as the wizard, with his secret powers and wicked pacts with the forces of evil. At least, she assumed he made wicked pacts. How else would he know what he knew?

He let his eyes drift over her, slowly, assessingly. Probably regretting his foolish agreement the night before, that he would take her in place of her sister. She held her head high, wishing God had granted her just a few more inches of stature if he were going to grant her such a tall husband.

"I thought you were the docile one,'' he murmured.

"Yes, my lord," she said meekly, afraid he was going to change his mind. "Compared to my sister, my lord."

"And you're the smart one as well? Even though you were going to put horse dung on an infected wound?"

"Yes, my lord." She straightened her shoulders. "And the plain one."

His eyes were like a sly weapon, all soft, lingering caresses while he stood just out of reach. "I think you're a fraud, Lady Alys. You've yet to convince me of any of those three things. Now come along and stop arguing with me. The longer our patient suffers the worse it will get."

She moved then, struggling to keep up with his long-legged stride. "Our patient?"

"She won't accept help from me. Obviously you'll have to deliver it. You may take all the credit for her miraculous cure, and she won't have to worry about whether her children will be eaten. It works out quite neatly, don't you think?"

"Quite neatly," she said breathlessly, racing along behind him.

She was expecting to follow him up to his tower rooms, but instead he veered away from the keep, toward one of the outbuildings that lined the curtain wall. It was far removed from the chapel, well away from the cook houses and the laundry. But far too close to the stables and the mews for her state of mind. She wasn't overly fond of hunting birds either.

The door was heavy, iron over wood, but when he pushed it open it made no complaining noise. It was silent, as enchanted as most of the things that surrounded the magician.

The room was dark, with branches of unlit candles standing like sentinels. There was a hole in the roof above the brazier, and a fireplace at one end, but very little natural light entered the tomb-like place.

He moved to one end of the long, narrow room and pushed a curtain aside, and fitful sunlight filtered in, complete with a view of the stables. Alys managed to control her sudden start of fear.

It smelled of spices. Of herbs and rich, heady scents that teased her nose and caressed her skin. The room was warm; she could see the coals burning in the fireplace, and she wondered when he'd last been there, working. He'd been in his sleeping rooms the night before, she knew that much. But there was one thing she didn't know.

"How did I get back to the room I share with my sister?" she asked abruptly.

He had his back to her, busy with something on the wide, scarred worktable, and he didn't bother to look at her. "On which occasion?"

He was annoying, she had to grant him that. "Last night," she said. "After I came to your room and threw myself on your mercy."

"I have no mercy," he said coolly. "And in the future, I would prefer it if my future wife refrained from visiting men in their sleeping chambers."

"How did I get back to my own room?" she persisted.

"After you slid off your chair in a faint?"

"I don't faint!" she protested.

"Perhaps you're unused to the amount of wine your brother serves," he said serenely. "I would also prefer a wife who didn't drink to excess."

She bit back the retort that begged to be spoken. She'd made this bargain with the devil—it was no wonder he was testing her. If she backed out now it would be Claire who would pay the price.

"I didn't drink enough of Richard's wine to make

myself giddy," she said with deliberate calm. "As it happens, the stuff you gave me was far more potent."

He turned to look at her through the darkness, and his amber eyes glinted with amusement. "It was, wasn't it?" he said.

The truth of it was so obvious she was breathless. "You drugged me." Her voice rose with accusation.

"How could I have known you would seek me out?" he countered.

"How could you know anything?" she said bitterly. "Through your pact with the devil."

He laughed softly. "I made no pact with the devil."

"That's not what people say."

"You would be wise not to listen to what people say, Lady Alys. You will avoid a lot of misinformation and speculation."

"Then who should I listen to? You, perhaps?"

"Shouldn't a wife listen to her husband? Be guided by him in all things?"

It was the expected response, and yet she'd never had time to consider it. The majority of her life had been spent under the strict rule of the Sisters of Saint Anne, and she'd been dutiful enough. But then, the sisters had encouraged her love of learning, her interest in experimentation, even as they'd deplored Claire's willfulness.

None of that time had been spent around men, with the dubious exception of Brother Emory. She knew her duty well enough—a woman was a servant to her husband, bound to him in all matters. She just hadn't considered the reality of the situation.

"I suppose so," she said slowly.

She hadn't realized he'd moved closer, so that he towered over her. He probably did it to intimidate her, and it worked. "But you don't like it, do you?" he murmured.

"It's the way things are," she said, wishing she could back away from him, unwilling to demonstrate just how much he unnerved her. She was used to a calm, ordered life. He set things on end, wickedly so.

"Ah, but life is full of possibilities. Full of change," he said. "Maybe you'll poison me and run off and become Queen of the Gypsies."

He startled a laugh out of her. "That's more likely what Claire would do. I would suffer in a martyred silence, hoping a plague would carry you off. And besides, I don't like horses. Gypsies always have horses."

"I'm notoriously resistant to plagues," he said. He was too close to her. He was wearing black chased with silver, and he was warm. Strong. Distressingly strong. "And it would take rather a large amount of poison to even slow me down. Why don't you like horses?"

She considered lying a sin, not to mention a waste of time. She was a very poor liar. "I'm afraid of them."

"Why?"

"I was almost trampled to death when I was very young. I don't remember much of the circumstances, I only remember the huge creatures surrounding me, their hooves flashing. I was only four years old but I still remember that day."

"Four? Wasn't that the age you were taken from your mother?"

His knowledge appalled her. In the ensuing years she'd tried to separate those two occurrences, even though they were inextricably entwined. The horsemen, chasing after her mother as she tried to escape with her only child. The rough hands that had ripped her from her mother's arms, only to drop her in the midst of the angry, restless horses.

"You know far more of my history than I would have expected, my lord," she said, trying to keep the resentment and pain from her voice. "I cannot imagine why you should be concerned." For sixteen years she'd worked very hard at carving a calm, safe life for herself. Now in a few days' time that life had been shattered.

"Knowledge is power, and I set a great store by power. I like to know things," he said, his voice low and oddly appealing. It danced across her skin like a warm summer breeze, and she wanted to shiver, to shake it away, even as she wanted to bask in its warmth.

She looked up at him, keeping her gaze level and fearless. "And I like privacy in some matters."

He touched her. He'd kept his twisted hand hidden, though she wasn't bothered by the sight of it, but he lifted his strong, good hand and brushed it against her cheek. It couldn't be called a caress, more an odd act of claiming. She froze, helplessly aware of the unexpected beauty of that one hand, the long, graceful fingers, the narrow, well-shaped palm. A clever, well-made hand, gifted with talents.

"You will be my wife," he said. "You will have no secrets."

"Will you?" It was an outrageous question, and another man would have beaten her for it.

But Simon, avowed monster that he was, merely smiled. "Always, Lady Alys," he murmured. "Always."

Chapter Six

Sir Thomas du Rhaymer stared down at his hand. It still amazed him that she'd managed to draw blood—he would have thought his hide was thicker than that. The wound was small, and on any other occasion he would have ignored it. But knowing it had come from *her,* from her sharp white teeth, made it burn.

As he would burn, in hell, for the thoughts he was having. Richard and his wizard knew human nature far too well. He was a man who'd lived a cold, celibate life for years, but he was a man with eyes to see beauty, a mouth to taste it. For three years he had been impervious to all womanhood, including his bewitching, errant wife. And now, suddenly, he was vulnerable. Wanting.

It merely gave impetus to his determination, he told himself, climbing the broad stairs with a deliberate pace. The best battles were the fiercest, the most hotly contested. The battle for his immortal soul would doubtless be a monumental one, and with the stakes so high, he shouldn't expect it to be easy.

But neither had he expected to be lured by a vain, tempestuous beauty. Or touched by her as well.

He'd become a dour, disapproving soul, and he knew it. His squire had told him that, with the tactlessness of youth, and Thomas had accepted it willingly enough. Until he'd met Gwyneth of Longmead he'd been a reasonably simple, straightforward man. A dutiful son, a dedicated squire, a worthy knight who served his liege lord. But his lust for Gwyneth had shaken him, and her betrayal had shattered him. He'd built his life back, a steady, simple life devoted to God and Lord Richard, and now a new siren had come to tempt him again.

As long as she continued to hate him he was safe. And he had few delusions on that score. He was a good ten years older than she was, battle-scarred and hard, and he had every intention of keeping it that way. It was fortunate she was such a lively, high-strung creature. It was child's play to infuriate her, and that fury would distract her. She would never even realize he had an errant, sinful thought about her. The small, high, perfect breasts that pressed against her soft green gown. The glowing eyes, full of mischief and anger and unexpected humor. That mouth that had closed over his wrist and bitten the hell out of him.

He would be cold, and hostile, and he would be safe. She would never think twice about him, except to hate him.

And he breathed a deep sigh of relief as he mounted the stairs to the solar of Richard the Fair's sisters.

Married, Claire thought, not for the first time, pacing the room in barely controlled rage. She heartily pitied his poor wife. He must have made her life a living hell. Doubtless he beat her, often and severely. Doubtless she'd been sensible enough to run from him before his brutish temper resulted in her untimely death.

She had no idea why Richard had set such an ogre to watch over them, but then, Richard the Fair had proven to be a great disappointment to his younger sister. She'd always stubbornly clung to the notion that he'd just happened to forget their existence, but sooner or later he would ride down on the convent, his golden hair gleaming in the sun, and rescue the two of them, restoring them to their rightful place at Summersedge Keep.

Well, in effect he'd done that. But his golden hair was straw-like and thinning, his eyes were cruel, and if it were up to Claire she would have spent the rest of her days in the convent, safe behind those walls, with her sister for company and her precious Arabia for love.

She wanted to go back. She wanted to rescue Alys from that tall, strange creature who haunted Richard's side; she wanted to force her onto Arabia's back and ride off into the forests, never to be found again.

But that was only a dream. She had no way to get to her horse, and her guardian ogre would be watching her.

Not to mention the fact that Alys would rather be torn limb from limb than get within ten feet of a horse.

Who would have thought serene Alys would be crippled by such a fear? It made no sense to Claire, but then, little in this world was logical. At least she had been given a reprieve from marriage for the time being. Alys had sacrificed herself to the monster, but Alys was made of calmer stuff. She would endure, she would bend, not break under the burden of such a loathsome marriage.

She didn't even seem to consider it particularly loathsome. And in truth, Simon didn't seem particularly

Grendel-like. Apart from the twisted hand he kept hidden in the folds of his tunic, he was not ugly. There was, she supposed, even a strange kind of beauty in his distant, elegant face.

If only he didn't have those eerie eyes. Ghost eyes. That stillness that clung to him, like a mantle. He was a creature unlike any that Claire had ever imagined, and she could only hope Alys was fully aware of the danger she'd gotten herself into, by making such a noble sacrifice.

The alternative, of course, was far worse. Alys had a strong chance of surviving. Claire wouldn't.

"My lady, the knight is waiting outside your door."

Madlen, the serving woman, was hesitant as she broke through Claire's abstraction. "Which knight?" Claire asked, though she knew only too well.

"Sir Thomas, my lady. He bids me ask if you wish to take the air before the evening meal."

"If I wish to take the air I will do so," she snapped. "I certainly don't need his approval."

Unfortunately Sir Thomas was not conversant enough with polite behavior to keep his distance. He'd already ducked beneath the low portal of her room, and he glowered at her impressively. "I'm afraid you do, my lady. Neither you nor your sister are to step outside the keep unaccompanied."

Claire immediately retreated to the deepest window, perching herself on the broad expanse of stone beneath it. "My serving women will attend me."

He shook his head. "You may apply to your brother, my lady, and he will tell you what I have told you. Neither you nor your sister are to venture anywhere beyond your room or the great hall without my protection."

"There are two of us, and only one of you, Sir Thomas. How can you be in two places at the same time?" she demanded. "For that matter, where is my sister now? Perhaps she's being tortured and assaulted by Saracens. . . ."

"There are no Saracens at Summersedge Keep, Lady Claire. And the Saracens do not make war on women."

He caught her interest, much as she deplored it. "Did you go on Crusade, Sir Thomas?"

"Yes, my lady."

"And was it to seek forgiveness for sins already committed, or to be prepared in case the urge to sin overcame you later in life?"

"Sin is always in the midst of us, Lady Claire," he said.

"But I'm certain you manage to avoid it better than most." She shifted, moving closer to the window as she felt a soft breeze blowing in the unshuttered opening, stirring her hair. She pushed it back with annoyance. "Unless you call mistreating women a sin. I imagine you wouldn't."

"Have I mistreated you, my lady? I see no marks on your body."

He had a bandage wrapped around his hand, and Claire knew a moment's shame. She was too hot-tempered; Alys had tried to reason it out of her, the nuns had tried to beat it out of her, but the fact remained that she was far too quick to anger. And there was something about handsome Sir Thomas with the distant expression that made her want to stir him.

"You've been looking at my body, Sir Thomas? For what reason? Surely that's a sin as well. And you a married man!" she chided.

The arrow hit its mark, quite nicely. Faint color deepened his already sun-dark skin, though in the end she couldn't be sure which of her words had disturbed him. The mention of her body, or his wife.

"My immortal soul is not your concern, my lady. Nor is my wife."

"And what is my concern, sir knight?"

"That you behave yourself chastely and modestly at all times, that you prove yourself worthy of the husband your brother chooses for you, that you love God and esteem your betters, that you strive to be grateful for the gifts God has given you and the instruction of your elders."

"And is your instruction one of the gifts I'm supposed to be grateful for?" Her voice was arch.

He ignored her question. "You've been gifted with high-birth, good health, and family. Few people are so lucky."

"Are those the only gifts I should be grateful for?"

"Aye, my lady. For your undeniable beauty is nothing more than a curse, for you who bear it and for those, like me, who are sworn to protect it."

She should have been furious. And she was. But she was enchanted as well, and she wondered at the foolishness of his pretty wife, who unimaginably had found someone more desirable.

"Shall I wear a veil, Sir Thomas? To cover my distracting face from the sight of clamorous men?"

"You'll need sackcloth and ashes as well," he said gloomily. "And a wimple for your hair."

"Are these compliments?"

"No, my lady. Statements of fact."

If he hadn't sounded so doomed she would have laughed out loud. "I doubt my brother would agree to it," she said, and an unconscious shiver ran across her body at the memory of the unholy look in Richard's pale eyes. Imagination. Alys had always told her she allowed her fancies too much free rein, but this particular illusion had to have sprung from some dark, poisonous part of her brain, something she'd never realized existed. Either that, or it hadn't been her imagination.

"Lord Richard wants you kept safe," Thomas said.

"Yes, but for what reason? To make me a more valuable possession?"

"Surely for love of a sister?"

Alys was the one who excelled at keeping her emotions hidden. Claire always let her stormy responses out for all to see, and the very notion of Richard's brotherly love sent a shiver down her spine.

This time she did her absolute best to keep her expression serene, and felt proud of her abilities. Until Sir Thomas spoke.

"Why does that distress you?"

She slid down from the deep stone window. "You asked if I wished to take the air. I would, though I'd rather do it in the company of my women or my sister."

"Certainly they may accompany you, my lady. You'll simply have to bear with me as well."

At least she'd managed to distract him. For some reason the thought of Sir Thomas' keeping her company was not nearly so loathsome. He was overbearing, annoying, and humorless. He was very handsome, and very married, and he disapproved of her most profoundly. Which was utterly fine with her. Sparring with him kept her mind off her worries. About Alys and her accursed marriage. About Arabia. About her half-brother who was, more likely, Richard the Foul.

She shook her head, letting her long mantle of hair flow free. She knew from old what it would look like—a curtain of gold, shimmering down her slender back. She allowed herself a sly glance at Sir Thomas, to see his reaction to her flaunting gesture.

He didn't even blink. Immune to her.

Claire sighed. "Let us go for an evening walk, Sir

Thomas, and you can further instruct me on my maidenly duties." She held out her delicate arm, and after a moment's hesitation he placed his beneath it. His forearm was strong, well-muscled beneath the woolen sleeve of his tunic. Warm, living flesh.

She had seldom touched men in her life. They were different from women, harder, warmer, more disturbing. Or perhaps it was simply Sir Thomas who disturbed her.

She wasn't about to let him know it. She was strong as well, from schooling horses. Her half-brother was right, Arabia was no lady's mount, but Claire had the strength to handle her. If she could control a mare of that weight and strength, surely a puny human knight would be child's play.

Except that Sir Thomas was far from puny. He was tall, and solid, honed by years of fighting to an iron-tempered strength. And besides, Arabia loved her and wanted to do her bidding. The man beside her was a different case indeed.

"Are your thoughts disturbing, Lady Claire?" Sir Thomas asked, and it took Claire a moment to realize she'd been standing there, her arm in his, staring up at him in an abstracted manner.

Quickly she gathered her wandering wits. "I was thinking of horses, Sir Thomas," she said with complete truth.

For a moment he didn't look nearly so severe. "The air by the stables is not the freshest, my lady. But we could still walk in that direction if it pleases you."

It took her a moment to realize what he was saying. At least she would be able to see Arabia, to touch her, to croon soft, comforting words in her pale ear. It was a far cry from riding, but more comfort than she had imagined.

"I thought your job was to keep me away from my horse."

"My job is to protect you and your sister, to accompany you if you step outside the keep. If your path takes you by way of the stables it will be no fault of mine. I'm simply keeping you safe."

Her hand trembled, but his arm was strong beneath hers, and she found she could manage a very small, very real smile for the tall, disapproving knight. "You have a kinder heart than I would have suspected, Sir Thomas," she said softly.

He looked as if he were about to argue the point with her. But instead he simply nodded, leading her from the solar, his handsome, somber face averted.

She was a witch, Simon decided. Quite simply a witch. In his infinitely varied life he'd seen and heard many things, learned tricks and seeming powers, enchantments and healings, magic that was nothing more than clever manipulation of the gullible. He'd learned the power to draw men and women, to make them believe the impossible. But he'd yet to run across a creature such as Lady Alys de Lancie.

He'd known witches, both men and women, and in truth, they weren't that different from the monks he'd lived with in Switzerland. They all had their own form of magic, their own incantations, their own herbal powers that transcended most human understanding.

Alys was possessed of none of that. Her knowledge of herbal healing was laughably rudimentary, and knowledge of Greek and Latin, which she was purported to possess, had never been known to have any particular arcane effect on mankind. She was no great beauty, though he found her oddly pleasing. And yet she seemed to have exerted more influence on his waking and dreaming hours than anyone in his memory.

He had a grudging, distrusting fondness for women. For their soft bodies and sweet sighs, for their gentleness and appalling resilience. If women had fought the Fourth Crusade, they would have taken Jerusalem again, by wit rather than by force. They wouldn't have been distracted by the rich booty of Constantinople into forgetting their holy mission.

Not that he considered women particularly holy. They were practical, of the earth rather than the spirit, and he'd enjoyed them as such. Gypsies and countesses, whores and Saracens, peasants and even queens, they were all sisters in their delightful flesh.

Lady Alys was far more complicated. If she was earthy, it was disguised by shyness. And it wasn't merely his body that was distracted by the thought of her. She seemed to be distracting his mind and spirit as well, a dangerous state of affairs for a man who lived by his wits.

If he were any other man he would go to his priest for confession and absolution. He would ask for strength to avoid temptation.

But he was a man who liked temptation, who enjoyed resisting it almost as much as he enjoyed giving in to it. Lady Alys was temptation personified, and letting her leave his workshop, the healing salve safe in her little leather pouch, was disturbingly difficult.

He had potions he could have plied her with. Herbs to loosen her tongue and her morals and her gown, spices to make her need him. As he had suddenly, unexpectedly begun to need her.

It was ridiculous, of course. A stray fancy, borne of indolence. Richard the Fair had yet to apprise him of the full scope of his ambitions, though it didn't take an unholy wizard to guess where Richard's sights were set. He was a greedy man, unlikely to settle for anything less than the crown itself. And he would want his pet monster, his Grendel, to help get it for him.

He would want to tie Simon to him first, by the marriage vows. Since he seemed in no hurry to see Simon wed to his studious half-sister, then he must also be in no hurry to make his move.

Simon could be patient as well. Up to a point. He doubted he was going to wait for Richard's sanction to bed his shy bride. And he wasn't necessarily going to wait for the church's solemn rites.

He and Brother Jerome kept their distance from each other. The good monk knew when he was outmatched, and if it came to a battle of power, Brother Jerome would be banished from the comfortable household of Richard the Fair and the wicked wizard would triumph.

Both of them were careful to ensure that it didn't come to that point. No mention was made of the fact that Simon did not attend confession, whereas even Richard received absolution for the occasional minor sin he happened to recall. And Simon made very certain he didn't interfere with Brother Jerome's duties.

But Brother Jerome would expect to officiate at the wedding of Richard the Fair's sister and his chief advisor. Confession and penance and absolution would be a necessity. If Brother Jerome were given the chance, he would probably insist that a good scourging would cleanse Simon's soul.

Simon much preferred his soul dark and unrepentant. But he would wed Lady Alys of Summersedge Keep, with all the pomp, dignity, and rite that Richard and the Holy Church would demand. The power that an alliance with the House of de Lancie would bring was indisputable, and he could mouth the hypocritical words if need be.

He'd claim his reward first, however. A taste, perhaps, or the full course if he desired it. He would feast on Alys's small, soft, plump body, a feast of the senses, and when she took her vows she would be so besotted she would be no danger to him whatsoever.

She was afraid of horses. She was afraid of him, even though she was determined not to show it. Brought up in the strict confines of a convent, she was most likely terrified of men's bodies, and of what men expected of a woman.

He would calm her fears. Of horses, not of him. Her barely controlled nervousness gave him an edge that he wouldn't readily relinquish.

When he finally got around to taking her body she would be well beyond fear. She would be his, body and soul. And his claiming would be his triumph.

And hers.

Chapter Seven

The evening meals, Alys decided, were the worst. As in most great houses, dinner was served in the midst of the day, when work was still in progress. Richard would keep his magician by his side in close conversation, and Alys was left to her own devices, a pleasant enough occurrence. Claire was seated on the far side of her brother and his advisor, so there was no way the two of them could converse, and one of Lord Richard's elderly knights usually kept Alys company, if such it could be called. Sir Hector was more interested in his ale and his trencher than polite conversation, and Alys had to move fast if she were to get her share of food. Despite the deficiencies in the housekeeping during Lady Hedwiga's absence, the table was a good one, and Alys had no strong desire to share her meal with a gluttonous, drunken old soldier.

Unfortunately my lord Simon did not seem to eat at these lavish banquets. No shared trencher of bread was placed before him, though his goblet was filled with wine, and he seemed more interested in observing others and conferring with his lord than in sustaining his body.

But the evening meal was far worse. Richard was less interested in his duties as lord of the castle and much more concerned with wine and whatever young woman seemed to have attracted his fancy. As far as Alys could tell there were any number of them, well-bred, well-dressed and very beautiful, who earned his favor. It was a wonder to Alys, with the strict notions of morality that had been drilled into her by the nuns, but Brother Jerome seemed to turn a blind eye to it, concentrating instead on his own meal, failing to look up when Richard plunged one hand down the front of a young girl's gown, laughing uproariously at her sly shrieks.

"This displeases you, Lady Alys?"

She looked up to see the wizard standing over her. She hadn't realized he'd moved, and Sir Hector hastily stumbled out of his chair, knocking it over in the process, in his haste to get away from Navarre. If Simon were aware of his panic he made no comment, merely taking the seat the elderly knight had abandoned, using his good left hand.

"I am a modest soul. I'm unused to such a display of affection. . . ."

"I'd hardly call it affection," he said, his deep voice wry. "Animal lust, perhaps."

The girl shrieked again, laughing, as Richard poured wine on her partially exposed breasts. Alys averted her gaze hastily, but not before she saw Richard's hand fumbling at the hem of the lady's robe.

"You're shocked, my lady? You disapprove of a married man disporting while his wife is away?" Simon pursued the subject, watching her out of his still, golden eyes. "Most people are prey to lust. It's a healthy enough urge."

"For the men, perhaps," she said. "You have yet to convince me that women suffer from the same flaw. Or that it would be in any way healthy if they did."

"You don't think women feel lust?"

"Not decent women." Even as she spoke the words, she could hear the nasal tones of Reverend Mother Dominica with her endless lectures on the duties and trials of womankind. Since the Reverend Mother had managed to dispense with most of those trials and duties she wasn't, perhaps, the best expert on the subject, but Alys hadn't had much choice in the confines of the cloister. Sister Agnes, she of the hearty appetites and the genial nature, had hinted that perhaps a woman's lot outside the convent held surprising pleasures, but she'd never elaborated, and now it was too late to ask.

"I think you were in the convent too long, my lady."

"Not long enough," she muttered gracelessly. "And lust is a sin."

"You don't strike me as much of an expert on sin, Lady Alys," he murmured.

"And you certainly know far too much about the subject," she shot back, startling a laugh out of him.

Obviously the household of Richard the Fair was unused to hearing the magician laugh. Even Richard himself stopping pawing his willing partner to stare at Simon of Navarre.

"Something amuses you, my Grendel?" he demanded. The young lady had somehow ended up on his lap, and he pushed her off, so that she landed with a muffled shriek among the bone-strewn rushes.

"You have been gracious enough to gift me with a clever wife, my lord," Simon said.

"A clever woman is a curse," Richard said flatly, eying

Alys with profound distrust. "Change your mind, my friend. Choose the pretty one."

"My lord," said Simon, "I did."

It was stated as simple truth, shocking Alys into momentary silence. The fact that anyone could prefer her to her gay, lovely half-sister was a wonder. He was a brilliant, devious man—surely he could have a reason for such an unlikely preference?

But she could think of none. The conversation had once more built into a muffled roar, and she turned to face the man whose bed she would eventually share. "You are most illogical, sir," she said. "Have you fallen madly in love with me then?"

He laughed softly, as she meant him to. "I feel about love as you feel about lust, my lady. A sin and an abomination, a waste of time and a danger to the soul. Will you convince me otherwise?"

"I know as little of falling in love as I know of lust," she said. "And I think, like you, I prefer to keep my acquaintance with that emotion limited. Life would be far tidier all around."

His answering smile was cool and calculating, and utterly bewitching. "Life is seldom tidy, Lady Alys. And if you wish to fall in love with one of Richard's stalwart young knights I will make no objection. After I acquaint you with the many and varied delights of lust."

His face wasn't that close to hers, and yet she felt caught, trapped, drowning in his golden eyes, the rich timbre of his voice. An enchanter, they called him, and she could well see why. He was enchanting her, against her will, enchanting her with indecent promises and sensual lures, and Alys had always fought her senses.

As she fought the profound effect he was having on her. "Is that future supposed to make me happy?"

"It should. Isn't that what women want most? Prosperous, advantageous marriages and the freedom to love wherever they choose?"

"One person cannot control another's love."

"No. But I grant you the freedom to act upon it."

"You give me leave to cuckold you?" she demanded, incredulous.

"I give you leave to bestow your love and your favors upon a worthy knight or noble if your heart demands it."

"You believe the heart can demand such things?" she asked.

"I believe gullible humans can convince themselves of it," he replied.

"You make it sound as if you're not one of us. Human, that is," she said.

"I'm certain most people wonder the same thing. Even Richard at times suspects I'm the embodiment of some ancient monster with fierce powers."

"And does he fancy himself Beowulf?"

"God knows," Simon replied. "I imagine Richard sees himself as the hero of any number of heroic tales."

She glanced over at her brother. The very notion of Richard the Fair had seemed heroic indeed, and yet she'd never trusted in that particular fantasy. She had reason not to, with the faint memory of that day, so long ago, the plunging horses and her mother crying out for her, a memory that had somehow become connected with Richard. Unlike Claire, she'd never dreamed of being rescued from the convent by a forgetful, loving brother, though she'd kept herself from passing on her doubts to her younger sister.

She glanced down at her trencher. Most of the food lay there, untouched, yet she was unable to make herself eat. She would regret it, she knew she would. Hours later she would be famished, and she would spend the night that way. But right then she couldn't even imagine secreting a piece of bread in the leather pouch attached to her girdle.

A bowl of water was presented to her, and she dipped her hands in, cleansing them. She noticed that no one offered the ewer to Navarre. Logical enough; since he hadn't eaten anything, he would have no need to wash his hands. But she suspected it had more to do with what lay hidden beneath the folds of his dark robe.

"What happened to your hand?" she asked before she could think twice. She was immediately filled with horror at her own gaucherie, but Simon seemed amused.

"Do you realize you're the first person who has ever asked me?" he replied. "Most people just avert their eyes and cross themselves."

"I was wondering if there was anything that can be done to help you? Herbs, poultices. . . ?" Her voice trailed off before his skeptical expression.

"You'll probably be wanting me to dip my poor hand in horse dung," he said. "I hate to shatter your pride in your medical abilities, but I've already done everything possible. But I do appreciate your tender concern."

She should have been chastened into silence—doubtless he'd meant that to happen. But Alys was a stubborn woman.

"You still haven't answered my question," she said patiently.

"No, I haven't, have I?" he said. He rose, looming over her, and she had no intention of scrambling to her feet, only to emphasize the disparity in their heights. But Simon of Navarre wasn't particularly interested in her intentions. He put his good hand beneath her elbow and pulled her up, with a simple strength that was astonishing.

"Where are you going, Grendel?" Richard called out drunkenly. The wench was on his lap again, and her gown was halfway up her thigh. "You'll not be taking her maidenhead, not till you're properly wed!"

She'd fought her habit of coloring up all evening, but this last was too much for her. She turned her head away from the curious on-lookers, but to her dismay Simon of Navarre could see her reaction far too clearly. Doubtless it amused him.

He was still holding on to her arm with his strong, good hand, and it felt oddly possessive, oddly protective for a man who seemed to feel neither of those emotions. "I was planning on instructing Lady Alys in the proper use of healing herbs," he said coolly.

Richard waved a greasy hand in his direction. "So be it," he said grandly. "Just keep her away from the dreaded manroot." And he roared with laughter, a laughter echoed throughout the Great Hall. There were only a few unamused by Richard's ribaldry. One was Claire, sitting on her brother's right, a pale, unhappy expression on her lovely face. Another was the stern, handsome knight who sat beside her, watching her.

"My lord can trust me in all things," Simon said coolly. He swept Alys from the room, from her sister's presence, before she could protest.

It took her a moment to accustom her eyes to the dim light. A thick tapestry covered the door behind them, muffling the sound beyond, and a torch sent skittering shadows into the empty passageway. In the distance Alys heard another comment from her brother, one she just began to understand, when Simon pushed her toward the stairs with unceremonious haste.

"He's had too much wine," she said, stalling. "I don't like to leave Claire there without protection. . . ."

"She has more than sufficient protection. I doubt Sir

Thomas would let Saint Paul himself come within ten feet of the girl, and Saint Paul was a dried up woman hater.''

Such blasphemy left her utterly speechless, an unusual occurrence for one such as Alys. Simon noticed, of course, and he paused in the act of pushing her toward the stairs. "Close your mouth, my pet," he murmured. "There are good men and bad men everywhere, even among Christ's saints."

She pulled her scattered wits back together. "And you, of course, are perfectly willing to sit in judgment on them?"

He smiled down at her with sudden, unexpected sweetness. "If their teachings annoy me, yes."

"Brother Jerome could have you excommunicated."

"Brother Jerome enjoys a philosophical disagreement as much as the next man. He knows I'll go to hell anyway, and he's not averse to arguing with me before I go there."

Once more he'd managed to shock her. "Aren't you worried about your immortal soul?"

He looked down at her, almost pityingly. "I lost it years ago, my lady. Trust me, it makes life a great deal more convenient if you don't have to worry about such things."

"Life isn't supposed to be convenient any more than it's supposed to be tidy," she said, harkening back to their earlier conversation.

"Ah, but humans do have a way of trying to make it so."

There it was again. The reference to humans. He did it on purpose, she thought, to unnerve her. Unfortunately, it worked most effectively.

"But Claire. . . ." she said stubbornly, getting back to her original concern. He had a wicked way of distracting her from what she most needed to know, and she was finding it extremely irritating.

"Sir Thomas is more than up to the task of safe-guarding your sister. His sense of honor and duty is awe-inspiring."

"And why do I get the impression you're mocking rather than praising him for that?" she said sharply.

"Because you're already beginning to understand me quite well, my lady. And because I'm a cynic, a man who's seen too much and done too much to be impressed by a blind adherence to morality with no thought or choice involved."

She looked at him sternly, but he seemed totally unmoved by her disapproval. "I weep for you, my lord," she said.

"Weep for yourself, my lady. You'll be shackled to me for life."

"Ah, but you're forgetting," she said blithely. "I'll have all those stalwart knights to distract and entertain me."

He laughed, and it was a strangely charming sound. "Unless you drive me to murder you first."

"Do you murder women, then, my lord?"

"I haven't yet, my lady. I usually restrict my murderous activities to those who deserve them. But I'm open to new experiences."

It shouldn't have been a matter of jest. Men did kill their wives, in rage, in cold blood. And Alys had no doubt whatsoever that Simon of Navarre was capable of killing.

But he was no threat to her life, she was certain of it. To her peace of mind, doubtless. To her well-being, to her immortal soul, perhaps. But he would never hurt her.

Would he?

"This hall is drafty," he said with great patience, "and I have no strong desire to haul you up the stairs when you have two legs that can carry you up there."

"And why are you taking me upstairs?"

"Not to swive you," he said. "I've decided you need some training in the healing arts. If you keep putting horse dung on people they'll all be dead, and I like having my needs attended to by servants. They won't be able to do that if they're dead. Therefore, their health is of concern to me, and since they're all terrified of me, you seem the best choice to administer the proper herbs."

She looked at him, taking this all in. "Yes, my lord," she said with dubious meekness.

He wasn't a gullible man. "Yes, my lord . . . what?"

"Yes, I do firmly believe that you have no interest in the welfare of anyone but yourself and your only concern for others is that they are well enough to see to your comfort," she parroted. "And I will be more than grateful to learn whatever it is you wish to teach me."

He let his eyes slide down her body. "I am not convinced of that, my lady."

She fought hard against the color that rose to her cheeks. "I wish to learn about the healing arts. I'll endeavor to pass on your treatments to those in need."

He looked as if he were about to argue further, then thought better of it. "Then stop dawdling," he said in a sharp voice, and started up the winding tower stairs. Leaving her little choice but to lift her heavy skirts and scurry after him, cursing his long legs and his rapid pace.

She was a demon, sent to bewitch him, Thomas thought morosely, setting his goblet back down on the table. It was bad enough when she was tossing her sun-bright hair, teasing him, fighting with him.

It was far worse when she was sitting at the table, a woeful, lost expression on her far too beautiful face. He couldn't fight with a waif, no matter how lovely. It roused all his protective instinct, it made him want to draw her away from the rude voices, the bawdy comments floating through the air, to place her pretty face against his shoulder and cover her ears.

He was a careful man, and he kept his expression absolutely blank, but beneath it he mocked himself. She was a jade, there was no way she could be anything but, and her current megrims were doubtless due to a fit of sulks that she couldn't have her way. Though at this point he had no idea what her way was.

And in truth, she'd been oddly beguiling in the presence of that huge daughter of Satan she called a horse. She had crooned to the giant creature, stroked her silky nose, whispered loving things in her attentive ear. And Thomas had watched, and wondered if his wife had ever loved any creature on earth half so much as this pampered beauty loved her horse.

He couldn't help but approve. He had a knight's appreciation for a worthy horse, added to a natural fondness toward all animals. You knew where you stood with four-legged creatures. They were honest and true and incapable of deceit, and it grieved him to think that Lord Richard would hand such a magnificent creature to the highest bidder for his half-sister's hand. And he told himself it troubled him not at all that she, too, would be handed over to some elderly, wealthy baron who'd probably buried several wives already.

He'd been mesmerized by the sight of her hand, stroking the sleek, well-muscled flank of her horse. She wore no rings, which surprised him. He would have thought she'd be far more interested in gold and silver than a good horse. Her hand was pretty, well-shaped, but surprisingly strong-looking. But then, she'd have to have strong hands to rule an oversized creature like her mare.

Her days of riding her precious mare were done, whether she knew it or not. Lord Richard would see to it that she suffered a different kind of ride, and she would doubtless be well-pleased with her lot, as most women were. All they needed were creature comforts and the adoration of all the men surrounding them. And few men would be foolish enough to deny Lady Claire their besotted admiration.

There was a coarse laugh from beyond Lady Claire, and he looked to see Richard, wine-befuddled and belching, reach out and press a loud, wet kiss on his half-sister's mouth. "Gad, you're a pretty thing!" he shouted. "Damn me if I'm not half-tempted to keep you for myself."

The others laughed at his absurd, ribald sally, even Brother Jerome. But there was something in Lady Claire's wide green eyes, and in the furtive way she wiped the dampness from her mouth with the back of her hand once her brother had turned away, that made Thomas uneasy.

He looked closer at the faintly green tinge to her clear skin. She was going to hurl all over his lordship's trencher if he didn't get her out of there, and he decided it was his Christian duty to remove her. It mattered nothing that that was clearly what she was desperate to do for herself.

He rose, and Richard cast a curious glance at him. "Your sister is unwell, sire," he said politely. "I'll see her safely to her room."

"Sick, is she?" Richard bellowed. "Not used to good food. Take her away, Sir Thomas. And there's no need to warn you to behave yourself—that's why I chose you. I doubt you even know how to use a woman anymore. That witch Gwyneth unmanned you.''

Sir Thomas didn't even blink. Claire had risen to her feet, albeit unsteadily, and he put a strengthening hand beneath her elbow. She was shaking, and it struck him that perhaps she really was sick.

''Don't worry, I'll have Grendel whip you up a potion to put starch back in the old blade,'' Richard said. ''In the meantime, give us a kiss, dear sister.'' He reached for her, one meaty hand clawing at her wrist, and Thomas wondered whether they were about to indulge in a tug of war. Granted, Richard was his liege lord, but he wasn't about to release Claire when she could barely stand.

Lady Claire took care of the problem most efficiently. She look at her brother, focusing on his wet, bewhiskered mouth, and promptly spewed her supper all over him.

Richard leapt up, cursing furiously, but Thomas had already drawn her away. ''I warned you she was unwell, sire,'' he said, trying to keep his voice deferential.

''Sickly bitch,'' Richard fumed, ripping his soiled tunic from his body and revealing his coarse, thickly muscled body. ''Take her to her womenfolk before she hurls again!''

''Yes, my lord,'' Thomas said meekly. Claire looked entirely capable of it, one trembling hand pressed to her mouth, and he hurried her from the room before she could disgrace herself again.

She sagged against him, and he drew her to the stairs, sitting down and pulling her weak body against his. She was trembling, shaking so hard he thought her bones might break, and an odd, choking sound signalled that she might be ill again.

And then she looked up at him, and her green eyes

were full of mischievous delight, and he realized she
was shaking with laughter, and the choking sound was
her attempt to stifle her amusement.

"He'll think twice about kissing me again," she said
breathlessly, a stifled giggle in the back of her throat.

He wanted to jump up, denounce her as a foul, deceit-
ful strumpet, but he didn't move. He had seen a look
in Richard's eyes that he didn't dare interpret, but he
sensed that Richard deserved such punishment and
more.

"You're a dangerous woman, Lady Claire," he said.
"That's a formidable weapon you've got."

She still looked faintly green. "It doesn't require
much," she said brightly. "Just have Richard kiss you
on the mouth and you'd be able to spew as well."

Beaten. She deserved to be beaten. And he deserved
to be punished for not chastising her. But he found he
couldn't. He looked down into her unrepentant green
eyes, and thanked Christ and all his saints that she'd
just thrown up.

And that her soft, wicked mouth was no temptation
for his. For the moment.

Chapter Eight

She had fallen asleep again, Simon realized. It was quite an odd habit she had, of simply drifting off in his presence. He'd worked hard at presenting a formidable appearance to all the inhabitants of Summersedge Keep, and indeed, Lady Alys was frightened of him. But quite obviously not frightened enough to keep awake.

It was one thing when he'd drugged her wine with sweet poppy. Tonight he expected her to be alert, ready to learn of the herbs he showed her, ready to argue and banter with him as she had at dinner. It was a rare thing to have anyone capable of talking back to him, and the novelty enchanted him. The fact that it was a woman he desired made it even more interesting.

But she'd sat on the pile of cushions on the floor, watching him out of her calm, steady eyes as he started to tell her of the dangers of wormwood, and then those eyes drifted closed, and she slept, her back against the thick stone wall, her legs curled up beneath her. He watched the rise and fall of her breasts with complete fascination, almost as if he'd never seen breasts before. And he had, unclothed, wondrous breasts. The soft swell beneath Lady Alys's monumentally ugly gown shouldn't have absorbed him with such intensity.

But then, he'd already accepted the fact that there was no reason to his fascination with Richard the Fair's half-sister. It simply existed, and he accepted it. Without question it would disappear once he'd bedded her. In the meantime he could simply enjoy the uncharacteristic ache she inspired within him.

He rose, moving toward the simple desk. No one was allowed to clean his rooms but Godfrey, his manservant. No one was privy to his secrets but Godfrey, and Godfrey was mute, his tongue removed by a spoiled German prince who wanted to assure himself that his servants wouldn't talk.

The German prince himself would no longer talk— Simon of Navarre had killed him, and Godfrey had followed him with patient, intelligent devotion ever since. He was the perfect servant, friend and confidante, devoted to his master, deft in his handling of herbs, thoughtful and learned. It mattered not that Godfrey could write and therefore pass on the secrets that had been silenced from his mouth. Few people—and Richard de Lancie was not one of them—were able to read.

The inhabitants of Summersedge Keep would wonder why a man with a crippled right hand would have the kind of desk used in a scriptorium. If they knew. But since very few people saw the inside of his rooms, very few people thought to question.

He took the seat, then stretched his scarred hand out fully, reaching for the quill. The page of the herbal was just as he had left it, the colors clear and bright. Transcribing manuscripts had been his self-imposed treatment during the years he spent with the good monks. At first the pain had been unbearable, and his hand had shaken so badly with it that the manuscript had been unreadable. But he had persevered, through pain and stiffness, day after day, moving from the simple copying of biblical text to his own work of compiling an herbal, and the drawings were magical, vivid, glowing things.

It was his life's work, and he tended to think of it as penance for his sins. Not that he believed in penance. His sins were too great for absolution, and he no longer sought it. He simply followed his instincts, both noble and selfish, knowing he was doomed to whatever after-life had already been decreed.

He worked for a bit, occasionally glancing over at the sleeping woman. She kept her hair tightly braided, presumably in purposeful contrast to her sister's flowing tresses. She wore a veil, and a thin circlet of gold, but the headpiece was begining to slip. He wondered how she would look with her hair unbound, her full mouth smiling. He wondered what her mouth would taste like.

He would bed her. He would marry her. And he would leave her, and all of them, when he no longer needed them. And perhaps, if she showed herself an adept enough pupil, he would leave the finished manuscript with her.

A sudden, unexpected thought came to him. Would he leave her with more than the pages of wisdom acquired from his worldly travels. Would he leave her with a child as well?

He knew how to avoid it, both by Eastern and Western means. His knowledge of herbs was incomparable, bordering on what others might call witchcraft, and his knowledge of the rhythms of a woman's life was equally profound, garnered from the physicians and wise men in the holy lands who took delight in a broken knight who wished to learn, not to kill and maim. They'd mended his smashed body, and in watching them he'd learned what to do about his twisted hand when it had healed sufficiently.

He realized he hadn't moved in several long minutes, as the memories of the past swept over him. He wasn't usually prey to wasting his time on an ancient past, but neither was he a man to deny what life demanded. He watched Alys in her gentle sleep, and thought of her lying in his arms, in that same trusting sleep, her belly round and swollen with his child.

He pushed away from the desk in sudden anger. These were the dreams of an ordinary man, not one such as Simon of Navarre, who had spent long years creating the creature who effectively terrified all who strayed into his path.

He moved to the deep set window to stare out over the night-shrouded castle. There were lights in the bake house, and he could see the tiny glow of candles from the small chapel. Brother Jerome would be praying diligently, begging forgiveness for nonexistent sins, both his own and those of his people. Little did he know the true horror of real sin.

"What were you doing at the desk?"

Alys's voice was sleepy, soft, curious. He hadn't realized she was awake, and watching him. A mistake—he needed to be preternaturally aware of her.

"Reading," he said, willing to answer her this time, even with a lie. "Your company was less than inspiring."

She sat up. Her circlet was askew, and attempts to straighten it were lamentable. He wanted to go to her and take the thing off her head, with the veil as well. He wanted to loosen her thick plaits and wrap them around his hands. Around his strong, scarred, wounded hand that symbolized all he had been through.

He curled his right hand up into its customary, claw-like position, certain she was too sleep-fuddled to notice. "I'm sorry," she murmured in her oddly beguiling voice. "I don't usually fall asleep like that."

"Perhaps my company is soporific."

She smiled at that, a small, delightful upturning of her full mouth. He liked her sleepy, her guard down. "Unlikely, my lord. Though this time the wine couldn't have been drugged. You didn't have the chance to get near the stuff I had tonight, and it lacked the sweet, dreamy taste of the night before."

"Your imagination is very energetic." He managed, as always, to keep his reaction hidden. He needed to learn that he shouldn't underestimate her.

"That is, perhaps, the only energetic thing about me right now," she said with a yawn, stretching with unconscious sensuality. In general she wasn't a sensual creature—she'd spent too many years with the nuns, too many years looking after other people's needs and ignoring her own. But he suspected that beneath her careful behavior there was a ripe sensuality waiting to be awakened.

And he was growing rapidly more impatient to awaken it. Outside the wind had picked up, whistling through the narrow arrow-slits in the thick castle wall, stirring the flames in the deep fireplace, ruffling the thick, dark tapestries.

"There's a storm brewing," he said, pushing away from the window. "We'll have rain by morning. The serfs will be glad of it."

Oddly enough, Lady Alys appeared less than pleased. "A s-storm?" she said, the nervous stammer almost imperceptible. But he was a man who missed very little.

"Have you a dislike of rain, my lady?" he questioned gently.

"Only when it interferes with my outdoor activities," she said, rallying.

"And what are those? We've already ascertained that you're terrified of horses. You seem frightened of rain as well. What else terrifies you?"

"Don't be ridiculous," she said, clearly forgetting that one of her fears was Simon of Navarre. "I'm not afraid of rain. I'm just not overly fond of thunder and lightning."

He glanced out the narrow slit of window once more. In the distance he could see a fork of lightning shiver in the inky dark sky, but it was too far away to be of any moment.

"Horses, thunder and lightning, me," Navarre said softly. "Is there anything else that terrifies you?"

She didn't deny it, wise creature that she was. Her eyes met his quite calmly, her hands folded gracefully in her lap. "If there is I shall do my best to keep it secret," she said.

"You can try," he said, moving away from the wall and closer to her. She smelled of lavender and roses, of sweet wine and womanhood, a heady combination for his deliberately controlled senses. He knelt down beside her, and with his scarred hand reached up and brushed her cheek. She didn't flinch away in horror, as he half expected her to. She was afraid of ridiculous things, horses and thunderstorms. But a badly scarred hand left her calm.

More than calm. To his horror, she reached up and gently caught his hand in hers, and it was all he could do not to stretch it out from its false, cramped position and capture her small hand. She had good, strong, warm hands. The hands of a healer. The hands of a lover. He wondered if she'd ever touched a man with love.

It was a simple enough matter to find out. She wasn't

paying attention to anything but the scarred hand in hers, and she barely noticed when he put his good hand beneath her chin, lifting her face to meet his merciless eyes.

She noticed when he kissed her.

It was no chaste salute of courtly love. It was a lover's kiss, and she tried to jerk away, startled, but he was already prepared, sliding his right arm behind her shoulders and keeping her trapped against him as he took his time, his open mouth against hers in a slow, deliberate, experimental kiss. She trembled against him, but she couldn't fight or resist, he'd already seen to that, and she simply held still and let him kiss her.

Kissing was an overlooked art, one he'd trained in during the time he spent in the Near East as well. He knew how to use his tongue with skill and wicked delight, he knew how to kiss a woman into a weak mass of mindless longing. Even an obvious virgin like Alys of Summersedge.

He felt her small hands on his shoulders, not to push him away, but to hold him, her fingers digging into the flesh and muscles beneath his robes, clinging to him. She made no sound, when he would have desired it, but the tremors that shook her body were a satisfying enough proof of her surrender, and he was hard enough to take her, right then, amidst the scattered pillows that lay along the rush-strewn floor.

His bed was only a few feet away, in an alcove beyond one of the dark tapestries, and he thought he might carry her there, stripping the ugly gown from her body, stripping the fear from her soul, when his instincts ripped him from the sensual haze that was washing over him. Someone was approaching.

Very few dared, without a specific invitation, and he

controlled his snarl of frustrated rage with great effort as he lifted his head to look down at Lady Alys.

She lay passive in his arms, a dazed expression on her face, her mouth damp and reddened from contact with his. And then passivity vanished, replaced by shock and panic.

But no disgust, he was pleased to note. He released her when she squirmed, but he caught her elbow when she almost collapsed onto the floor again, easing her into a comfortable position before rising. Just in time to greet Richard the Fair as he stormed into the room with his usual burly energy.

"There you are, Grendel!" he said, failing to notice the small, huddled figure of his sister as she leaned against the cushions. "I grow impatient!"

"You often do, my lord," Simon murmured with faint weariness, knowing he could get away with it as no one in Summersedge Keep could. "What would you have of your humble servant?"

"Are you my humble servant?" Richard demanded, peering at him through the shadows. "Sometimes I doubt it very much indeed. Do you share my vision? My ambitions? You do realize that the higher your lord rises, the higher you do?"

"Indeed," he answered. "And I wouldn't deny I am an ambitious man in my own way. But I doubt anyone is capable of sharing the true breadth of your visions."

Richard preened visibly. "Still, you're a clever man. The cleverest man I know. You must have a sense of where this is leading. Of what you can do to help me. Do I have to spell it out, man?"

He turned his head, slowly, toward Lady Alys, the motion a simple, direct warning to Richard the Fair. His lordship turned bright red, sputtering in fury.

"What by the holy rood are you doing here, strumpet?" he demanded, striding across the rush-strewn floor and reaching down for her with one meaty hand. "I would have thought it was the younger one who would be eager to lift her skirts, not the perfect little nun. What have you done with her, Simon? She looks like she's been tumbled by a blacksmith with a twelve inch rod."

Simon said nothing, watching his intended bride's face turn bright red with embarrassment. Her brother hauled her to her feet with more roughness than Simon would have liked, but he decided now was not the time to interfere. Like as not Richard would escalate his bullying, and then Simon would have no choice but to do something from which there was no turning back.

"I've been instructing her on the use of herbs in healing, my lord," Simon murmured. "She's a very quick learner."

Richard stared down at her small, stubborn figure and let out a lewd bark of laughter. "I can imagine. What else have you been teaching her, you blackguard? Have you been showing her the other uses mouths can be put to?"

"Lady Alys was generous enough to grant me the boon of a chaste kiss," he said, still watching Alys's pale face.

"Doesn't look chaste to me." Richard brayed with laughter. "Perhaps we'd better hurry the wedding along. We don't want a brat appearing in six months' time. You'll fill her belly once you're wed and not a moment before, eh?" He put his thick hand on Alys's stomach, squeezing, and she bit her lip to stifle a cry.

Simon moved then. He had enough sense not to put his hand on Richard—there was a limit to what his liege lord would tolerate, and he was too far gone in wine to be sensible. If it came to a fight Simon would kill him quite easily, but he wasn't ready for Richard to die.

"My lord," he said, and Richard wheeled around, forgetting his sister. Alys shrank back, a trembling hand pressing her stomach. "If you wish I can send the wench away."

"Do that," Richard said with a wave of his hand. "Can't stand the silly creatures most of the time. They belong on their backs, you know, with their legs spread. Send the bitch away, and we'll have a glass of wine and talk about the future."

Simon had little choice in the matter. The seduction of Alys of Summersedge would have to wait. At the moment she looked both faint and confused, and if the reddening of her mouth had lessened, the reddening of her cheeks was still bright. Time would only be to his advantage. She'd liked that kiss—it was no false pride that told him so. He'd felt the softening in her flesh, the faint yearning that had begun to blossom. Given a few days to think about it, that yearning might come to full flower.

Before he could say a word Alys turned and ran, disappearing from his tower room like a frightened rabbit. She was an interesting mixture of bravery and fear. He had little doubt she'd face a dragon for those she loved. But for her own sake she was more than willing to run away and hide.

Richard, with his usual single-mindedness, walked directly past the damning desk with its page of illuminated manuscript. He poured himself a goblet of wine and tossed it down, ignoring the red trails that dribbled into his beard. "Damn me if you don't have the best wine in the castle," he said, belching. "I know that can't be the truth of it, but every time I drink in your rooms it tastes sweeter."

"Perhaps it's the company," Simon said in a dulcet tone.

Richard blinked at him drunkenly, missing the irony entirely. "As you wish," he mumbled, waving an airy hand. "So you're teaching m'little sister about herbs, are you? Knowledge such as that can be dangerous in the hands of the frailer sex."

It was taking Richard a surprisingly long time to get to the point, but Simon was prepared to be patient. "Dangerous, my lord? How so?"

"Herbs can be wicked things. Dangerous, even deadly. What if a wife takes it into her head to choose a new husband? Couldn't she administer something deadly in his wine, and no one would ever know?"

"It is always possible."

"There are such things, aren't there?" Richard pressed the issue, moving closer. He smelled of sweat, sour wine, and ever so faintly of vomit, none of which odors was unexpected. "Drugs that can be fed a man, or even a child, that would kill him without a trace."

"Perhaps. Though most physicians and barbers could recognize the signs of poison easily enough."

"But there are other potions, herbs and the like, that can simply put a man into a deep sleep, are there not? Nothing harmful, unless, of course, one made the mistake of taking too much. I remember hearing of such a matter. Prince Edward of Normandy's wife was used to dosing herself with various herbs, and one night she simply took too much, and never woke up."

"There were, of course, rumors that the prince assisted her in making such a fatal error," Simon said gently.

Richard beamed at him. "Exactly! That can happen, can it not? A perfectly reasonable medical mistake, and the unwanted person is conveniently disposed of."

"It's been done since the beginning of time, my lord," Simon said, lowering himself into the seat by the fire, his right hand hidden in his long robes. "And who is it you would have me kill?"

Richard blinked, momentarily disconcerted. And then he roared with laughter. "That's my Grendel," he shouted. "Always ready with a quip. Poison's not my weapon—I prefer to meet someone on the field of battle. I leave the sneaky stuff to those best suited for it."

"Such as myself?" Simon murmured.

"You came highly recommended, Simon of Navarre. An expert at exterminating . . . difficulties."

Simon allowed himself a small, cold smile. "You still haven't answered my question, my lord. Exactly what difficulty did you wish exterminated?"

"All in good time, my Grendel. All in good time. There do exist such potions, do there not?"

"Which potions do you mean?"

"Sleep potions," Richard said irritably. "Elixirs which do no harm in moderation, but might prove dangerous if taken in excess. Herbal concoctions that might only make a strong man drowsy, but could kill a frail boy of twelve."

The silence was absolute. In the ensuing stillness the only sound was the faint crackle of the fire, and the sound of the wind whistling through the arrow slits.

The king of England, Henry the Third, was a frail boy of twelve. Second cousin to Richard de Lancie, who was several steps removed from the throne. But those steps could be easily surmounted if the throne were rendered empty by a tragic accident, a fatal miscalculation of a herbal potion intended to soothe.

It was no more than Simon had suspected of his amoral liege lord. Murdering a child might be a hideous crime, but murdering a child-king was simply a matter of political expediency.

"It could be done, my lord," Simon said slowly. "There are rare potions, spells that I learned in the East, that could bring about the desired results."

"We must be very careful. We cannot allow such things to fall into the wrong hands."

"My herbs are safe in my rooms," Simon said. "No one would be able to touch them without my permission. No one would dare try."

"Do you have that potion made up?"

"No, my lord. Such concoctions are complicated, delicate matters, not done easily. There is very little call for it. It would take time to prepare it."

Richard moved closer still. "Be very careful, my Grendel. There are dangerous people in the world, those who wish ill of ones such as my dear cousin, the king. We are all sworn to protect him with our lives."

Odd, Simon thought, staring up into his face with no expression whatsoever. His bad hand was clenched in a painful fist beneath the enveloping robe. He wouldn't have suspected Richard's machinations would disturb him. But then, he'd always been foolishly sentimental about the lives of children. One of his few weaknesses.

"I am yours to command, my lord," he murmured. "I'll prepare that potion and keep it safe."

"How long will it take you?" Richard didn't bother to disguise his eagerness.

"It could be a matter of days, or a matter of weeks, my lord. It has to do with making certain I have the correct ingredients. Some may be difficult to come by."

"You are my best and dearest lord," Richard said fondly. "Do it quickly, my Grendel. And you'll have anything you want as a reward."

"Your sister is reward enough."

Richard grimaced. "And you're a very odd man. Not a bit like me."

Simon looked up into the conscienceless eyes of his sworn lord. "Yes, my lord," he said in a slow, deep voice. And if he'd still believed in God he would have thanked him that it was so.

Chapter Nine

Sir Thomas du Rhaymer was an interesting man, Claire decided as she scrubbed her mouth with fresh water and mint leaves. Every now and then she suspected there might be a human being behind those flinty eyes, that stern expression on his handsome face.

She'd asked the servants about him, of course, and come up with a variety of answers. He had a wife, all right. Gwyneth du Rhaymer had run off with a wealthy baron whose land bordered the distant reaches of Summersedge, and she was great with child.

It was rumored that she'd been pregnant before, by her handsome husband, and that she killed the babe, rather than bear it. It was rumored that her husband had beat her often and severely, causing her to lose the unborn child. It was rumored that she'd been pregnant by Richard himself, and he'd made his sorcerer give her drugs to rid herself of the child.

Claire didn't know what to believe, and in the end she believed none of it. In truth, the man had an unfaithful wife. And he was dour, disapproving, and far too handsome for a man who wanted to give his life to a monastery.

Madlen was full of useful information, most of it reasonably reliable. "Such a shame," she'd muttered, rolling her eyes. "Such a handsome man, and what a waste! He could do so much more good out in the world. Think of what pretty babies he'd have!"

Very pretty babies, Claire had thought, remembering his icy blue eyes and silken hair.

"But he's out to make a hermit of himself, and even if Lord Richard won't let him, he'll be a hermit knight if he has his way. He's a stubborn young man, far too interested in his soul and not enough concerned with the life he's living."

"He needs a new wife."

"And where's he going to find one? He's still married to that heartless jade."

"Couldn't he have her put aside? Have the marriage annulled? With Richard's help he would be certain to. . . ."

"What makes you think Richard would help?" Madlen demanded with a coarse laugh. "He was the one who made the match in the first place, knowing he was marrying a whore to a saint. He'd only interfere if he thought it would aid him, and having Sir Thomas miserable and cold and angry suits him very well indeed. It makes him a better fighter, and that's all Lord Richard cares for."

"It seems so sad for him."

"Don't you be breaking your heart over his pretty blue eyes, mistress," Madlen had warned in her motherly way. "He wouldn't accept an annulment if one were granted. He's not one to set aside the vows he made to

God, even if the pope himself gives him leave." She sighed heartily. "Don't you just hate noble men?"

Claire rinsed her mouth and spat the water in the bowl, still thinking of Madlen's words. In truth, noble men were the very devil. They didn't laugh, didn't dance, didn't compliment a girl on her hair or her eyes. They just looked at you and glowered.

She wondered if she could make Thomas du Rhaymer smile. He wasn't a monk, not yet at least. Not in his heart. She didn't know why she was so certain of that fact, but she was. For all his stern disapproval, there was something in the way he looked at her. Something that kindled a strange, longing fire deep within her, something she'd never felt before.

Just her luck, she thought sourly, kicking her long skirts out of her way as she crossed the solar she shared with her sister. God had granted her a glorious gift of beauty, and the only man she longed for was the one who didn't want her. Couldn't have her. Didn't need her.

Except that Sir Thomas du Rhaymer did need her, quite badly. He needed her to teach him how to smile. And she needed him to teach her how to. . . .

"Claire!" Alys rushed into the room as if the hounds of hell were pursuing her. Her veil was half torn off her neat plaits of hair, her cheeks were flushed, her eyes suspiciously bright. She didn't look the slightest bit like her usually staid self, and Claire gave up the disturbing tenor of her thoughts to concentrate on the unlikely tumult of Alys.

"What's happened to you?" Claire demanded. Alys had tears in her eyes, another first, and her mouth looked slightly swollen. "Did that . . . that creature hurt you? He hit you, didn't he? Tell me he struck you and I'll steal a sword and run him through! How dare he lay a hand on my sister! I'll gut him, I swear. . . ." Her furious voice trailed off in the face of Alys's sudden laugh.

"I'd like to see you try, dearest," she said. "Of course he didn't hit me."

"Your mouth is swollen," Claire said accusingly.

"He kissed me."

Claire was dumbfounded. "I will kill him," she said, quite calmly.

"No, you won't. I am pledged to him—he has every right to kiss me." She sank down on the bed, pulling the veil and circlet from her head.

"What was it like?" Claire asked finally.

"Like?"

"The kiss? Was it nasty? Hurtful? Did he kiss your mouth or your cheek or. . . ."

"Of course he kissed my mouth, Claire," Alys said with deceptive calm. "I'd hardly be this disturbed by a chaste kiss on the hand."

Claire felt a chill in her heart. "So there was nothing chaste about this kiss?" she forced herself to ask.

She half expected Alys to deny it. Instead a strange, distant expression came into her eyes, as if she were remembering something long in the past, when it couldn't have been more than an hour ago. "No," she said in a small voice. "There was nothing chaste about his kiss."

Claire's curiosity overcame her. "Why did he kiss you? What did it feel like? Was he gentle, or rough? Did he ask leave to kiss you? Did he. . . ?"

"Does Simon of Navarre strike you as the sort of man who would ask leave to kiss someone?"

"He doesn't strike me as the sort of man who'd be interested in kissing," Claire said bluntly. "Does he you?"

"No," Alys admitted. "But he is. No one could be quite so adept at it without possessing a great deal of interest in the subject."

"Adept?" Claire shuddered. "I don't know how you could bear it. I know that he is not precisely ugly, if you don't notice that twisted hand of his, but I still can't imagine it. So he kissed you on the mouth. What did you say?"

"I didn't have much of a chance to say anything. It wasn't a brief kiss."

"What do you mean? How can a kiss be other than brief? Lips touch, and then part."

"There's more to it than that. He put his mouth against mine, and I thought that would be all there was to it. And I told myself I must submit. But then, when he used his tongue . . ."

"His tongue?" Claire shrieked in horror.

"I tried to pull away. But I hadn't realized he was holding me so that I couldn't escape. I could only stay there and let him kiss me."

"Oh, my poor angel," Claire moaned. "That you had to endure such a terrible thing."

"But it wasn't," Alys said. "At first I was quite shocked, but since there was no way I could get away from him I simply let him kiss me. And it grew very dark and strange, Claire. The room seemed to glow, and I felt as if I were sinking into a deep, soft pillow made of velvet, and darkness was all around me, but it was lit with stars, and I knew I had to hold on to him or I would fall, but he was there, and quite strong, and I knew I should be safe, and. . . ." Her voice trailed off as she noticed Claire's stupefaction.

"You did like it," she accused her.

"I don't know," Alys said in a practical voice. "Perhaps I'll have to try it again to make certain."

"Alys!" Claire was shocked.

"I don't know what would have happened if Richard hadn't suddenly arrived," Alys added. "I felt faint, and oddly weak, which I imagine was what he had in mind. Lord Simon's motives could never be simple."

"He was trying to cloud your mind. He probably used one of his filthy potions on you, and your addled brain is the result of drugs, not his kissing," Claire said sternly.

"Does my brain appear addled?" Alys sounded wistful. "I'm not surprised. And yet I've always prided myself on my sharp wits."

"It's witchcraft."

"It's nothing of the kind," Alys said sharply. "And there were no potions tonight, nothing to make me weak and pliant. For all that he likes to frighten people into thinking he's some sort of dread monster, Simon of Navarre is only a man. No more, no less."

"And you still intend to marry him? You're still willing to sacrifice yourself for me?" Claire was unaccustomed to feeling guilt, but all her sister's protestations were unable to allay the feeling.

Alys lifted her head and met her sister's gaze, and for the first time there was a trace of her older sister's usual serenity, her calm good humor. "Claire, my sweet," she said in a soft voice, "I begin to suspect that it will be no sacrifice at all."

Claire stared at her in disbelief. This wasn't the staid, plain older sister who'd always looked out for her, always cared for her. With her shining eyes and flushed cheeks, with her hair awry and her lips reddened, she looked absolutely lovely. Not at all the perfect little scholar and would-be nun. She looked like a woman, a woman whose first concern was no longer her sister Claire.

She swallowed her moment of panic with admirable calm. "Perhaps Grendel is preferable to the convent.

You know I have never approved of your supposed vocation. But you know you have only to say the word."

"And what, my love?" Alys asked. "Will you step in and take my place as the virgin sacrifice? Or will you skewer my betrothed?"

"You mock me. I would do either, if necessary," Claire announced with great dignity.

"There will be no necessity. Simon of Navarre and I are very well suited. He is a man of many talents and interests. I know I shall enjoy learning from him."

"And what exactly is it that you'll be learning, sister dear?"

And to Claire's dismay, steady, stalwart Alys turned a bright, embarrassed crimson.

Simon of Navarre stood by the narrow window slit and stared out at the castle. He preferred his rooms in the north tower to all others—from his vantage point he could see the mountains to the east, and the thick, dark woods of Summersedge Forest which stretched for countless miles to the rocky sea coast. He could see the rich, fertile valley below and the rustic buildings that comprised the town. And he could see across the rest of the castle, the battlements and windows, the towers.

His betrothed was still awake. Either she or her sister still moved about in the room in the east tower he'd manipulated Lord Richard into giving them. He'd chosen it for that very reason—that he could see it well from across the empty space over the rooftops and the battlements. He could watch her.

He was a wise, distrustful man, and keeping an eye on all those who might do him damage was a habit he'd learned early on. He told himself he had no other interest in keeping watch over Lady Alys. He cared not if she had a lover or two, as long as she was discreet.

Except that now he'd had a taste of her virgin mouth, he found he wanted to be the one to explore the rest of her innocence. He'd never been a man particularly attracted to virgins. They wept, they were almost impossible to pleasure, and they were usually ugly as sin, else they wouldn't still be virgins by the time he got to them.

But for some reason he didn't fancy the notion of some other man between her legs, taking her maidenhead, claiming her. He wasn't a greedy man, having learned early on that most possessions were as easily lost as won, but he found that he had the most uncharacteristic desire to possess Lady Alys of Summersedge.

The soft glow of candlelight lit her deep window, and he thought he could see a woman's shadow cross in front of it. There was no long ripple of hair, no flounce in the gait of the pacing woman, and he knew it wasn't the younger one. The silly flirt, the supposedly pretty one.

He'd given Alys something to pace over, something to trouble her mind and her spirit. He wondered if it troubled her body as well. It assuredly troubled his.

There were women he could have, quiet, discreet women who knew how to share pleasure, but somehow he couldn't summon up any interest in them. It was little wonder he wanted to possess Alys. For some reason she had managed to possess him.

He left the window, moving to stand by his partially completed manuscript. There were no pages describing what Lord Richard had asked for, and he wondered whether he would commit the ultimate, foolish act, and detail the herbal concoction that would kill a king. Complete with glowing colors and careful illustrations. He expected that he would.

He didn't bother to look down into the courtyard to make certain his workshop was dark. No one dared enter the place—they were convinced that ghosts and creatures of the devil haunted the rooms when he wasn't there. Of course, they believed that he was, in truth, a creature of the devil, so it made little difference whether he was there or not. In daylight or darkness they gave his workshop a wide berth.

Of course he had lied to Richard about the poisonous concoction. It was simple enough to make, and the ingredients were to be found almost anywhere in England. The proper proportions were crucial of course, but it was something he was experienced in using. He'd killed twice using that herbal remedy, with care and forethought. The patients had died, peacefully, an old woman with unbearable pain and rotting limbs as her only future, a middle-aged merchant who'd just beaten his second wife to death and wanted to ensure that he slept well before he wed his third victim.

They had died in their sleep, in no pain, though he might have wished that the merchant had suffered a bit more. He could only hope the hereafter, which he wasn't sure he believed in, would take care of punishing the brutal merchant with suitable severity.

The young king would feel nothing, and it would doubtless be a kinder death than countless others had in store for him. Being a king was a profession filled with danger, and the life expectancy was almost as short as that of a sickly babe. Henry the Third would die sooner or later, probably sooner, probably painfully. In truth, Simon of Navarre would be doing him a service.

His own cynical laugh surprised him. He hadn't realized quite how far he'd gone, down the spiral of death and evil. He'd never killed a child, either by malice or in battle. It had been the deaths of children, hundreds of them on that cursed crusade, that had sealed his own fate and made him who he was. And yet now he was ready to commit that very crime, to justify it, for his own ends.

Human frailty, his own in particular, always amused him. He sank down in his chair and stared into the fire, clenching and unclenching his hand. He would assemble the ingredients for the lethal sleeping draught. But whether he would actually let Richard the Fair administer it was yet to be determined.

Whether Simon of Navarre had truly lost his soul was still a question better left to those who judge. Brother Jerome would insist that there was salvation. Richard the Fair would bid him dance with the devil.

It was a simple choice. All the power and wealth that Simon had ever desired was within his grasp. The boy wouldn't make it to manhood anyway, not in these perilous times.

But he wasn't a man to be rushed into any choice. He would most likely do it, for the simple reason that it would give him exactly what he wanted. Perhaps he'd have Lady Alys do the actual mixing of the concoction. After all, she was so very eager to learn.

The fire was dying, but he made no move to stir the coals. In the distance he could see a flash of lightning, and he remembered Alys's fear. Was it the lightning that kept her awake and pacing? Or was it the memory of his kiss?

It certainly wasn't a guilty conscience that kept her from her bed. Alys was truly innocent, untouched, unsoiled by the darkness that roamed the earth and seemed to have settled in Simon's soul.

He would soil her, and part of him regretted that fact. But in truth, it was only a very small part, the tiny

piece of his conscience that still remained. He managed
to push it aside with no great difficulty.

He would make the fatal draught, and he would swive
Lady Alys. And the devil could take his soul. If he hadn't
already.

He slept, sitting in the chair, dreaming of Alys
wrapped in nothing but her silken hair. He dreamed
of Alys, her mouth opened in a scream of horror.

And then he saw them. The children. Slaughtered
along the road to Damascus. Bought and sold as amuse-
ments for depraved soldiers. The Children's Crusade.
The last frail hope in a world gone mad, now blighted
by horror. And there had been nothing he could do to
save them, nothing at all.

And he woke with an anguished cry.

Chapter Ten

Sir Thomas du Rhaymer awoke in a cold sweat, sitting upright on his straw-filled pallet, shaking in the frigid morning air. As a knight he was deserving of better sleeping accommodations, but the narrow pallet on the stone floor was suited to his nature, and he slept hard and well upon it.

Not that night, however. His dreams had been tormenting, restless, wicked dreams, and as he scrambled out of bed to splash his face with icy water, he thanked a merciful God he couldn't remember them. The evidence still remained on his wayward body—he was hard as a pikestaff—but he told himself it was no more than the need to relieve himself. And he knew he lied.

It was early, even for the most energetic of the Keep's inhabitants. He could smell fresh bread baking on the cool, pre-dawn air, but the garderobe was empty, and all around him people slept.

He washed and dressed quickly, his early morning plan simple. He would head for the chapel and morning prayers, then find a quiet place in the still, cool air to contemplate his sins, both real and imagined. By the time the spoiled beauty roused herself from her bed he would be fully prepared to resist any temptation she might throw in his way.

There were two chapels inside the castle walls: the small, family chapel in the Keep itself, and the larger one that abutted the curtain wall. With luck Brother Jerome would be about, and Thomas could make his confession. Brother Jerome would be too lenient with him, but Thomas could add to his own penance. Indeed, his proximity to Lady Claire of Summersedge was a penance in itself.

A few stray dogs were slinking about the courtyard as he made his way to the larger chapel, shivering in the crisp air, but there were no people about. He was just reaching for the door, when he heard the distant whirrup of a horse.

He froze. That noise could have come from any number of the horses lodged in the vast stables at Summersedge Keep. It could have come from a workhorse, or one of the knights' steeds. It could be a gentle lady's palfrey, restless in her stall.

But he knew it was no such thing. He slowly turned, in time to see the huge mare flash by in the murky pre-dawn air, a pale figure clinging, saddleless, to its broad back. And there was never a question in his mind who that stubborn creature was.

He moved quickly, speed an essential part of his soldier's training, telling himself there was no way in heaven she could get beyond the castle walls. At that hour of the day the drawbridge should be up, the portcullis down, all entry and exit barred even in this less than hostile time.

But he'd underestimated the treacherous female. He

didn't know who she'd managed to bribe, or cozzen, but the entrance to the castle was free and clear, and no soldier of Lord Richard was about to put a cross-bow bolt in a lady's back if she refused to halt.

He was cursing under his breath as he ran for the stables, too furious even to notice the wickedness of his language. He'd ridden since he was a child—he had no more need of a saddle than that hell-bent female—and he found Paladin easily enough amidst the horses. Within moments he was thundering out the gate after her, but she was so far away, a mere speck in the distance, that he doubted she knew she was being followed.

He hadn't ridden bareback, without armor, in years. He bent low on Paladin's neck, urging him faster, and a sense of glorious power filled him as the wind tore through his short cropped hair. It was a cool, damp air, redolent of mist and dry leaves, and for one brash, wild moment he thought of simply urging Paladin faster, faster still, until he passed the troublesome wench, leaving her in the dust. Leaving all of Summersedge Keep in the dust, the memory of his wife, his duty to a corrupt lord, his troublesome urges that had chosen a fine time to reappear and torment him.

He could just imagine the expression on Lady Claire's beautiful face as he soared past her, ignoring her. He could equally imagine Richard the Fair's shock that his most holy of knights had turned his back on duty and honor and simply returned home to his neglected estates in the north.

It wasn't to be. His liege lord might be unworthy, but Thomas had made his vows to him, just as he had to his faithless wife. If he were to damn his eternal soul by breaking his God-given vows, then he'd rather do it with Lady Claire than by running away.

He wasn't going to do either, and he cursed himself

for even thinking such a thought. She was out of sight of the castle now, just beyond the copse of trees, and he cursed again. Summersedge Forest was no place for the likes of her. It was a wicked place, filled with wild animals and evil spells, and the paths were strewn with dangers, low hung branches, up-shot roots. She could be swept from her horse, her fragile bones smashed against the ground, and he would have to carry her corpse back to her brother.

But her bones weren't fragile, they were strong. And she was too good a rider to take foolish chances. He was a halfwit to worry about her. Besides, it wasn't Lady Claire he was worried about, it was facing her brother with no good excuse.

He couldn't find her. She had melted into the forest like the first snow on a bright day in December. The leaves were thick along the narrow trails, and he couldn't even attempt to track her.

He waited, he searched, he called for her, knowing full well she wouldn't answer even if she heard him. In the end he turned back to face his punishment. If Lord Richard wanted him hanged from the battlements, so be it. There were far worse futures he could face.

The castle was awake and a-bustle when he rode back over the drawbridge. His squire, Alain, was waiting for him, but the boy had the sense to keep his questions to himself and simply take Paladin's reins and lead him back to the stables.

Lord Richard would be in the Great Hall, breaking his fast. Most of the castle would be there as well, either eating or serving. It was as good a time as any to confess his transgressions. That way a hunt could be mounted for the missing beauty as quickly as possible.

He didn't pause during his headlong dash into the hall, and the doors banged loudly as he pushed through, causing an uncustomary silence to wash over the busy place. He strode down the middle of the huge room, past the side tables, skirting the huge fire, coming directly to the dais and the curious, merciless eyes of Richard the Fair.

"What kept you, Sir Thomas?" he demanded, taking a deep draught of his morning ale. "Have you forgotten your duties? Overslept, eh? And with whom? None of the serving wenches claim any knowledge. Perhaps you prefer young boys?"

Thomas didn't even blink, so intent was he on confession and punishment. "Your sister, my lord. . . ." he began in a rough voice.

"Don't tell me you've bedded my sister, for I'll know you for a liar," Richard said with a coarse laugh. "She's been here this last half hour, wondering where her chaste champion had gotten himself to."

He hadn't seen her. Too intent on confession and punishment, he hadn't even noticed that she was seated next to her boisterous brother, albeit as far away as she could manage. He stared at her in dumbstruck disbelief. Her hair was chastely plaited, with a loose veil and circlet covering its golden glory. Her clothes were somber, her eyes utterly calm as they met his.

"So?" Lord Richard demanded. "Where were you, Sir Thomas?"

He managed to pull his gaze away from Lady Claire, but only with supreme effort. "Er . . . I was lost in prayer, my lord."

Richard's contemptuous snort was reply enough. "That's no way to watch over a high-bred filly like m'sister. You'd best watch yourself, lad. She could lead you a merry chase."

Thomas cast a sudden, suspicious glance at his liege lord, but Richard had no idea how very close he'd come to the mark. "Aye, my lord," Thomas said in a dutiful voice. "A thousand pardons."

"A mere handful is enough, and see that it doesn't happen again. If my little sister continues to behave herself, you might find her a nice little palfrey and allow her a gentle ride within the castle walls. Something suitable for a lady. You'd like that, wouldn't you, my dear?" he demanded of his sister.

She lifted her willful chin. "You are too generous," she said sweetly.

Thomas looked at her doubtfully. He couldn't believe her sudden docility; he couldn't believe the neat hair and calm demeanor that suggested a woman just risen from her bed. She seemed a far cry from the hoyden he'd chased through the forest. Her color was high, but Richard's crude jests could be the cause.

Old Sir Hector was seated next to her, drooling over her, and Thomas had to content himself with a seat at the lower table, where he could look up at her and torment himself with his indecision. His morning ride had increased his appetite, and indeed, Lady Claire seemed equally hungry. She never looked in his direction; she kept her face down and her expression demure, but he told himself he wasn't fooled.

Richard stood up abruptly, signalling the meal was at an end, and the others hastily followed suit, a few of them choking on their ale-soaked bread. Thomas vanished back into the shadows of the hall, waiting his chance to accost the devious wench, to find out the truth.

But luck was still against him. She came sailing by on Sir Hector's arm, flashing a brief, triumphant smile in his direction. "There's no need to hover, good Sir Thomas," she murmured. "I'm certain Sir Hector can be trusted to keep me safe."

The elderly Sir Hector preened, and Thomas knew a sudden, unworthy desire to kick the old man's cane out from beneath his gnarled fist. "As you wish, my lady," he said, bowing slightly as they moved past.

And then her ladyship looked back at him, and there was a wicked smile in her eyes. "You might spend your free time improving your riding skills, Sir Thomas. You never know when you might find yourself caught up in a chase."

He watched her go, and now he could see the dew-bright dampness on her thick plaits. And he wondered, quite absently, whether anyone had ever spanked her. And he wondered if he were going to break his self-imposed rule against violence to women, and administer that punishment.

"You seem quite cheerful this morning, Sir Thomas," Brother Jerome observed, coming up beside him. "It's not often that the morning finds you smiling."

Thomas jumped guiltily. "You must have misread my expression, Brother Jerome. I was thinking of someone quite troublesome."

Brother Jerome followed his gaze quite pointedly, looking at Claire's disappearing figure. "Some of the most delightful creatures in God's creation are troublesome indeed, my son. We missed you at morning prayers."

"I . . . was called away," Thomas mumbled, aware that he was treading perilously close to telling the good brother a lie.

"Were you?" Brother Jerome glanced at Claire again. "I am not the man to remind you of your vows—you are much harder on yourself than our Savior would ever be." He leaned closer, putting a gentle hand on Thomas's clenched fist. "Trust me, my boy. There's nothing wrong with smiling."

* * *

She found him in his workshop. It was a small blessing—Alys had no desire to broach Navarre in the intimacy of his solar. In truth she had no desire to face him at all, and her reaction to his absence at the breaking of the fast was relief tinged with anxiety. The longer she put off seeing him, the worse it became. She would have much preferred facing him in public. The memory of last night was still too strong in her senses, and she wanted to avoid a replay, or even worse, an escalation of last night's kiss. She had been tormented, unable to sleep, pacing the floor for long hours as she listened to the distant crack of thunder. For once it wasn't her fear of storms that kept her awake. It was her fear of Simon.

Not that she was about to let him see it. He was busy at the far end of the low, narrow building, and when she stepped inside he didn't look up; he was absorbed in whatever potion he was concocting, completely unaware of her presence. Or seemingly so—with Simon of Navarre one could never be certain of anything.

It gave her a chance to study him at her leisure, with no one as witness. Viewing him dispassionately, she should have found nothing to be afraid of. He was a man, with all the frailties of mankind, no doubt, even if he had yet to display any. He wore his hair long, a thick rich brown streaked with lighter colors, as if he'd spent many hours in the sun. And yet he was a creature of shadow and darkness, was he not?

His skin was a faintly golden color as well, matching his light, amber eyes. He looked a bit like some exotic being, not quite human, and he doubtless did what he could to reinforce that impression. His long robes were better suited to an older man—they were elegant, made of rich fabrics in jewel-like colors. The dull gold that he wore today matched his gilded features, and she imagined him as some great wild beast, a huge cat, perhaps, sleek and dangerous.

He moved with elegant, unhurried grace, and his back was lean and straight beneath the robe. He lived among books and herbs and healing, away from far more natural and tedious male pursuits such as hunting and riding and fighting. Why would he be interested in something as mundane as kissing?

Except that there had been nothing even remotely mundane about last night's kiss. Even with her total lack of experience she knew those moments with his mouth upon hers were unlike what most people felt from such embraces. She had endured it, and then she had revelled in it. And now it frightened her.

The room smelled of spices, thick and mysterious, and she could feel the smoke dancing through the air, swirling toward her, calling to her. She felt herself sway toward it with sudden longing, and she wanted to reach out her arms and embrace it, embrace him, when cold, wicked sense shattered the illusion, and she saw there was no smoke swirling in the room, and the man at the far end was watching her with his calm, jewel-like eyes.

"Did you wish to see me, my lady?" His voice made her skin shiver. She wondered why. It was low, even, but in all, very powerful. Another weapon that he used wisely, she told herself, struggling for equanimity. And failing to find it.

"I didn't mean to disturb you," she said, summoning the manners Sister Agnes had drilled into her. "You hadn't realized I was here, and I planned to come back later. . . ."

"I knew you were here," he said, watching her. "And you make a habit of disturbing me."

She flushed, her nervous fingers pleating the ugly brown stuff of her loose-fitting gown. "I'm sorry, I've never been particularly good at being demure and fading into the background. You would think I'd learn the art of dutiful silence with a glorious creature like my sister to revel in being the center of everyone's attention, but I've always had difficulty controlling my tongue and my thoughts. You wouldn't believe the penances I've suffered, and they've failed to curb my questioning mind. The nuns had given up hope of me." She stopped abruptly, realizing that she'd been babbling.

"Merci, mon dieu," he said softly. "There are different forms of disturbance. You manage to disturb me when you're sound asleep." He glanced toward the dim daylight beyond the open door to his workshop. "I assume you aren't about to fall asleep again, are you? You would probably find better rest in your own room."

The memory of her sleepless night assailed her, and she grimaced. At least he could have no notion of how restless she'd been. "I'm not tired," she said, a bold-faced lie.

"Astonishing," he said softly. "Considering that someone spent most of the night pacing in your room, and it could scarcely be your silly-headed sister, I would have thought you'd be in dire need of a rest."

She froze. "You were watching? You set spies on me? How could you do such a thing?"

"Quite easily, in truth, but I did not. If you had managed to keep your eyes open during one of your nocturnal visits to my solar, you would have realized that I have a view of both the surrounding countryside and most of the keep. I can see the room you share with your sister simply by looking out a window."

"Did you watch me undress?" The sharp question was out before she could call it back.

Her mortification was increased by his laughter. "My eyes are not that good, and I keep my looking glass in the workshop. Though now that you mention it, perhaps I should have my servants bring it up to my room so that I can peruse your naked body at my leisure."

"You enjoy tormenting me," she said stiffly.

"You are so very easy to torment," he murmured, and she realized he was very close indeed. She hadn't even been aware of his moving toward her; he'd accomplished it with his usual stealthy grace. "If I wished to watch you take off your clothes I would simply arrange to have you brought to my room and make you do so."

"Don't you think my brother might have some objection?"

The look in his eyes failed to reassure her. There was a bitter humor that was entirely lacking in warmth, and even in the heated room Alys suddenly felt chilled. "Your brother needs me, Lady Alys," he said. "I expect he would deny me nothing."

She believed him. She would believe almost everything bad of Richard, and Simon of Navarre was not the man to make idle boasts. "What does he need you for?" she asked.

"Everything his heart desires, my lady," he said with a cynical twist of a smile.

For a moment she said nothing, perusing the shadowy confines of his workshop. The brazier glowed at the far end of the long, low room, and the scent of spice was in the air. "My brother wants power," she said. "He wants wealth."

"I can give him those things."

"He wants women as well."

"I can provide him with herbs that will make the most recalcitrant of females overeager."

She froze. "Is that what you put in my wine?" she demanded in horror.

He was too close to her. He touched her chin, tilting her face up to his so he could view it with care. "No, my lady. Why do you ask? Have you been feeling over-eager?"

She pulled away from him, stumbling back over her long skirts. "No," she said. "But I have no doubt you think I'm the most recalcitrant of females."

"It's part of your charm," he murmured.

"You should have no wish to wed an unwilling woman."

"Ah, but I thought you were willing. You offered yourself so sweetly in the place of your little sister. Have you changed your mind?"

"I cannot imagine what you would want in either of us," she said bluntly.

"An alliance with the house of de Lancie is not to be taken lightly. Lord Richard is a very powerful man, and with my help, that power may increase. It would be a prudent marriage for me."

"And you are a prudent man?"

"Not particularly."

"Then why have you agreed to marry me?" She wasn't absolutely certain she wanted to hear the answer, but she was sure she wouldn't rest until she knew.

He smiled down at her, a cool, wintry smile that didn't reach his golden eyes. "Because I was bored," he said. "And you seemed far more likely to interest me than your silly little sister."

She believed him. He was a strange man, one who'd marry out of boredom, one who'd give his loyalty to a man far less worthy. A man would own her, possess her, body and soul. She was afraid of him, it would be foolish to deny it.

But she was also fascinated by him, like a fat, juicy mouse being hunted by a snake, all she could do was stand still and quiver, looking at him out of her wide eyes. . . .

She laughed at herself, breaking the spell he'd cast over her. She half expected fury on his part, but he simply looked at her with a question in his eyes. "Something amuses you, my lady?"

"My own over-active imagination," she confessed. "There is no reason on earth that I should be frightened of you. Is there?"

"Is there?" he echoed.

And in the distance, she thought she could hear the faint hissing of a snake.

Chapter Eleven

Simon of Navarre had one strong, immediate need. To strip that phenomenally ugly brown dress from Alys of Summersedge.

It wasn't a need to have her naked, though that was a strong enough motive. He was used to holding his desires at bay—it sharpened them, and made their fulfillment all the more satisfying.

But the sheer ugliness of her clothes was an affront. She was standing at a work bench, her narrow sleeves pushed up her forearms, her neatly plaited hair escaping from the restraining veil and circlet. The warmth of the brazier had caused a faint sheen to glisten on her broad, calm brow. The sweet, clean scent of flowers and soap mixed with the richness of spices.

The dress was laced up the back—he could simply take a knife and cut the ties, and with luck it would fall at her feet. Except that he would need two good hands to accomplish such a feat, and he wasn't about to trust Lady Alys with the truth.

She was concentrating on the task he'd set her, a simple enough mixture of horehound and rosemary that would cure all but the most stubborn case of body lice. She was a quick enough learner, exact in her measurements, steady in her gestures. He enjoyed watching her move. She did so with a certain calm grace that was both unhurried and profoundly alluring, and yet he doubted she had any inkling of her sensuality. The kiss he'd given her last night had left her shaken, but he'd done his best to lull her into feeling safe and secure with him once more. He'd let her stay that way. For a while, at least.

"Do you intentionally seek out the ugliest clothing you can find?" he asked, leaning against the high work table and surveying her. "Or are you merely lacking in taste?"

Her flushed face darkened. "It would be very vain and foolish to wear costly garments."

"Vanity and foolishness are expected in women."

The glance she cast in his direction was wonderfully derisive. She said nothing—she didn't need to.

"You could ask your sister for advice," he continued, wickedly interested in forcing a reaction from her. "Her clothes are graceful and appealing. She could help you choose something new."

"I choose my sister's clothes," Alys said. "If it were up to her, she would dress in stable clothes all the time. And when one is possessed of Claire's beauty, everything is flattering."

"Trust me, Lady Alys, muddy brown complements no one."

It was working. She bit her lip, casting a troubled glance at him, obviously torn between hurt and annoyance. "If my lord Simon finds me that ugly then I wonder why you should agree to marry me?"

"It's your clothes that I find ugly," he murmured. "Fortunately clothes can be removed."

He'd scared her this time. Not enough to make her jar the careful mixture she was stirring, but enough to flame her cheeks. "Or I can have prettier clothes made," she countered.

"There is that alternative," he agreed. "One does not necessarily preclude the other."

"One may delay the other," she shot back.

"True enough," he said, enjoying himself. "Though it could work in any number of ways. I could strip you of your clothes and be so enchanted that I would wish to keep you in that particular state. Alternatively, prettier clothes might make me more impatient to take them off you."

"There is always the dire chance that once you saw me without clothes you would be so appalled you would make haste to keep me properly covered."

He laughed at that, unable to stop himself. She was a dangerous woman indeed, with a quick tongue and a ready wit, and a slow, sensual grace that was driving him to distraction despite the clumsy clothes.

A moment later he knew his timing could not have been worse. The doorway to his workshop darkened, and he knew instinctively who was there.

"Did I hear my Grendel laugh?" Richard the Fair demanded in his deceptively boisterous voice. "Surely I must be mistaken. Such a fearsome creature as my most trusted advisor would never laugh over some trifle."

Simon said nothing, watching as Alys stiffened, immediately plastering a plain, quiet expression on her face. She didn't like her half-brother, not a bit. But she wasn't afraid of him, she who was afraid of so many things. Her future husband included.

"He was laughing at my clumsiness," she said, stepping back from the worktable.

"Oh, I don't think so," Richard replied, stepping into the room, his great bulk casting the entryway into shadows. "He's not the sort of man to find humor in something so commonplace. You are reputed to be wiser than most of your sex, little sister. It is a rare woman who can make Simon of Navarre laugh. I may have underestimated you."

Richard the Fair was gifted in the art of making subtle threats. Alys blinked, aware that she was in some sort of danger but unused to the machinations of her elder brother, and Simon deemed it time to intervene.

"It's never wise to underestimate anyone, my lord," he murmured. "Even the most humble of vassals might prove to be unexpectedly dangerous."

"And my sister is hardly a humble vassal, is she?" Richard replied in a silky voice seemingly full of good cheer. "I forgot—she's the smart one, the other's the pretty one. I still say you made a bad choice, Grendel. But now that you have, I'm not in the mind to let you change. I have other plans for the pretty one."

"I have no wish to change my decision, my lord."

"You're a deep fellow, Grendel," Richard said, shaking his head. "I'll never hope to understand you. Keep the girl busy. I have received word that Hedwiga will return tonight, and I have things to accomplish before she does. I don't want anyone getting in my way." He was gone as abruptly as he arrived, leaving Alys staring after him with a perplexed expression on her face.

"Why does he call you Grendel?

"Surely a wise child such as you would know who Grendel is?"

"The bone-cracking, blood-drinking monster that

Beowulf slew," she replied. "I fail to see any connection."

"You flatter me. Richard likes to see me as his pet monster, someone who can terrify his people into instant obedience."

"I find Richard far more frightening."

"No, you don't. You're quite immune to his bullying. But all I have to do is move close to you and you shake like a frightened rabbit confronted by a hungry wolf."

"I rather saw myself as a white mouse," she said, lifting her head to meet his gaze. "And you as a snake."

He smiled slowly. "In the garden of Eden? Do I tempt you, Lady Alys?"

He already knew the answer to that question, even if she didn't. He could sense it in the faint quiver of her mouth, the distant look in her changeable eyes. He could feel it in the air surrounding her. Dampness, heat and longing.

She wisely ignored his question. "Why did Richard tell you to keep me busy? Why should my presence be a constraint to him? I'm not likely to intrude on his private rooms uninvited."

He'd hoped she hadn't noticed the oddness of Richard's request. She was too sharp, and he doubted she would believe even the most likely of lies.

"I imagine it's *your* room that *he's* intruding on, in truth. And your sister."

She stared at him. "What business would he have with Claire?"

"Her future, perhaps?"

"But why should I not be there?" she persisted.

"I can think of any number of reasons," he said, hoping to placate her. "He might think you'd interfere."

"Interfere with what?" Her voice had risen alarmingly, and Simon cursed silently. So his observant lady hadn't missed Richard's lascivious glances at his half-sister. "And what does his wife's return have to do with it?"

She'd started toward the door, almost at a run, and he had no choice but to catch her around the waist, pulling her back against him with his unscarred hand. She struggled, but he was very strong, even using only one arm, and she was wise enough to know she was outmatched.

He could feel the breath storm through her body, her heart pounding against his chest. He breathed in the rich scent of her perfume, letting it taunt him. "You won't do any good rushing up there," he said with deceptive calm. "He'll have a guard stationed at the door."

"You knew what he was going to do?"

"No. I still don't know, I simply know the way Richard's mind works. He wants your sister, and he's not a man to ignore his hungers."

"She's his sister as well!"

"I'm certain he's figured a way around that little problem. Richard is not possessed of a great brain, but he can be very cunning in getting what he wants in this life."

She tried to pull away from him, but he had no particular desire to let her go. "And you intend to stand around and do nothing while he . . . while he. . . ?"

"I don't know what he's planning to do. And it is never wise to interfere with Richard's pursuit of pleasure."

She kicked backwards, connecting with his shin beneath the heavy robe. It startled more than hurt him, but he released her anyway, sure he could recapture her if she were fool enough to rush to her sister's rescue.

"You're afraid of him!" she accused him.

"No."

"Then why won't you stop him?"

"An interesting question," he said in a measured voice. "I've seen men do far worse and been unable to stop them. On the scale of atrocities, a man deflowering his half-sister is fairly mild."

"Mild?"

"I've seen children raped and murdered," he said in a cool voice. "I've seen an army of bound prisoners hacked to pieces. I've witnessed torture and barbarity that you can't even begin to imagine."

"And done nothing to stop it?" she cried.

He lifted his scarred hand, careful to keep it bent. "Where do you think this came from?"

"And so you gave in? Let the horrors go on around you, unchecked? If it were me, I wouldn't have ceased fighting until they'd torn my body apart. And even then I'd curse them, haunt them. . . ."

"I thought you were the quiet one," he said softly.

"Not when my family is in danger. Not when innocent people are being hurt. And if you don't move out of my way," she said fiercely, "I'll curse your black heart till the day I die."

"Ah, Lady Alys," he murmured, "I have no heart. Black or otherwise."

He'd heard Godfrey approaching, always alert. Godfrey knew everything—he would be well aware of Richard's intent, and prepared for his master's wishes.

Alys was fool enough to think the distraction of Godfrey's arrival was enough to let her escape. He caught her again, spinning her around and pressing her face against his shoulder. She didn't stop struggling, but this time he could use his scarred hand without her noticing.

"Godfrey," he said in a casual voice. "Go find Sir

Thomas du Rhaymer and have him attend Lady Claire in her solar. Impress on him the urgency of the situation.''

Godfrey disappeared in the silence with which he arrived, but Simon had no doubt that even without a tongue he'd be able to convey the message to Sir Thomas. It would have to do.

He glanced down at the woman struggling in his arms. She chose that moment to sink her teeth into his shoulder, a mistake on her part. It aroused him.

He waited until her sharp white teeth released his flesh, then shoved her away from him, pushing her up against the daub and wattle wall of the workshop. She was too angry to be intimidated, and she glared up at him in mute fury, tears glistening in her hazel eyes.

"The only one who stands a chance of stopping Richard is Thomas du Rhaymer," he said patiently. "He has a tediously rigid view of right and wrong, and he's been pledged to guard your sister."

"But Richard was the one who ordered him to guard her!"

"It makes no difference. Thomas has accepted the task and he will perform it. He will die rather than let Richard hurt her."

"But he hates Claire. She said so!"

"You already know my opinion of your sister's intellect. Sir Thomas would defend his worst enemy in such a situation, but you may trust me on this, his feelings toward your sister are far more complex."

She'd lost some of the wildness of anger and fear, and he almost missed it. "How do you know?" she whispered.

"I watch people. It is the surest way to gain knowledge, and knowledge is power. If anyone can protect Claire, he can. Or he will die trying."

She took a deep, calming breath, and he backed away

from her, only a bit, enough to give her the illusion of freedom. "Very well," she said in a deceptively brisk voice. "I think I'll just go for a walk to calm my. . . ."

"No," he said. "And it's a waste of time to stare at me with such fury, I'm immune to your disapproval. You will stay with me until Thomas brings your sister here."

"What makes you think he will?"

He smiled, a cool, wintry smile. "Experience. Magic. Take your pick."

She looked at him with great calm. "I hate you."

"No, you don't. You're very angry with me right now, but when your sister is safely brought here you'll decide that I'm not such a monster after all. Despite this." He lifted his twisted hand deliberately, just to watch her reaction.

She didn't even blink. "Having a wounded hand does not make you a monster," she said.

"True enough."

"It's your wicked nature that does it," she shot back.

He wanted to laugh, but he had enough sense not to push her beyond bearing. In truth, he had no idea whether Thomas du Rhaymer would arrive at the solar in time. Perhaps he'd misread the lustful determination in Richard's eyes, but he seldom made mistakes. And if Claire struggled, and fought, Richard was entirely capable of killing her. He'd done it before.

He wasn't about to share his doubts with Alys—she was already furious enough. "Go find a place to sit, my lady," he said gently. "Fall asleep again. I'll make certain no one disturbs you."

The look she cast him was full of hatred and bitter contempt, but she knew there was no way past him. She was trapped in the workshop, trapped into waiting. It was small wonder she hated him.

She would hate him even more, he expected. He wondered if she would love him as well. He hoped not. Women's love was an irrational thing, and it would only bring her pain. He could hope to spare her that.

At that moment love was the furthest thing from her mind. She stalked past him, her ugly brown robe trailing after her, and sank down into a corner, wrapping her arms around her knees. She didn't look at him, or anywhere else but the packed earthen floor of the workshop. But he truly doubted that this time she would fall asleep.

Claire was sitting by the deep-set window, making little progress on her needlework, when she heard the heavy sound of booted feet approaching her solar. She closed her eyes with a sigh, then allowed a tiny, wicked smile to play about her mouth. Doubtless it was Sir Thomas, come to watch over her once more, to glower and lecture. It had been absolutely grand that morning, racing through the thickly rising mist of dawn, Arabia strong and sleek and sure beneath her, the dour knight following at her heels. She wondered what would have happened if she had let him catch her?

She'd been unexpectedly shy at the thought. She knew about men with an instinct as old as time, not from any practical experience, and she knew that beneath Sir Thomas's fierce disapproval lurked a dangerous longing. One that called to her.

She'd been a fool to prance away with Sir Hector, who was, without a doubt, the most boring creature in all creation, not to mention the fact that he liked to pinch her cheeks. She'd only done it to increase Sir Thomas's rage, but the advantage had soon paled beside the penance of listening to Sir Horace's heavy-handed flirting. She certainly hoped her brother had no fancy to wed her to the elderly knight. Even the terrifying Lord Simon would be preferable.

The footsteps were coming closer, and she smoothed her thick curtain of golden hair, not bothering to retrieve the light veil she'd worn earlier. She had no qualms about appearing before the very noble Sir Thomas looking her best. She tugged at the neckline of her simple gown, wishing it were cut lower.

The heavy door slammed open without so much as a knock, and Claire's good-humored anticipation vanished in sudden dismay. She was already tugging her neckline upward when Richard the Fair strode into her room. "See that we're not disturbed," he said over his shoulder, and the door was closed behind him, leaving the two of them trapped inside the spacious solar. Leaving Claire alone with her half-brother.

She had risen, nervously, but she was smart enough to know that one should never show fear in front of a dangerous animal. Therefore she smiled, setting down her needlework and advancing on Richard's burly form. "Dear brother," she murmured, reaching up to plant a chaste kiss on his bearded cheek, "how kind of you to honor me with a visit. I'll have one of my serving woman go find Alys and we can. . . ."

He caught her arm in his meaty grip. The expression in his slightly reddened eyes was unreadable. Disturbing. "No need to bother the serving women, or your sister," he said. "As a matter of fact, I've seen to it that they won't be bothering us. I thought it was time that the two of us became better acquainted."

She wondered whether she could vomit again. Unlikely—it had been hours since she'd eaten, and despite her uneasiness her stomach was sadly calm. She took a step back, but he still gripped her arm with his strong, rough hand. He reached out and caught a strand of her hair, pulling it toward him painfully.

"Pretty," he murmured thickly. "Pretty hair, pretty girl. Give us a kiss, love. I haven't been kissed by such a pretty girl in a long time."

"I just kissed you," she said, trying to still the terrified beat of her heart.

"Not that way. I want a real kiss." He hauled her toward him, but she was strong, used to controlling Arabia, and she was struggling, pushing him away.

"We are brother and sister," she said fiercely. "To touch me would be an abomination in the sight of God and man."

"As for that, I'm thinking maybe we're no kin at all. Your mother lifted her skirts for my father—who's to say she didn't do the same for a dozen others? A whore is always a whore. You might just as well be the daughter of some handsome knight who wouldn't take no for an answer. One like me."

She squirmed, struggling desperately, furious. "You're neither a knight nor handsome," she spat at him. "Let me go or I'll scream."

"Then I'll have to shut you up." And he covered her mouth with his.

His breath was rank, foul, his mouth wet, and she slapped at him, pulling his thinning hair, raking her nails down the side of his face until he thrust her away. She fell, hard, breathless, against the floor, staring up at her half brother in horror.

His eyes were narrow, amused, and the long red streaks on the side of his face showed where her nails had traveled. "I like a lass with spirit," he said. "But you do that again and I'll kill you before I fuck you."

He was fumbling with his breeches when she screamed, as loud as she could, scrambling across the floor through the thick rushes. He leapt for her, but she was too fast for him, and she was almost to the door when it opened.

Sir Thomas du Rhaymer stood there, calm, strong, a faint trickle of blood at his mouth.

"What the hell are you doing here?" Richard screamed. "Get out, damn you!"

Thomas didn't even blink. "You bade me watch over Lady Claire and make certain no man molested her. I'm doing your bidding."

"I'm the one who gave the orders, damn it. Get out of here."

Thomas didn't move. Claire cowered against the stone wall of the solar, terrified that he might leave her. "I can't do that, my liege. I gave my oath before God and I am bound to keep it."

"Stupid bastard," Richard fumed. "Guard!"

"Your man and I already discussed the situation," Thomas said, touching his faintly bloody mouth. "He was moved to agree with me."

"Agree with you about what, you impudent bastard?"

"That your gentle sister be brought to Brother Jerome to make her confession."

Claire opened her mouth to protest, then shut it again, wisely, at a quiet signal from Thomas.

Richard took the opening he was given. "And well she should," he said, straightening his clothes and wiping his mouth on his sleeve. "She has been unseemly. And you have not watched her closely enough, Sir Thomas. This was in the nature of a test, to see how well-guarded she was. A test you have failed miserably."

"Aye, my lord," he said, lowering his head dutifully. "I will endeavor to improve."

"I'll be finding someone else to watch over the girl. Someone I can trust. In the meantime, keep a close watch on her and don't let anyone talk to her. You understand? Or I'll have your heart on a stake."

"Aye, my lord," he murmured again, making no protest.

"Take her away, damn it," Richard mumbled, heaving his bulk onto the bed. "And have someone bring me some wine. I find I'm in sore need of it. Unless you killed the guard, you bloodthirsty bastard?"

"Only . . . disarranged him a bit, my lord." He held out his arm for Claire, and for a moment she just stared at him, unwilling to trust even him for a moment.

The alternative was far worse. Her brother was watching her out of brooding eyes, and she could still taste the foulness of his mouth on hers.

But she had been well-taught, by Alys and the holy sisters. For all Richard's excuses, she knew she was the daughter of a lord, and she stiffened her back and accepted Thomas's proffered arm.

"God give you peace, brother," she murmured politely as she started out the door.

And in her heart she cursed him to hell and back again.

Chapter Twelve

She clutched Thomas's arm so tightly he felt pain as he led her from the room. He could have tensed his muscles, but he didn't, letting her hurt him, letting her fingernails dig deeply into his flesh.

They stepped past the unconscious guard, but Claire didn't even glance down at his body. If she had, she probably wouldn't have seen him. She had the blind look in her eyes that Thomas had seen before, on women who'd seen more than they could bear, on soldiers who had done more than they could bear. Her rich blue dress was torn, and he could see the marks of rough handling on her pale skin. Though Lord Richard looked far worse, with those red streaks down the side of his face. How was he going to explain that to his lady-wife upon her return to the Keep? Lady Hedwiga was one of the few people able to make demands on Lord Richard, and he usually complied. What would be his excuse?

Claire's face was absolutely expressionless, eerily calm.

Her mouth was swollen, her hair disordered, but as far as he could tell he'd gotten there in time.

He wondered what his liege lord would do when he realized that Thomas had stopped him in his unholy pursuit. He'd only gotten Lady Claire away from him by sheer luck, and it would take all his ingenuity to keep her safe.

He wouldn't be able to do it alone. Brother Jerome could be counted on to prick Lord Richard's conscience and keep him from such an atrocity. And the most unlikely allies of all, Simon of Navarre and his mute servant, had given him warning in time. As far as he knew, Lord Simon had never done a thing that didn't benefit himself.

Certainly Lady Claire's older sister would be distraught. But Grendel had no need to impress his future wife. And he risked endangering his relationship with his lord if Thomas had told Richard who sent him.

Simon of Navarre was not a man to be trusted. But he was a man whose aid could be used.

The woman beside him stumbled as they started down the winding stone steps of the east tower, and he caught her other arm, peering at her in the dimly lit confines of the stairway. She was still calm, and when he released her she stood steadily enough, looking at him out of her clear green eyes.

"Could you leave me for a moment, Sir Thomas?" she requested in a calm, polite voice that for some reason caught at his heart.

"It's not safe. . . ."

"My brother won't come after us. He'll have to think of another excuse before he tries it again. I'm perfectly safe. Just walk ahead a bit and I'll catch up with you in a moment."

He stared at her, torn. She seemed so reasonable,

and in soldierly confusion he tried to imagine some intimate female thing she had to take care of that would require his absence. He could scarcely ask her to explain.

"I'll wait for you around the next turn," he said finally, reluctantly, and she nodded, seemingly accepting.

He knew how to listen, and he couldn't rid himself of the notion that she might race back upstairs and try to cut out her incestuous brother's heart. It was the sort of thing she'd probably dream of. But there was no sound of running footsteps as he paused one turn down on the curving staircase. Only a faint, animal-like sound, muffled, silenced.

He knew how to listen, and how to move. He remounted the steps, his thick leather boots silent on the stone, to find Lady Claire huddled in a tiny heap on the landing, her fist in her mouth to silence her sobs. She was shaking, so hard he thought she might shatter with it, and the tears were streaming from her beautiful eyes and turning her face into a mottled, miserable mess.

The muffled sound became a choked sob, and he told himself he should disappear back down the stairs, to give her privacy until she could compose herself. He hated women's tears—like most men he felt helpless in the face of them, and a hasty retreat seemed the better part of valor.

But he couldn't do it. He couldn't leave her there in a crumpled heap to cry her eyes out. He took a step closer, but she didn't notice. He stared down at her for a long moment, and then he simply reached down and pulled her up on legs that could barely hold her, wrapping her shivering body in his strong arms and holding her against him.

The sobs broke free, noisy, ugly, wrenching. She was no beauty when she cried, and he couldn't resist her. He stroked her hair, smoothing it away from her tear-streaked face as he murmured soft, soothing words of comfort. And she clung to him, Lady Claire did, crying her heart out, accepting the solid comfort he could give.

Gradually the crying lessened to a few stray sobs. She shuddered, took a deep breath, and he was about to release her and step back, telling himself he wasn't reluctant, when she caught his arms and shook him.

Her beautiful green eyes were red-rimmed and swimming with tears, but her anger and fierceness were back. "I want you to kiss me," she said.

He couldn't quite believe her words. "What?" he said stupidly.

"I want you to kiss me," she repeated. "I need you to kiss me. I don't care that you're married, I don't care that you disapprove of me and think I'm a silly, stupid female. I don't care that kissing me would be endangering your immortal soul. I want you to kiss me so that I don't have to think of *him* kissing me." Her voice was deep with loathing.

"It won't endanger my immortal soul," he said slowly, sure of no such thing. And he swiftly brushed his lips against hers in a chaste kiss.

"No," she said. "Not like that. I want you to kiss me the way *he* did." And she reached up and put her open mouth against his, twining her arms around his neck.

He hadn't kissed a woman in years. Gwyneth had never been fond of kisses, or at least of his, and he'd been chaste since she left him, never even tempted. And now the first woman who'd been able to get past his stern morals and strict guard was pressing her body against his, demanding he kiss her, and it would have taken a saint to resist. And Thomas du Rhaymer, much as he regretted it, was no saint.

He cupped the back of her head with his hand, holding her still, calming her, and then he began the process of showing her what a kiss should be like, slowly, using his mouth to gentle her, nibbling lightly at her lower lip. She shuddered in his arms, and then she stilled, tipping her head back to allow him better access, pressing her body up against him so that he could feel her breasts through the layers of clothing that bound them.

He'd forgotten how sweet a woman could taste. Or maybe no woman tasted as good as Claire of Summersedge—he was entirely ready to believe that. She kissed with complete innocence, following his lead, letting her tongue touch his, as she moved closer still.

He slid his fingers through her tangled hair, slanting his mouth across hers, deepening the kiss, feeling his soul slip away and no longer caring. He could make his confession later. He could repent later. But how could he repent of something that felt so miraculously wonderful?

He was out of breath, and so was she, and yet he didn't want to break the kiss. Neither did she. Once he pulled away, regret and recriminations would follow. As long as his mouth was caught with hers there existed nothing in the universe but the two of them.

A sound broke them apart. A distant shout from the courtyard beyond the window, and he fell back, away from her, horrified at what he'd done.

"I must beg your forgiveness, my lady," he said in a rough voice. "I should never have touched you. . . ."

"I made you do it," she said in a small voice.

He was afraid to look at her, he who was afraid of nothing, even death. "No," he said, shaking his head.

"You were distraught, you didn't know what you were asking. I took advantage of you."

"Oh, stop it," she snapped, strength returning to her voice. He forced himself to look at her, and the color was back in her cheeks. Her eyes were bright, and the life had flooded back into her body. If she'd looked brutalized and beaten before, now she looked radiant.

"It was my fault, not yours," she continued in a practical voice. "And you were noble indeed to indulge me. I'm the one who took advantage, not you."

"We shall have to disagree on that," he said stiffly, returning to his usual stern self. "I'll find someone else to guard you."

"No!" she cried, the panic back. "You can't! I don't think anyone else could keep me safe from Richard. You know it as well as I do."

The problem was, he did know it. It was a simple choice. If he kept watch over her, his immortal soul was in very grave danger, for all that he denied it to her. He wanted her, it was that shameful and that simple. He was a man accustomed to resisting his needs, but his ache for Claire of Summersedge was stronger than anything he had ever felt in his life. Stronger, perhaps, than his love of God.

But if he abandoned her, she would be lost. No one would be willing to protect her from Lord Richard, and she would be helpless. And he would be damned as well, for denying his duty to protect the weak.

She didn't look particularly weak at the moment. She looked determined, tear-stained, and well-kissed. And he wanted to kiss her again.

"It will never happen again," he said in low voice. "It will never be repeated."

She kept her eyes chastely downcast, and perhaps she was agreeing. Or perhaps not.

She wouldn't know the power of that kiss, she who'd only been kissed by a man she hated. She wouldn't know that few kisses could shake one to the soul the way that one had. The one they'd shared.

He wasn't about to inform her. Years from now she might remember the passionate kiss they had shared on the landing at Summersedge Keep, and she might wonder why no kiss had ever been quite as glorious. Or maybe she'd be lucky enough to forget.

He knew he wouldn't be so blessed. He'd remember her mouth, the feel of her small, soft breasts pressing against him, he'd remember the tears and the taste and the scent of her. He'd remember the kiss until his dying day.

And he hoped it would come soon.

"I'll take you to Brother Jerome," he said shortly.

"I'm to confess my sins immediately?" she asked with a trace of laughter.

It was his sin, for all she denied it, not hers, but he forbore to argue it with her. He would do the confessing; she would take shelter from the rapacious men that surrounded her. Himself included.

"I told your . . . Lord Richard I was taking you to see Brother Jerome," he said. "It's best if we stick to the original design."

"He is my brother, you know."

"I know. There was a stronger resemblance when he was younger, but there's no doubt the two of you are close kin."

She shivered, but there was nothing she could say. She lifted her head, and her small smile was very brave. "Then let us go find Brother Jerome," she said.

And he took her arm, cursing himself under his breath.

* * *

"She's safe."

Alys jerked her head up to stare at the wizard. She had done her best to ignore him for the last, endless stretch of time, too busy concentrating on controlling her fears. So much of her life was beyond her control. In the convent she'd been able to watch over Claire, to keep her safe from her wilder urgings, and there had been no men to threaten her.

But now, out in the real world, their greatest threat had come from one who should have been their greatest protector, and Alys was helpless to do anything about it.

She looked up at the man towering over her, anger and hope warring within her. "How do you know?"

"My servant came and informed me. Sir Thomas has taken her to Brother Jerome for safety and succor."

"I didn't hear any voices."

"Godfrey is mute."

"Then how do you know. . . ?"

"We have our own ways of communicating. Suffice it to say, your sister is safe."

"For now," she said bitterly. "What if Sir Thomas isn't around to guard her the next time my brother decides to break God's laws?"

"Richard spends most of his life breaking God's laws, not to mention his own," Simon said in a pragmatic voice. "But by tomorrow Lady Hedwiga will have returned, and if Richard is afraid of anyone, it is his sour-tongued wife. And I expect Thomas will keep a closer watch on her from now on. Before he simply thought he had to protect her from her own foolish impulses."

"How can he protect her from his liege lord?"

"The same way he does everything. Sir Thomas is a man of tiresome nobility and integrity. He will forfeit his life to protect your sister. And Richard may demand just that," he added, unmoved at the prospect.

"Would you?"

"Would I?" he echoed, perplexed.

"Would you give up your life for the sake of another? A woman?"

"You, perhaps?" he said lightly, and Alys kept the color from mounting to her cheeks by only the strongest effort. "I doubt it. I have learned to keep my own best interests in the forefront. If a woman dies, there is always another to replace her."

He sounded perfectly reasonable, and yet for some reason she didn't believe him. The serving woman's burnt arm came to mind, and his efforts to secure Claire's safety.

"You are a liar, my lord," she said abruptly.

His golden eyes narrowed. "Husbands have killed their wives for saying less," he warned her.

"But I am not yet your wife. And I suspect you are loath to kill, particularly a woman."

There was no denying the bitterness of the smile that curved his mouth. "And you, my dear Alys, are a dreamer. Don't make the mistake of thinking I value human life above my own comfort. I don't. People are a bountiful commodity. If someone dies there is always someone to replace that person, be it a woman, a servant, or a king."

There was no reason why she should think his words were anything but idle banter. And yet there seemed a thread of meaning beneath that Alys found profoundly disturbing.

"I'll take you to your sister," he said abruptly, before she could question him more closely. "Doubtless she is completely distraught and will need the comfort and care of another woman even more than Brother Jerome's tender ministrations."

For once Simon of Navarre was proven wrong. When they entered the chapel building the room was smoky with incense, and Alys could see a figure prostrate in repentance in front of the altar. But it wasn't her sister, it was a man, and as she started forward she recognized Sir Thomas du Rhaymer.

Navarre caught her arm, drawing her back before she could stumble in on the man's private communion with God, and turned her toward Brother Jerome. His kindly face was drawn and troubled.

"A bad business," he said, shaking his head. "A bad business indeed. Lord Richard must have been plagued by dishumors, to have been so disordered in his mind as to assault his sister. We must pray for him, Lady Alys."

That was the last thing Alys wanted to do, but she'd been strictly raised, and knew her duty. "Of course, Brother Jerome."

He smiled at her benevolently. "Your sister is in the herb garden. Go to her, my child, while I discuss this sad affair with Lord Simon."

Claire was seated on a stone bench amidst the lemon thyme and lavender, her face pale and set. Alys's first instinct was to rush toward her and envelop her in her motherly arms, but something about Claire's demeanor stopped her. She approached slowly, knowing her sister was aware of her, and sat beside her on the bench, saying nothing.

After long minutes Claire reached out and put her hand in Alys's, still not raising her eyes. There was blood on her fingernails, doubtless from Richard, and Alys found she could rejoice with bloodthirsty simplicity.

"I was frightened, Alys," she said eventually, in so low a voice Alys almost couldn't hear her.

"I know, love," she replied.

"I didn't know what it was to be frightened. I didn't know what it was to be so helpless. He wouldn't listen to me, Alys. He wouldn't stop."

"But Sir Thomas came in time," she reminded her.

"But what if he doesn't the next time Richard conveniently decides I'm not really his sister?" She turned to look at Alys, and her great green eyes were dark with stormy tears. "He might not be there. . . ."

"He will be there, Claire," Alys said firmly. "Lady Hedwiga will return, and Brother Jerome and Lord Simon will aid us."

"That horrible creature?" Her voice was raw with disbelief. "How could he stop Richard? Why should he bother?"

A slight trace of annoyance slid into Alys's compassion. "He's responsible for alerting Sir Thomas this afternoon," she said sharply. "He sent his servant to warn him. If it hadn't been for him, no one would have come to your rescue."

If she had hoped Claire would be chastened she was disappointed. Her sister merely looked perplexed. "Why would he care? Why would his risk his liege lord's displeasure?"

"Why did Sir Thomas?" she countered.

"Because of a vow," Claire said bitterly. "That's all he cares about, his vows and his honor. He would have rescued a sow he'd been sworn to protect, and risked his life in the process."

"I doubt he looks upon you as a sow."

"No, I'm a great deal less useful and more inconvenient," she said with a weary sigh.

"But far prettier," Alys said lightly.

It was the wrong thing to say. "Curse this prettiness," Claire said bitterly. "If it brings me the attentions of my own brother, I would rather look like. . . ."

"Like me?" Alys supplied lightly.

Claire turned to look at her for a long considering moment. "No," she said. "And if I were you, I'd give a care about Richard. You are looking far too lovely recently, and he might have a preference for swiving his blood kin."

Alys didn't know whether to laugh or to weep. "Let us go to our solar and dress in our ugliest clothes," she said. "We can smear our faces with dirt, tangle our hair, perhaps pluck out a tooth or two. If you can bear to do it, I can too."

She managed to lure a small, rusty laugh from her sister. "I dread to inform you, dear sister, but you are already wearing your ugliest clothes. Perhaps I'll borrow from your wardrobe. It might give Richard a disgust of me that nothing else has managed."

Alys put her arms around her, and Claire clung to her, shivering in the bright autumn sunlight. "If he touches you again, I will cut out his heart," Alys promised fiercely.

"And I'll hand you the dull knife to do it with," Claire said. And her rough little laugh caught with a sob.

Chapter Thirteen

There were times when discretion was called for, and times when it was best dispensed with. Simon of Navarre was a man who trusted his own judgment in such matters, and he was seldom mistaken.

Richard the Fair was seated in his solar, a cool, herb-soaked cloth laid against his scratched skin. Simon could smell the tangy scent of lemon balm, and he wondered who had treated Lord Richard. There were other remedies, more efficacious and less painful, but Richard deserved all the discomfort that could be visited upon him.

Lady Hedwiga was probably responsible for the remedy. She was sitting by the embrasure, stitching dutifully, and her disapproving face was pinched and sour, as if she had never been absent on one of her interminable religious retreats. It was a fortunate thing that she spent the majority of her narrow-minded, disapproving life either on pilgrimage to holy places throughout England or in private retreat in her solar, speaking to no one but her servants and Brother Jerome. If Richard had had to spend much more time with her he probably would have had her strangled.

As usual she refused to acknowledge Simon's presence. Hedwiga ignored anything that didn't fit within the neat little boundaries of her life, including her husband's peccadilloes, her bastard half-sisters-in-law, the needs of the people of Summersedge, or the social niceties of castle life. She kept to her solar and lived a life of austere chastity.

"I rejoice to see you looking so well," Simon said with a deliberate drawl as he approached Lord Richard. The buxom serving girl who was attending to him scuttled away at Simon's approach, crossing herself hastily.

"The bitch clawed me," Richard said gruffly.

Lady Hedwiga didn't look up, determined to ignore both of them. "Which bitch is that, my lord?" Simon inquired blandly.

"The woman who calls herself m'sister. Which I take leave to doubt is the case," he added self-righteously. "I was never too certain about it in the first place, and the more I see of her, the more I'm certain she's some other man's by-blow. Her mother knew a good thing when she saw it, saw how honored Alys was, and sought the same for her bastard."

"I gather Lady Alys was torn from her dying mother's arms and locked in a convent for the next sixteen years of her life. It hardly seems that attractive a prospect."

Richard didn't even ask him how he knew of Alys's past. "It just goes to show how little you know of life, Grendel," he said, as he dropped the herb-soaked cloth to expose his mauled cheek. Lady Claire had done a thorough job. "Claire's mother got rid of her infant, knowing she'd be well-provided for, and then went on with her life of frivolity. It isn't to be wondered that she lied."

"Where is she now? If you have real doubts you might ask her. . . ."

"She's dead these ten years past. Died of a pox, I suppose, though I don't really know. Nor care."

"Brother Jerome is concerned."

"Brother Jerome's always concerned," Richard said in a peevish voice. "He should know well enough to leave me be. He's to look out for the women—they're the sort that need his infernal interference. Not me."

"I believe that's exactly what he is doing," Simon said blandly. "He is concerned for your sisters."

"She's not. . . ."

"She is, my lord," Simon broke in with steely firmness. "One has only to look at the two of you side by side to recognize it. Only blood kin could have such similar beauty." He wasn't averse to outrageous flattery if it served his purpose, and Richard was vain enough to swallow it whole. "I know not what evil demon made you think she was anything other than your sister, but that wicked suggestion has not served you well."

Richard would need a scapegoat, as Simon well knew. He could only hope that onus wouldn't fall upon some poor innocent who would undoubtedly be put to death in order to assuage Richard's conscience, or at least his reputation, but that was the very least of his worries. Life was hard, and death was always close at hand.

"Demon," Richard muttered. "You say it truly, Grendel. It was the work of Satan and his helpers, of that there is no doubt. I will think hard on it, and see if I can remember who first suggested such a thing."

He would think hard on it, all right, and decide which of his household was the most inconvenient. If he had a score to settle, an old injury to soothe, it would be dealt with quite handily.

Simon glanced over at Hedwiga's bowed head, her pursed lips and wattled chin all that showed in her averted profile. Richard would have given anything to rid himself of his lady wife, but her family were too wealthy and powerful for him to get away with it. He was stuck with her, a barren, carping creature, and there was nothing he could do about it.

Simon didn't even pause to consider why he should exert himself to rescue the beauteous Claire. He disliked thinking that he had a sentimental streak in his body, and he considered Lady Claire to be a spoiled creature of far less interest than her older sister.

But he had a . . . passing fondness for Lady Alys, and Alys wished her sister protected. Which was reason enough, Simon supposed.

"It's a fortunate thing that Thomas du Rhaymer came in search of his charge," he continued. "He saved you from committing a very great sin."

Lady Hedwiga's head jerked slightly, but she didn't turn or otherwise betray that she was listening.

"Sod him," Richard muttered with real invective. And then he laughed. "Aye, Saint Thomas will meet his reward in heaven, no doubt. He's not interested in any from the Lady Claire."

The deed wasn't done until Richard claimed her as his sister. "You chose well," Simon persisted. "You may count on Sir Thomas to keep your sisters safe."

"Alys needs no protection from you, does she? She'd hardly the type to make a man lose his head. Unlike the younger one," he added broodingly.

"A man may lose his head over a great many things," Simon murmured. "I've yet to see a woman who was worth it."

4 BESTSELLING HISTORICAL ROMANCES BY YOUR FAVORITE AUTHORS CAN BE YOURS, FREE!

Kensington Choice, our newest book club now brings you historical romances by your favorite bestselling authors including Janelle Taylor, Shannon Drake, Rosanne Bittner, Jo Beverley, and Georgina Gentry, just to name a few! Each book is filled with passion, adventure and the excitement of bygone times!

To introduce you to this great new club which is part of Zebra Home Subscription Service, we'd like to send you your first 4 bestselling historical romances, absolutely free!   And once you get these 4 free books to savor at home, we'll rush you the next 4 brand-new books at the lowest prices available, as soon as they are published.

The way the club works is that after your initial FREE shipment, you will get our 4 newest bestselling historical romances delivered to your doorstep each month at the preferred subscriber's rate of only $4.20 per book, a savings of up to $7.16 per month (since these titles sell in bookstores for $4.99-$5.99)! All books are sent on a 10-day free examination basis and there is no minimum number of books to buy. (A postage and handling charge of $1.50 is added to each

shipment.) Plus as a regular subscriber, you'll receive our FREE monthly newsletter, *Zebra/Pinnacle Romance News*, which features author profiles, contests, subscriber benefits, book previews and more!

So start today by returning the FREE BOOK CERTIFICATE provided. We'll send you 4 FREE BOOKS with no further obligation: A FREE gift offering you hours of reading pleasure with no obligation...how can you lose?

We have 4 FREE BOOKS for you
as your introduction to
KENSINGTON CHOICE!
To get your FREE BOOKS, worth
up to $23.96, mail the card below.

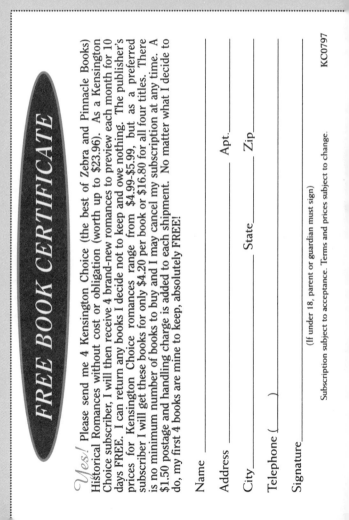

FREE BOOK CERTIFICATE

Yes! Please send me 4 Kensington Choice (the best of Zebra and Pinnacle Books) Historical Romances without cost or obligation (worth up to $23.96). As a Kensington Choice subscriber, I will then receive 4 brand-new romances to preview each month for 10 days FREE. I can return any books I decide not to keep and owe nothing. The publisher's prices for Kensington Choice romances range from $4.99-$5.99, but as a preferred subscriber I will get these books for only $4.20 per book or $16.80 for all four titles. There is no minimum number of books to buy and I may cancel my subscription at any time. A $1.50 postage and handling charge is added to each shipment. No matter what I decide to do, my first 4 books are mine to keep, absolutely FREE!

KC0797

Name _____

Address _____ Apt. _____

City _____ State _____ Zip _____

Telephone (___) _____

Signature _____

(If under 18, parent or guardian must sign)

Subscription subject to acceptance. Terms and prices subject to change.

4 FREE
Historical Romances
are waiting
for you to
claim them!

(worth up to
$23.96)

See details
inside....

KENSINGTON CHOICE
Zebra Home Subscription Service, Inc.
120 Brighton Road
P.O.Box 5214
Clifton, NJ 07015-5214

It was the right approach. Richard laughed. "You're a wise man, Grendel. I've chosen well for my chief advisor. No woman's worth the trouble they can cause. See to it that Sir Thomas keeps a closer watch on both my sisters."

Simon bowed. "As you wish, my lord."

He was halfway down the hall when Hedwiga's nasal, carping voice came to him, raised in anger. Richard's mumbled replies were less audible, and Simon found he was smiling. Lady Hedwiga would punish Richard, far more thoroughly than any of Brother Jerome's penances.

Not that he could count on Richard's forbearance to last any length of time. Claire was a choice temptation, and Richard had never been one to deny himself. He was forestalled only.

There was only one remedy, and that was to distract Richard from his lust. Richard's appetite for power was stronger than any of his other insatiable needs, and concentrating on his machinations might keep him busy. To save one young woman, he needs must sacrifice a child. He shrugged. Sacrificing that child-king had been a probability from the very beginning. He wouldn't allow himself to dwell too long on the unpleasant prospect. When a nasty job had to be done, it was best to get it over with.

His workshop, however, was not the best place for such a project. These things must be done with delicacy, and for all that he'd managed to scare away most of the inhabitants of Summersedge Keep, he preferred the confines of his tower room for matters such as these. No one dared breach the fastness of his private quarters except Richard himself, and even he was usually too wise. As for Alys, she was a complication he would deal with later.

He was proven right in his surmise within the hour. He was in his workshop, making a mental list of all he would have Godfrey fetch to his room, when a shadow appeared at the door, blocking out the late afternoon sun, and he knew, to his regret, that it wouldn't be the distracting Lady Alys.

Sir Thomas du Rhaymer stood in the doorway, tall, acutely uncomfortable, looking as if he'd just stepped into a nest of vipers, or a fresh pile of horse dung. Simon had no illusions as to what Thomas thought of him. He'd worked hard to engender fear and distrust and superstitious horror, and the noble Sir Thomas had always reacted just as Simon had planned.

"You do me great honor, Sir Thomas," Simon greeted him smoothly, allowing just a trace of irony into his voice. "I trust Lady Claire and Lady Alys are safely bestowed?"

"They're back in their solar, with Brother Jerome keeping them company," Sir Thomas said slowly. He was a handsome man, a stalwart young knight, Simon thought. Not so very different from the young man he had once been, so very long ago, it seemed.

He shook that thought from his head, never one to waste time on foolish memories. "I've spoken with Lord Richard. Lady Hedwiga should keep him well-behaved for the time being, though it seems best if you keep a close watch. Our liege lord is a man of impulse and strong actions, and he seems uncertain that Lady Claire is truly blood kin."

Their eyes met briefly, both of them knowing that was a convenient lie. Thomas took a deep breath. "Even were she not, she is a lady worthy of gentle treatment and respect."

"But who in this life gets what she or he deserves?" Simon countered, leaning against the workbench.

Thomas hadn't come to him for a discussion of philosophy, nor to report on the condition of the two sisters, but he seemed curiously loath to get to the point. Simon was willing to wait.

"Our reward comes in the next life," Thomas said stiffly.

"Will you have a true and faithful wife in the next life, Thomas?" he questioned softly. "A just lord, lands of your own, children to raise?"

"I have estates," he said.

"But there's not much use in holdings if there's no one to share them with, is there?" He wasn't quite sure why he wanted to taunt the young man. Thomas had lost almost as much as Simon had, and yet he still clung to his faith, to his honor. Such blind devotion annoyed him.

He'd pushed Thomas too far. The knight turned and started toward the door, and Simon was half-tempted to let him go. But curiosity was one sin he cultivated. "Leaving so soon, Sir Thomas?" he said. "I thought you came to ask me something."

Thomas halted, turning to look at him, his face pale and set in the murky light. "Why would you think that?"

"You would hardly bother to inform me of the ladies' well-being. You dislike and distrust me as much as everyone else in this castle, with the exception of Brother Jerome."

"Brother Jerome is too good and too forgiving," Thomas said sharply.

"To me?" Simon inquired. "Or to you?"

Ah, he was torn, and Simon found it vastly amusing. He wanted to storm from the workshop, cursing Richard's wicked wizard. But there was obviously something he needed even more.

Thomas took a deep breath, steeling himself to do

commerce with the devil. "I have need of your services."
It came out in a rough whisper, and Simon moved
closer, keeping the triumphant smile from his face.

"I am honored, good knight," he murmured. "And
what can I do for you? A healing salve for boils, a spell
for making money? A cure for impotence, a posset to
cleanse the bowels? Or are you, perhaps, interested in
a love philtre?"

"Are there such things?" he asked hoarsely.

"There are indeed. It is only a sorrow that the people
of Summersedge are too afraid of me to seek my help."

"You like to frighten them," Thomas said.

Simon's opinion of the young man rose a notch.
"Indeed, I do. Very astute of you. Only the bravest dare
seek my help or disturb my work. So tell me, sir knight,
what can I grant you? I have things to accomplish before
the evening meal, and while I find your company stimu-
lating I'm afraid I must forgo its pleasure before long.
You want a love charm, I assume? I needn't ask for
whom—it's quite clear to anyone with eyes. You want
Lady Claire to fall into your bed."

"No!" he cried in real horror.

"No? You intrigue me. Then what is it you want?" he
said with a trace of impatience.

"Something . . . something that would have the opposite effect," he said in a harsh voice.

"The lady is too eager?" It was cruel of him to taunt
the miserable young knight, but Simon couldn't resist.

"No!" Thomas said.

"Be clear, and be brief, Sir Thomas. Tell me what
you wish, and I will grant it if it's in my power."

"I want you to give me something to . . . to strengthen
my will. To make me oblivious to the charms of . . . of
a lady. I need the very opposite of a love potion. Some-

thing that would make me immune to base longings and desires.''

Simon didn't laugh, much as he wanted to. Indeed, the poor, noble young man could almost break his heart, if one still beat within his scarred body. "I can't do it,'' he said in a surprisingly gentle voice.

"Why not? Is it not within your powers?''

"I know of several ways to accomplish what you seek. None of them are pleasant, and all of them are too far reaching.''

"I'm not afraid!" Thomas said.

"You're willing to take an herbal remedy that will make you cold and hurtful and without conscience toward all you meet? It can't be refined into dislike for one person, I'm afraid. Or would you prefer a simple surgery? I've seen it done, even assisted in the process, and you'd most likely survive. I could remove your testicles and then no woman would have anything to fear from you.''

Sir Thomas turned a lovely greenish shade. "I . . . er. . . .''

"Or you could simply continue as you have been, praying for deliverance from the distraction of womankind. Their sights and their scents, their soft sighs and gentle movements. You've resisted so far, surely you can continue to be strong?''

"I hadn't counted on Lady Claire," he muttered.

"She is a temptation, isn't she?" Simon said softly. "But I have faith in you, Sir Thomas. You'll find it in your heart to resist her siren's lures.''

The look Thomas cast at Simon was full of anguish. "It isn't her fault," he said. "It's mine. And I can resist lust. I can resist lures.''

"Then what is it you cannot resist?''

"Love," he said flatly.

Simon didn't laugh. "If it's that bad, Sir Thomas, then maybe you'd be better off caponed."

Sir Thomas turned on his heel and stalked toward the door in a righteous rage. He paused at the last minute, unable to stop himself.

"Promise me one thing, wizard," he said.

"If it is within my power," Simon said lightly.

"Don't give any love philtres to Lady Claire."

"Are you afraid of her succumbing to Lord Richard?" he asked softly. "Or to you?"

Sir Thomas was at the far end of his tether, and if Simon were to push him much further he would regret it. But Simon was always one to push things. "Do anything to hurt the lady," Thomas said grimly, "and you'll be the one who's caponed."

It was irresistible. "Ah, but Sir Thomas. Who's to say I'm not already?"

The castle was alive with rumors. Lady Hedwiga had returned and refused to give audience to her husband's bastard sisters. Richard the Fair had retired to his own solar with enough wine to drown an army. And Brother Jerome was running all over the castle looking greatly troubled.

But that was nothing compared to the more delicious rumors that currently flourished. Sir Thomas was far too noble to indulge in idle gossip, but the courtyard of Summersedge Keep was a busy place so close to the evening meal, and at least three servants had been listening quite avidly. Within the hour it was public knowledge that Sir Thomas du Rhaymer had been bewitched, that Lady Claire had seduced the poor knight, and that Lord Richard's mysterious advisor was lacking a vital portion of his anatomy. The kitchen workers hadn't had as much fun since Christmastide.

It took longer for the word to reach the two sisters, since neither of them went down to eat. They stayed alone in the solar, window shutters flung wide to let in the cold, cleansing autumn air and rid the place of Richard's foul presence. It wasn't until Madlen arrived back, her plain face alight with mystery and pleasure, that they first heard.

Madlen was a woman possessed of a kindly heart and a very small amount of tact. While Lady Claire was in the garde-robe, she informed Lady Alys of the rumors concerning Sir Thomas and Lady Claire. Enough time had passed, along with Richard's careful intervention, that it was now believed that Lord Richard had come upon the two of them, rutting in Lady Claire's solar.

No one quite believed it, of course. Lord Richard would scarcely bear the scars of a woman's hand on his face, and Sir Thomas would not be alive if it were the truth. But it made a lovely story on a quiet night.

But Richard's pet monster was always more interesting, and Madlen couldn't bear to wait until she was alone with Claire. The other women would be arriving soon, and would spoil her delight in passing on such shocking information.

Alys stood at the window, staring out over the castle below, remembering Simon's words. He'd watched her the night before, seen her pacing in front of the windows. She peered into the darkness, trying to orient herself. Which tower was his? Which lighted window belonged to the Wizard of Summersedge Keep? Would he be watching again tonight? If she went to him, would he kiss her again?

A wild, foolish fancy, and she pulled away, only to see Madlen busy whispering in Claire's ear as she brushed her long, silky hair. Claire's expression was one of utter horror, until she noticed her sister's curious attention. She muttered something sharp and dismissive to the servant, taking the brush from her hand and continuing to attend to her own hair.

"You may go, Madlen," Claire said with unaccustomed dignity. "We have no further need of you tonight."

Madlen looked toward Alys uncertainly, but Alys simply nodded. Claire was more than able to unlace her sister's cumbersome gown, and Alys was suddenly, mortally tired.

"And we shall have no need of any other of the women attending us tonight," Claire added sharply.

"Yes, my lady." Madlen curtseyed, but there was no denying the real pout on her plain face.

Alys waited until the servant was gone, her footsteps dying away in the distance. She waited long minutes while Claire brushed her hair, her face averted, her back turned.

She waited until Claire looked up, a determinedly cheerful expression plastered firmly on her pretty face. "I'll brush your hair for you, Alys, if you wish. I'm sorry I sent Madlen away but she was so rough tonight she was giving me a headache."

"I don't mind," Alys said pleasantly. "As long as you tell me what it was you were whispering about. It must be something quite awful."

"Nothing."

"Lying is a sin, Claire," she said gently.

"So is being kissed by your half-brother," she shot back.

"His sin, not yours, Claire. What did Madlen tell you? I promise I won't be unreasonably angry. Has

Richard been telling lies? Has he disparaged you in
any way. . . ?''

"It's not about Richard," she said, never able to keep
a secret in all her seventeen years. "And it's not about
me."

"Then what is it?"

Claire reached up and caught her sister's hands, pulling her down to sit beside her on the bed. "Are you
certain you want to marry Simon of Navarre?"

Alys kept the calm expression on her face by force.
"I wasn't aware there was much of a choice in the
matter," she said, avoiding commitment. "It was either
you or me, and we decided that you wouldn't thrive in
such a circumstance."

Claire bit her lip. "Perhaps it's for the best," she said,
more to herself than to Alys. "This is probably very good
news indeed. At least you'll be spared. . . ."

"What news, Claire?" Alys couldn't keep the faint
tone of impatience from her voice. "Has something
happened to Lord Simon? Is he hurt?"

"Not recently," Claire said.

"Would you please explain yourself?" Alys didn't
wonder at the tension in her voice. She was growing
accustomed to experiencing heightened emotions
when it came to the man who would wed her.

"Apparently Simon of Navarre's hand is not the only
useless part of him."

Alys looked at her blankly.

"He's been castrated."

Chapter Fourteen

It didn't take long for Simon of Navarre to understand the odd looks he was being given. He sat beside Lord Richard at supper, barely touching his food, intent on his own thoughts and nothing else, when he began to realize that he was being paid even more attention than usual. The inhabitants of the Keep were always wary of him, always casting furtive glances his way as if to ward off roaming evil, but tonight there was even more revulsion than usual. It wasn't until he remembered his conversation with Sir Thomas that he guessed what must have spread around the castle like wildfire.

He'd lived a seemingly chaste life during the two years he'd been at the Keep—there would be no one to deny that he was less than a man. The thought amused him. It had only been an errant taunt, and yet he could turn it to his advantage. If Alys heard the tale, and she was bound to, she would make the mistake of thinking her chastity was safe.

Even Lord Richard was giving him odd glances, and

it took all Simon's concentration to keep his face expressionless. The meal was likely to last for several more hours—there were musicians and jugglers to keep the revelry going, but Simon had had enough. Godfrey had already brought the important herbs and philtres to his solar. He could work in peace tonight, secure that no sleepy female would intrude upon his solitude and his concentration.

He ought just to bed her and have done with it. She'd become far too much a part of his waking hours, and he should resent anything that distracted him. As he did resent her, for disturbing his concentration, for arousing him, for making him doubt his life's course.

Richard looked almost relieved to dismiss him from the table. Like most men, he probably had an obsession about his genitals, and the thought that another man might be lacking made him feel vulnerable as well.

Simon was enjoying himself completely.

There was a strong wind blowing that night, ruffling the tapestries on the walls in his tower room, and he peered out into the night, finding his gaze traveling automatically toward Alys's window. It was still bright—which was no wonder. The hour was not that advanced, and it had been a tumultuous day for the two sisters. He wondered if she'd heard the tale yet.

He turned his back on the window, on Alys, moving to the makeshift workbench and stretching out both hands, loosening the cramped right one. He couldn't afford any more distractions. The potion needed to be completed, that much was certain. Whether he ended up giving it to Richard was yet to be decided.

He pushed his hair away from his face, rolling up his long sleeves. He would concentrate on his work with single-minded diligence. And he wouldn't think of Alys at all.

Except to wonder if she'd heard and believed.

"He's been what?"

"Castrated. Unmanned. Like a gelding," Claire explained with great patience. "Surely you've heard of that?"

"Not with people," Alys said. "What makes you think that?"

"Because he told Sir Thomas."

"Sir Thomas doesn't strike me as the sort for gossip."

"The servants overheard the conversation."

"And how did it go? 'Oh, by the way, I'm missing my manly parts?' "

"You don't believe me," Claire said, shocked.

"Oh, I believe you were told that. I just don't believe it's true," Alys said calmly.

"It would be a blessing if it were. No risk of dying during childbirth, no submitting to his beastly desires . . ."

"It is our Christian duty to submit to our husbands' beastly desires," Alys pointed out. "And children are worth the risk."

"You could get the marriage annulled. Marriage is for the procreation of children, and if there's an impediment. . . ."

"Marriage is for political purposes, and for that matter, there's been no marriage," Alys said sharply.

"Pray God that there never will be."

Alys stood up abruptly, striding away from her sister as she rubbed her arms. It was a cold night, and she was restless, troubled. "I thought castration changed a male. Turned them placid, like a gelding, or plump, like a capon. Simon of Navarre is neither placid nor plump."

Claire rose too, pushing her golden hair away from her face. "Since you're so doubtful, why don't you simply ask him?" she said in a sharp voice.

Alys turned. "I think I will."

"Alys!" Claire shrieked in utter horror. "You're not going. . . ."

But Alys had already left the room.

It was late, but the Great Hall was still noisy with revelry. Alys kept to the shadows, moving silently toward the tower steps that led to the wizard's rooms. She was cold, and she wrapped her arms around her body, shivering slightly as she mounted the curved steps. The wind blew through the arrow loopholes. The noise and music from the Great Hall receded in the distance as she climbed.

She had to be mad. Was she really going to barge in on Simon of Navarre and ask him about the state of his genitals? It was one thing to tell her sister that she planned to do it, another actually to accomplish the deed.

She was tired of being a quiet little mouse. She was tired of rumors and whispers and hushed threats. She was tired of lies.

Of course, there was always the chance that it wasn't a lie. She paused on the landing, leaning against the cold stone wall as she considered that unlikely possibility.

What would she do? Would it be cause to rejoice, as Claire had said? He wouldn't be able to possess her, deflower her. For all her convent upbringing she knew perfectly well what went on between men and women. She'd even seen them coupling in corners in the Great Hall, in the stable yards. The thought of doing that with Simon of Navarre was both terrifying and fascinating.

But maybe she wouldn't be doing that with anyone at all. If Richard married her to an impotent man, she would live out her life in chastity, like the very nun she had wanted to be. Surely that was cause to rejoice?

And hadn't he told her she could bestow her favors where she wished? Perhaps it had been his way of telling her he had no use for them himself.

It was driving her mad. She wasn't afraid to know the truth, and she wasn't afraid to ask him. At least, not much.

His servant lay outside the door, and his eyes opened as Alys approached. He was a gentle looking man, though Alys suspected he could be quite fierce in defense of his lord, and he scrambled to his feet as she drew closer.

"I wished to see . . ." she began, but he'd already opened the door for her, and she let her words trail off, moving ahead before her nerves could fail her.

He stood at a makeshift table, not bothering to look up as the door closed behind her. This time she didn't make the mistake of thinking he wasn't fully aware of her.

"Your servant let me in," she said.

He didn't look up. "Godfrey has orders to admit you whenever you come looking for me. How may I help you, Lady Alys? Were you seeking another lesson in herbalism? Or are you perhaps interested in alchemy?"

"Alchemy?" she said, momentarily and gratefully distracted from her quest. "You are versed in the alchemic arts? Can you make gold?"

"I know any number of things," he said, and he looked up at her. His hair was pushed back from his face, and his golden eyes were still and watchful. "What were you wishing to learn?"

The question jumped to mind, but stopped at her

lips. She moved into the room, doing her best to appear casually interested in her surroundings. If she didn't know better she'd think he was amused. That he had guessed what information she was in search of, and he found it entertaining.

"How is your sister? Is she recovered from her ordeal?" he asked, watching her as she circled the room.

"As well as can be expected. She's very angry right now."

"A healthy sign," Simon said. "And what of you? You seem to be plagued with a disordered mind this evening, Lady Alys. What is disturbing you?"

No, she couldn't come right out and ask him. She was just as big a coward as she'd always thought.

Stalling for time, she moved to the cushioned chair and sat down, pulling her long skirts out of the way. Claire was right, she thought absently. It really was an astonishingly ugly dress.

"Why do you wish to marry me?" she asked abruptly.

He leaned against the table, surveying her. "For the usual reasons."

"And what are they? Because you care for me? Because you want children to carry on your lineage?"

He threw back his head and laughed, and the sound was hateful. "How very young you are, Lady Alys. I tend to forget that. People marry for money and power, my child. Not for love. You come with a generous dowry and a blood connection to the royal family of England. Whereas I am a traveler, with no lands or family that I care to claim. Your properties will give me stability and respectability.

"I doubt anything could give you respectability," she muttered.

He looked amused. "No? I expect you're right."

"And how will I benefit from this marriage? What will

be my great boon? How will it differ from the life of a nun?'' She couldn't have asked him any more plainly, and she waited impatiently for his answer.

She shouldn't have underestimated him. ''You'll have far less power,'' he said. ''If you'd stayed in the convent I imagine you would have ended up an abbess. Perhaps even a saint. Married to me you'll end up martyred like most women, without the public praise to go with it.''

''Will I have children?'' She waited, holding her breath.

The glint in his eye was by no means pleasant. ''I would suppose anything is possible if you arrange things wisely.'' He moved closer, leaning over her, putting his strong left hand on the arm of the chair. ''Let me ask you again, sweet Alys. Why are you here?''

She stared up at him, hands clasped tightly in her lap, lost in the wicked gleam in his golden eyes. He wouldn't let her escape, she knew it, without admitting what she sought. ''They have said . . .'' she began. ''. . . there are rumors . . . that is to say . . . I wanted to know. . . .''

He waited, saying nothing, merciless, and finally her temper was roused.

''I wanted to know if you were capable of fathering children,'' she said in a furious rush, feeling the color flood her face. She lowered her head, refusing to look him in the eye, embarrassed and angry and miserable.

He didn't move, and she knew with sudden certainty that he wouldn't answer her until she looked up. The moment stretched on, seemingly forever, and the only sounds were the wind rushing around the stone battlements overhead and the crackle of the fire.

When she could stand it no longer she lifted her head to glance at him. There was no reading his expression; he was adept at covering his reactions, and he seemed merely curious. "I have spent a great deal of time in the East," he said. "And I have learned there are many ways to conceive a child, even when it seems unlikely, and many ways to avoid conception when the time is not right. Are you so interested in being a mother?"

"Most women are."

"Are you?"

"Yes."

There was a lengthy silence, and then he spoke. "Be brave, sweet Alys. Ask your question." His voice was a taunt, and there was unexpected humor in his eyes.

She bit her lip. "Are you less than a man?"

"More than a man, most would say," he replied. "Be more specific."

He was tormenting her, enjoying her discomfiture, and she couldn't stand it any longer. "Have you been gelded?"

He caught her chin in his hand before she could look away, his long, strong fingers cradling her face. "You'll find out eventually," he said, and put his mouth against hers.

She was too stunned to react. She simply sat there, letting him kiss her, letting him cup her face with his hands, his thumbs stroking her cheeks as she closed her eyes and gave herself up to frightening, floating feeling.

He moved back, and she let out a little cry of disappointment, opening her eyes to stare up at him dazedly. "Why do you tease me?" she whispered.

"Because it's so much fun," he said, brushing his mouth against her cheekbone. She moved her face, to give him better access, and she found she was shivering. He felt it too, drawing back with a frown that should have been terrifying, but for some reason his frowns no longer frightened her.

"You're cold," he said. She didn't deny it. "It seems

I should do my best to warm you up." Before she realized what he'd intended he scooped her body up in his
arms. It wasn't that difficult a task—though she was
plump she was small, and Simon of Navarre was quite
strong. He carried her across the room to the alcove,
mounting the dais that held the big bed, and set her
down carefully, covering her with a fur throw. She was
still shivering, though she knew she shouldn't be cold,
and she stared up at him mutely, waiting, wondering.

"That should warm you up," he said, tucking the
cover around her. "I think it would be better if I didn't
lie down with you."

"Why?" She was beyond being shocked at her own
temerity.

"Because I don't think you're ready to find out the
truth," he said lightly, starting to turn away.

"I'm still cold," she said in a very small voice.

He paused, his tall body rigid in the dim light. And
then he turned, looking down at her as she lay, helpless
and waiting in his bed. She wasn't sure what she wanted
from him. She only knew she was cold.

"As you wish, my lady," he murmured. "Never let it
be said that Simon of Navarre couldn't be chivalrous."
And he lay down on the bed beside her, the fur throw
between them, and pulled her shivering body into his
arms.

It took her a while to realize that that was all he
intended to do. To hold her against the warmth of his
body, her face pressed against the rich wool of his dark
robe, to let her feel the steady beat of his heart against
hers through the heavy fur, to let their breath rise and
mingle in the night air. She could smell spices, rich and
fragrant; she could smell his skin, the scent of wine on
his breath; she could close her eyes and revel in the
sounds and scents and feel of the night around her.

And she did, relaxing her tense body, and slowly the shivers began to leave her. She lay against his arm, blissful, drowsy, as he slowly brushed her hair away from her cheek, his long, delicate fingers stroking her skin. And then she slept, his body pressed up against her, his fingers entwined in her hair.

She slept, and dreamed of wizards.

His precious little virgin bride was as innocent as he suspected, Simon thought, staring down at her sleeping face. He was hard as a rock, pressing against her leg quite insistently, and she probably thought it was his magic wand. He wanted to laugh, but for some reason his sense of humor had fled.

She looked very young lying in his arms, far too young for a jaded soul like him. It wasn't a matter of years—there might not be ten years between them. It was a matter of all he'd seen and done. He'd lost something, something there was no regaining, and if he were possessed of any decency he would let her be, rather than soil her by taking that precious innocence.

But he had no decency, only a certain devious common sense. Much as he wanted to take her, here and now, he was going to deny himself that pleasure for the time being. She slept in his arms, and he was content to have it so. And when she awoke, he would teach her how to mix poison that could kill a king.

She was half-besotted with him, and he knew it, even if she failed to recognize the symptoms. He told himself he should be displeased, but in truth, he found he enjoyed it. She was a fascinating combination of cowardice and bravery, primness and sensuality. She responded to kisses with a natural delight that suggested even greater pleasure in the offing. Perhaps he should push

Richard into formalizing the marriage. This all might disappear overnight—war and illness and death were common, and each of those disasters could change his course of action, and his life. He would hate the thought of leaving Summersedge Keep without claiming Alys of Summersedge's virginity.

And he wanted more than that. He wanted more than the awkward, messy first coupling. He wanted to take her on a journey of sensuality that left her breathless and heartstruck. He wanted to try everything with her that he had learned in his travels, and some things he'd only dreamed of during long, fever-ridden nights.

He wanted her almost to the point of madness, a dangerous, vulnerable state for a man like him.

He had lain down on the bed beside her for a reason. Not to warm her—within moments the heat from the fur throw would have penetrated her chill bones. Not to seduce her, though his body was crying out with the need for it. Not to comfort her, because he liked her wary and uncertain. It made things easier for him.

He had lain beside her on the bed to prove to himself he could resist her. He was still stronger than her irrational allure, his furious appetites, his needs, and his hungers. He could torment himself by breathing in the scent of her hair and remain unmoved.

Or at least, unmoving. He could lie beside her, hard as a rock, and not do a damned thing. Even if it killed him.

As he was beginning to suspect it might.

He'd never been overly fond of celibacy, even in his most idealistic days, but there was nothing he could do about it. He'd already fixed it so he couldn't find release with a willing kitchen maid—the rumors had spread so quickly it would become the talk of the castle if he found himself miraculously regenerated.

No, it would wait. He wasn't sure for how long. The only reason not to take her right now was to prove to himself that he didn't have to.

Once he was certain he had his hunger under control he could take the steps to assuage it. He could strip off her ugly, ugly clothes, toss them into the garderobe, and keep her naked in his bed for days and weeks and months, and to hell with Brother Jerome and Richard's murderous plans.

Or maybe he'd wait until he'd done Richard's bidding, as he knew he would, eventually. He'd come too far along this particular path to turn back now. If Richard managed to seize the throne in the aftermath of the young king's death, there'd be a place of unlimited power for the advisor who happened to be his brother-in-law. It would give him everything he wanted, and he would be content.

He rolled over on his back, and she curled closer, letting her head rest on his shoulder. There were times he doubted if he knew what contentment was, or ever had. Years and years ago, when he'd been a child living in the north, on his parents' estates, he'd been hopeful, foolishly believing in a forgiving God and an honorable mankind.

He'd learned the folly of both, and that contentment was a sham, a lie to trick weaklings.

But even now, lying amidst the furs with Alys of Summersedge sleeping by his side, so trusting, so small and sweet and delicious, he could feel the first dangerous trickle of peace. The kind of peace that would strip away everything he'd worked for. The kind of peace that would allow him to make the mistake of caring for Alys of Summersedge, only to have her die in childbirth and her child die with her.

The kind of peace that would slaughter innocent children and turn him into a weak, useless coward.

He wanted no peace like that. He would remain as he was, invulnerable, clever, wicked as he could be.

And he would survive.

Chapter Fifteen

Richard the Fair had a knack for choosing his weapons. His knights were among the bravest and the strongest in all of England, his servants were devious and skilled, and his chief advisor, Simon of Navarre, was feared throughout the land.

Simon had no doubt that whoever was foolhardy enough to sneak into his tower room in the middle of the night would be well-armed, and sent by Richard in search of the deadly herbal concoction. Richard was an impatient man, and Simon had put him off for too long.

He lay perfectly still on the wide bed, Alys asleep beside him with the thick fur throw chastely between them. It was just as well he hadn't given in to temptation and deflowered her. Lovemaking, when done properly, took too much away from the participants. He needed to be in full control of his senses to defeat the intruder.

The man would be entirely ready to kill him once he found the potion. It would simplify Richard's life enormously—there would be no witness, no accomplice to pay off, and he could hand his older sister to a wealthier prospect. Therefore, whoever was in his rooms must be possessed of intelligence and judgment as well as ruthlessness. Richard wouldn't entrust such a decision to just anyone.

It wouldn't be Thomas du Rhaymer. Thomas wasn't willing to do Richard's dirty work, and Richard knew it. He saved Sir Thomas and his formidable fighting skills for straightforward battle. He used others to commit murders.

The man moved with great stealth—that narrowed the field down to Aidan of Montrose, a squire to Sir Horace and a young man totally without conscience. Simon slid from the bed in utter silence, leaving Alys sleeping still.

Aidan didn't hear him coming. Simon moved up behind him like a wraith, absently aware that he was unarmed and Aidan had a long dagger that had cut more than its share of throats. He had little doubt he would prevail, and little concern if he didn't. And then he remembered the woman lying asleep in his bed.

Something alerted Aidan, for he spun around, dagger already drawn and flashing outward, and Simon acted instinctively. His right arm shot out, his hand closing tightly around Aidan's thin neck as he slammed him against the stone wall by the window. With his left hand he caught Aidan's knife-wielding wrist, twisting it until he heard the bones snap, until the dagger clattered onto the floor and Aidan gasped in pain and fury.

"Were you searching for something, Master Aidan?" Simon said softly, tightening the iron hold he had on Aidan's slender neck. It would be a simple enough matter to crush the life out of him, leaving him to strangle on his own blood, and it would be no more than what he deserved. Simon had seen the corpses of the men and women whose throats Aidan had cut. Doubtless on Richard's orders, but he was a young man who took pleasure in his work.

Simon was not. He had killed enough people to last him through this lifetime and the next, and he didn't want even a pimple on the ass of humanity like Aidan of Montrose on what was left of his conscience.

"I mistook your room . . ." Aidan gasped, but Simon shook his head with a chilly smile.

"Don't bother, Master Aidan. I know why you came, and I know who sent you here. You'll have to report back to your master that you failed, and that I am greatly displeased with him."

There was pure malice in Aidan's eyes. "I don't like failure," he said, "and there's nothing wrong with your right hand at all, is there? Lord Richard would be interested to know that, don't you think?" With a superhuman effort he jerked his arms up, trying to break Simon's hold, but he'd underestimated his opponent. The force of the ensuing blow sent him reeling back, toward the window that overlooked the courtyard.

Simon had released him abruptly. Aidan of Montrose made no sound at all as he went through the open window, and there was no terror in his face as he disappeared into the deep well of the night. Only acceptance.

Simon heard the distant thud as the body smashed against hard stone below. No one would be likely to find him until morning, and it would be impossible to tell where he'd fallen from. Richard would know, of course. And Richard would be warned.

He closed the wooden shutters, not bothering to look down into the darkened courtyard below. The wind was still strong, the room was chilly, and he felt that strange, empty feeling that came over him when he least expected it. If any man had deserved to die it was the

murderous Aidan of Montrose. If his fear of Simon had
made him clumsy, that was his own fault. He wouldn't
be able to carry tales of the miraculous cure of Simon's
twisted right hand; he wouldn't be around to try again.

If Simon had any sense at all, he would be rejoicing.

"Is he dead?"

Alys stood there, sleepy, her long plaits hanging down
to her waist, her plain dress rumpled and disordered.
He wondered how long she'd been watching.

"Undoubtedly."

"Shouldn't you check?"

"If he's not dead now he will be before long. If I go
down and find he still breathes, I'll have to cut his
throat, and I have no desire to get blood on my robes."
He kept his voice cool and unfeeling, hoping to shock
her.

Alys of Summersedge didn't shock easily. "You
already have blood on your robes, my lord," she murmured. "He must have hurt you."

He glanced down at himself in surprise. Even in the
dim light of the banked fire he could see the dark stain
of blood against his side. He hadn't even realized that
Aidan had managed to cut him.

"I'll have someone see you to your room ..." he
began, but she moved toward him.

"I'll take care of you," she said.

"I'm entirely capable of tending my own wounds."
He sounded disgruntled, but he didn't care. He wanted
her out of there, now. He wanted to patch his torn skin,
to bathe the blood and the sin from his hands and body.
He was hurting, and he wasn't about to share his pain
with anyone.

"Take off your robe, my lord." Her voice was completely calm as she moved toward the basin and ewer,
pouring fresh water into the bowl. There were clean

cloths near at hand. But he wanted her gone from this place.

"I told you, I can take care of it. Even with one useful hand I can see to it, and if I need assistance I'll have Godfrey attend me."

She came up to him, setting the basin on the table. "You have two useful hands, my lord. I know it as well as that poor man did. Are you going to throw me out the window as well?"

"Don't tempt me," he muttered.

"I have done my share of nursing, my lord," she said. "I'm comfortable with the human body. Take off your robe and lie on the bed and I'll see to your wound."

He gave her a cool stare. "The good sisters allowed you to tend men in the convent infirmary? And what were those men doing there?"

"There were no men, my lord. But a body is a body— I don't see why such a fuss has to be made about it."

She was trying to sound so practical. He found that even through the bleak mood that had settled over him he could be amused by her stalwart determination to tend his wounds, by her insistence that one body was much the same as any other.

If he were sensible he would ignore her, send her back to the tower room she shared with her sister, and take care of his own body. He was more than capable of stitching his torn flesh without flinching. He wondered if she was.

But he wasn't feeling sensible. He was hot, angry, reckless. A man lay dead beneath his window, his side was bleeding, and a woman he wanted stood before him.

"As you wish," he said abruptly, moving to the heavy iron candelabrum he used to light his work. He'd dowsed the flames earlier, but now he simply stuck the end of it in the glowing coals until the tapers ignited, throwing a bright, warm light throughout the room. "You'll need to see what you're doing." He took only a small step back from her and stripped the heavy, embroidered robe over his head.

Beneath it he wore breeches and a loose white linen shirt that was already stained dark red with blood. He stripped that off as well, standing before her clad only in breeches, and waited for her reaction.

At first her attention was only for the gash in his side. He could tell that it was nothing of note—a mere slice that wouldn't need stitching, for all the blood. "Sit down, for heaven's sake," she said, and when he did as she bid she knelt down in front of him without hesitation, pressing a cool wet cloth to the wound, turning it, soaking up the blood that had already begun to thicken and slow.

He looked down at her bowed head, momentarily bemused as she tended to him. It had been many years since he'd allowed anyone else to tend his body. Since he'd left the Saracens his own knowledge of healing had surpassed everyone else's, and he was safer seeing to his own care.

But her touch was gentle, soothing, and he leaned back in the chair, closing his eyes, letting her touch him, simply breathing in the pleasure of it. Her arms were resting on his thighs as she pressed the damp cloth against his side, and it was exquisite torment. He wanted to pull her closer, so that her arms encircled his hips, her head resting against him. He wanted her to use her mouth on him, as he'd learned in France, he wanted that and more. . . .

His eyes shot open, his erotic fantasies fading, when he realized she wasn't moving. She knelt between his legs, looking up at him, wonder and curiosity in her eyes as she surveyed his scarred torso. Wonder, curiosity, but no disgust.

"What happened to you?" she said in a soft voice, and she let her small, soft hand reach up to touch the ancient mark of a sword cut across his left shoulder. Her fingertips traced the thick white line, coming to a knife wound that had grown infected before it had healed. "Who did this?" Her voice was filled with pain and anger, as if she could rage at an ancient enemy long dead.

"Saracens," he said. "Knights. Gypsies. Robbers. I've traveled to many distant places in my life, and this world is a dangerous place." He kept his voice even as her fingers brushed against the place where Raddulf the Red had speared him.

"Saracens and knights?" she murmured, seemingly intent on exploring his lean, scarred body. She looked up at him. "Were you on crusade?"

Of course he should deny it. What would Simon of Navarre, the evil wizard of Richard the Fair, have been doing on a crusade to free the Holy Land?

Exactly what he had done. Slaughtering innocents in a quest based on greed. Not his own, but other men's, making his guilt all the worse. Until he made a vow that he would kill for no man's greed, no man's dreams, but his own. And he'd kept that vow in the years since.

"Don't answer," she said, when he hesitated. "You'll only lie to me. Your body speaks more truthfully than your words."

Little did she know. If she moved closer between his legs she would discover exactly how truthful his body was, though in her convent-bred innocence she might not realize just how hard he was for her. The touch of her hands against his ancient wounds, the soft mercy of her voice, the scent of her, the feel of her pressing against his legs, combined to arouse him in ways he hadn't thought possible.

Her delicate fingers led her to the worst of his wounds, where a battle axe had cloven deep into his side. A battle axe belonging to a fellow crusader, madly determined to protect his plunder from one who had no interest in it.

He'd left Simon for dead beneath the hot Constantinople sun. It was there El Adhir's men had found him, and brought him to be healed. And begun to teach him the wisdom of the East.

Her hands traced the horrific wound almost reverently. "You must have been very close to death," she said in barely a whisper.

"Yes." His own voice was strained, but she didn't seem to notice. Instead she bent her head and placed her lips against the wound that had brought him new life.

He caught her face, gently, in his hands and drew her away, unable to bear it. She simply turned her head and kissed the scarred right hand that had killed a man that night.

He would die at her hands. He knew it, with sudden lightning clarity. The man he had struggled so hard to become, the all-powerful, all-knowing Simon of Navarre, would be destroyed by a woman's heart. If he had any sense at all he'd toss her out the window after Aidan of Montrose. He could find someone else to follow in his quest for wealth and power. Another country, another lord without Richard's weaknesses for flesh and wine.

It wasn't as if he hadn't killed women before. He'd followed orders and set fire to the building in Constantinople that had housed helpless women and children. It mattered not that he hadn't known who or what was inside until he heard the helpless screams of the dying.

He could kill this tender young girl who was so very great a threat to him. It would be so simple to snap her neck.

She looked up at him then, with wise eyes. "What are you thinking, my lord?" she asked simply.

"That you'll be the death of me. And that I should kill you before you destroy me."

She didn't blink. Reinforcing what a formidable opponent she was, to accept his honesty without flinching. Another woman would have run screaming from the room. Another woman wouldn't have been there in the first place. Alys of Summersedge didn't even draw back.

"It would probably be the wisest course," she said with great calm. "But you won't do it."

"Why not?"

She smiled then. A very small, utterly bewitching smile, one that put to a lie the notion that Alys was the plain sister. He stared at her, momentarily, dangerously lost. "Because, my lord, you are not nearly as heartless as you devoutly wish to be. Despite your best efforts to prove otherwise, you are an honorable, caring man. You would no more murder a helpless woman than you would fly."

He stared down at her, and in the distance he could still hear the screams of the dying, the crackle of the fire as it consumed the old building thousand of miles, thousands of years away. "I thought your sister was the witless one," he said harshly. "If you have neither brains nor beauty, what's to recommend you?"

He watched the color drain from her face. There was more than one way to kill a woman, he thought distantly. You could lure her into thinking you saw her true worth, and then mock her.

Alys of Summersedge sat back on her heels, no longer touching him, staring up at him in shock and dismay.

He wanted to reach out and draw her back to him, to pull her arms around his bare, scarred waist and kiss the pain from her eyes. But he did nothing. Knowing that that was the cruelest thing of all.

Godfrey was too wise and knowledgeable a servant to simply barge in, or even disturb him by knocking. But Simon knew he was there, and he rose from his chair, careful not to touch the young woman who was still kneeling on the floor, her head bowed.

One look at Godfrey's face told him that Aidan of Montrose had been found. "Take Lady Alys back to her room, Godfrey," he said in an even voice. "Make certain no one sees you—there'll be enough gossip as there is."

Godfrey's mournful face was too expressive as he nodded. Alys was struggling to her feet, but Simon made no move to assist her. Afraid that if he touched her he wouldn't be able to let her go. After a moment's hesitation Godfrey went to her side, offering her his strong arm as she struggled with the trailing skirts of her ugly, hateful dress.

He should have torn it off her. He should have slaked his lust in her soft young body; he should have taken her again and again until he was blind and weary of it and her. Taken her as the gypsies did, taken her as the Arabs did. Taken her with dark teeming lust and cruel, tender love.

Instead he'd wounded her, deliberately, and the wounding hurt him most of all.

At least she would leave him alone. She would no longer look at him out of hopeful eyes; she would be wise enough to be wary of a dangerous man such as he. He didn't move as she came towards him. The wound in his side had stopped oozing blood. The rest of his scarred body was thrown into relief by the crackling fire, casting his face in shadows. He stood over her, and he knew that he terrified her, and he rejoiced in it.

Except that she stopped, despite Godfrey's best efforts to lead her away. She stopped in front of him, and he expected to see the shimmer of tears in her eyes. They were clear and determined.

"Simon of Navarre," she said in a calm, stern voice. "You are a very wicked man. But you're not getting rid of me so easily." She had the absolute temerity to reach up on her tiptoes and brush a soft kiss against his set, grim mouth. And then she was gone, leaving Godfrey standing there, astonished and amused.

"Get after her!" Simon snarled. "That should have convinced you she hasn't the sense a baby chick has. See her safely to her room or I'll. . . ." He couldn't think of a proper threat, she'd managed to addle him so completely, and Godfrey simply grinned, damn him, before he took off after her.

The room was silent at last. He could still smell the flowery scent she used. He could still feel the warmth of her lips against his. The wisest thing he could do would be to have Godfrey bring him a willing serving wench to rid him of his lust, but, he reminded himself yet again, his random lie had ruled out that particular notion. He was trapped in his celibacy.

And she still didn't know the answer. Hell's imps, of course she did, he mocked himself. She saw him far too clearly, saw past his sorry attempts at evil, past his subterfuges and fancies. But she hadn't seen Aidan of Montrose's body smashed into a lifeless pulp on the flagstones beneath. She hadn't seen the charred corpses of the women of Constantinople. She still had no idea how evil men could be.

And he was a man, there was no denying it. One who had done more than his share of terrible things. There would be no forgiveness from a merciful God for sins of such magnitude. And Simon would be damned before he would forgive God for creating a world where men could commit such atrocities.

He moved to the window and pushed the shutters open again. Torchlight illuminated the scene beneath the tower. Aidan of Montrose hadn't fallen as far as Simon had hoped, and there was little doubt from which window he'd plunged. One of the servants looked up to see him standing there, watching, and he quickly crossed himself. They all feared and hated him, exactly as he wanted them too. This would only solidify their beliefs.

He had earned their hatred. He had earned his own. Stepping back, he pulled the shutters closed once more, and Alys's pale, shocked face swam in his mind's eye. And he took his strong right hand, tightened it into a fist, and slammed it into the fresh wound in his side, bringing it away covered with blood.

She wouldn't have left him if Godfrey hadn't appeared. In the end, she had no choice, but at least she'd left him shocked and bemused. He'd struck her a painful blow, one that stunned her with its cruelty, but it wasn't a killing one.

It was odd that she, who considered herself totally without vanity, would be wounded by his words. Perhaps because he'd insisted that he did see beauty in her, and she'd wanted to believe that a man could.

Beauty faded. It was no gift to Claire—it brought her pain and unwanted attentions, even the possibility of incestuous rape. Surely they would all be better off without it.

But Simon of Navarre had looked at her with a gleam

in his golden eyes; he'd touched her with his two strong hands, stroked her skin, kissed her, and she knew he wanted her. No matter what cruel words he flung at her.

Godfrey was hurrying her along, and she struggled to keep up with his longer legs. Trust Simon to have a mute servant, one incapable of spilling his master's secrets. Alys had no need of Simon's secrets. She only wanted the truth about who and what he was.

She drew back at the foot of the tower stairs. There was no one around; they'd made their way through the night-darkened castle without witness, and she was breathless and feeling stubborn.

"Did he cut out your tongue?" she demanded abruptly.

Godfrey stopped, looking down at her out of his sad, aging eyes.

"They tell me he did. That he cut out your tongue so you couldn't spread the truth about him to anyone. But I don't believe it of him, even if he'd want me to. He didn't, did he?"

A faint smile lit Godfrey's thin mouth, and he shook his head.

"And he's not the bad man he wants me to believe he is?" she persisted.

Godfrey's response was not as encouraging this time. He shook his head again, but less emphatically. He pointed to the stairs, but she refused to move.

"He's really a good man, isn't he, Godfrey?" she asked, hearing the note of pleading in her voice and hating it. "He's capable of love and decency, isn't he?"

And slowly, slowly, Godfrey shook his head, his eyes full of sadness.

She turned and ran then, holding her skirts up. Madlen slept on the floor by the door, snoring lightly, oblivious to her mistress as Alys skirted her sleeping form and slipped into the bedroom she shared with Claire.

She half expected Claire to sit up and demand to know where she'd been. But Claire had suffered too cruelly that day, and she lay in exhausted sleep, sprawled in the middle of the bed.

Alys didn't have the heart to move her. She'd slept well in Simon's bed, in Simon's arms. And she wasn't about to believe his words, or his servant's sorrowful assurances, or gossip, or common sense. She wasn't sure when it had happened, but a change had come over her, a shift in her life. She belonged to Simon of Navarre, and he would belong to her. And nothing would get in her way.

She sat down on a pile of pillows, wrapped her arms around her knees, and began to cry in utter silence.

Chapter Sixteen

"I am not pleased with you, Grendel," Richard growled. His pale blue eyes were red-rimmed as he sat at the small table in his solar, picking apart a piece of honey bread. There were no servants about, which could only be on purpose. Richard must have been expecting him.

"Neither am I pleased with you, sire," Simon said in his cool, emotionless voice. "I thought you trusted me to see to your best interests."

"It was taking too damned long!" Richard said in something very close to a whine. "And it cost me one of my best men. Aidan of Montrose was a very talented young man, most happily unburdened by a conscience. I had great hopes for him."

"It is indeed a tragedy to see a promising life snuffed out too early," Simon said with only a trace of irony. "I gather he fell from the battlements."

"You can gather all you like. You and I both know you tossed him out your window when you caught him in your rooms," Richard said with a disapproving sniff. "I didn't expect you to behave in such a manner. You didn't have to be quite so brutal, you know."

"I beg your pardon, my lord. I suppose I should have allowed the young creature to cut out my liver."

Richard's eyes lit up. "Did he try to stab you? I knew the boy had the makings of greatness in him. There are very few people in Summersedge Keep who would go anywhere near you."

"Aidan of Montrose was brave to the point of foolhardiness," Simon said.

"And now I've got to make excuses to his mother, who's some kind of kin to me." Richard's whine was back. "And what's this I hear about you being unmanned? You never said anything about that."

"You never inquired."

"My sister will want children."

"And you are very concerned with your sisters' desires, are you not?" Simon said smoothly.

Richard laughed. "Still, I don't trust a man with nothing between his legs. It's not natural."

"Neither is attempting to fornicate with your sister."

Richard slammed his fist down on the table, and the dishes jumped. "She led me on," he said. "Besides, I'm not convinced she's my sister after all."

"If you persist you'll lose another of your best men. Thomas du Rhaymer might be burdened with a conscience, but he has few peers when it comes to fighting. I doubt you'd want to dispense with him, and the only way you'll get your hands on Lady Claire is to kill him."

Richard glared at him. "You're annoying, Grendel. Did you know that?"

"It's a rare talent," Simon purred.

Richard leaned back in his chair, wiping the crumbs from his tunic. "I can't afford to lose any more of my most trusted men," he said slowly. "Neither my fighting men nor my advisors. But I'm not a man possessed of patience. When I decide on a course of action I see to it."

"Some things are out of your control, my lord."

Richard stared at him blankly. "No."

Simon shrugged. "I wish my concentration were as perfect as yours, my lord. I find myself distracted far too often. By strangers sneaking into my rooms, looking to disturb my work. By weeping women needing protection."

"I doubt Lady Claire came to you for protection, Grendel. You have a less than comforting demeanor."

"Her sister trusts me."

"Does she indeed?" Richard sat upright. "Do not tell me you've won the creature's heart? She'll be much distressed when she finds you don't come fully equipped."

"Perhaps she'll be relieved," Simon murmured.

Richard looked at him for a long, thoughtful moment. "Send Brother Jerome to me," he said abruptly.

"Do you plan to make your confession?"

"Ha! I have nothing to confess. Send Brother Jerome, and then send someone in search of those two supposed sisters of mine. A thought has come to me."

Simon looked at him warily. He'd learned never to underestimate his liege lord, and Richard's ideas usually boded ill for everyone but Richard himself. "As you wish," he murmured. "I'll spend the day working on the sleeping remedy you requested."

"Certainly," Richard said, waving a blunt hand. "I'll summon you when I require your presence."

Simon hid his reaction with the ease of long practice. "I would have thought you'd prefer me to work on your commission."

"There's time for everything," Richard said, ignoring the fact that he had just sent a man to steal the item in question from his trusted advisor. "I think I'll go visit Hedwiga."

"I'm certain your wife will be honored," Simon replied politely.

"I'm certain she won't, but she knows she's to do my bidding, whether she likes it or not." Richard rose, rubbing his thick hands together with anticipation.

An anticipation that filled Simon with grave misgivings.

"I won't go," Claire said flatly. "I don't ever want to see his face again."

"I don't think we have much choice in the matter, my love." Alys struggled for the calm she seemed to have lost over the last few days. "If Brother Jerome is to be there as well we truly have nothing to fear. It is always possible Lady Hedwiga has finally chosen to grace us with her presence. And I expect Sir Thomas to be hovering nearby as well. He takes his responsibility to you very seriously."

There was no reading Claire's odd expression. "He takes life too seriously," she muttered.

"You don't think it's a serious matter?"

Claire made a face. "To be sure, it's a serious, sad, painful business where everyone dies at the end, most of them sooner than they should. But that doesn't mean we have to spend our days in mourning for what might never happen. It doesn't mean we cannot let a smile cross our lips. It doesn't mean that joy can't be found, stolen, snatched away from a jealous fate."

"What has Sir Thomas got to do with joy?" Alys asked.

"Absolutely nothing," Claire said gloomily. "You won't let Richard touch me?"

"Not on my life. Nor on Sir Thomas's life, for all his gloom. I expect Richard simply wants to apologize for his behavior." Alys didn't truly believe any such thing—Richard was not a man who recognized his own faults—but she wasn't about to share her doubts with Claire. At least they would have protection. Madlen, in bringing the summons, had come directly from Brother Jerome, who'd been ordered to appear as well.

There was no word as to whether Simon of Navarre would be present at the audience, and Alys wasn't sure whether she was ready to see him again. He'd managed to confuse her totally, she who prided herself on her sharp brain and steady nature. He was a sham, a trickster, a man who killed quite easily and without compunction. Alys had seen men die before, but never so swiftly. At one moment the man stood there, Simon's supposedly crippled hand wrapped tightly around his throat, and in the next he was gone, smashed onto the paving stones below.

"You have a far more hopeful outlook than I do," Claire said with a frown. A moment later Madlen reappeared, carrying a swathe of deep rose-colored material trimmed in yellow gold. "Lord Richard said you were to wear this, my lady," she announced, draping the gown across the bed.

It was a glorious thing, Alys thought with a faint longing. The prettiest shade of rose she'd ever seen. Long, bell-like sleeves lined in rich golden yellow. A beautiful dress for a beautiful woman.

"I'm not wearing it!" Claire announced sharply. "I won't let him dress me up for his pleasure. . . ."

"It's not for you, my lady," Madlen announced flatly. "It's for Lady Alys."

Claire's astonished expression would have been comical if Alys hadn't been shocked as well. "You must be mistaken, Madlen," she said after a moment. "This dress is clearly suited to Lady Claire, not to me. I couldn't. . . ."

"Lord Richard said you were to wear it, and I don't fancy dealing with his anger if he's disobeyed, do you?" Madlen said with great good sense. "It'll look a rare treat on you."

Claire struggled for words. "It's too fine a dress," she said flatly, touching it with a faintly covetous stroke. "What need would my sister have for such a thing?"

"I have no idea, my lady," Madlen replied. "Perhaps he wants to please his sister."

"I don't think our happiness is of any particular interest to my brother," Alys said, edging nearer the dress. What would Simon of Navarre think when he saw her in it? Would he still call her plain? Or would he stare at her with that deep, unsettling look in his eyes? Would he kiss her again? And again?

"I'm to take you to Lady Hedwiga as soon as you're ready," Madlen continued. "And I don't think either the lord or his lady are in the mood to be kept waiting."

Alys did her best to hide her dismay. "You see, Claire," she said. "I was right. Lady Hedwiga has finally chosen to welcome us to Summersedge Keep. There is nothing to fear, is there, Madlen?" She turned to the serving woman. "Lady Hedwiga is a good woman who spends her life on prayer. She could hardly wish us ill."

Madlen shrugged her thick shoulders. "As to that, I'm sure she's a holy woman, though I can't say why she wants to see the two of you. She's never spent much time on anything but her religion."

Claire made a face. "Maybe she found out what Richard tried to do and she wants him to apologize."

"I doubt it. More likely she wants to berate you for leading him on," Alys said wryly as she presented her back to her sister for unlacing.

"Wretch," Claire muttered under her breath. "You're probably right. But then, why would you be summoned as well? In such an unsuitable dress?"

Alys slipped her ugly gown off, casting a wistful glance at the glorious swathe of rose and gold. "It will probably look hideous on me," she said warily.

"If it's as bad as you think you can give it to me," Claire said with her usual artless generosity, helping her sister into the heavy folds.

Alys went to stand in front of the wavery reflection of the mirror. Her hair was a tangle down her back, in sore need of replaiting, and the unlaced gown drooped loosely around her. But Alys didn't need Claire's in-drawn breath or Madlen's sigh to know the truth.

"You're not getting this gown, Claire," she said flatly. "Lace me up."

Claire did so with swift competence, moving out of the way as Madlen approached with a brush. "No plaits today, my lady," she said in a voice that brooked no disagreement. "You have very pretty hair when you don't hide it away. No wimple or veil either—just a ribband around your hair."

"I prefer to have my hair covered." Alys's voice was uncertain.

"Madlen's right," Claire said. "If you're going to be a beauty you might as well go all the way. She's right— your hair is lovely and I never realized it. It has glorious streaks of gold and brown and honey amber. Why in the world do you always hide it away?"

Alys didn't bother to explain. She knew perfectly well that no matter how beautiful her dress, how pretty she was, she would always pale next to her glorious sister.

And since she spent her life in her sister's company, false vanity seemed an absolute waste of time and energy.

But at that moment, looking at her reflection in the glass, she was ready to kill before she gave up that dress. She wanted Simon of Navarre to see her in it. She wanted him to weep at what he'd thrown away.

Except that he hadn't thrown her away. He'd insulted her, dismissed her, but as long as he wanted her, fate and her brother decreed that he would have her.

And as long as he wanted her, she was willing to pay the price. As long as she could divine a way to make him suffer regret.

She didn't know if he was a man who felt regret. He didn't seem as if he would, but she had a strong suspicion that he was very different from the mysterious creature he appeared to be. She already knew his lame hand was only a sham. His supposed unconcern for the people of Summersedge Keep was belied by his dung-free remedies.

She suspected he had a strong reason for speaking those cruel words last night, but she couldn't even begin to imagine what that reason could be. She would be a fool and a half to suspect him of any noble motives, and she had never been a fool. He had sought to demoralize her and drive her away, at least temporarily. She could only wonder why.

Lady Hedwiga was not, at first glance, that intimidating a woman. She was ordinary looking, a good ten years older than her husband, with a pinched mouth, dark, disapproving eyes, and thin, claw-like fingers that fondled a large crucifix attached to her girdle. Alys had spent her life among the professionally religious, from merry Sister Agnes to the dour Reverend Mother Dominica, but never had she seen someone as coldly removed from the warmth of everyday life as her half-brother's wife.

"My lady," Alys greeted her with determined friendliness as she advanced into the room. Claire held back, and Alys gave her a surreptitious shove in the small of her back, propelling her forward. "How joyous it is to find a new sister. . . ."

She'd been planning to plant a respectful kiss on the woman's pale, papery cheek, but Hedwiga held up a restraining hand.

"We are all sisters in Christ," she said, with an expression that suggested she found that fact very ill-managed of Him.

Alys halted, and Claire stumbled into her. "Indeed," Alys said brightly, still making an effort. "Your generosity in taking us into your home has touched us both."

"It is duty, no more, no less," Hedwiga intoned. "I have no time to waste on social pleasantries. You are here at my husband's request." She made the word "husband" sound like a curse, which, in Richard de Lancie's case, it was.

"How may we serve you?" Alys asked politely.

Lady Hedwiga sat in her throne-like chair, staring with raw dislike at the two young women. "I'm to instruct you in your marital duties," she announced abruptly. "My husband has deemed it time for you to know what's expected of you, and he has requested that I inform you. Sit down."

Ordered was more like, though Alys would have thought that Hedwiga didn't obey orders from anyone, even her bullying husband. She cast a furtive glance at her sister, but Claire was looking oddly pale as she sank gracefully down on the narrow bench at Lady Hedwiga's feet.

Alys sat as well, careful not to crumple the glorious

folds of rich rose material, clasping her small, capable hands in her lap as she tried to still her apprehension. Why would Richard decree that she learn of her marital duties? The obvious answer was too disturbing to contemplate.

"You must submit," Lady Hedwiga began in her nasal voice that was not much better than a whine. "Marital relations are women's punishment for Eve's sin. It is a trial and a torture, an abomination that women must endure."

This was hardly a surprise to Alys, as she'd heard the same from the Reverend Mother and the other nuns. However, those august ladies had been speaking from a total lack of experience, something Lady Hedwiga didn't share.

"Torture?" Claire echoed in a nervous voice.

"Hideous torture," Lady Hedwiga said, with a grim nod of her head. "It is brutal, painful, wet, and disgusting. . . ."

"Wet?" Alys echoed in surprise.

"You will bleed and wish you were dead," Hedwiga continued, ignoring the interruption. "And there is no escape from the horrors until you either quicken with child or die. The latter would be preferable, since once the child is born your husband will want to commence his foul rutting once more."

Alys said nothing, glancing once more at her sister. Claire's skin was pale, her eyes wide, her expression a mixture of shock and fear, and Alys's immediate temptation was to panic as well. It took a supreme effort to plaster a faint, calm smile on her face.

"If it's so horrible, Lady Hedwiga, then why do people persist in doing it?" she asked with perfect sense.

Lady Hedwiga glared at her. "If it were up to womankind it would be stopped."

"And then there'd be no mankind," Alys said in her most polite voice.

It wasn't meek enough. "Pert," Hedwiga declared with a mighty glare. "It must be endured by certain women to ensure the continuation of the race. But there is no other reason. As for men, they are beasts, foul and unreasonable."

"But Lady Hedwiga," Alys said, "exactly what does this foul and unreasonable act entail?"

Claire made a choking sound beside her, and Lady Hedwiga turned red with fury and embarrassment. Alys had hoped the question would serve to silence her, but she had underestimated her adversary, and there was no question that Hedwiga was exactly that.

"It requires you to lie still, close your eyes, and submit," she said through gritted teeth. "That is all you need to know. Allow your husband no liberties."

"I suspect, my lady, that what one may or may not *allow* Simon of Navarre has little to do with what will happen." She was trying to sound calm and philosophical, but there was no denying the wistful note in her voice.

"He's the spawn of Satan," Lady Hedwiga hissed. "He will seek to destroy your soul for his Evil Master."

"Surely Richard isn't evil," Alys said, not sure of any such thing. "A bit hot-headed, I grant you, but. . . ."

"I'm talking about the devil, wench!" Hedwiga jabbed a pointy finger at Alys's chest. "Simon of Navarre is a witch, a wizard who serves one master on earth and one master in hell. Take no pleasure from his foulness. Hold your mind aloof as he practices his wickedness upon your body."

"How could I take pleasure if it's disgusting, torturous, and evil?" Alys asked.

"Not to mention wet," Claire added helpfully.

"It's the devil's work. Part of his cunning plan to steal your soul. There are rumors that Simon of Navarre has been gelded. Do not count on God's being so merciful."

"God is always merciful." Brother Jerome stood in the doorway, and Alys felt her heart and stomach plummet. He was dressed in holy vestments, prepared for a holy rite, and since it didn't appear as if anyone was about to die or be baptized, there was only one disturbing alternative. "Trust in Him, Lady Alys, and be obedient."

Richard shouldered his way past the slender priest, his thinning blonde hair damped and draped over his skull, his impressive paunch decorated in a tunic of scarlet that clashed with the deep rose of Alys's dress. He paid it no mind, hauling Alys off of her bench and imprisoning her within the reach of one meaty arm. "You're prettier than I would have thought, lass," he said, leering down at her. "Perhaps I've been too hasty in promising you to Simon of Navarre." He caught her chin in his rough hand, pinching her painfully. "After all, he's pledged to me, and it would be a foolish man who dared betray me."

She knew he was there, she could feel his presence, even though Richard's bulk obscured almost everything. And she knew now why she'd been given a glorious rose-colored dress and ordered to appear at her brother's side.

She turned her head, and Simon stood there, dressed in black robes, a silver dragon adorning the front of his long tunic. If he were astounded, humbled by the sudden improvement in her appearance, his face didn't give it away. As usual, his expression was impossible to read, and his golden eyes moved over her with what seemed like distant curiosity.

"Perhaps Lady Alys should have a say in the matter,

my lord," he murmured. "Marriage to me, now, or later to a different man of your choosing."

Richard laughed. "What say you, lass? Marriage to my Grendel, with a withered claw and probably a withered rod as well, or would you rather wait and see who else turns up?"

She couldn't believe he was really offering her the choice. She looked around her, at the faces of those in Lady Hedwiga's chilly solar. She glanced at Claire's stricken face and opened her mouth to speak, but Simon was already ahead of her.

"You have my bond whether I marry your sister or no," he said to Richard. "And I have no interest in the younger one. I'll take Lady Alys if she wishes, or continue as I am."

"You hear that, sister?" Richard said. "Not many women are given a choice in matters like this. Shall you marry my pet monster or live in celibacy for a bit longer?"

They waited for her answer. She didn't for one moment believe that she really had a choice—Richard would do with her as he wished, dispose of her as it pleased him. Whether she refused or accepted, it had all been preordained.

Simon stood a little apart from the others, tall, aloof, even forbidding, his right hand hidden beneath the folds of his black robe, his face expressionless, his mouth unsmiling. His mouth, that had kissed her and taunted her. His mouth.

"I will marry Simon of Navarre," she said in a clear calm voice belied by the tremor in her hands.

Simon looked neither gratified nor disappointed. He merely nodded, his golden eyes cool and distant. "Let it be done, then," he said. And coming up to her, he took her icy cold hand in his left one, taking her away from Richard's possessive grasp.

What am I doing? she thought in sudden panic. Why in heaven's name did I agree? Torture, Hedwiga said. Blood, pain and despair at the hands of a monster. . . .

He pressed her hand, tearing her attention away from her panicked thoughts, and she looked up at him in swift surprise. His hand was warm, strong, holding hers, and there was an odd expression in his face. One might almost have thought it was reassurance, except that Simon of Navarre wouldn't care if she were frightened.

"Brother Jerome," Richard said, his voice rich with satisfaction, "marry them."

And the words were like a death knell.

Chapter Seventeen

She sat by his side, small and still and frozen. His little bride, a virgin sacrifice to the monster Grendel, eating little of her wedding banquet, drinking less as she awaited her doom. It should have amused him, but Simon wasn't in the mood to be amused.

The rest of the castle seemed inclined to celebrate the wedding despite the fate of the innocent bride. Richard was roaring drunk, grasping at every female within reach; both his sisters were kept well out of his way. The only person who looked more miserable than the bride was her younger sister, who watched the proceedings with real fear in her admittedly beautiful green eyes. Sir Thomas stood behind her, a glowering protector, and not even Richard dared approach. At least Lady Alys could be assured her sister was safe as she faced her own ruination. A virgin sacrifice indeed.

He hadn't been surprised when the summons had come. He knew Richard too well, had played chess with him too many times not to know when Richard would decide to use his bishop. He was fully prepared to be wed to the quiet little woman by his side, and she had accepted him, when he had done his best to make it clear there was no need.

Of course, Lady Alys was wise enough to know that all the promises in the world were no protection against fate. She'd barely met his eyes, though she'd let her hand rest in his without pulling away. He wondered how badly he'd wounded her the previous night. Quite badly indeed probably. He wondered if she had some stray notion of punishing him.

It would take more than a woman's tears and displeasure to punish Simon of Navarre. And the soft, sweet little wren that he'd married was singularly unversed in feminine wiles. She would be no match for him if it came to a battle.

They shared a trencher, but she made no move to offer him some of the choicest bits of food, nor did she eat much herself. And he watched her, like a peregrine falcon eyeing a tender white rabbit, wondering when he would choose to pounce.

He rose, abruptly, and the Great Hall fell into silence. Without a word he held out his left hand for his lady, looking down at her, daring her to ignore him, to show her panic, to try to escape.

She did none of those things. Her eyes met his, and for a moment he was shocked. There was fear in her eyes, yet there was a surprising tenderness. She placed her hand on his arm and rose, managing a tremulous smile.

"If you need some help ploughing the field I'm sure any number of my knights can oblige you!" Richard called out drunkenly. "Sir Emrick, what say you?"

Richard had overestimated the courage of his knights.

They might face a horde of Saracens without flinching, but none was willing to risk Simon of Navarre's anger.

Simon smiled faintly. He could feel the tremor in Alys's hand, and he wanted to lift his scarred right hand and cover hers, comforting her. He did no such thing. Comfort was an illusion, only delaying the painful truth. The truth that life was a bad business at best, full of pain and treachery, and the only reward was money and power.

Money and power he would claim with his bride. Richard's settlement had been generous, but Simon had no illusions that he was expected to enjoy it for long. Richard would take what he needed from Simon and then dispense with him. If he could find another tool like Aidan of Montrose, one who was a little more deft.

And if Simon were fool enough to relax his vigilance once he gave Richard what he wanted.

He took her arm and led her away from the hall. No chattering horde of women tried to accompany them. She was left to face the marriage bed alone, unprepared. Out of the corner of his eye he'd seen his sister-in-law struggle to her feet, but Sir Thomas had quickly subdued her. A wise move on his part. Alys had made her decision, but her sister's distress would distract her.

The halls were still and deserted as they climbed the stairs with stately grace, the torchlight flickering wickedly across her pale face. She was lovely, but then, he'd always known that, despite her ugly clothes and her tightly plaited hair, her downcast eyes and her demure behavior. She was lovely, and he wanted her with a need so fierce it frightened him. So fierce that he had no choice but to deny it.

The women hadn't even come to his room to prepare the bridal bower, but Godfrey had done his best. There were dried rose petals in the rushes that covered the floor, perfuming the air with sweetness, and soft linen covers on the wide bed where he'd already held her. Where he would take her innocence, and leave her with . . . what?

He could, in fact, be kind. He was, occasionally, even if he regretted the necessity. He much preferred when people had no notion of his random charitable acts.

But Alys of Summersedge had done no harm. When he finished with her, and with Richard the Fair, he would see her safely to a convent, where she could live out her life in peace and contentment, happy in her books and the company of women.

Godfrey closed the heavy wooden door behind them as he left, and Simon looked down on his young wife. She was very small, very vulnerable.

"Do you know what happens in the marriage bed?" he asked abruptly, releasing her arm.

She stepped away from him, moving toward the bed as if in a dream. "Yes," she said.

"And where does this expert knowledge come from? The nuns?"

She stiffened her back beneath the flowing rose colored gown. "They are learned women."

"Not in the ways of sex."

She blushed. He hadn't seen her blush before—it made her pale skin glow. He wondered absently if she blushed all over her small, lush body. He wondered how long he would keep himself from finding out.

"I've been in plenty of farmyards," she said with comical dignity. "I understand the mechanics. And Lady Hedwiga instructed me in proper comportment."

He laughed. It wasn't a pleasant sound in the shadowy room, but he wasn't feeling particularly pleasant. He was tense, frustrated, and angry. Angry at the woman who was willing to sacrifice herself to Grendel. Angry at himself for becoming a monster who frightened children and old men and young women. Sweet, soft young women.

"And what is proper comportment in the marriage bed, Alys?" he murmured.

"To submit."

"How arousing." His tone was sarcastic, but she was obviously too nervous to notice.

"I shouldn't cry or scream, no matter how painful, how degrading and disgusting," she continued in a voice marred only by a slight quaver. "If I close my eyes and lie very still it will soon be over. Madlen assured me that no one ever dies from it."

He could see them, the women of Constantinople, their bodies strewn in the streets. "Madlen is wrong," he said in a bleak voice.

It was hardly what she wanted to hear. "I could die?"

He roused himself. "No," he said. "Because I am not going to take you."

She blinked, staring at him, her mouth slightly opened in surprise. He wanted to kiss that mouth. He wanted to get as far away as possible from her. He wasn't going to do either.

"You won't?" she said breathlessly. "Or you can't?"

He knew that his smile was far from warming. "It doesn't matter. All that matters is that you'll lie in that bed alone tonight. I don't sleep much in the best of times, and there's work I have to finish. More important work than deflowering a nervous bride. Get in bed and dream of monsters, wife. And dream of noble knights to save you from devouring demons."

"I don't want one," she said in a very small voice.

"Don't want what?"

"A noble knight to rescue me."

She was braver than he'd imagined, standing there small and proud in his tower room. Brave enough to take him, perhaps, and he took a reluctant step toward her, unable to help himself.

The sizzle of lightning skittered past the wide window through which Aidan of Montrose had made his descent, followed by a low rumble of thunder. It was far away, but Alys jumped as if she'd confronted a dragon, and he halted, both relieved and disappointed.

"And I don't want a woman who'll submit."

His innocent bride looked shocked. "You want someone to fight you? You prefer rape?"

At that he did cross the space between them, cupping her face in his hands to tilt it upward. Her eyes were solemn, questioning, but she made no effort to break away. "For a wise woman you can be very stupid, Alys," he said gently. "There is such a thing as pleasure." He gently stroked her cheeks with his thumbs.

"Pleasure?" she echoed blankly, as if the word were in Arabic, even as her body arched towards his, unconsciously seeking him.

"Pleasure," he said, his voice low and beguiling. "Shimmering, endless longing and delight, touch and taste and delicate wonder." He moved his head closer, let his mouth hover over hers. "Heat and dampness and yearning," he whispered. "An empty aching that finally explodes into a small death that is like no other."

She stared up at him in a trance, caught by the magic of his words, the promise in his mouth. She wet her lips with a nervous tongue, still caught in his gaze. "It sounds terrifying," she whispered finally.

"My lady," he whispered, "it is."

And he pulled away from her, turning his back on her without another glance, heading toward his worktable.

"Go to bed, sweet Alys. Dream of safety. I have work to do."

He half expected her to protest. To follow him, put her hand on his shoulder, and then he would turn and pull her into his arms, lift her up onto the high table and take her there and then, amid the tumbled herbs and elements, teach her the true terror and wonder that awaited her.

But the thunder rumbled again, only a low warning, and with a muffled cry she scampered toward the bed.

There was no one to get her out of her dress, and he wasn't about to offer. He couldn't afford the distraction. He was too close to getting the proportions just right in the lethal sleeping draught. A few more hours of work and it would be done. And then he could decide what to do with his bride.

He had no idea what he would do with the poison. Whether he would, in truth, hand it over to Richard the Fair and let him kill an innocent child.

Not that any child of Plantagenet blood could ever be innocent. Particularly a son of John Lackland, the worst king England had yet known. And the chance of an early death for the monarch was high—if Richard didn't see to it then someone else would likely do the job.

Still, Simon hadn't decided. And he wouldn't decide until the sleeping draught was made, tested, and hidden away from Richard's prying servants.

His virgin bride fell asleep almost immediately, which shouldn't have come as a surprise to him. There was something infinitely restful about the ease with which she slept, particularly in his presence. He was accustomed to unnerving people, and he had little doubt that Alys found him unsettling. Just not enough to keep her awake.

He stripped off his enveloping robe, moving about the room in his tunic and hose, his sleeves rolled up to bare the scarred hand and arm. She slept and he would resist her. He worked and she would dream of him.

And it would be a long, stormy night indeed.

Thomas had no choice but to drag her from the room. Claire had watched her sister depart, horrified tears filling her beautiful eyes, and she'd risen, obviously planning to go after her, to pull her sister away from Simon of Navarre.

It would have been foolish and useless, but Thomas felt a grudging softness in his heart for her. He'd shielded her smaller frame with his large one, drawing her into the shadows by force as Richard was distracted by a troupe of acrobats.

She fought him, but he simply wrapped his strong arms around her slender form and held her tight against his body, one hand clamped over her mouth as he half carried, half dragged her through the arched portal into the darkened hall beyond. She kicked him, her soft leather shoes negligible against his tall boots, and he half expected her to aim for his balls. She didn't though, and he considered she might not even know where a man was most vulnerable.

Ah, but she did know. She could knee him between the legs and he would writhe with pain, but it was nothing compared to what she could do to his carefully protected honor.

He waited until they were out in the courtyard before he released her mouth, and he was rewarded with a shrill, furious scream, one that was echoed in the stables. Thomas had no doubt which horse was answering his mistress. "Bastard," she said furiously. "Cowardly dog! I won't let her be sacrificed! I'll stop it, I swear. . . ."

She tried to turn and run, but he caught her around the waist and dragged her back against him. She was panting with fury and exertion, her silken hair was tickling his nose, and he could smell the heady scent of musk perfume that she wore. It aroused him, as always, a fact he deplored. Her rounded buttocks were pressed against his hips, and he knew he was growing hard, and he knew there wasn't a thing he could do about it. Prayers and repentance had no effect except to make him feel more guilty. No matter what his soul and honor said, his body knew the truth.

"There's nothing you can do," he said grimly, letting her wear herself out. "He's her husband, she spoke the wedding vows. No one forced her—it was her choice."

"She did it for me!" Claire wailed. "She went with that . . . that monster for my sake, and I can't let her do it! If you won't help me, at least let me go and save her myself. If I don't hurry it will be too late!"

"She's only been gone a few minutes," Thomas said wryly. "It'll take him that long to get her up to his solar."

"What if he stops to kiss her on the stairs?"

There was sudden silence between them. He had done just that, kissed her on the stairs, kissed her with his heart and soul and body, and if he were any other man it wouldn't have stopped there.

"No one has the right to interfere between a husband and wife," he said, fighting back the memory of Gwyneth and her lascivious baron. "She's made her choice."

"For me!" Claire wailed.

He spun her around, his temper shredding. "The world does not revolve around you, Lady Claire! If you weren't so busy thinking of your own concerns you would have realized that Lady Alys was more than willing to marry Simon of Navarre, and her reasons had less to do with you and more to do with her own wants."

"How could she have wanted to marry him?" Claire demanded, aghast.

He shook her, hard enough to startle her out of her self-absorption. "Not every female on this earth is shallow and vain and stupid," he snapped.

She was suddenly very calm. Dangerously so, like the center of a huge storm before it began to blow once more. "Well," she said, "that's a small improvement. At least you are no longer convinced that all women are worthless, even if I still fit that category."

"You're not worthless."

"But I'm shallow and vain and stupid, aren't I?" she snapped back.

"Shallow and vain," he said, no longer caring about the risk. "And stupid if you think you can stop whatever's going to happen in that tower room. Don't let your sister's act be a waste. She went with him willingly, and it wasn't only for your sake. But if you blunder up there and set everything at odds, it will all be in vain, and neither of you will end up happier. Let it be, Claire."

It was the first time he'd used her name, but she didn't seem to notice. She blinked back the ready tears, and he knew he could have been lost in her eyes. He couldn't blame witchcraft, or evil spells. He could only blame his errant heart.

She looked up at him with a face full of hope and fear, longing and despair. She looked up at him, and he knew that what he'd once felt for Gwyneth had been a boy's foolish fancy, tempered by the promise of a sensible marriage. Richard had offered lands and gold to the man who married Gwyneth, and Gwyneth had promised wondrous fleshly delights sanctified by the church.

In the end, neither had been enough. In the end, he wanted nothing more than to run away with the slender, beautiful, tiresome creature who confronted him, her beautiful mouth quivering, her eyes bright with unshed tears.

There was a storm brewing. The wind whipped her golden hair, catching it up and hurling it toward him. Overhead lightning spat through the sky, and he could smell the rain approaching.

"Let me take you to your solar, Lady Claire," he said stiffly. "Your women will stay with you, and I'll keep watch. No one will harm you."

"But what about my sister?"

"She has her husband to guard her."

"It's her husband I'm most afraid of." She pushed the hair away from her face. "Can you do nothing, Thomas?" Her voice was so gentle and plaintive that he wanted to slay dragons for her.

"Nothing, my lady," he said.

She glanced up toward Grendel's tower, her eyes troubled. A dim light pooled outward, but there was no sign of movement within. "If he hurts her, I will cut out his heart."

"I've heard that he doesn't possess one, my lady," Sir Thomas said.

She turned to look at him with devastating calm. "A problem that afflicts most of the men in this castle, Sir Thomas." And she started ahead of him, toward the east tower.

It was done. He had no idea of the hour, he only knew his back hurt, his neck was stiff, and his eyes were stinging from concentrating too hard. He stretched, glancing over to the darkened alcove where his bride slept so peacefully, her gown twisted around her sweet young body.

There were other places he could sleep. A trundle bed, a pallet in the anteroom where Godfrey usually kept watch. He was going to do neither. He would lie beside his bride in the big, fur-covered bed, and he wouldn't touch her.

He glanced down at the clear purple liquid. There was enough in the small stoppered bottle to kill a number of times over. It was a potent draught, and it only remained to be tested. Two drops would promise deep, restoring sleep to a large man. Four drops would kill him.

Or at least, that's what he presumed. He had every intention of testing it first, and this time he didn't dare use one of the servants, not for an experiment that could lead to high treason. He would drink it himself, and sleep beside his young bride totally oblivious to temptation.

He measured two careful drops into a wine goblet, then splashed some warm red wine on top of it. He was about to carry it to his lips when a noise beyond the door caught his attention. He set the glass down again in complete silence and moved stealthily toward the door, his right hand curled protectively against his side.

Richard de Lancie stood in the hallway, swaying slightly, his face flushed from drink, but Simon didn't make the mistake of underestimating his opponent. He slipped through the door, closing it behind him, closing it so that Richard couldn't crane his neck and see what lay beyond.

"Did you swive her?" he demanded in a piercing whisper. "Did you get between my little sister's legs and show her what a man is for? Show her what she's got to look forward to for the rest of her life?''

"It's hardly your business, my lord," Simon said with mocking politeness.

"Then again, perhaps she won't have to put up with it much longer. If you were to die, perhaps I'd let her go back to the convent. She'd be happier there, and God knows she's no prize like Claire. You were lucky enough to get her, but some of the more powerful barons around here wouldn't be quite so eager. I could get her into a nunnery with less expense."

"Not while I'm alive," Simon said with deceptive calm.

"Ah, but life is short. We both know that. Who's to guess when an assassin will turn up, with an ancient grudge? Or a piece of bad shellfish could finish you off."

"I have no fondness for shellfish," Simon said. "As for ancient enemies, they don't exist."

"You mean to tell me that there's no one on this earth who wants to kill you?" Richard scoffed. "No one who wants nothing more dearly than to cut your throat?"

"No one left alive," he said gently.

Richard made a faint choking sound. "I want the sleeping draught, Grendel," he said abruptly.

"It's almost ready."

"You said that before."

"Then you should learn not to waste your time repeating questions. The draught will be in your hands very soon. Once I test it."

"You're going to kill someone to see if it works? Let me make a few suggestions. . . ." Richard's voice was eager.

"It is a sleeping draught, my lord," Simon corrected

in a reproving voice. "A dangerous one, taken in the wrong dose, but when properly used, absolutely harmless. I intend to try the dosage on myself."

"You're mad, Grendel!"

Simon smiled. "So you've always said, my lord."

"I want it by tomorrow. If you're dead beside my sister then I'll search your rooms till I find it."

"I won't be dead," Simon said.

"Harrumph!" Richard's disapproval was extreme. "Bring it to me tomorrow whether it works or no. We can always try it on Sir Hector when he's being particularly annoying."

Simon waited until he was out of sight, down the circular stairs, before he went back into the solar. The fire had died down, but the room was warm, almost overheated. The smell of spices and wine lingered in the air, the smell of perfume and flowers and crushed, dried rose petals. He looked at the bed and saw Alys sitting up, a goblet of wine in one slim white hand.

"I wondered where you were," she said in a sleepy voice. "Was that my brother I heard?"

He nodded, momentarily distracted by her voice. By the fact that the dress had loosened in sleep and was drooping around her slender shoulders. She had beautiful pale skin. "He wanted to make certain you survived your ordeal," he said.

"He wanted to make certain I *had* an ordeal. Did you tell him you declined to deflower me?" She spoke the words boldly, but the color still flushed her pale cheeks.

"I didn't consider it his business. He's already planning my successor as it is."

"He wants a new wizard? I mean, advisor?"

"He wants a new husband for you. Though he's strongly considering the convent."

"I don't want to enter a convent."

"That was your original request. What made you change your mind?"

"You."

The word was simple, her voice was husky and beguiling, and he knew he couldn't resist her. He stayed where he was, rooted to the stone floor, telling himself he didn't need to do it. She sat in his bed, her gown drooping around her, her hair a curtain down her back, and he wanted to go to her. To lay her back among the fur throws and cover her body with his. And he knew he wasn't going to resist her.

And then he froze, as she lifted his goblet to her lips and drank deeply. Of the honeyed wine. And the sleeping potion.

Chapter Eighteen

He heard the sound from a distance, a great roaring noise that somehow came from his own throat. "Noooooo!" But she'd already brought the goblet, his goblet, to her lips, and he threw himself across the room, onto the bed, covering her, dashing the cup away from her so that it skittered across the floor, the drugged wine soaking into the rushes.

Alys sat utterly still, gazing at him in shock. He was straddling her, and he cupped her face in desperation, staring into her eyes, looking for signs of death or madness. "How much did you drink?" he demanded hoarsely.

He'd frightened her, but he didn't care. It took her a moment to answer, and her voice was quavery. "I'm sorry," she said. "I didn't think you would mind if I had a sip of your wine."

"How much did you drink?" he repeated.

"Not much at all. Just a sip or two, I think. Is there something wrong with the wine?"

He closed his eyes for a moment, forcing himself to breathe slowly. When he opened them she was staring up at him, her expression bewildered. "It will just make you sleepy," he said in a deceptively calm voice, praying it was true. "I was working on a simple sleeping draught. Lady Hedwiga has need of it." It was a stupid lie, but he was much too shaken to think clearly.

"Why was it in the goblet?"

"I planned to test it on myself before giving it to others."

"You were planning on spending the night in a drugged sleep?" She sounded more confused than outraged, and he could see by the darkening of her pupils that the drug was beginning to work. She would be unconscious in moments, and she wouldn't remember a thing of this conversation.

"It seemed a practical enough idea. It would be the only way I could sleep beside you without touching you."

"Why wouldn't you touch me?" she whispered.

She wanted him. His sweet little virgin bride, convent raised, afraid of horses and thunderstorms and most men, wanted him, the monster of Summersedge Keep. She didn't know what she was asking for.

He tilted her head back, and her neck was long and delicate beneath her stubborn chin. He wondered what she would do if he put his mouth against her pulse.

She was slipping down on the bed as the drug took possession of her, slowly, languorously. "I'm afraid of you," he said, knowing she wouldn't remember. "I'm afraid of loving you."

She blinked, dazed. "You're afraid of making love to me?" she said, her voice gently, sweetly slurred.

"No," he said bleakly. "I'm afraid of loving you, when I haven't loved anyone in years. It would destroy me."

Her eyes drifted closed, but a sweet smile curved her mouth. "Then perhaps," she whispered, "you need to be destroyed."

She was asleep. But whether it was simply a deep, restoring sleep or a more wicked one, leading towards death, he couldn't tell. He could only watch her, the rise and fall of her breasts beneath the rumpled gown, the faint tremor in her blue-veined eyelids, the sleepy whispers as she shifted and stirred.

He stretched out beside her on the bed, his body shielding her as she slept. She was a restless sleeper with the drug working its wickedness—she moaned and stirred, and strange words tumbled from her mouth, words of fear and longing. She opened her eyes once, to stare at him in drugged confusion, until she managed to focus on his face. He half expected the terror to increase, but instead she sighed with relief and closed her eyes again, trusting him.

He hated that trust. He hated her. He hated the tenderness he felt for her. He could summon Godfrey and have him keep watch over her. Godfrey was a learned man; he would be more than capable of observing her reactions to the drug, more than capable of writing them down. There was no need for Simon to lie there beside her, watching, worrying, needing her.

He couldn't move away from her. Occasionally he let his hand drift across her, across her sleeping face, across her restless body, his scarred hand a contrast to her unmarred skin. He had no idea what he would do if she died. Too many people had died, too many women, too many children, too many brave young men and old cowards. Too much death, and if she died at his hands he didn't think he could bear it.

It was close to dawn when she opened her eyes once more, and they were clear and calm as she looked up at him with no surprise whatsoever. He had seen death too often not to know when it was imminent, not to recognize the eerie calm that preceded a soul's passing, and he was frozen with despair and rage.

She reached up and touched his face with a gentle hand, and it had been so long since someone had caressed him. "Am I going to die?" she whispered.

"No." It was a lie.

The slow smile that lit her face was impossibly erotic. "Good," she murmured. "I don't want to die a virgin bride." And she lifted her head and kissed his mouth.

He was too startled to do more than hold still, motionless, as she pressed her untutored lips against his. She pulled back, a faint frown wrinkling her brow beneath the tumbled hair. "Didn't I do it right?"

He was past resisting her and his own desperate need. Without thinking he rolled on top of her, pressing her down into the soft furs as he cradled her neck in his left hand. "You need practice," he said, and set his mouth against hers, feeling her open to his pressure, the softness of her lips, the smoky, drugged taste of her. It should have distracted him, but he was beyond that, his appetite was fully aroused, and he needed her, needed her mouth, needed her soft, sleep-drugged body, needed the sweet forgetfulness she could give him.

He was rock hard, wild with wanting her, and she moved beneath him, warm and trembling, needing him as well. Her laces were already loose from her disordered night's sleep, and it was simple enough to pull the gown down her arms, to her waist.

Her breasts were small and round and perfect beneath the thin linen of her chemise, and he put his hands on them, cupping them, feeling the nipples harden against his fingers. He lifted his head to watch her, and her eyes were lost, dazed, dreamy. She was his for the taking; they were married and alone in his big, soft bed, and there was no way he could deny himself. Whatever reasons he had for keeping away from her had vanished in the heat and the darkness. He knew he wouldn't stop.

He put his mouth on her breast, sucking the sweet flesh through the thin material, and the sound she made was a soft cry of pleasure as she arched beneath him, restless, seeking what her instinct told her she needed.

She slid her arms around his waist, pulling him closer to her, and her drugged eyes were wide and confused. He put his hand between her legs, and she jerked, startled, frightened, still needy, and she pushed against his hand with her hips, silently begging for more.

He pulled up her skirts and she whimpered suddenly, the small sound of a frightened angel. She stared up at him in mute fear and longing, as a bit of reality began to pierce the drugged cloud that surrounded her. He knew he should stop. And he knew that Grendel, the monster, would not.

Her hands slid up his chest, pulling the loose shirt away from his body. The room was dark and her eyes were now closed. The feel of her hands on his skin was exquisite torment, and in sudden impatience he ripped his shirt off, throwing it across the bed.

She was no longer frightened of him, and he could blame the drug for that, but he didn't care. Drugged or not, conscious or not, she was his, and he would take her, and deal with the consequences tomorrow.

He wanted to seduce her, arouse her, please her, but the feel of her hands on him set a kind of madness upon him, and all he could think and feel and taste was her soft skin, her voice, her warm, clinging body.

He would have her, and there was no room for the

tears she wept as she clung to him. He cursed his ungentle hands but he couldn't stop himself from wanting her, taking her. He moved between her legs, pushing in deep, breaking past the frail barrier of her innocence. He hurt her, and she cried. He kissed her, and she kissed him back. He touched her, and she came.

Tight around him, damp and breathless and lost, she lay beneath him, holding onto him with a possessive fierceness that managed to shock his tangled brain. He expected rage and sorrow and recriminations. A thousand curses on his head for his rough passion.

Instead he got love.

Her face was wet with tears. He gently brushed them away, wondering what words he could find. Should he ask her to forgive him? Or should he demand more?

She hiccupped, a soft, lost sound that cut him more deeply than her faint protest. She opened her eyes to look at him, and in their glazed depths he could see a mass of tangled emotions.

"I hate you," she said.

"I know."

"If you touch me again I'll see to it that you really are unmanned."

"I know."

Her furious eyes met his. "I love you," she said, her voice rich with loathing.

"I know," he said, and kissed her.

Her eyes fluttered closed, and she began to snore very delicately.

He froze, staring down at her in disbelief. And then he collapsed beside her on the bed. And then he began to laugh, out loud, as he hadn't laughed in years. His bride slept on beside him as he laughed, at himself, at her, at the complete madness and unpredictability of life. She wouldn't die, his sleeping bride.

Nor would he kill a boy-king for the sake of power and money. He was twice as smart and nearly as ruthless as Richard the Fair, and Richard was no match for him. Simon would figure a way out of his current predicament, with Richard none the wiser that his plans had been thwarted. With any luck, Simon would be able to convince him it was his own decision.

Alys moved closer to him in her deep sleep, murmuring beneath her breath, and he reached out to caress her face, smoothing her long, thick hair back. She sighed, nuzzling against his hand like a sleepy kitten, and he knew it was too late. She would probably try to kill him when she awoke and remembered her rude deflowering. He didn't care. He was lost, captured by an innocent, destroyed by a would-be nun, and there was no way the monster, Simon of Navarre, Richard the Fair's Grendel, would ever be the same.

Claire lay alone in the bed she had shared with her sister, dry eyed and desperate. Sir Thomas had left her at the door, coming no further, and there was no sign of her serving women, including faithful Madlen. She was alone, with no one to attend her, no one to come to her rescue if her lecherous brother should once more decide to ignore the laws of God and man.

She had reached out a hand and placed it on Thomas's strong right arm, feeling the bone and muscle and heat through the rough wool of his tunic. "Stay," she pleaded. "I'm frightened. Help me."

But Thomas had withdrawn his arm with hasty gentleness, looking at her as if she carried the pox. "No one will come near you, my lady. I've given my vow to keep you safe, and nothing will stop me."

"I don't want to be alone in that room," she said

desperately. "I need you to guard me. There's a trundle bed that Madlen. . . ."

"No!" He took a step away from her, and she half expected him to ward her off with the sign of the cross. "I'll keep you safe, I'll fight for you, I'll die for you, but I won't lie at your feet like a tame dog. I won't be led into temptation."

"Temptation?" She stared at him in amazement. "Are you telling me I tempt you?" The very notion was absurd.

Except that she met his wintry eyes, and they were no longer so cold. They were hot with pain and longing, and she took an instinctive step backwards, shaken by such naked need.

"You tempt me to my complete destruction, my lady," he said in a harsh voice. "And even if I had no care for my immortal soul, I could not destroy you as well." And he turned and walked away from her before she could stop him.

The night was endless. She could hear him pacing beyond the door, his heavy boots steady and reassuring and maddeningly distracting on the stone floor. Every now and then he would come closer, and she would hold her breath, waiting for the door to open. But it never did.

She dreamed of him. She had never heard him laugh, but in her dreams he did. He put his arms out to her, and she went to them, gladly, weeping with joy, only to have him turn to ashes in her arms. She looked up into his face, calling for him, but all she could see was Richard with his lecherous, blood-shot eyes, and she woke up screaming.

"There, there, my lady." Madlen scurried to her side, her plain face knit with worry. "You must have had a bad dream, and no wonder. Sit up and I'll help you out of that accursed dress."

It was morning, gray and overcast, and somehow Claire had managed to sleep. "Have you seen my sister?" she questioned, turning her back so that Madlen could unlace her.

Madlen shook her head. "She's with her husband still. If it were any other bride I would say we won't see her for a day or two, but there's no telling with Grendel ... Lord Simon." She hastily corrected herself. "But don't you worry, my lady. I'm certain she's fine. These things are difficult for convent bred ladies, but she'll grow accustomed to it eventually." Madlen looked more doubtful than her calming words. "In the meantime, you need to eat something, and you need some fresh air. Sir Thomas said I was to accompany you to the stables where you might see your brother's horse, but by no means was I to leave you unguarded."

Claire froze. "Where is Sir Thomas?" she demanded. "He swore he'd watch over me, protect me. . . ."

"He's left, my lady. He's been called away. Who would he be protecting you from, my lady?" Madlen asked with deliberate innocence. "No one wishes to hurt you."

"Except my brother," Claire said bitterly.

"Nay, my lady. Lord Richard wouldn't harm a hair on your lovely head, I'm sure of it," she said earnestly, ignoring the faint bruising that still remained on her mistress's neck. "And Sir Thomas should return by late today, I'm certain. In the meantime I expect Sir Hector would be happy to keep you company. . . ."

"Sir Hector is no match for my brother."

"No one is, my lady," Madlen said softly. "He's the lord of this castle, and no one is going to stand up to him."

"Except Sir Thomas, who's abandoned me."

"He had reason."

"And what was that? A prayer retreat?" Claire didn't try to contain the bitterness in her voice.

"He had to see to his wife's burial."

Claire dropped the brush she was holding. "What?"

"Word came last night, and Richard sent for Thomas to tell him. His lady wife died in childbirth two days ago at Hawkesley Court and her babe with her."

"Oh, no!" Claire cried, shocked out of her own panic. "To lose his wife and his child. . . !"

"Not his child, my lady. Nor his wife in anyone's eyes but the law. Gwyneth of Longmead ran off with Baron Hawkesley, and she was carrying his child when she died." Madlen shook her head. 'Tis a sad thing, but Brother Jerome would tell us it was God's judgment."

"God wouldn't kill a child to punish a woman," Claire said firmly.

"I've seen it happen too many times to doubt it. He'll be back tonight, after he's taken Lady Gwyneth's body back to her family holdings. You can keep yourself safe that long, can't you?"

"You'll take me to see Arabia?" she asked, her mind turning feverishly.

"Aye, my lady."

Claire smiled, a devious, obedient smile. She could do nothing for her sister, trapped with the demon in the north tower. And Sir Thomas could or would do nothing for her. He would be mourning his fallen wife.

But she could do something for herself. She could climb on Arabia's back and escape this place, and this time she wouldn't come back. She could disappear into the thick forest, survive on nuts and berries and wild game if she were clever enough, and no man would ever touch her again.

Not even the man she longed to have touch her.

"Just let me change, dear Madlen," she said sweetly, "and we'll take the air."

And Madlen was fool enough to take her at her word, nodding comfortably.

She awoke in his arms. She couldn't move—her limbs felt bound by velvet ties, her head was stuffed with feathers, and her mouth tasted of rabbit's feet. She opened her eyes and then quickly shut them again, as searing pain lanced through her skull. Even in the dimly lit tower room it was far too bright. Even her teeth hurt.

She forced herself to breath lightly, slowly growing accustomed to her circumstances. He lay up against her side, warm and strong and oddly comforting, and one arm rested across her waist, possessive, protecting. He was wrapped in a fur coverlet. She could see his shirt lying on the floor and a sudden foreboding filled her. He slept on beside her, despite the lateness of the morning hour.

He looked like a different man when he slept. No monster at all, with his golden eyes closed, his thick lashes resting against his tawny cheeks. Without the force of his personality to cloud things, he seemed oddly vulnerable, something she would never have thought of Simon of Navarre.

And beautiful. She hadn't realized it before, but his forbidding face had a kind of unearthly beauty. His cheekbones were high, his nose thin and strong, his mouth wide and surprisingly generous. If he weren't so intent on terrifying everyone into submission he could have probably charmed them into doing his will.

The room was chilled, but no one had come to see to the fire. They probably didn't want to interrupt the bridal couple in the throes of ecstasy. Not that Alys had been in the throes of anything, ecstatic or otherwise. She had slept like the dead, and her memory of the night before was filled with strange and incomprehensible dreams.

She glanced down at the bare arm lying across her body, scarred, muscled and strong. And then she realized that her glorious rose colored gown was tangled about her, pulled down to her waist, rumpled up to her hips. She turned to stare at him in shocked surprise but he slept on, oblivious to her reaction.

She was able to slip from underneath his arm. The rushes were damp beneath her feet, and she had no notion where her thin slippers were. She wasn't about to look. Her head hurt her so badly she thought she might weep with the pain, and for some reason the sight of Simon of Navarre, sleeping so peacefully, so chastely in the bridal bed, wounded her deeply. If he didn't want her, why had he married her?

Silly question. He'd married her for the settlement Richard had given him, for the power of being brother-in-law to his liege lord. He'd married her out of boredom and spite, most likely.

If only she had a similar excuse.

She'd married him because she wanted to. Because she wanted him. Because she was enchanted and terrified, fascinated and bewitched. She'd married him because she wanted him to kiss her again, to tell her he'd lied, and that she was beautiful. She'd married him because she'd fallen in love with the monster in the cave, and no amount of common sense could talk her out of it.

She needed to find her sister. She needed some of the comfort and wisdom she'd dispensed so generously to Claire; she needed to regain some of her distance. She had no illusions about Simon of Navarre—he was a cold, dangerous man. He would destroy her if he had to, even if he regretted it. He had more of a conscience than he pretended to have, but not enough to ensure her safety.

She tried to pull her gown around her, but the results were less than impressive. She couldn't reach the lacing, her hair was an impossible tangle, and her shoes were missing. Her mouth felt bruised, swollen, and her breasts ached. She felt strange and damp between her legs as well, something the nuns had taught her to ignore. Her monthly courses must be upon her again, though it seemed as if she had just finished with them. She glanced back at the sleeping man with sudden doubt, but he didn't move, seemingly innocent. He couldn't have debauched her without her knowing, could he? He couldn't have deflowered her while she slept?

In truth, she had no idea. She couldn't remember a thing. Perhaps he'd done all he was capable of doing. Perhaps he really was less than a man, incapable of bringing her children, or the pleasure he'd talked about the night before.

But she didn't believe it for one moment. Simon of Navarre was a trickster, a liar, a charlatan and a cheat. He was a man who did exactly what he wanted to, no more, no less. She only wished she knew what it was he wanted.

Her foot knocked against something in the rushes, and she bent down to pick up the jeweled goblet she had seen the night before. It was dented, as if someone had flung it against the wall, and there was a faint, sticky residue at the bottom of the bowl. She stared at it, trying to remember, but her aching head made her mind numb. She'd held that goblet the night before, and he'd shouted at her. The rest was a blur.

She set the damaged goblet down on the table, lifted her skirts and ran from the room, ignoring her stockinged feet, ignoring the fact that a good deal of her chemise was visible above the drooping dress. She needed her sister, and she needed her now.

When Simon woke he was alone in the bed. It still smelled of her, musk and roses and soft skin. He was so hard he almost reached down to take care of it himself when something stayed his hand. He could lie on his back, think of Alys, and bring himself some ease. But that would only increase her hold over him.

Besides, he had more important things to attend to. He had to destroy that foul draught and the written page of instructions he'd inserted in his herbal before anyone could get their hands on it. His decision was finally clear, and he wanted no chance to change his mind. He pushed himself out of the tumbled bed, reaching for his abandoned clothes, and headed for the work table and the silver vial of precious liquid.

It wasn't there.

He didn't bother searching the room—it would have been a waste of time. He didn't summon Godfrey to question him—Godfrey wouldn't have the answers. Simon already knew the truth. This time Richard the Fair had chosen the proper tool. Someone had made his or her way into the wizard's forbidden room and stolen the sleeping draught, and Simon had either been too enmeshed in his sleeping bride to notice or foolishly asleep himself.

And if he didn't do something about it, a child would die. There was enough of the draught in that vial to kill at least half a dozen people, and he had no doubt Richard would use it sparingly. Six more people on

Simon's conscience, when it had already been so heavy-laden that it had snapped and broken.

Somehow it had rebuilt itself. Somehow he had regained a troubling sense of honor. He could keep his mouth shut, knowing that Richard would say nothing, knowing that his future was, for the time being, secure. Chief advisor to the king of England was a position that was both powerful and dangerous. He was afraid of nothing—surely this would fill his needs.

Unbidden, the memory of Alys of Summersedge came to him. Alys of Navarre, with her trusting eyes and her fierce nature. She deserved a peaceful life, a home in the countryside, surrounded by trees and flowers and children. She would be a good wife, a good mother, a kind and fair lady of the manor.

But she needed the proper husband for such a blissful future. She needed a country at peace. She was unlikely to get either of those rare commodities.

He had to find her. To find out what she remembered about last night, and whether she suspected anything untoward in the silver vial that had rested on the work table. He had no illusions about Lady Alys—if she realized the vial was dangerous she would take it, and it was far too lethal to fall into the wrong hands.

He could taste her on his mouth. Feel her skin against his hands. He could hear her muffled, shocked cry when he made her climax.

He cursed himself. That damnable stuff had seemed to work as an aphrodisiac on his shy wife—and he must have inhaled too many fumes himself. Sex was the least of his worries. Alys's soft, plump body was of no particular importance. Even if he couldn't stop thinking of it. Of taking her, again and again and again, until they were both too weary to do more than sleep. And then wake, and do it again.

He had to find Alys, and he had to make certain the vial was in Richard's hands. Dangerous hands, undoubtedly, but at least Richard would know the power of the liquid. There would be no tragic mistakes, only deliberate ones.

He had to find Alys. He had to make certain she was safe. And then he could start the arduous task of rearranging his life.

Chapter Nineteen

She'd been a fool to run away, Claire knew it deep within her heart, as much as she wished to deny it. It had been ridiculously simple—without Sir Thomas to watch over her, escape was easily arranged. Richard's stable men were stupidly lax, and her glowering guardian hadn't warned them that she was adept at getting her way. All she had to do was distract Madlen, send her off on a fool's errand, and she was away before anyone realized she had left.

It was growing late now, stormy. The wind had picked up, swirling the dry dead leaves around Arabia's delicate feet as she picked her way deeper, ever deeper, into the forest. Claire had been riding for hours—she'd lost track of time, and only as the sky grew darker did she begin to realize she might have been a bit hasty in running away.

She wondered if they even knew she was gone. She'd smiled sweetly at the guards who watched over the drawbridge of Summersedge Keep, and they'd stared at her with the same besotted expression they or their compatriots had shown the first time she ran off. She'd belted up her petticoats and jumped onto Arabia's back the moment she thought it was safe, and there had been no cries of alarm. And now she found herself wishing that there had been.

Alys had tried to warn her against her impetuous nature, and Claire had never listened. Alys's prudence had landed her in the bed of a monster. Claire's foolishness had probably led her to her death.

She'd never realized how very tall the trees were. It was dark in the forest, but whether it was from the storm, the approaching night, or the thick growth of greenery, Claire couldn't tell. She only knew she was frightened.

It was an entirely unpleasant sensation. She had spent most of her young life relatively fearless. She was brave and reckless when it came to horses and her own safety, and if she ran into trouble her sister was always there to extricate her, to plead with the nuns, to take the blame and the punishment on her behalf. And Claire had let her.

Just as she had let Alys be wed to a creature of darkness. She had let Alys sacrifice herself for her, and at that moment she felt completely unworthy of the trouble.

She heard the rumble of thunder, and Arabia sidestepped nervously. That was one weakness shared by her sister and her horse—a strong dislike, even a fear, of thunderstorms. Claire could never understand why. She reveled in the wildness of nature, hungered for the strong wind to toss her hair, the rain to soak her skin.

Though to be entirely honest, she wasn't in the mood for it at that particular moment. Right then she would have been more than happy to be safe inside the east tower of Summersedge Keep, with Alys to keep her company and Sir Thomas to keep the monsters at bay.

But Thomas had deserted her, when he swore he would keep her safe. He'd left her for his faithless wife, and Claire knew she was impossibly selfish and evil to begrudge a dead woman that small dignity.

But she did. She wanted Thomas to watch over her, she wanted him to keep her safe, she wanted him to . . . she wanted him to. . . . She wanted him.

It was that shockingly simple. She wanted a man she could never have, a man who despised her and thought she was his personal path to eternal damnation. She wanted a poor knight, who didn't want her and couldn't have her even if he changed his mind. Her brother would see to that.

Her brother would see to a great many other things, Claire reminded herself, and that was why she had run. She couldn't save Alys, she could only save herself.

The Convent of Saint Anne the Demure was somewhere on the other side of this vast forest. Alys had said they would not welcome her, but Alys didn't know the force of Claire's charm when she chose to exert it. Even the stern Mother Dominica had been helpless before Claire's practiced, wistful smile and huge, tear-filled eyes.

They'd take her in all right, particularly when she told them what her brother had attempted. They would keep her safe, as they always had, and eventually the wizard would tire of Alys and she would join her. And everything would be as it was, but safer.

Claire had lost her taste for adventuring. She no longer wanted to run through fields, to have men fall at her feet. She was content to live a chaste life, as long as it meant Richard couldn't get anywhere near her. If she couldn't have Thomas, she didn't want anyone else.

It was growing colder. It was too early for snow, but there was a bite in the air that cut through her thin wool gown. She hadn't been able to bring anything when she'd left—Madlen was simple and accepting but even she might have grown suspicious if Claire had gone for a simple walk loaded down with cloaks and extra food.

They said this forest was haunted. She didn't want to believe it, but each rustle of leaves, each tiny scuffling made her chilled skin shiver in fear. She was tired, and it was starting to rain, icy little pellets that stung her skin. She needed to find shelter, someplace warm and dry until the storm passed.

She finally settled for a small clearing in the woods. Two of the ancient trees had toppled to make a rude shelter, and she nudged Arabia forward to investigate, the reins held lightly in her hand.

The crackle of lightning was shockingly close, the heavy rumble of the thunder shaking the ground beneath her. Arabia let out a panicked whinny, rearing into the air.

Claire hadn't been thrown from a horse in over three years, despite her recklessness, but the day had been long, her emotions were raw, and her concentration shattered. She could see the ground hurtling up at her, the crossed branches of the fallen tree, and she reached out her hands to shield herself, to break her fall, but it was too late, she was falling, trapped amid the branches, and Arabia was gone, deserting her in a mindless panic.

Claire lay amid the branches, struggling for the breath that had been knocked from her body. It took endless moments for it to return, and with it came a sudden, blinding pain in her arm. She bit her lip, forcing herself to stay conscious, but the rain grew heavier, colder, and all she could do was crawl through the maze of branches and huddle beneath the uprooted trunks of the huge old trees.

Another crash of lightning, and Claire let out a muffled shriek, pulling herself into a tight little ball of pain and cold and misery. She was protected from the rain, but just barely, and with her luck some ferocious wild animal would stumble upon her and have her for dinner.

She didn't care. She had never been more miserable in her life, and worst of all was that she couldn't even feel sorry for herself. She had brought it on herself, she had done nothing to help her sister, and she deserved all the misery that had come her way.

She would have given anything to see the proud, disapproving Sir Thomas again. She would throw herself at his feet, beg his forgiveness, beg him to rescue her, and promise to spend the rest of her life chaste, docile, and holy. She would have her head shorn, dress in sackcloth and ashes instead of her fine clothes, and walk barefoot to the convent if only she could get out of this mess.

But there was no one to save her this time. No strong, handsome knight, no willing sister. Even her horse had deserted her. She cradled her hand in her lap, pulled her knees up to her chest, and silently began to cry.

Richard was waiting for him. He sat alone in his solar, a mug of strong ale in his hand. He looked up when Simon appeared in the door. "You're much later than I expected," he said. "It's well into the middle of the day. I thought you weren't going to emerge from the bridal bower at all."

"I had things to do," Simon said coolly.

"I'm certain you did." Richard smirked. "And where is the blushing bride? Did you fuck her bowlegged?"

"Your concern for your sister is touching," he murmured. "Godfrey tells me she's resting in her room in the east tower."

"How could Godfrey tell you anything? You cut out the man's tongue," Richard said in his cheerful voice.

"In fact, I wasn't the one who maimed Godfrey. He'd hardly be my devoted servant if I had done it. And we have no trouble communicating, I assure you."

Richard grimaced, taking a huge gulp from his ale. "So why are you here, Grendel?" he demanded. "Have you changed your mind about which sister you want? If you haven't managed to take her maidenhead then I suppose we could see about an annulment, though I can tell you right now I'm not about to part with the other one."

"Such brotherly protectiveness is admirable."

"I told you, I don't believe Claire's any kin to me at all. Her mother was a whore, like all women. Of course she'd lie about the girl's parenthood, since my own father was dead and couldn't deny it."

"You say all women are whores. Does that include Lady Hedwiga?"

Richard laughed at that. "Would that she were, my friend. She'd be a lot more interesting than she is now. What do you want from me?" His red-rimmed eyes met Simon's without wavering.

That was part of Richard's particular strength. He had no qualms about his sins; he committed them boldly, without conscience.

"We both know what I want, Richard," he said gently. "The draught is not yet tested. It could be dangerous. . . ."

"The draught?" His face held the innocence of a gifted liar. "You told me you were days away from perfecting it."

"It's not perfected yet. It could have unfortunate, unexpected effects. . . ."

"And you think I stole it from you? Which means, I gather, that it's missing? That it's fallen into the wrong hands?"

"Indeed," Simon said. "Dangerous hands."

Richard looked up at him from beneath his thinning blonde hair, and his expression was bordering on smug. "Then you'd best find it, before someone gets killed."

Simon didn't move. The warning was implicit, and yet there was nothing he could do about it. He had no proof—he could scarce accuse his liege lord of high treason against the young king. As long as Richard stayed at Summersedge Keep then the king was safe, it was unlikely that Richard would trust anyone to commit the murder without him there to oversee it. Richard had an inflated opinion of his own abilities, and he would assume that none of his minions could perform properly without instructions. Simon had time.

"That would be a great tragedy," he said slowly. "Perhaps I simply misplaced it. You may be certain I'll be more careful in the future."

Richard's grin was smug. "I'm certain you will, Grendel. I know I can always count on you in the end."

"Always," Simon agreed, lying effortlessly.

Alys slept, a deep, dream-crazed sleep, tossing and turning in the wide bed in her tower room. There had been no sign of her sister when she'd entered the room, only Madlen sitting by the fire, placidly working on her stitchery. She'd taken one look at Alys's face, made a comforting, clucking noise, and quickly divested her of the rumpled rose gown and tucked her into the bed. Alys never heard her leave.

Her dreams were strange, tumbled things. They were pure sensation, touch and scent and taste that made no sense at all, and when she finally awoke the day was almost spent, and she was shivering.

She sat up in her bed. Long shadows moved across the tower room, and the wind blew through the narrow slits, stirring the heavy wall hangings. Her headache was gone, but her mouth felt thick and sluggish, and her brain wasn't functioning properly.

"I thought you might be wanting a bath, my lady," Madlen's voice penetrated the sleepy haze that still befogged Alys's brain. "Seeing as how you spent last night, that is."

Alys blinked. How would Madlen know how she spent the previous night?

"Are you in much pain, my lady?" she asked, her solicitousness doing little to cover her avid curiosity.

Alys didn't know what to answer. She tried to remember the horrors that Lady Hedwiga had warned her of. Pain and blood, she'd said. Wet and disgusting. For some reason she had yet to associate Simon of Navarre with things that were disgusting, but then, he hadn't wanted her. That in itself was fairly disheartening.

"I'm fine," she said shortly. "A bath would be lovely, but I would like privacy as well."

"My lady, if I may be so bold as to say so, at times like these women need the advice of other women," Madlen said, not giving up easily.

"Lady Hedwiga has already been more than helpful."

"You've seen her today?" Madlen sounded doubtful.

Alys was becoming an adept liar. "We had private converse," she said.

"But Lord Richard said she was unwell—unable to see anyone."

Hell's blood, Alys thought, adding cursing to her rapidly growing list of sins. "I brought her a posset," she said. "An herbal concoction I learned from the nuns, to ease her discomfort." She summoned a learned smile. "I'm entirely able to take care of myself as well."

Madlen looked doubtful, as well she might. Alys knew full well that Madlen was twice her age and had outlived two strong young husbands and one elderly one. She knew more about women's bodies than most midwives, and the last thing Alys wanted was to expose herself to Madlen's prying eyes.

"As you wish, my lady," she murmured politely, lowering her curious gaze. "If you change your mind you have only to summon me."

There was blood on her thighs when she lifted her chemise, blood staining her clothing, and she knew a moment's horrified uncertainty as she slid into the warm, fragrant bath. Had she been mistaken all this time?

The heated water was a blessing, and she dismissed her sudden suspicions. He didn't want her, he'd made that clear. She must have been wrong about her monthly flow.

She leaned back in the tub, letting her long hair soak up the water, and she shut her eyes, resting her head against the linen covered wood. She felt wonderfully peaceful, floating, almost ready to sleep some more.

She let her drifting mind go chasing down the odd dreams that had plagued her, and the caress of the water against her skin reminded her of other caresses, touches, strange and dangerous delights that enticed and frightened.

She sat up abruptly, splashing water over the floor and her discarded clothing. "Madlen!" she shrieked.

As expected, Madlen was hovering, her plain face alight with avid curiosity. She glanced at the pile of clothing on the floor, but fortunately no blood stains could be seen. What a fool she'd been, Alys thought bitterly. So innocent and so trusting.

"Bring me fresh clothing at once," she said. "And send my sister to me. I have need of her. . . ." Her voice trailed off as she saw the look of utter panic on Madlen's plain face. "What's wrong?" she demanded. "Has something happened to Claire? Where is Sir Thomas? Has Richard been near her, harmed her . . . ?"

"In truth, my lady, I do not know," Madlen said miserably. "We went for a walk in the courtyard earlier today and she just . . . disappeared."

Alys rose from the bath, oblivious to her nudity, the chill in the air, and Madlen's curiosity. "Is her horse gone as well?"

"I don't know."

Alys tried to still her rising panic as Madlen helped her into dry clothes. "And what of Sir Thomas? Did he go after her?"

"Sir Thomas isn't here. Oh, my lady, forgive me, but I didn't know what to do, and I thought she would return sooner or later!" Madlen wailed.

It was almost full dark outside, and the rumble of thunder was ominously close. "Does my brother know she's missing?"

"No one does. My lady, where are you going?" Madlen's voice rose, but Alys had already fled.

She had no idea what she was going to do. Turning to Richard for help was out of the question—Alys trusted him no more than Claire did. Nor was she particularly eager to turn to her husband. Not if he'd done what she suspected. And if she was wrong it would make things even worse. She was only dimly aware of what had passed between them the night before, and she wasn't sure she was ready to ask for his help. Sir Thomas was gone, Madlen said, and Alys trusted none of the other knights who filled Richard's hall.

She had reached the bottom of the east tower stairs when she barreled into a strong male figure, so intent on her sister's whereabouts that she didn't look where she was going.

"Lady Alys." The voice was grim, cool, but blessedly welcome as she looked up.

"Sir Thomas!" she cried, and without thinking flung her arms around him. "Thank God you've returned! I need your help desperately."

Sir Thomas was not dull-witted. "Your sister. Where is she?" he said in a sharp voice. "Has anyone laid a hand on her?"

"She's run away. I was asleep, and that fool Madlen didn't watch her carefully. I haven't checked to see if her horse is missing but I'm certain it is."

"If the horse is gone, then so is your sister," he said. "I knew something was amiss." He spun around and headed out into the courtyard, with Alys scampering along behind him, trying to keep up.

"You'll go after her?" she pleaded. "You'll try to find her?"

"I *will* find her," he said sharply, and she believed him. She had no other choice. He paused and looked down at her, taking her small hand in his large, gloved ones. "Your sister will be safe with me, I promise. I will bring her back to you safely."

Alys found treacherous tears filling her eyes. "I know you will," she said, and flung her arms around him, planting a grateful kiss on his cheek.

She stayed where she was, alone in the storm swept courtyard, watching him as he disappeared into the stables. The wind was tossing the heavy skirts of her gown about her ankles, whipping her long, wet hair against her face, and she pushed it back with an absent hand. There was nothing she could do now but wait.

She turned, and froze. Simon of Navarre stood there in the courtyard, dressed in black, watching her, his face cool and distant.

"How long have you been there?" She wondered at the calmness in her voice.

"Long enough to watch your touching farewell to your brave champion. You forgot to give him a love token to wear into battle."

She ignored his taunt. "My sister has run away."

Simon nodded. "I assumed it was something like that. And du Rhaymer is going in search of her?"

"Yes."

"Then I suppose he deserves your kisses," the wizard said idly.

She moved closer to him, flinching as lightning sizzled in the sky. "My lord, you have no cause for jealousy."

"My lady, I am not jealous." He said it with simple honesty, and she should have felt relief.

She didn't. She felt a slow building rage, curdling deep in her belly, she who had always avoided anger and passion. She came up to him, close enough that his long black robes caught and mingled with her gown in the swirling wind. She pushed the hair from her face to glare up at him, and her last ounce of proper behavior fled in the wash of emotion.

"Of course," she said bitterly. "You have to care about someone in order to feel jealousy. And you've already given me leave to take a lover. I would think Sir Thomas would do very well. As a matter of fact, that's what we were doing before we reached the courtyard. We had an assignation in my room, and he . . . and he. . . ."

He smiled down at her, very gently. "Sir Thomas is besotted with your sister, and even if he weren't, he's far too noble and stalwart a knight to seduce a married woman. Not to mention that he's far too wise a man to make an enemy of one such as I."

"Why would it make an enemy of you?" she said in a hushed voice, her anger vanishing as quickly as it came, replaced instead by anticipation.

He put his hand to her face, and lightning sizzled in the air. She shivered, but she didn't pull back.

"What do you remember of last night?" he countered.

"Very little."

"Then come upstairs with me now," he said, "and I'll remind you."

Chapter Twenty

She ran from him. She ran from his touch, suddenly terrified. She ran across the courtyard, and he made no move to follow her, stop her. She knew if she looked back Simon of Navarre would be watching her out of his still, golden eyes. But she didn't dare look back.

If she did, she might stop running.

What had happened last night? What had he done to her? Why couldn't she remember? She was supposed to be unnaturally wise for a woman, learned and thoughtful. How could she have forgotten the loss of her maidenhead?

Her mind had forgotten, but her body remembered. His touch on her skin had sent waves of sensation washing over her. Her stomach had knotted, her breasts had tingled, and between her legs she felt hot and wet.

What had he done to her?

The lightning sizzled behind her, and she let out a terrified shriek as she stumbled up the short flight of stairs to the Great Hall.

"Marriage has turned you into a slattern, sister dear."

Richard stood there, a dark, unreadable expression on his ruddy face, staring down at her, and she knew a sudden, unreasoning fear.

She touched her damp, tousled hair, unrestrained by circlet or wimple. She wore no jewels, and her feet were bare. "I . . . was in a hurry, brother dear," she said. Belatedly she came up to him and pressed a dutiful kiss on his bearded cheek.

"And why were you rushing about, sweet Alys? Were you in search of your sister? I've yet to see her today, and I confess, I miss her pretty face." It was said with great innocence, but Alys wasn't fooled.

"She's sick," Alys said abruptly. "She has the stomach grippe. Madlen has been holding a basin, and you think there'd be an end to what she can get rid of, but she keeps spewing. I don't think you'd want to see her. Her face isn't the slightest bit pretty when it's green."

Richard was looking slightly green himself at the picture she'd conjured up. "A reasonable excuse," he said, nodding. "Then if you've just been with her, where were you running to? Your husband's side? I wouldn't have thought Grendel would be the sort to kindle that strong affection. Or were you, perhaps, running away from him?"

Curse the man and his father as well, Alys thought, not caring that it was a father they shared. She'd never even seen old Lord Roger of Summersedge, but he sounded like a womanizing, unprincipled bastard, and his lecherous son took after him.

"I am a most dutiful wife," she said meekly, hoping she looked it.

"Of course you are, my dear," Richard said. "I would expect no less of you. And I'm certain you don't want to spend your days being ogled by the servants while they guess exactly what kind of member your husband has. I'll see that you're taken back to his solar for privacy."

"No! That is, I'm ready for company . . ." she began, but it was already too late. Richard had signaled for two of his menservants to approach.

"Which reminds me, dear Alys. I'm as curious as the next man. What kind of member *does* Simon of Navarre have? Does it work? Is it forked like the tongue of a snake?"

The two men had taken her arms and were leading her away. She could have struggled, but she suspected it would have been useless. They would take her back to Grendel's lair, throw her in, and fetch her broken bones in the morning. She made one last attempt.

"I need to speak with Lady Hedwiga again," she said, squirming in their tight grip. "I need her wise counsel. . . ."

"My lady wife is indisposed," Richard said with a doleful expression on his face. "She hopes that the posset you brought her will help, but we can only pray."

"Posset?" Alys echoed, but she was already being dragged toward the stairs of the tower, and it would have been useless and undignified to fight.

At least the tower rooms were empty. A fire blazed brightly in the fireplace, and the room smelled of spices and dried roses. The bed hangings were drawn back, the coverlets neatened, the rushes on the floor were fresh and strewn with dried flowers. She looked at the bed with dismay, trying to will her memory to return.

She was rewarded with a crack of thunder, and she moved away from the window in sudden panic, taking a seat by the fire. Lightning storms were bad enough on the ground—up high in a tower they were well-nigh unbearable.

Her sister was out on a night like this, with only a high strung horse for company. A horse who hated thunderstorms as well. Alys could hear the rain pelting against the heavy stone walls of the tower, mixed with the intermittent sound of thunder, and she forced herself to calm down. Claire wasn't afraid of storms. Claire wasn't afraid of anything at all, and even on a stormy night like this she would somehow manage to find shelter, keep herself safe until she was found.

There was nothing more Alys could do for her. If she went out searching for her she would get lost herself. She had done her best—lied to her brother to keep his suspicions calm, and sent the one man she could trust to find Claire. If Thomas couldn't find her, no one could. And Thomas wouldn't rest until he did.

The thunder cracked again, and Alys shivered. Her stomach was empty, her nerves were stretched tight, her whole body felt tense and strained and abnormally sensitive to everything around her, heat and light and sound. But she was safe within the thick walls of the tower, safe at least from the storm. Only if she were fool enough to climb the final flight of winding stairs to the parapet would she be in any danger from the lightning, and she had no reason to do such a foolhardy thing.

She would stay by the fire and await the coming of her husband. There was no escaping him, much as she wanted to. She was afraid of him as she had never admitted before. Afraid of the dangerous depths of his golden eyes, the touch of his hands on her skin. Afraid of his mouth, touching hers. Afraid of everything.

She would lose herself. Just as she had lost part of her memory of the night before, if she came to his bed the rest of her would simply disappear. She had begun to think of him as a Grendel monster after all. He wouldn't devour her body and drink her blood—he would eat her soul.

She slumped in sudden despair as the door opened, but it was only Godfrey, Simon's mute servant, carrying a tray. Dinner, she realized with a longing sniff. Warm pheasant and baked eels and cakes, sweet white bread and cheese and a ewer of wine as well.

He set it in front of her, and she saw with relief that there was only enough food for one. Only one goblet. She would have a peaceful last supper, at least.

She looked up at Godfrey's sober face, smiling her thanks. "Will my . . . will Lord Simon be joining me?"

Godfrey shook his head.

"Will he be coming later?" Stupid question, Alys chided herself, picking at the bread. Where else would he go?

But Godfrey shrugged, expressing uncertainty, and for some reason Alys's nervous stomach knotted even more tightly. She didn't want him there. But she didn't want him gone either.

"Where is he, Godfrey?" she asked, knowing he couldn't answer.

Few men could write. Fewer women could read. Godfrey moved to the tall desk and made a few laborious marks, then handed the paper to Alys. "On the parapet," it said. And for emphasis Godfrey jerked his head upward.

Overhead, in the storm. Alys crushed the paper in her hand, forcing a tremulous smile to her lips. "Thank you, Godfrey," she murmured.

She almost called him back when the door closed behind him. What in God's name was Simon doing up there on the battlements? No one was storming the castle, and in this kind of weather he wouldn't be able to see anything at all. Did he have a sudden longing to be struck by lightning? Or was he really empowered—could he control the elements, thunder, lightning, and rain? There were times when she almost believed it to be so.

But to believe that, she would have to believe that he worked with the powers of darkness, for there was no doubt whatsoever that Simon of Navarre was a far cry from a godly man.

He'd managed to wipe clean her memory from the night before. He managed to draw her to him so that she dreamed of his touch like a wanton, she who was frightened of men, she who should have been a celibate nun. He'd bewitched her, enchanted her, and she had no idea whether it was magic, witchcraft, or something far more elemental.

She forced herself to eat, though she had little appetite. She sat in the curved chair and stared into the fire, hypnotized by the dancing flames. She could hear the intermittent thunder, the lashing of the rain against the stone of the keep, and from the Great Hall she could hear echoes of raucous laughter. All would be well, she told herself, more a prayer than a certainty. Claire would be found, and protected.

Could he really be up on the battlements? What possible reason could Simon of Navarre have for walking along the parapet above his tower? The storm was fierce and deadly, the lightning coming so close at times she could smell the odd scent of it on the air. If he stayed up there he would die.

And she would be a widow. Free, perhaps, to enter the convent that had once seemed the only possible happiness for her. If she had any sense at all she would go lie down on the bed and sleep, praying for his death.

But she seemed to have lost all her sense. The wise, careful young woman had vanished, and she knew she was going up into the maw of danger, the gaping mouth of death, to find Simon of Navarre. To find her love.

Her feet were icy cold on the tower steps. She clung tightly to the twined rope that served as a handrail, and her gown trailed behind her on the stairs. By the first half turn the stone steps were wet from the rain dripping down from the opening, and she wished she'd worn shoes. But her shoes were in the east tower, with the rest of her few possessions and those belonging to her sister. It was an appealing thought—to race back across the rain-drenched courtyard and take shelter in the bed she had shared with Claire.

But there was no shelter to be found. The noise from the Great Hall faded away as she climbed, and she felt as if she were climbing into the sky, into the very heart of the storm itself. The past and safety lay behind her, Simon of Navarre lay ahead of her, and she had made her choice. She would stop fighting it, when it was what she wanted, and needed.

She was afraid of horses and storms and men. She was afraid of heights as well, and this was the first time she had ever climbed to the top of one of the four towers that surrounded Summersedge Keep. It was dark, and the pennons flapped wetly in the wind. She paused in the opening, cowering and hating herself for it as she tried to accustom her eyes to the darkness.

There was no other access to the turret. They were alone. He could throw her over the side with no one to witness it, and the only one who would mourn was Claire, who might already be dead in the forest.

She could see him now, standing with his back to her, facing into the pitch black night. Lightning sizzled all around him like a tapestry of stars and she watched in awe as it danced in the air about him. It sizzled downward, crashing onto the north tower, but he didn't flinch, even as Alys cowered in the opening to the parapet. He was dangerous, god-like, elemental, part of the night and the storm, as terrifying and powerful as a bolt of lightning.

He must have felt her eyes on him. He turned, slowly, to look at her huddled in the entryway. He'd discarded his formal robes. His thin cambric shirt was drenched, clinging to his body, and his hose were wet as well. He leaned against the parapet, watching her, not even blinking as the rain washed down his bleak face. Watching her, as the thunder echoed around them. Watching her.

She wanted to turn and run, as she'd wanted to ever since she first set eyes on the creature. The man, for that was what he was. But the fear and the longing fought against each other, bringing her closer, ever closer. Bringing her up a twisted flight of stairs in the dark of night, to face her nemesis across a wind-swept expanse of stone. She hadn't come this far just to run away.

She needed a sign from him, a word, but he'd given her none. She couldn't even remember what had gone on between them in the dark hours of the night before, but she knew it had been monumental. She was finally ready to surrender, body and soul, but she needed to know he would accept the sacrifice.

The rain had let up, turning into a thick, soft drizzle. "What do you want, Alys?" he asked in a cool, weary voice.

You. The answer was clear in her head, but she was afraid to say it. "It's raining," she said.

"Very observant." He pushed his long wet hair away from his face, sluicing some of the water away as well. "Did you come up to inform me of this?"

"There's lightning. It's dangerous."

"I know that as well. I'm not afraid of thunder and lightning, sweet Alys. I'm not afraid of horses or men or death or even the wrath of God. I'm not afraid of anything."

A faint ribbon of memory danced through her mind, and she spoke before she could think twice. "Except me," she said.

He froze, a statue in the dark, rain-swept night. "I have no reason to be afraid of you, Alys. Your own terrors will keep you well away from me." He moved his arm, and the lightning sizzled, followed by a loud clap of thunder.

Alys stumbled back onto the steps, and he laughed. It wasn't a pleasant sound. "You see," he said. "You don't know what you want, and even if you did, your fears won't let you reach for it. Go to bed, Alys. I won't touch you again."

Again. There was the word, proof that what she had forgotten had really happened. "Did you bed me last night?"

He smiled faintly. "Indeed. You weren't sure whether you liked it or not, but in the end you were quite . . . amenable."

"Why don't I remember? Is it witchcraft? A spell of some sort?"

"Drugs," he said succinctly. "You drank wine that was not meant for you, and the effect was calamitous. You were quite demanding, my love. A virgin bed was no longer an option you chose to accept."

She could feel her cheeks flame red, the only warm part in her frozen body. He seemed oblivious to the cold and the wet, standing out there in the light rain. "Is that why I forgot?"

"Either because of the drug, or the shame of remembering that you wanted me."

His eyes were cold. She didn't think golden eyes would ever be cold, but his were. Colder than the rain.

"Why have you come here, Alys?" he asked again. "What do you want?"

She had no answers, and he turned his back on her, staring out into the stormy night once more.

She took a step upward, bare foot on icy wet stone, and a streak of lightning sizzled nearby. She took another as the thunder followed it, and the rain began to increase.

She was being tested, and she wasn't sure who was doing it—a cantankerous wizard or a mischievous God. In the end it didn't matter. She took another step, out into the opening of the turret, certain that something or someone would strike her dead.

"What are you doing, Alys?" He'd turned to watch her, and his expression was disbelieving.

She'd emerged from the winding staircase to stand out in the open, but she hadn't yet been able to make her feet move further. "Facing my fears," she said in a wobbly voice.

"Courting death?"

"Are you going to kill me?"

"The lightning might."

"Are you going to kill me?" she persisted, flinching when the thunder rumbled again.

"Would you ride a horse for me?" he countered.

"Yes."

"Would you walk across this parapet to come to me?"

"Yes." And she started forward, shivering, as the rain lashed down around them.

He watched her with the quiet intensity of a man watching an acrobat walk across a narrow wire. He said nothing, made no gesture, as she slowly came toward him. She halted just out of reach, lifting her head and throwing back her shoulders with quiet determination.

"Would you come to me?" she asked him.

"Yes," he said. And he crossed the last few feet of parapet and pulled her into his arms, kissing her mouth.

He was wet, and his shirt clung as she pulled it off him. He tasted of rain and the night, and he ripped the laces in her gown as he stripped it from her, throwing it on the hard stone floor to make a pallet. He lowered her down onto it with surprising care, tearing at her thin chemise, and then she was lying naked beneath the rain and the storm, the angry heavens and Simon of Navarre's golden eyes.

She wanted him to take her quickly, so that she could remember, but he moved slowly, almost in a trance, as his scarred hand moved across her body, touching her, and everywhere he touched she was warm, blazing. He kissed her mouth, using his tongue, and she kissed him back, sliding her arms around his waist and holding him, reveling in the feel of his rain-slick flesh, the sinew and muscle and the terrible tapestry of scars. He kissed her throat, the tips of her breasts, and she arched up with an inarticulate cry, needing more. He put his hand between her legs, and she was frightened, but she parted them willingly enough, letting him touch her, stroke her, leaning back and closing her eyes to the rain as he moved down and put his mouth where his hand had been, put his tongue where his fingers had been.

She wanted to cry out, but she didn't dare. She was speechless, voiceless, lost in a liquid haze of frantic desire that was beyond her understanding. The lightning sizzled across the sky, and reaction sizzled across her body in perfect harmony, a spiking, shattering clash of feeling that made her stiffen and cry out.

The thunder rumbled and roared, and her heart pounded, drowning it out. She was panting, weeping, and she wanted him to stop his wickedness, but it was too glorious, and she arched off the scattered clothes, searching for something that she couldn't understand.

He slid his fingers deep inside her as he touched her with his tongue, and she convulsed into a sudden darkness that felt like death. All around her demons beat their wings, or were they angels? She didn't know or care, lost in a torrent that tore her apart.

She had barely caught her breath when he was moving up, over her, resting between her legs where he'd kissed her. He caught her hands in his, the right hand so terribly scarred, the left smooth and elegant, and she watched him, watched his eyes drift closed as he pushed deep inside her, filling her.

There was no pain this time, no resistance. She was sleek and wet and ready for him. Damp, she'd been told. Gloriously damp. And she was.

Her body already knew the rhythms, even if her mind had forgotten. She arched her hips willingly, taking all of him, and his thrusts were deep, steady, rocking her back against the discarded clothing.

She wanted more. She wanted him to open his eyes and look down at her, to know who he was with. His wet hair hung down and tangled with hers, the rain beat down on their naked bodies, but there was heat everywhere, her body was on fire, and she wanted more.

He knew. He opened his eyes and looked at her as the pace increased, and she was caught in the tangle of his eyes, staring up at him as her body received him, faster now, harder, deeper, and she still wanted more. She was crying, she wasn't sure why, but he licked the tears from her face and kissed her with them. She wanted to hold him, but her hands were trapped beneath his, and all she could do was absorb him, take him, as he was taking her, steal his soul and make it her own.

She wanted more. She wanted his love, she wanted his child. She was greedy now, and wanted everything. Her skin felt hot and prickly, her breath was fighting against her pounding heart, and she knew she would die. She didn't care. She wanted more.

"Now," he said. It was a whisper, a mere breath of sound, his mouth at her ear. And she was the one who gave, everything in that very moment, convulsing around him, lost and given, death and rebirth, body and soul.

And he was with her.

Chapter Twenty-One

Simon wrapped his wife in her discarded dress, lifting her limp body from the stone floor of the turret with ease. She laid her head against his chest and closed her eyes as the water sluiced down over her, but she was too drained to do more than simply breathe.

He carried her down the winding stairs to the bedroom. The fire was blazing, filling the room with light and warmth, and he laid her down on the bed with exquisite gentleness, tossing the ruined clothes on the floor, and covering her with soft fur throws. He pushed the wet hair away from her face, framing her cheeks with his two hands, and looked down into her eyes. He wasn't sure what he would see there. Regret, condemnation, confusion.

She reached up and covered his hands with hers. Their hands, pressed together, seemed almost painfully intimate, but she wouldn't let him escape. "You are mine," she said in a fierce little voice.

The words startled him, but he didn't move. She was

a woman who claimed very little, who sacrificed all that mattered to her for the sake of others.

But she wouldn't sacrifice him. She held his hands against her face and stared up at him with calm determination. He was hers, she said. And she was right.

"Go to sleep, Alys," he said gently, letting his thumb caress her swollen mouth. He'd kissed her too hard, and he should regret it. Regret the marks his loving had made on her body.

But he didn't. Instead he reveled in them. She was his, he was hers, for however long fate granted them, and that was enough.

He tried to pull away, determined to let her rest, but she caught his arm, and she was strong. "Not without you," she said.

He looked down at her. Her wet hair was spread out beneath her, her face was pale and dreamy. She looked well-loved, and that was the unbearable truth. He had loved her. He did love her. And that would be his downfall.

He should move away, kiss her lightly and dismiss her. He'd entered into this marriage knowing it would only last as long as it suited him, as long as this life suited him. When things became tricky he would disappear, abandoning his young wife and whatever he had earned, and take only Godfrey and what wealth was easily transportable.

And Alys of Summersedge, Alys of Navarre, was not easily transportable. She was afraid of horses, she couldn't ride, and as fate would have it, speed would be an important part of his escape. She would hold him back and destroy him, and the sooner he pulled away from her, the better.

Her hands were light against his, insistent. He could break free with no trouble at all. "I won't leave you,"

he said. And he lay down on the bed beside her, pulling
her into his arms.

When Alys awoke the tower room was deserted. She
lay naked in the bed, alone, the fur throw pulled tight
around her. The gown she'd worn lay in a sodden heap
on the floor, the fire had burned low, and cool sunlight
pierced the windows, sending bright shadows across the
floor. The storm had passed, and she should have been
relieved.

"I won't leave you," he'd said, and he'd come to bed
with her, and the night had been endless and shatter-
ingly beautiful. He had done things she couldn't imagine, coaxed her into touching him, tasting him, taking
him until she was weeping and shaking, lost in some
strange world where only the two of them existed.

But he was gone, and she was alone.

She sat up, trying to still the sense of uneasiness that
washed over her. Something was wrong. Something was
dreadfully wrong. She scrambled out of bed, searching
for something to cover herself with. None of her clothes
were there, and she settled for one of Simon's plain
black tunics. It was so long it trailed on the floor, and
the sleeves draped halfway to her knees, but at least she
was decently covered when the soldiers burst through
the door.

"You'll come with me, my lady." She didn't recognize
the knight in charge of them, nor would it have done
her any good. Her questions were ignored, her protests
stifled, and she was dragged from the tower room with
uncaring force.

She screamed for Simon, but someone clapped a
hand over her mouth, silencing her. She kicked, but it
was useless against the heavy leather boots of the sol-

diers. She bit, and an arm caught her along the side of her head, and everything went black.

She awoke in blackness, in a darkness so thick it was like death. She was freezing cold, lying on something hard and unforgiving, and she could hear the soft, scuffling noises that could only be rodents' feet.

She didn't scream. Much as she wanted to, she clamped her teeth shut, stilling the panic that threatened to break forth. She was afraid that if she started screaming she would never stop, and the stone walls would echo with her madness.

She forced herself to breathe slowly, deeply, summoning calm in the midst of her panic. She knew where she was. Even though she'd never seen them in her life, the knowledge was immutable. She was locked in the dungeons of Summersedge Keep.

Who had put her there? Only Richard had the power to command such a thing, but why in God's name would he do so? She had done him no harm, except to protect her sister from his twisted urges.

There was another, far more sinister possibility, one she shied away from even as it sprang into her mind. Had he locked her away at the request of his favored advisor? Had his wizard told him to dispose of an unwanted wife? With the marriage and the bedding her political worth had been exhausted. Perhaps she had no more value and was simply being put away, to be forgotten until decades from now when someone came across her bones?

She sat up, shivering in the damp chill, and peered into the darkness surrounding her. A faint light emanated from the far wall, and she rose, moving toward it, toward the iron grille that kept her prisoner. Beyond lay another room, dimly lit, though this one looked more like a crypt than a dungeon. A woman lay stretched on the stone slab floor, but Alys had little hope she was alive. The form was too stocky to be Claire, and for that she breathed a heartfelt prayer of thanks.

One bar of the grille obscured her vision, and she rose on tiptoes to get a closer look, peering at the face of the dead woman. She fell back with a cry of horror.

Lady Hedwiga would give no more misguided lectures on comportment in the marriage bed. She was well and truly dead.

"It's quite simple," Richard said smoothly. He was dressed in full mourning, and he'd wept, openly and fulsomely, as he'd accepted the condolences of his people. His eyes were still red-rimmed as he closeted himself with his wizard, but his mask of mourning had transformed into smug glee.

"Simple, my lord?" Simon echoed. He knew when to be wary, when life had taken a particularly dangerous turn. As it had this morning, when he'd come down to the news that Richard the Fair's lady had died in her sleep.

"You shouldn't underestimate me, Grendel," Richard said, smoothing his beer-dewed mustache with a stubby finger. "I can be just as clever as you can, in my own way. Hedwiga has always been burdensome. The sleeping draught needed to be tested. Unfortunately my lady wife proved frailer than I expected."

"You murdered her," Simon said, keeping his voice calm. It should have come as no surprise. Richard was capable of that and more. If Simon hadn't been so besotted by his wife he would have seen it coming. Not that he would necessarily have stopped him, but he had a dislike of surprises.

Richard smiled sweetly. "Whether she was murdered or not remains to be seen."

"Why?"

"It may have simply been a tragic accident. After all, Alys didn't realize how strong the draught was when she gave it to my sickly wife. Or, at least, that's what I would hope. I would hate to think my sister was a cold-blooded murderer."

"Alys?" He showed absolutely no emotion. He was beyond reaction. "Why would Alys have murdered your wife?"

"Now that part troubled me," Richard confided. "Why would a demure, practical creature such as Alys want to murder Hedwiga? Apart from the fact that anyone who met her would want to murder Hedwiga," he added cheerfully. "The fact remains that several of my servants and men at arms saw her enter Hedwiga's room with a goblet and vial just before evensong. She was the last person to see her alive."

"Alys was in my solar. . . ."

"No one saw her, Grendel. And no one would believe you."

"She had no reason. . . ."

"Witchcraft, Grendel. She was invaded by demons that forced her to commit such a hideous act." He took another leisurely sip of ale.

"Then it's not her fault."

"Ah, but how do you get rid of demons? Only by destroying the host. You know what they do to women convicted of murder, don't you? They're buried alive."

"Where is she?" He kept the hoarse desperation from his voice by sheer willpower.

"In the dungeons. In a cell next to the body of my wife, where she may look upon her and contemplate her sins."

"You can't do this."

"Simon of Navarre, I have."

He could kill him, quite easily. Richard was thickly muscled, but he'd grown soft with age and meat and drink, and he'd be no match for Simon's height and skill. But that wouldn't help Alys.

If it weren't for Alys this would all be very simple. He would kill Richard the Fair and escape.

If it weren't for Alys he would never have been caught in this trap in the first place. Richard would have no power over him, other than his own greed.

He sat down, leaning back in the chair, surveying his lord with deceptive idleness. "So what is it you want, my lord?" he asked in a curious voice. He already knew the answer.

"What I have always wanted. Your loyalty and devotion. Your dedication to my best interests. Your assistance in helping my plans come to fruition."

"You want me to kill the king."

"Such bluntness!" Richard protested. "But in a word, yes."

"What made you think I wouldn't be willing to do it for you? Your interests are mine. I would rather serve the King of England than a second class earl."

Richard's face darkened for a moment. And then he laughed. "Ah, Grendel, your boldness enchants me. And I have no reason to doubt your loyalty. I merely believe in making certain that my allies are well-motivated."

"And I'm supposed to care whether Lady Alys is judged guilty of a murder she didn't commit, and sentenced to a brutal death?"

"Don't you?" Richard asked, eyeing him curiously.

"Not particularly. She's a clever enough wench, but no great beauty. Her main value is in her kinship to you, and if you choose to dispense with that kinship, and her, then she's of no value to me. I would do as you bid, regardless.''

"Almost, dear Grendel, I believe you. But you must confess you were surprisingly laggard in your production of the sleeping draught. And you've been . . . odd, recently. Distracted. I assumed my stone-hearted demon had fallen prey to Cupid's dart.''

Simon just looked at him, and Richard laughed.

"Foolish me," he said. "I should have realized you would be impervious to such weaknesses. Now the other one, Claire, she's a tidy handful. It's easy to grow foolish over such beauty. But you're such an odd creature, you didn't even want her.''

"I leave her to you, my lord," he said in a silky voice.

"And I believe I'll take her," Richard said. "As soon as she recovers from the stomach grippe. Can't abide spewing women. Hedwiga cast up her accounts before she died, you know. I was afraid she'd purged herself of the poison, but God was on my side.''

"Indeed," Simon murmured.

Richard leaned forward across the table. "You know the truly horrifying thing about the whole affair? She became amorous!" He shuddered in ghastly remembrance.

"It does have that effect," Simon murmured, his brain working feverishly. So Richard didn't know that Claire had run away. That might be put to good advantage, though at the moment he couldn't see how.

"I almost had to strangle her, which would have complicated matters, but fortunately she spewed and died.''

"Fortunately." Simon kept his right hand twisted beneath the long sleeve of his robe. It was clenched in a tight fist of rage. "When do we leave for court, my lord?''

Richard beamed at him. "That's my Grendel. I'm a man in mourning, but the young king and his regent will overlook that detail in my zeal to present my condolences. After all, Hedwiga was a cousin to the boy as well."

"And what of Alys?" he asked with what sounded like no more than idle curiosity. "If you don't intend to charge her then you might as well set her free."

"You care so much for your plain little wife?"

"You should know me better than that. I have no need of her, and she's an annoyance. Send her back to the convent if you like. One with a vow of silence. Then she need trouble us no longer."

"But what if she's with child?" Richard asked with cunning sweetness. "Or is she still a maid?"

It was a question Simon had no desire to answer. No desire even to contemplate. But he had to be extremely careful with exactly what he divulged to Richard. "She's no longer a maid," he said casually. "Though I doubt she'll quicken with child."

"Some of your Arab tricks, eh, Grendel? Well, I like 'em that way myself on occasion."

"So you'll have her released from her captivity?" He made it sound as if it were of the least importance to him.

"Oh, no, Grendel. I would fear for her life. I'm afraid too many of the servants have been gossiping, and they're afraid of her. They think she's been tainted by her association with my wizard, and they firmly believe she killed my wife. They're afraid of you, but they're perfectly willing to put her to death." He smiled sweetly. "Besides, I need guarantee of your good behavior. We'll take her with us."

"You don't need any guarantee, and I have little interest in what happens to her."

"Then why do you keep asking about her?" Richard counted.

Simon managed a cool smile. "Guilty conscience?" he suggested. "She's only an innocent."

"You have no conscience, Grendel, and I would have said you have no heart. Nevertheless, Lady Alys will accompany us to court, and we will present her case to his majesty."

"She'll be an inconvenience. She doesn't ride." He kept the desperation out of his voice, but he doubted Richard was fooled.

"That's not a problem, dear friend. She'll be traveling in a barred cage."

For Claire the night had been endless. Somehow she managed to sleep, curled up in a tight ball beneath the fallen trees. Her clothes were soaked from the rain above and the ground below, her wrist was swollen and throbbing with pain, and she was desperately hungry.

She wasn't alone in the woods, she knew that much. She wasn't sure which she feared more—wild boar or civilized men. Both were deadly; neither could be reasoned with. And Claire was beyond reasoning.

When she awoke it was close to dawn, though the light barely penetrated the darkness of the ancient forest. The rain had stopped at last, with not even a stray rumble of errant thunder. She ducked her head out from her makeshift shelter, and her hair caught on one of the branches. She reached up to release it and gasped with pain. Her wrist was bruised and swollen, throbbing with such pain that she could barely raise it. She yanked her hair free with her other hand, leaving long, silken strands enmeshed in the fallen tree, and moved into the clearing.

There was no sign of Arabia. At least she was bridle-
less; there were no trailing reins to get caught in the
trees as she ran in desperation. For that matter, Claire
was righteously annoyed with her beloved mare. Had it
not been for Arabia's skittishness she would never have
fallen, and she wouldn't be cradling what was likely a
broken hand.

She sneezed, loudly, three times in a row, and her
temper didn't improve. She wanted warm dry clothes,
she wanted something to eat, and she wanted her sister
to fuss over her, to wrap her damaged hand in herb-
soaked bandages to bring down the swelling. She wanted
to be taken care of, but there was no one to turn to but
herself.

She kicked her long skirts out of the way and started
walking in what she hoped was a north-westerly direction. Back to the Convent of Saint Anne the Demure,
back to safety and the stern care of the nuns.

She found berries to eat, and fresh water to drink.
The sun grew hot enough that the rain-soaked forest
grew moist and sticky, but still she walked, her wet
leather shoes sloshing uncomfortably around her feet.
The thought of Alys, trapped with the cruel and heartless wizard, panicked her, but there was nothing she
could do but pray that her sister pass through her time
of trial and torment with as little pain as possible.

She prayed for herself as well—that she might stop
her endless wanderings and find a clear path to safety.

She prayed for her brother too, though she doubted
that God would grant those particularly bloodthirsty
petitions.

She even prayed for Arabia, ungrateful beast that she
was, that she'd find safe shelter, not in her brother's
stable, but someplace where she would be appreciated
and loved.

It was the same that she wished for herself.

There was one more soul to pray for, one she'd avoided thinking about. Sir Thomas du Rhaymer deserved her prayers, for the loss of his wife, for his stern attention to duty. She should thank God he was stalwart and honorable.

She tripped over a root and went sprawling, her injured hand taking the brunt of the jarring. She was wet and hungry and miserable, and she lay in the muddy grass and wept, ugly, noisy tears of pain and sorrow and regret. She wept for all of them, for her sins and her selfishness. And in the end she wept for Thomas, wanting him, needing him.

She was lying in the mud having a temper tantrum, there was no other word for it. Thomas had heard her angry squalls from a long way away, and he'd known with a certain grim humor that it was his quarry. His lady love, his heart's delight, lying in the mud, kicking her heels and howling like a babe.

She was a spoiled brat and he knew it. She had spent her short young life getting her own way by dint of her beautiful face and her wheedling charm. Someone should have spanked her lovely little arse when she was a child, but he suspected that no one had had the heart to.

It was too late for that now, even though it might have done her some good. He'd married Gwyneth, and now he'd buried her, and in her grave he'd buried his regrets and dour soul. He was a free man, and his love lay sprawled in the mud, screeching. In faith, it was a glorious day.

She didn't even hear him approach, so caught up in her self-pity that she was oblivious to everything. He slid off his horse and tethered the reins to a nearby bush. Not that Paladin would run off—he was properly trained, unlike her ladyship's spoiled mount. But Thomas was a careful man at all times.

He came to stand over her, and even within the shadowy forest he blocked the fitful sunlight. She grew suddenly still, but she didn't dare look up.

"You should be glad I'm not a wild boar, or you would truly have something to weep about," he said in his most practical voice.

He was unprepared for her response. In seconds she was on her knees, and then she launched herself at him, throwing herself into his arms.

He was unprepared for it, and he went down beneath her, his arms coming around her immediately, cushioning their fall. She looked a sight—her face was streaked with tears and mud, her nose was running, her hair was tangled and full of snarls and brambles, her once pretty gown was ripped and torn and filthy. And to his smitten eyes she had never looked lovelier.

"Thomas," she cried, and there was an ache in her voice that he couldn't resist. "Thomas." And that was all she said, as she wrapped one arm tight around him and held him as if he were her only link with safety.

He should get up and disentangle himself. He should put a distance between them. She was a young, foolish, willful girl who didn't know her own mind, and he needed to be wise, to protect her from men like himself.

"Thomas," she said again, with a sigh of relief that sounded perilously close to love. He put his hand beneath her chin to tilt her tear-swollen face to his, to assure her he would keep her safe, but she looked so lost, so woebegone, that he couldn't resist her. Leaning down, he kissed her, when he knew he shouldn't, pulling her damp, bedraggled body closer to his, deepening the kiss as she opened her mouth for him, and he knew that he was lost. Hopelessly, irrevocably lost.

And he wasn't going to let her go back.

Chapter Twenty-Two

It was a slow, laborious procession northward. King Henry the Third, the boy king of England, was in residence at one of his castles near York, and the trip from Somerset seemed to take forever.

Not that Simon of Navarre was in any particular hurry to arrive there. He had yet to figure out a way to extricate Alys from her captivity, and each day as they drew nearer he felt his options vanish.

Richard had seen to it that he'd had no chance to talk to her. She was kept closely guarded in that damned cage that at least resembled a carriage. She had cushions and throws and plenty to eat, her every comfort seen to. Richard had a certain wicked cunning—he knew that if he abused her too sorely he would lose Simon's unwilling cooperation. But if he released her he would no longer have anything to hold over Simon's head.

Simon kept his expression blank, his gaze forward as they plodded along the rutted roads heading toward the north of England. It was growing colder with each passing day as the winter approached, and his fur-lined mantle was little protection against the bitter wind. He was heading north, for the first time since he'd left, and with each tedious day of travel he felt disaster looming ever larger.

He was eighteen years old when he left the North of England, young and pious and newly knighted, filled with a crusader's zeal. He would right the wrongs of this world, he would. Free the Holy Lands and win his place in heaven. He would return, loaded with riches and honors, and win back his family's place in the world. He would regain the lost manor house and lands that King John had torn away from them and passed to another favorite. He would live in peace and harmony, with justice for those who served him.

God, he'd been young! Even then he knew there was no bringing back his mother, dead from cholera, or his father, dead from a drunken accident during a tourney that might just as well have been deliberate suicide. And he'd learned in the ensuing years just how ephemeral peace and harmony were, just what a joke the very notion of justice was.

The only way to survive was to see to your own interests. He'd learned that hard lesson, and all the good men he'd met over the years, the monks of St. Anselme's, the physicians of Arabia, the gypsies of Lombardy, and the ascetic scholars of Switzerland, had failed to convince him there was any alternative. His plan had been simple: amass all the wealth and power he could in the shortest amount of time. And keep himself inviolate from the people that surrounded him.

Alys of Summersedge had destroyed that notion. He should hate her for it, and part of him did. He was no longer the center of his own life, and that made things damnably complicated.

Killing the child of King John should never have been
a moral issue. King John had destroyed his family on a
whim—it was simple justice that Simon return the favor.
But he'd been reluctant from the very start, and he
wasn't certain he could blame that on Alys. Even before
she arrived at Summersedge Keep, he'd felt unsettled.

He refused to look back at the traveling carriage that
held her prisoner. He hadn't met her eyes since she
was brought forth from the dungeons—if he did he
might lose the icy composure that was one of his major
weapons. He had no idea what she thought of him, or
if she understood what had happened to her. That she
would despise him was a given. That she blamed him
was also likely. How would she feel when he freed her?
If he freed her?

He huddled deeper into his cloak. She had piles of
fur throws in her litter; she had curtains drawn against
the wind, and against curious eyes. She would be safe
enough for the time being. And if she was sentenced
to die he would strangle her himself before he let her
endure the torture of being buried alive.

She was being taken to her death. Alys knew it with
calm instinct. The endless days of bouncing over the
horrible roads made execution seem almost a delightful
alternative. Almost.

She had no intention of going quietly, however. She
had refused to confess to witchcraft and the unholy
murder of Lady Hedwiga, despite Richard's pleasant
assertion that her confession was not needed and would
only make things easier for her. There were enough
witnesses, her husband included. And Alys didn't know
who to believe, who to trust. Or whether, in the long
run, she even cared.

Would they burn her? She hoped not. She had never seen anyone burned, but she suspected it would be the most unpleasant of deaths. Having her head lopped off would be a marked improvement. She had seen the severed heads of criminals and found them extremely unsettling, but if it were her own head then she would no longer have eyes to see it.

Perhaps they'd toss her into the sea. She couldn't swim, of course, but she'd heard that drowning was not an unpleasant way to die.

Or would they choose the cruelest, kindest death of all? Would they have Simon of Navarre administer the same poison that he'd used to kill Lady Hedwiga before laying the blame on her?

Would he be merciful? Would he make certain her death was swift and sure? She no longer cared.

She lay back amidst the fur throws, closing her eyes. Why had he done it? Why had he denounced her as a murderess? For that matter, why had he killed a querulous old woman who was essentially harmless?

The answer was simple. He had done it for gain. He had done it for his lord and master. Richard had bade him do it, and it was done.

Perhaps they would hang her. Would Claire come and hang on her body, to speed the process? Or was she safely away, with Thomas du Rhaymer to protect her? Alys tried to summon anxiety but found she couldn't. For once in her life her own situation took precedence. Claire could fend for herself.

They had stopped for the night. Alys pushed the curtains aside to watch the soldiers dismount, and Simon of Navarre moved into view. He was muffled in black, his long streaked hair flowing in the wind, and he looked cold and merciless. She could hear her brother, the new-made widower, laughing somewhere out of sight, and she half expected Simon to join him.

She willed Simon to look in her direction, fiercely determined that he should see what he had done. He was strong enough to resist the lure of her gaze, but he turned anyway, his expression as bleak as the harsh wind that swept down over them.

Richard came up behind him, slapping an arm around his shoulders. "We need some warm ale and warm women," he said. "Damn this blasted weather!"

Simon turned to look at him, and Alys waited, hopelessly, for him to denounce him. To demand her freedom, to threaten him, kill him, if he didn't release her.

"I'll settle for the warm ale," he said evenly.

Alys flung herself back against the cushions. Another night in her luxurious cage, huddled beneath the thick fur throws. In truth, she was probably more comfortable than the creature who was her husband, but she felt trapped, crazed by the bars that surrounded her. She had never had a fondness for dark, enclosed places, and day after day of imprisonment was wearing at her soul.

They were going to see the King—she'd been told that much and little more by the men who guarded her, and by the pale, frightened Madlen who'd been brought along to attend to her needs. She would be brought before the child king and he would pass judgment on her crimes.

If Claire was safe she no longer cared what happened to her. She would endure, as long as she must, and if she died she would come back and haunt Simon of Navarre like Grendel's mother—a vengeful hag to drive him mad.

She despised him. She despised herself, for her weakness, for her futile attempts at discerning a reason for

Simon's betrayal. There could be no reason, no justification.

And the worst part of all were her dreams. She would dream she lay in his arms, his face pressed against hers, his scarred hand cradling her. She would dream that he loved her, when he never had. And when she woke she would weep silently in her elegant cage.

Thomas might have lost his head and betrayed everything he held dear if Claire hadn't cried out in sudden pain. Her mouth was full and sweet beneath his, her damp, bedraggled body warm and irresistible, and she kissed him back with such desperate fervor, and he wanted her so urgently, that he might have forgotten everything and taken her there among the moss and fallen leaves, and she would have welcomed him.

Her reluctant cry of pain was followed by a strangled protest as he pulled away from her, but sanity had returned, whether he welcomed it or not. She sat amidst the lichen and the leaves, her gown tattered and mud-stained, looking up at him with such soulful longing that he almost reached for her again. And then he saw the swollen wrist she was trying to hide from him.

"Is it broken then?" he asked, his voice unnaturally harsh.

She didn't flinch. "I don't know. I fell on it when Arabia threw me."

"Your horse threw you?" he echoed in astonishment.

"She's afraid of lightning." Claire straightened her back, immediately defensive.

"I thought you were a better horsewoman." He said it deliberately, to push her away, when he was so afraid he'd reach for her again.

"I thought you were a better protector," she shot back. Her eyes filled with fresh tears.

"I failed you," he said evenly, taking her swollen hand in his with infinite gentleness. She bit her lip but didn't cry out as he slowly, carefully examined it. "I will never forgive myself for that."

"Don't be silly," she said, immediately contrite. "You had more pressing obligations."

"To a woman who had already relinquished all claim to my care, and who no longer needed it." He set her hand back in her lap. "I don't think the bone is broken."

"It hurts," she said, faintly fretful.

"It will heal in God's time."

"How do you know?"

"I have faith," he said simply.

She lifted her eyes to his face, and he wished he could force himself to turn away. He couldn't. She could see the hopeless love in his face if she chose to recognize it, and he could only hope she would ignore it.

A foolish hope. She leaned forward and pressed her soft mouth against his in a sweet, tempting kiss. "Will you marry me, Thomas du Rhaymer?"

He jerked back from her in shock. "What?"

"Will you marry me?" she repeated. "I have decided that I want no one but you, and I am very used to getting what I want in this life."

"Your brother would never allow it."

"We won't ask him. We won't go anywhere near him. We can sail for France and wander the countryside. You can live by your sword and I'll cook for you," she said, growing more enthusiastic.

He stared at her, bemused. "You can cook?"

"No," she confessed. "But I'm certain I can learn."

"There is no need, my lady," he said in a reproving

voice. "I will keep you safe, I've sworn my life on it, and I won't fail you again. I have houses and lands of my own. My mother will make you welcome."

"And you will marry me?" she persisted.

He shook his head. "You need to marry a man with far more wealth than I possess, my lady. You need a man with a light heart and a merry soul."

"I'll lighten your heart, Thomas," she said.

Little did she know she was tearing his heart apart. He shook his head, doing his best to keep his expression distant and austere. "No," he said. "I will not marry you."

He wasn't sure whether he expected relief or displeasure from her. He got neither. She simply nodded. "Very well," she said calmly. "I shall simply have to be your leman." And she launched herself against him, ignoring her wounded wrist.

He fell back among the leaves as she covered his face with inexpert kisses, and he reached out to push her away, only to find that his hands were kneading her arms, and he was kissing her back with an unholy fervor, drinking the honey sweetness of her mouth.

He tried to extricate himself, but she clutched him tightly, despite her injury. To get away from her he would have to hurt her, and that was something he simply could not do. He tried not to respond to her kisses, but that was another thing beyond his suddenly limited capabilities. He could no more keep from kissing her than he could keep the sun from rising and setting. He loved her, and there was no way he could deny it, or her.

Her breasts were small, beautifully shaped, and she took his hand and placed it on her, and his fingers cupped her instinctively. He tried to sit up, but she simply climbed astride him, so that she was cradled in his lap, and he told himself he could stop fighting, at least for a moment.

She was breathless, laughing, when she lifted her head to look at him. "You'd best change your mind, good knight," she said. "If you won't wed me I'll seduce you, putting both our souls in mortal danger."

"My lady . . ." he protested helplessly.

The light vanished from her eyes. "Thomas," she said simply, "don't you want me?"

She looked as if she might cry once more, and he knew he couldn't bear it if he were the cause of her tears. "Claire," he said, "a man would be mad not to want you. I want you with every breath in my body, every drop of blood that moves through my veins. I want you so much I could die from it."

An impish grin lit her face. "Then have me."

And he knew he would. He would have her without her family's blessing; he would have her knowing she could do so much better for herself. He would have her, and he would never let her go.

He moved with surprising swiftness, surging off the forest floor, and she would have landed in an ignominious heap if he hadn't caught her good arm and dragged her up against him. "Not without a priest's blessing."

She blinked in disbelief. "You'll wed me? Because I forced you?"

He was perversely pleased to see his love could be as irrational as most women. Now that she'd gotten her way she seemed suspicious.

"No, my lady," he said with great patience, picking the leaves out of her tangled hair. "I'll wed you because I love you."

"Why? Because I'm comely?"

It was an obvious enough reply, but he had the sense to know that his bride wouldn't be pleased with it. He picked a twig out of her hair. "My love," he said with great patience, "your hair is a rat's nest. Your eyes are swollen from weeping, your nose is red, your clothing is tattered, and your face is streaked with mud. You are still beyond passing fair, but not enough to tempt my immortal soul." He wiped a patch of mud from her delicate cheekbone. "I love you because you have a fierce heart, a brave soul, a tender touch, and a woman's grace. I love you for a thousand reasons that I can't even begin to understand, when I didn't want to love you at all. I love your mind and your heart and soul, and yes, I love your pretty face as well. But I'll love you when you're an old crone as well."

"I'll never be an old crone," Claire said with great confidence, clearly pleased with his confession. "I expect I'll be a great beauty even when I'm fifty."

"I expect you will," he agreed solemnly. "And why would you be marrying me? For my strong right arm?"

"Of course not," she said briskly, picking twigs out of her gown. "I've had a long time to think about it. I love you because you can't resist me, no matter how much you disapprove of me. I love you because you're not afraid of my brother, you're not afraid of the wizard, and you're not afraid of my frowns. I have a thousand reasons as well for deciding that only you will suit me, but I think that most of all I'm marrying you for your pretty face."

He threw back his head and laughed, the sound ringing through the forest, and she looked at him in shock. "I've never heard you laugh before," she said ingenuously. "You should do it more often."

"You'll have to ride pillion with me. Paladin is strong enough for the extra weight, and I'm in no mind to see if that devil mare of yours decides to return."

"We're in a hurry?"

"We need a priest, my lady. You may have no care for your immortal soul, but I'm not so lax about such matters. I'll have you with the church's blessing and not before."

She looked at him, and there was a look in her eyes that in any other but an innocent he would have called pure desire. "Let's find a priest," she said, starting for his horse.

They dragged her from her sleep in the midst of the darkness, rough hands pulling at her, yanking her out of the cage. She could hear Madlen's useless protests as they hurried her away, and she wondered if they were going to kill her now, without further delay? If she weren't so weary she would probably care.

They took her to the magnificent tent that had been erected, one knight that she didn't recognize pushing her through the opening, his gloved hand painful on her upper arm. She tripped, sprawling on the thick carpet, and for a moment she kept her head down, keeping her hatred a secret.

"There's my little sister now!" Richard boomed in a cheerful voice.

She raised her head. Richard reclined against a vast pile of pillows. His beard was stained with grease, his face red from wine or heat, and he watched her from chill, evil eyes devoid of feeling. She didn't bother to look at the man beside him, knowing it was useless. Simon of Navarre would give nothing away. He would simply stare at her as if she were an insignificant insect.

Changing her mind, she allowed herself the luxury of glancing his way, just to solidify her rage, when the man who'd brought her to the tent gave her a rough shove with his foot, halfway to a kick.

Simon surged to his feet, and the man fell back with a muttered oath. "Touch her again," Simon said in a soft, silken voice, "and I'll feed your entrails to the crows."

Richard bellowed with laughter as the knight stumbled from the tent, away from Simon's golden eyes. "You're possessive of the wench, Grendel," he said, belching. "I wonder why?"

Simon sat again, and the furious glow in his eyes faded to watchfulness. "I have a dislike of seeing helpless creatures abused," he said mildly.

"Since when?" Richard didn't bother waiting for an answer, leaning forward and fixing his piggy little eyes on his half sister. "Are you ready to confess, Alys?"

"Confess to what?"

"The murder of my lady wife, of course. Unless you have other crimes to confess as well."

"I had no reason to harm Lady Hedwiga," she said helplessly.

"So you say. I care not for your motive. I have three servants who saw you with her. That will more than suffice for His Majesty." There was a faint note of ridicule in his voice as he mentioned the king.

"I didn't. . . ."

"You know what they do to women convicted of murder, don't you? They bury them alive. It takes a while, and they do tend to scream, at least until the dirt fills their mouths and weighs down their bodies."

She stared at her brother in horror. "No," she whispered.

"The executioner usually covers the head last. So the criminal has time to think on her crime and the justice being meted out." He took another gulp of wine.

"I didn't kill Lady Hedwiga."

"I say you did. And no one will dispute me, isn't that the truth of it, Grendel?"

"Leave her be." Simon's voice was sharp and cool, and Richard turned to stare at him in mock dismay.

" 'Leave her be?' " he echoed. "I swear you have a fondness for the girl."

"You aren't going to have her killed, and tormenting her is needlessly cruel."

Richard's thick lips curled in a smile. "Cruelty isn't needless," he said. "I enjoy it."

Alys rose with deceptive grace, thankful that her long skirts hid the trembling in her cramped legs. "If you have no further questions of me, brother," she used the term with deliberation, "then I would prefer to return to my cage."

"Just one, my pet. I must confess you're hostage for Simon's good behavior. He insists that you're an annoyance that he has no use for, but I find I cannot quite believe him."

Alys darted a shocked glance at him, but as usual Simon's expression gave away nothing at all.

"What I wish to know, dear Alys, is did he deflower you?"

She didn't blush. She could keep her own face equally emotionless. "Why would you wish to know?"

"Well, there's no telling how this little drama will end. You may die at the hands of an executioner, or Simon might very well end up with his head parting company with his body. Anything is possible. You're a commodity, Alys, a useful one, but no man wants another man's brat to inherit his lands. I want to make sure there's no bun in the oven if I choose to wed you elsewhere."

"I'm already married in the eyes of God."

"If he was incapable of fathering children then the

marriage can be annulled." He picked his teeth with
the point of his dagger. "I find that I'm not so eager
to let Claire go to some wealthy baron in return for
loyalty. I have . . . plans for her. So you will be the chosen
one. Answer the question, Alys. Did Grendel take your
maidenhead?"

"I know no Grendel."

"Don't be tiresome, wench. Did Simon of Navarre
tup you? Did he bed you as other men would bed you?"

"I've lived my life in a convent, brother. I know nothing of other men."

"You're a learned women!" he shouted. "And you're
no fool! Did he bed you as any other man would bed
you?"

She met Simon's golden eyes for a breathless
moment. "No," she said. Simon smiled faintly.

Richard let out a shout of triumph. "I thought not!
You may have some value after all, for such a plain little
creature. Behave yourself, and I just might forget about
this poison nonsense."

"Poison nonsense?" she echoed.

"Servants can be mistaken. They're barely human as
it is. Go back to your cage, Alys, and think on your sins.
Pray for forgiveness, and thank God I married you to a
creature like Grendel."

Simon reached for his own goblet of wine, seemingly
inured to his lord's insults. His eyes met hers over the
rim of the goblet, but there was no reading his expression.

"I do, my lord," she said truthfully. "I do."

Chapter Twenty-Three

It was sheer luck that brought Claire and Thomas to the tiny church at the edge of the forest. Sheer luck that Brother Jerome had stopped to visit an old friend, and was standing in the portal of the stone church, watching their approach with disbelief and joy.

Claire immediately ceased tormenting Thomas with her small, strong hands, ducking her head behind his broad back as she felt an unaccustomed flush mount her face. Thomas was right—she wasn't particularly well-suited to illicit delights. However, she suspected she was most gloriously suited to licit ones, and she poked her head around Thomas's strong frame to grin at the priest.

"Will you marry us, Brother Jerome?" she called out.

Brother Jerome's delight faded into worry. "Is there need for haste?" he asked, catching the reins of Paladin and looking up at them.

Thomas slid down from the horse, then turned and caught Claire around her slender waist, his hands strong and warm as he lifted her down. "Need you ask?" he said evenly.

"With you, my son, no," Brother Jerome said. "With Lady Claire as temptation, however . . ."

"Thomas is very good at resisting temptation." Claire didn't bother to disguise the disgruntled tone in her voice.

"I am happy to hear that," Brother Jerome murmured. "Does your brother approve this wedding? You must know that it could be declared invalid if the lady's closest kin has not given permission."

"Lord Richard has no say in the matter," Thomas said flatly. "Either he is no kin to Lady Claire, and therefore has no say in her disposal, or he is the most unnatural of brothers, and cannot be trusted to see to her welfare."

Brother Jerome said nothing, staring at the two of them searchingly. Eventually he nodded. "I would be happy to do God's will and unite the two of you in marriage. But have you thought, my son? Lord Richard is a dangerous enemy."

"I will keep her safe."

"I am satisfied that you will. I could only wish someone would be able to help poor Lady Alys."

Claire was jolted out of her happy anticipation with the rudeness of a blow. "What do you mean?" she demanded in a hoarse voice.

Brother Jerome's face was stern. "You do not know? Haven't you heard? She's been accused of murder. Lord Richard is taking her north to see the King, to put her to judgment. If she's found guilty she'll be buried alive."

"Oh, God," Claire cried out. "She killed him?"

Brother Jerome looked confused. "She's accused of poisoning Lady Hedwiga."

Relief flooded her. "Lady Hedwiga is dead? But that's

ridiculous! Why would Alys do such a thing? And where would she come across poison?''

"Her brother has accused her of trafficking with the devil," Brother Jerome intoned.

"Well, of course," Claire snapped. "He had her marry him. What's her lord husband had to say to all this?''

"As far as I know, not a thing. I was sent from the Keep when they left for York, and all I've been able to do is pray for a just outcome.''

"A just outcome? My sister is no murderer, and you know that as well as I!''

Thomas put a restraining hand on her arm. "Brother Jerome has not accused her, love. He's only repeating what he knows. Where have they gone?''

"They're heading north along the North Road. King Henry is in residence at Middleham Castle.''

"How fast are they traveling? Surely they aren't making Alys ride?'' Claire demanded.

"I saw her placed in a traveling carriage that . . . er . . . resembled a cage.''

"And her monstrous husband did nothing to stop this?''

"Nothing, my lady.''

She turned to Thomas. "We're going after them," she said.

"No.''

"You can't expect me to ignore my sister's plight! I have to do something, I have to save her! All her life she's taken care of me, sacrificed for me, and I've selfishly accepted everything she's done as if it were my due. Now that she needs me I can't turn my back on her.''

"I'm not expecting you to. I'm expecting you to wait here with Brother Jerome while I go after her.''

"I won't do it! What makes you think you'd have any

better luck than I would? He might have you killed on sight for deserting his household. . . .''

"He doesn't know that I have. As far as he's aware, I've gone to see to my wife's burial. If I show up he'll merely think I'm resuming my duties. If I show up with you he'll probably geld me.''

"You think he will listen to you?''

"No.''

"He'd listen to me,'' Claire said in a bitter voice. "I have something he might be willing to trade for my sister's life.''

"And what is that, my lady?'' Brother Jerome asked.

"Me.''

Brother Jerome crossed himself, uttering a hasty prayer. "You can't consider such an abomination,'' he said.

"I can consider anything to save my sister,'' she said fiercely. Thomas stood beside her, remote, powerful. "Are we going after them?'' she demanded. "Or do I leave you behind?''

"You should beat her,'' Brother Jerome said. "Often, and severely.''

"Once we're married,'' he agreed carelessly. "Have you a horse? Lady Claire lost hers.''

"That would leave me without a mount!'' the good friar protested.

"We'll bring it back to you,'' Thomas promised. "And you may marry us upon our return.''

"And if you don't come back, my son?''

"Then pray for our souls, Brother Jerome.''

If Richard the Fair, had had any sense, they would have avoided the market town of Watlington and the boisterous festival that spilled over into the countryside.

A man of robust appetites, he loved a fair as well as most, but he had more important things to attend to. There'd be time enough for feasting and whoring when they'd finished at Middleham Castle. Time enough once the king was dead.

Grendel would have to die as well—it was an unfortunate necessity. Richard was wise enough to know that he would never be secure as long as someone held the secret to his power. As long as he kept his plain, pious sister in her cage, Simon of Navarre would do exactly as he wanted. But that wouldn't work for long.

Richard found it vastly amusing that his partner in wickedness would have done anything as absurd as fall prey to a quiet little sparrow of a creature. In the years that Simon had been Richard's chief advisor he'd shown not a trace of weakness or partiality, not for women or other men or young boys. He had seemed powerful and inviolate.

But his sweet little sister Alys had brought a change to all that, and it had been sheer luck that had brought them together. Richard had never thought Simon would choose the plainer of the sisters, he had a love of beauty and finery, and to choose the lesser one seemed unlike him.

But he'd chosen Alys, and he'd become absurdly vulnerable. Not through anything as obvious as sex, since it was clear that Simon of Navarre had lost the ability to function as other men did. Perhaps Alys really was a witch after all, one who'd used her powers on the all-powerful sorcerer.

The reasons behind it didn't matter, only the results. Simon of Navarre would obey without question, and would continue to do so as long as Richard kept Alys hostage. Once he killed her, Simon would have no motive for loyalty other than his own self-interest.

In the past Richard would have assumed that Simon's self-interest would rule over any stray sentiment. Now he wasn't so sure. He would keep the two of them alive as long as he needed them. Until the king was dead and things were well in hand to ensure Richard's claim to the throne.

And then he would show great good sense and have Simon killed before he dispensed with his annoyance of a sister. It was never wise to underestimate the wrath of a wizard.

There was bear baiting and cock fighting in the market town. Roasted meats and music and magicians to entertain the crowds. He should have pressed on, gone the long way around the bustling town, but he was tired, bored, and hungry. The wise thing would have been to move onward. But Richard the Fair didn't waste his energy being wise.

They camped on the bluff outside the town, and the smell of food and livestock rose to mingle with the woodsmoke. They were two days away from Middleham, two days away from the start of his glorious future. He could afford a day of pleasure before he got on with his life's work.

He rubbed his balls absently. He wouldn't go back to Summersedge Keep once the deed was done. He owned lands and castles all over England, though the Keep had always been a favorite. He would move South, toward Kent, and send for Lady Claire. She would still be locked in her solar, as he'd commanded, and he had complete faith that his servants wouldn't dare fail him. They knew the punishment for mistakes.

He'd conveniently decided that Claire was no sister to him, and her beauty made the possibility of damnation worth the risk. But he found himself wondering about little Alys. What about her had managed to ensnare his all-powerful wizard? He couldn't reasonably deny his kinship with her as well, but he found himself wondering what lay beneath her ugly clothes. Perhaps he'd find out before he had her smothered.

The night was cold, drear, with only a quarter moon to light the sky. Simon of Navarre lay sleeping in the corner of the tent, wisely making no attempt to elude his liege lord's presence. He was a sensible man; he'd accepted the way things were and had made the best of it, sleeping the sleep of those without conscience, his imprisoned wife forgotten.

Richard the Fair grinned as he stretched out on his own bed. Maybe there was hope for Grendel after all.

Simon waited until Richard started snoring before he rose to look down at his liege lord.

He could cut Richard's throat and watch him bleed to death, speechless, in a matter of moments. But that wouldn't solve the problem of Alys's captivity. There were four men guarding the wagon, and they'd been told to be particularly suspicious of him. He knew he would have one chance, and one chance alone, to rescue her, and he had to make certain there were no mistakes. A diversion was simple enough to arrange, but it would have to be timed carefully so that he could be there to release her, and there had to be some avenue of escape. There was no question but that she would have to mount the back of a horse or accept death, and he hoped she would make the wise decision. If she couldn't, they would both die, and he wasn't particularly ready for death.

He rose, knowing from experience that Richard's wine-fueled sleep would be heavy enough to keep him from realizing his wizard was gone. He counted on his men at arms to watch him, and unfortunately they were very good at their job. So far it had proved impossible to get anywhere near Alys without an army of witnesses, and he had no intention of reassuring her and having word get back to Richard.

Not that he had any illusions. Richard no longer trusted him. Despite Alys's lie and Simon's own lazy protests, Richard knew that his wizard would betray him for the utterly ridiculous sake of a woman's life. But as long as the suspicions were unspoken, he had a small measure of safety. So he nodded and said nothing as Richard prattled on about the future, and dreamed of his head on a pike.

He needed an ally, and he had none. The frightened-looking serving woman who attended Alys would likely run screaming into the forest before she helped him, and it seemed as if Richard had chosen the men who accompanied them with special care. Every one of them had a particular grudge against Simon of Navarre.

Admittedly, it would have been hard to find inhabitants of the Keep who didn't hate Simon. He had done his best to intimidate everyone who'd come his way, and very few had proven resistant. Only Brother Jerome, and God knows where he was now. And Thomas du Rhaymer, off in search of Alys's silly little sister.

It was a cold night, but he didn't bother with his fur-lined mantle. He liked the cold, the icy nip of frost that danced across his skin. It went a small way toward cooling his blood. And he needed to be cool, to be calm and unemotional, in order to accomplish what needed to be done.

The wagon was off to one side, the thick curtains pulled tightly around it. He wondered if she was warm enough in there, if she slept soundly. If she dreamed, if she cried. If he somehow managed to come to her, to kill the guards that surrounded her prison and cut her free, would she take the knife from his hand and plunge it into his heart?

And he wondered if he would care.

The guards had moved away from the cart, closer to the warmth of the fire, but Simon did not think for a moment that they would simply watch as he approached the makeshift prison. He ignored them, ignored the wagon and the pale-faced woman who sat nearby, and walked into the forest.

"Guess even a wizard needs to relieve himself every now and then," one man said in a loud voice. Louder than he usually would have dared speak within Simon's hearing. One more sign that Richard's favor had been withdrawn.

"At least his John Thomas is good for something," another one said with a crude laugh. "Bet the little lady would like to know what a real man's like."

Simon paused at the edge of the woods, out of sight, his right hand clenched tight on his dagger. He was unmoved by the insults, but the suggestion of a threat to his wife was a more serious matter. It was more than possible one of those idiots would decide to climb into Alys's prison and find out whether or not she was still a maiden. It was more than possible that Richard would encourage them.

He'd never felt possessive in his entire life. He'd never felt helpless.

It was a small noise, and to a man less observant it might have sounded like a woodland creature, a squirrel or rabbit scuttling through the fallen leaves. But Simon seldom made mistakes.

He'd already drawn his knife when the creature hurtled itself at him, a bundle of rags and hair and fury, but at the last instant he dropped the blade, catching the enraged creature with both hands.

She made a choking sound of great pain, collapsing at his feet, and a moment later Thomas du Rhaymer hove into view, panting slightly.

"You need to keep better watch on your lady," Simon observed in a quiet voice, hauling Lady Claire to her feet and still keeping her hands imprisoned in his. He could see no weapon, but Lady Claire was a formidable young woman, and he had no desire to end up a real castrati.

"Bastard," she spat at him, struggling. "Murderer!" She gasped again, and he realized that one of her wrists was tightly bandaged, and that he was hurting her quite badly.

He shoved her toward her champion with a sound of disgust. "Keep hold of her, du Rhaymer. I have no particular desire to inflict injury on my wife's sister, but I'm not in the best of moods either."

Thomas caught her, holding her easily against him despite her struggles. "Are you going to call the guards?" he asked in a low voice.

"You don't really think I would, do you?" he replied.

Claire stopped struggling, though her face was still mutinous. "Calm down, my lady," Thomas said to her, and astonishingly enough, she did. The wonders of love, Simon thought bitterly. "His lordship is going to help us."

"Help us get killed," she shot back, but her voice was quieter now. "He hasn't made any attempt to rescue her yet. What makes you think he even cares?"

"I've thought of one plan," Simon said in a mild tone of voice. "You could take her place."

Claire opened her mouth to insult him again but her

stalwart knight simply clamped a hand across her face, silencing her. "How heavily is she guarded?"

"Four men at all times, and no one in the camp is likely to help. Between the two of us we might be able to manage, but why did you bring that tiresome creature along?" he demanded, looking askance at Claire. "No, don't tell me. I imagine you didn't have much say in the matter."

She knocked Thomas's restraining hand away. "I love my sister!" she said furiously.

His response was immediate but unspoken. He just looked at her coolly, and finally Thomas spoke.

"There's nothing wrong with your right hand," he observed.

Simon flexed it, leaning down to pick up the knife he'd dropped rather than skewer his sister-in-law. "No," he said.

"I imagine there's nothing wrong with any other part of you, either."

Simon smiled faintly. "I can't imagine that's any concern of yours."

"We like large families. Children and nieces and nephews," Thomas said.

"Let's see if we survive the next few days," Simon replied. "Then we can worry about procreation."

"I'm still a maid," Claire announced in a pugnacious tone of voice.

"My condolences," Simon murmured. "I'm certain Thomas will take care of that problem when he has the time. At the moment I think your sister's safety is of greater concern."

"There wasn't time for Brother Jerome to marry us," Thomas said. "We can wait until Lady Alys is safely bestowed."

"Bestowed where? In her husband's care? I doubt

she'll welcome that," Simon said coolly. "You could see her safely back to that convent she came from. I imagine that's as welcome a place as any. Or she can make her home with you if she so chooses."

"I can protect them from Lord Richard, if that is a concern of yours."

Simon smiled. "I don't anticipate that that will be a problem," he said gently.

Thomas nodded, understanding immediately. "I'll take her wherever she wishes to go."

Lady Claire had obviously had enough of being ignored. "What are we going to do?" she demanded. "I don't want her to spend another night in that horrible cage."

"The night is half over. If you can manage some patience we can free her tomorrow, during the fair. In the confusion you should be able to escape."

"You have a plan?" Thomas demanded eagerly.

"An idea," Simon replied. "It requires careful preparation and accurate timing. Richard doesn't know her spoiled little ladyship has taken off, or that you went after her. If he spies you tomorrow, he'll simply assume that Lady Claire is still locked in her solar and you've come to offer your help."

"Do you think he'll believe it?" Thomas said doubtfully.

"Richard has a great deal on his mind. He won't be wasting his suspicions on one of his loyal knights. In the meantime, keep that impatient creature quiet, would you? Take her somewhere and tup her while I work on it."

"We're not married, my lord."

Simon muttered a curse in Arabic. "Then bind and gag her and dump her in a ditch and we'll fetch her later."

Thomas turned. "She's not here," he said in an ominous voice.

"What do you mean?"

"I mean she's gone," Thomas said in a desperate voice. "And if I know my lady, she's gone after her sister."

"Hell and damnation," Simon muttered. And he started for the clearing.

Chapter Twenty-Four

It was a fortunate thing that Thomas du Rhaymer caught up with Lady Claire before Simon did. He tackled her before she reached the edge of the clearing, landing on top of her with a muffled "ooof." If Simon had been the one to catch her he might have delivered the sound thrashing she so richly deserved.

He kept walking through the forest, stepping over the entwined, bickering couple. She was blistering him in a shrill voice, Thomas was holding her still, and Simon moved on, shaking his head in wonder. How two sisters could be so dissimilar was a question not soon to be answered. Lady Claire was a rare handful, but Sir Thomas was more than up to the task of taming her. They'd deal a lot better with each other once they managed to get into bed.

And in truth, in certain ways Alys was more like her rebellious half-sister than one might first think. Her beauty was more subtle but undeniably luminous, her bravery quieter but surely as fierce. And he had little doubt her rage could equal Lady Claire's monumental proportions.

Lady Claire was silent now, and he could hear the faint, soothing murmur of Thomas's voice, the soft rustle of clothing as he left them behind, and he wondered vaguely which would prove stronger, Thomas's moral resolve or Claire's determination. Either way, the battle would keep them busy for the next few hours.

He paused at the edge of the forest, watching the encampment with wary eyes. The four guards usually stationed at each corner of Alys's makeshift prison had abandoned their posts and moved closer to the fire. They were passing a wine skin around, one had an arm slung around the serving woman's plump figure, and Alys had been forgotten.

He could go up to the back of the carriage and part the curtains. He had no idea whether there was lock on that side as well, or whether he'd be able to open it without a key. Circumventing locks was one of his many talents, but the stakes had never been so high.

What would she do if she woke up and saw him? Scream in denunciation? Cry out in fury? Either would get them both killed, but she had no reason to trust him, every reason to despise him. If he had any sense he would leave her alone in her cage, go back to the tent he shared with Richard, and see if he could complete a workable plan for tomorrow, now that he knew he had an ally.

He paused outside the wagon, hidden in the shadows and the looming forest. No one could see him; no one could hear him. He moved closer, hoping for a sound from beyond the thick curtains, but his wife slept. Hating him.

*   *   *

Alys lay huddled beneath the covers, desperate for warmth. Her head was cold, her nose was cold, but she couldn't bury her face in the animal throws without suffocating, and she had no desire to speed that particular fate.

She could hear the guards laughing. She wondered if Simon were laughing as well.

She could almost feel him watching her. His still, golden eyes moving slowly over her face, his hands reaching for her. The sensation became overwhelming, and she pushed the covers back, rose to her knees, and spread the heavy curtains that shielded the back of her carriage.

He stood there, as she knew he would. She opened her mouth to speak, but he moved quickly, putting his hands through the bars and covering her mouth as he shook his head for silence.

She closed her eyes, breathing in the scent of his skin, absorbing the warmth of his touch. She had gone most of her life without a man's touch—how had it suddenly come to mean so much? And not any man's. This man's hands, scarred and lying.

She turned her face and pressed her mouth against the scarred palm. He moved closer, up against the iron bars, and slid his fingers through her hair, caressing her. The bars were icy cold against her face, his hands were cold as well, and she could see her breath in the shadowy moonlight.

This was one time when she couldn't count on her knowledge, her wisdom, her years of study. She could only look into her heart. She plastered her body against the iron bars and reached for him.

The feel of his body against hers was heaven. He kissed her, but the bars kept him from deepening the kiss, and she shivered in frustration. It was a silent dance of longing and despair, mute reassurance that she could only take on trust, and he'd given her no reason to trust him.

It didn't matter. When he drew away he touched her with his elegant, loving hands, and she believed in him. She lay down on the pallet, and he drew the covers tight around her. And then he knelt in the cold, his arms through the bars, and held her until she slept.

When she awoke the next morning she wondered if she'd dreamed it all. If she'd conjured Simon of Navarre out of thin air in her longing for him. There was no sign he'd been there. The frozen ground behind the wagon left no trace of footprint.

She must have dreamed it.

The guards released her for her morning ablutions, and she stumbled into the woods with Madlen close at her heels to relieve herself. The forest was still and silent, no bird calls sounding in the frosty morning, and even Madlen was grimmer than usual as she led her prisoner to a swift flowing stream.

Alys knelt down and dipped her hands in the icy water, splashing it over her face. She could only hope that, as it washed away the sleep, it would also wash away the treacherous fantasy of the night before. If she was to escape from this current disaster with her life intact she would need all her wits about her, and no sentimental weaknesses to betray her.

She dipped her hands again. Madlen was looking toward the camp, a disgruntled expression on her face, and she'd wandered a few steps away from her captive, obviously believing Alys was too cowed to attempt an escape.

Escape was the foremost thing on Alys's mind. She looked up, across the narrow stream, trying to judge how fast she could move, whether she had any chance of getting away from her brother and hiding in the forest. It was unlikely, but it was the only chance she might have, and she tightened her muscles, getting ready to spring forward across the stream, when she saw a sight that shocked her.

It was a face in the undergrowth. A face she knew and loved. For a moment she thought she was dreaming again, that her hopeless wishes had conjured up the beautiful face of her sister.

Alys cast a nervous glance over her shoulder, but Madlen had wandered farther still, out of earshot but not out of sight, and Alys had no doubt she would move fast enough if her charge ecided to make a run for it. She wasn't a heartless woman, but she had her own well-being to consider, and her loyalty to her mistress had been easily abandoned. Alys turned back, wondering if Claire's face would have disappeared once more, but she was still there.

"We're going to rescue you," she whispered, the sound barely traveling across the burbling sream.

"We?"

"Thomas is here as well."

"Run away," Alys said desperately. "Don't risk your own safety. I'll be fine—Richard wouldn't really hurt me."

"He'll kill you," Claire said flatly. "And we both know it. They have some grand plan to release you but they're not telling me." She sounded aggrieved. "Just be ready to flee as soon as you're given a sign."

"Who. . . ?"

But Claire had already faded into the woods, and Madlen stood over Alys, looking stern.

"Who were you talking to, my lady?" she demanded, peering past her into the seemingly uninhabited woods.

"My reflection."

Madlen's response was a grim snort. "That's about the only help you're going to get," she said. "Come along, my lady. We've a long day ahead of us, and I'm hoping to enjoy myself."

"Enjoy yourself?"

"There's a market fair in the next town. Gervaise says we're to travel right through it on our way to Middleham. It's been a long time since I've been to a market fair."

"Won't it be difficult to carry my cage through the town?" Alys suggested in a purely practical voice. "What if I screamed for help?"

"No one would listen," Madlen said flatly, and Alys knew that was the truth of it. "I imagine the monster has some sort of plan for you. Maybe he'll cast a spell over you to keep you silent."

He could do that, Alys thought. He could make her do anything he wanted her to.

"I'll behave myself."

"I would expect you'd be wise enough to do so, my lady," Madlen said, leading the way back to the clearing, back to her cage.

It was only as she settled once more against the fur coverlets that she remembered Claire's disgruntled words. "They have a plan and they're not telling me," she said. Who could "they" be?

Sir Thomas, of course. And she knew without question who else would be working toward her rescue. The bleak, unloving creature who was her husband.

"What do you have to smile at, my lady?" Madlen asked curiously as she locked the bars with a heavy chain.

"It's a beautiful day," Alys said, "and we're going to a fair."

Madlen threw a doubtful look at the overcast sky. "You won't be enjoying the fair, Lady Alys," she said.

"Oh, even in my cage I'm planning to enjoy it tremendously," she said sweetly.

And Madlen waddled off, shaking her head at her mistress's lack of wits.

It required perfect timing. It required a far greater element of luck than Simon of Navarre preferred to count on. It required Richard the Fair to play his part, true to his nature, and it required Alys's trust, her selfish sister's willingness to follow orders, and God's will.

In all, there were just too many unlikely variables to depend on any chance of success.

But there was no alternative. By tomorrow they would reach Middleham Castle, and the path from then on was set. The child would die, most likely followed by Alys and Simon. He expected it would take Richard less than a year to get himself named king—the others who stood closer to the throne were as easily disposed of as a twelve-year-old monarch.

He could count on Claire's love for her sister. He could count on bravery from Sir Thomas du Rhaymer and Alys. He could even count on Richard's vanity to put the plan into motion.

But what he couldn't depend on was God's mercy.

He was more than willing to make a bargain with God. His quiet little wife was entranced by him, he knew that without smugness. But she would be much better off with some pious and stalwart knight. If he could manage to free her, and dispense with the evil incarnate that was her half brother, then he would willingly barter his own life. After all, he'd seen and experienced more in his thirty-four years than most men did in twice that time. If he had to die, he was willing that it be so. As long as Alys lived.

Richard rode up beside him, all boisterous good will. "Shall we pass through the fair, or stop to enjoy ourselves, Grendel?" he demanded.

He'd already made up his mind, of course, and his question was merely a taunt. But Simon had spent the last three years manipulating him, and he wasn't about to stop when the stakes were so high.

"I suggest we skirt the village," he said.

"I confess, that had been my original thought," Richard observed. "Too much distraction for the guards, and we wouldn't want Lady Alys to make a scene."

"Indeed. Though she could, of course, be silenced. And I doubt any of your men at arms would dare allow themselves to be lax in their duties."

"True enough. Then why don't you think we should stop at the fair?"

"The town of Watlington is known throughout the north of England as the birthplace of Thador the Magician."

"Thador? Never heard of him."

Since Simon had just created him that seemed logical. "He was the greatest wizard who ever lived, more miraculous than Merlin himself. Ballads are still sung of the wondrous things he did, and wizards and sorcerers from all over the world come to Watlington in hopes of impressing the people with their craft. Since the people are quite used to magic it requires a superior wizard indeed."

"Have you ever been here?" Richard eyed him curiously.

"No, my lord. I have never felt the need to prove myself to a bunch of peasants."

"Of course not," Richard agreed. "Nevertheless. . . ."

"Sire?"

"You say this town is well-known throughout England as the home of wizardry?"

"Throughout the Christian world, my lord."

"Then it would reflect very well on me if my personal wizard was proven to be a master at his craft."

He'd fallen for it, like a hungry carp for a fat worm. "My lord, I won't stand in the town square and conduct a magic show to astonish and amaze the people of Watlington."

"You will, Grendel. If you value Lady Alys's well-being."

"I have told you, my lord, I have no interest in what you do with Lady Alys, beyond a mild hope that she not suffer unduly," he said in a bored voice. "And if you really intend me to do this, I suggest you ensure that she doesn't escape while the villagers are distracted."

"Very wise, Grendel." He glanced toward an ill-dressed servant who was hovering nearby. "You there. See that Lady Alys is bound and gagged for our trip through the market town. And make certain the cage is securely locked.

The servant nodded, bustling off toward the rolling prison, and Simon breathed a faint sigh of relief. Things were working well so far. He could only hope that Alys would recognize Sir Thomas's blue eyes beneath the shabby disguise, of a servant and know that the binding would fall away with the right amount of effort.

Ah, but Lady Alys was observant and brave. She was the least and the greatest of his worries.

He turned to look at his liege lord, and his smile was wintry cold. "As my lord wishes," he said.

Richard de Lancie laughed. "That's my Grendel." And he spurred his horse down the steep hill toward the bustling town of Watlington.

The stage was set. Thomas had done his work well— a word here, a word there, and the townspeople were prepared, agog at the notion of a real live wizard in their midst. Lord Richard of Summersedge wouldn't lower himself to talk with the local peasantry; he would never hear that Simon of Navarre was the first magician ever to stop in their ratty little market town.

Braziers had been set at the four corners of the platform that had most recently held wrestling matches. The ropes had come down, and someone had managed to secure what doubtless passed for a decent chair here. At least they'd piled it with tattered velvet. Richard could watch the show in a manner befitting his station, on a makeshift throne.

They shouted the wizard's name as he and Richard rode through the surging crowds. Richard wouldn't like that, but he smiled benevolently. "You're popular already," he murmured to Simon above the roar of the crowd. "Do not shame me in front of these good people."

Simon glanced at him with icy curiosity. "Good people?" he echoed.

"They'll be *my* people before long," Richard said. "I want them to know I can control the powers of darkness. Fear is a wondrous motivator."

Simon could feel the icy trickles form in the pit of his stomach, something he hadn't felt in more than a dozen years. He hadn't cared enough about anything to feel fear. He felt it now.

"You are very wise, my lord," he said. An urchin

appeared out of nowhere, grabbing the reins of his horse as he threw them down. Lady Claire was equally as filthy as her beloved, and well nigh unrecognizable in the boy's garb she'd managed to filch. Only her beautiful eyes would give her away, and she was wise enough to keep them lowered.

He mounted the stairs to the platform, keeping his right hand well-hidden in the folds of his long black tunic, and the crowd chanted his name. Not his name—they called "Grendel, Grendel, Grendel . . ." and he paused with a theatrical flourish, waiting for his lord to precede him.

The carriage had halted by the corner of the platform, and someone had drawn the curtains. Alys sat in her prison with a cloth across her mouth, her hands bound tight in front of her, and he knew a moment's panic. Had Thomas been able to do his part? If he'd failed, this would all be for nought.

"My lord," he said to Richard, gesturing to the throne-like chair. Richard seated himself, prepared to be entertained, and laughed heartily when Simon tossed back his left sleeve and presented him with a goblet of sweet red wine.

It was a simple enough trick, but the crowd roared with approval, and Richard held up the goblet in an elaborate tribute before quaffing it.

He drained the goblet. Simon watched him do it out of slitted eyes, and when Richard finished he smiled, cat-like.

Richard was right about one thing—fear was a powerful motivator. The simple peasantry of Watlington knew their demons well. Simon moved to one brazier and sprinkled the first mix of herbs on the hot coals.

The explosion was muffled, the red smoke billowing outward in thick, fat roils. "I call on Belial," Simon intoned in his rich voice, "on the powers of darkness that fell from heaven, to aid my quest and do my bidding."

The townspeople gasped in horror at the demonic words, crossing themselves as they moved uneasily.

He moved to the opposite brazier. This time the explosion was louder, the smoke deep blue, wafting over the crowd. "I call on Astaroth, ruler of western regions of hell," he intoned, checking from beneath slitted eyes. His own horse had been tethered close to the stage, impervious to the smoke and noise, but the two by the wagon were moving restively. Everyone was too fixated on the wizard to wonder why two filthy creatures were standing ominously near the wagon with a pair of fine horses. Unfortunately, Alys was equally fixated, staring at him, making no effort to release her bindings. If she hadn't recognized Thomas she might not even know that she could.

He went to the third brazier, and the wagon was out of his view. It was the signal Thomas was waiting for, and there was nothing Simon could do to make certain she escaped.

He stood over the brazier, sprinkling the dust that Godfrey had gathered, and green sparks began to shoot outward, like crazed fairies. "I call upon Amon, demon of the underworld, who sets all prisoners free." He raised his voice to a shout, and opened his hand over the fire.

The explosion rocked the stage. He staggered back, coughing, unable to see through the billowing smoke. There were shouts and cries from the crowd, screams of terror, yet he could do nothing but pray.

He hadn't asked a thing of a merciless God in over a decade. He asked now. "Save her," he said.

Richard hadn't moved. He was sitting in his chair,

stunned, and Simon had no idea whether the poison had done its work or not.

He crossed to the brazier in front of Lord Richard. "I call on Fleurety, demon of poison herbs. Do my bidding!"

He'd overestimated the amount needed for the final brazier, but in the end it didn't matter. The final explosion was so powerful that the metal brazier split apart, sending shards of fire through the quickly scattering crowds. The smoke was thick and black and oily, and Richard rose to his feet, swaying, his pale eyes glazed.

"I want a woman," he said in a thick voice, oblivious to the chaos around him.

"It's been known to have that effect," Simon replied.

Richard's eyes opened wide. "You bastard," he said, drawing his sword and stumbling toward his sorcerer. He caught him in his burly grip, imprisoning Simon's left hand, holding a knife at his throat. "What's the antidote, Grendel?" he demanded hoarsely. "Tell me or I'll cut your throat."

He couldn't move his left hand—Richard had it imprisoned, and the bite of the knife was sharp against his skin. He couldn't even turn to see if Alys had made it safely away.

"There is no antidote," he said, flexing his crippled right hand.

"Damn it," said Richard. "You've killed me."

"Not yet." And lifting his right hand, he drove the knife into Richard the Fair's black, dead heart.

"Alys, come!" Thomas du Rhaymer's voice was urgent, but she couldn't move. The stage was covered with smoke, but somehow she could see the two men struggling and the flash of metal.

Thomas flung the cage door open and reached in for her. She'd already managed to rip off her bonds, but she hadn't realized the lock was broken. She should have known that Simon wouldn't leave anything to chance.

Thomas hauled her from the cage just as another explosion rocked the stage. She struggled against him, desperate. "I can't, Thomas! I have to find him!"

"It's no good, my lady," he shouted at her. "He's done this much for you, let him be." He scooped her up around the waist, ignoring her struggles.

"He'll kill him."

"Come." He picked her up and carried her through the teeming crowd, and she might have been as insignificant as a feather, for all that her struggles affected him. Her sister was waiting at the edge of the rioting crowd, barely controlling her horses.

"No," Alys cried, as she realized how they expected to get her away from the town.

"Yes," said Sir Thomas, tossing her up onto the beast's high back and following after her.

Her struggles were panicking the horses, but she didn't care. She screamed, fighting like a madwoman, determined not to leave Simon, but clearly Thomas had had enough. She never even saw the blow coming, only the merciful blackness that closed over her.

Chapter Twenty-Five

There had been a time when returning to the Convent of Saint Anne the Demure had been all that Alys wanted. As they rode through the stone gate that surrounded the abbey she tried to summon up some pleasure, but her capacity for it was as dead as her heart. She simply lay back against Thomas du Rhaymer's strong chest, imprisoned by his arms, astride the huge, monstrous horse that would likely trample her to death if Sir Thomas hadn't been controlling the creature.

She had gone beyond fear as well as hope. Even the sight of Sister Agnes's plump, welcoming face was no comfort.

They helped her down from the back of the horse, and she went with them willingly enough, shuddering with stray relief to be away from the creature. A moment later Claire was beside her, drawing her into her arms, weeping with joy.

"He's dead, Alys!" she said triumphantly. "I saw him fall! He'll never come near you again."

Alys froze in sudden despair. "You saw him? Are you certain?" If Simon was dead then she didn't want to live. It was that sinful and that simple.

"Without question. The blood was everywhere," she announced in ghoulish delight.

Alys swayed, feeling suddenly faint. "Who killed him?" she managed to gasp.

"That creature you married," Claire said in a disapproving voice.

Alys looked up at her in shock. "Simon killed himself?"

"Don't be ridiculous! Simon killed Richard."

Alys, with true sisterly devotion, grabbed Claire by the tattered tunic and shook her. "I don't care what happened to Richard!" she shouted furiously. "Where is Simon?"

"My child." Brother Jerome appeared out of the gathering darkness, gently removing Alys's grip from her sister's clothing. "No one knows what happened to him. Word has been flying through the kingdom. According to the witnesses, he disappeared in a puff of smoke."

"I believe it," Claire said cynically, as Sister Agnes swiftly crossed herself to ward off a curse.

"He couldn't have," Alys said flatly.

"He did," Brother Jerome assured her. "He's gone back to the realms of darkness from whence he came. We won't be seeing him again."

"He didn't come from darkness," Alys said in a cranky voice. "He's as human as you or I."

"None of us has the ability to disappear at will. It is said that his withered hand miraculously healed itself at the last minute, and it was with it that he killed Lord Richard."

"Miraculous," Alys muttered.

"You must face the truth, my child," Brother Jerome said solemnly. "He's well and truly gone."

She wanted to scream her denial. She wanted to fling herself on the ground and kick in rage and fury. They watched her, all of them, with wary eyes, as if they feared the dreaded sorceror had bewitched her as well.

He was no sorceror. He was a man, with all the strengths and frailties of the beast. She loved him beyond reason, and he was gone.

She summoned up her Good Alys smile, the gentle, obedient expression that had served her well for her twenty years. She could become Good Alys again. Sister Mary Alys, the good nun, the perfect aunt. The lost soul.

She stood silent by her bathed and beautiful sister as Brother Jerome read the marriage vows over Claire and Sir Thomas. She kissed Sir Thomas on his cleanly shaven cheek, hugged Claire, and smiled her Good Alys smile.

They put Thomas and Claire in the room the sisters used to share. They put Alys in the adjoining room, and there was much merriment from the celibate religious as the bridal couple closed the door.

Alys sat by the window, staring out into the moonlit night. Her body ached, but her heart was ripped in half. There was no way she could deny the truth of Brother Jerome's words. Simon had saved her.

Simon had left her.

She looked down at her flat stomach. Was a child already started? She sensed that it was so, but she was afraid it was merely a vain hope. She wanted his child. Most of all she wanted him.

She heard a crash from the room next door, and the muffled sound of laughter. "Yes, Thomas," her sister whispered in a husky voice. "There."

She rose abruptly. There was no way she would sit in

that barren room and listen to the sounds of her sister's joy. She wished them love and happiness and pleasure beyond knowing. She just didn't want to have to hear it.

The wind had picked up, scudding the dry leaves along the empty courtyard. The good nuns were already asleep in their cells. Brother Jerome was likely resting as well. There were only three people awake in the entire convent, and Thomas and Claire were fully occupied.

A stray, sensual laugh drifted out over the night air, and she moved more swiftly, following the moonlit path to the small clearing by the stream. It had been one of her favorite places to walk to when she was a child, a place of peace and comfort, things she always longed for. Perhaps if she curled up next to the icy stream, her borrowed mantel wrapped tight around her, she could find some sort of peace. Or at least she could give way to the kind of grief that tore her heart apart. There would be no one to see Good Alys weep.

She sat on a fallen log, huddled against the cold, and tried to summon forth tears. They refused to come. She thought of Simon, with his golden eyes and his scarred body, his clever mouth and his wicked ways.

There were no tears.

She thought of the years ahead of her, stretching out, alone. If she had a babe they would take it away from her, but Claire would raise it as her own, and she would have nieces and nephews as well as her own child to comfort her empty, worthless life.

There were no tears.

She thought of marriage to a goodly knight. Brother Jerome had assured her that her marriage to the sorcerer would be declared invalid, and she would be free to find a new life. She could marry a good man and forget Simon of Navarre had ever touched her.

There were no tears.

She thought of rising to her feet and wandering ever deeper into the woods, never to be seen again. By far the most pleasant of all the futures that lay before her, but a sin nonetheless, and she should get down on her knees and beg God's forgiveness for even thinking of such a thing.

There were no tears.

She heard the faint chink of a horse's bridle, and her life-long panic reasserted itself. She rose, ready to run at a moment's notice, when the horse appeared in the clearing.

She knew him. Huge and black, more terrifying than even Claire's wild mare, the horse halted, snorting. She didn't need to look up, way up, to see Simon of Navarre watching her.

"Why did you lie to your brother?" The words were unexpected, and she stared up at him like a lackwit.

"I never lied."

"You told him that I hadn't taken you as an ordinary man would."

She could feel the blush mount on her cheeks. It was a glorious feeling. "I didn't lie," she said again. "You didn't."

"How so?"

"I could hardly speak from experience, but I decided you must be far better at it than any ordinary man."

In the moonlight she could see the smile touch his eyes as it curved his mouth. "You're pert. Someone will have to beat you."

"I hear my brother is dead. The sad duty of instructing me will have to fall to you."

For a moment he said nothing. Then he spoke. "Will you come away with me?"

She looked warily at the horse. "Where?"

"To the far reaches of the world. To the isles of the north, where the wind is like ice. To the heat of the desert, to the mountains of Switzerland. Come away with me and you may never see England again."

It was a warning. She squared her shoulders, looking up at him. "Would I have to ride a horse?"

"Yes."

She tilted her head to one side, considering him. "Do you love me?"

"Love is a trick and a sham. A foolish plague and a lie and a torment."

"Do you love me?" she repeated, quite calmly. Knowing the answer.

"Yes, may it curse my soul."

"May it save your soul," she said. The horse moved, and she knew she could be trampled beneath his huge sharp hooves.

"Are you coming?" he asked.

"Take me," she said, holding up her arms. And he pulled her up in front of him, onto the huge warm back of the horse.

The creature reared slightly, but Alys simply leaned back against Simon as his arms came around her. And they rode off into the moonlit night, the dry leaves rustling beneath the horse's hooves.

DANGEROUS GAMES   (0-7860-0270-0, $4.99)
by Amanda Scott

When Nicholas Barrington, eldest son of the Earl of Ulcombe, first met Melissa Seacort, the desperation he sensed beneath her well-bred beauty haunted him. He didn't realize how desperate Melissa really was . . . until he found her again at a Newmarket gambling club—being auctioned off by her father to the highest bidder. So, Nick bought himself a wife. With a villain hot on their heels, and a fortune and their lives at stake, they would gamble everything on the most dangerous game of all: love.

A TOUCH OF PARADISE   (0-7860-0271-9, $4.99)
by Alexa Smart

As a confidence man and scam runner in 1880s America, Malcolm Northrup has amassed a fortune. Now, posing as the eminent Sir John Abbot—scholar, and possible discoverer of the lost continent of Atlantis—he's taking his act on the road with a lecture tour, seeking funds for a scientific experiment he has no intention of making. But scholar Halia Davenport is determined to accompany Malcolm on his "expedition" . . . even if she must kidnap him!